In The Haze

Praise for In The Haze

"I am officially addicted to all things Brittany and Charli! Holy moly, Emily Bourne outdid herself. She delves so much deeper into the twins' lives, and I didn't think that was possible." Becca C. Smith, *Author of The Riser Saga.*

"Emily Bourne does a wonderful job exploring all the characters in her book and making it all come to life." Katie, *Goodreads Reviewer*

"Emily Bourne submerges you into the world of these girls. You feel every heart break and every action as if you were on that rollercoaster with them." Isabella, *Amazon Reviewer*

"If you read *'In A Mirror'* and thought that was full of drama, well wait until you get a boatload of this novel! Raw, realistic, and touching." Gracie, *Amazon Reviewer.*

"Emily Bourne writes the themes as if she's experienced them first hand. The stresses of peer pressure when it comes to drinking, sex, and other potentially damaging behaviours are normal when you're a young adult." Dahlia Burroughs, *Newspeak Press*

Tragedy. Betrayal. Bond.

In The Haze

EMILY BOURNE

HCP

First Published by Halo & Claws Publishing 2020

IN THE HAZE

Copyright © Emily Bourne 2020

For information contact: https://www.emilybourne.net

Stock Images via Bigstock, Shutterstock
Editor Dahlia Burroughs, Newspeak Press

ISBN: 978-1-925990-03-4 (Paperback)
ISBN: 978-1-925990-02-7 (Ebook)

For anyone who feels lost or alone.

You matter.

1

Charli

"Stare them down or they'll never let you cross," a girl beside me says as I stand at a traffic light crossing.

My forehead tenses. "Stare them down?"

"As you walk across," she says, nudging at the cars driving over the crosswalk. "Stare at the drivers. They won't stop driving unless you show them confidence."

"That's crazy." I puff out a laugh. "They should stop when it's our time to cross."

"This is Italy," the girl says in an accent I can't place. The sun highlights her strawberry-blonde hair and freckled pale skin. "The rules are different here."

I follow her lead and stare down the drivers as we cross the road. The cars slow, yet I still fear for my life. *Please don't run me down,*

Crazy Italian Drivers.

My fingers smooth over the St Christopher pendant my sister gave me on our last birthday. I straighten my back, trying to act confident. Charli, you're in a foreign country and have the freedom to explore any part of the city you want. Where's your excitement gone?

"Thanks for the help," I say as we make it to the other side of the road. I recognise her from our school bus, but we weren't introduced. "I'm Charli, by the way."

The girl swats her hand. "That's nothing. I've come to Italy many times with my family. I'm Maja, I'm from Sweden. What accent is that? British?"

"No, I'm Australian."

"Wow, you're far from home. How long are you on exchange?"

"It's nine months total, so I'm almost halfway through." Every day I pinch myself to make sure this is real. My parents actually let me go to Spain for school and travel to other countries. Granted, it's only for school excursions, but how many kids back home get to say they're travelling through Europe at sixteen?

"Goes fast, huh?"

"Tell me about it. I don't want it to end," I reply.

"Are you liking the school?"

"School is fine. Different to what I was expecting."

"How so?"

"I expected more Spanish-speaking classes, but so many are in English."

"Yeah, that's typical of international schools. My dad's a diplomat, so I have been to many schools, giving me lots to compare," Maja says as we walk through a boutique district. "Every move gets less special."

"How many countries have you lived in?"

"I only count it if it's over six months, so I'd say eight."

"*Whoah*, that's a lot of moving," I reply. "I've never moved to a new house before. This exchange program is the biggest change I've ever made."

"It's very cool you've been able to travel so far from home. Your friends must be very jealous."

I smile. "A bit jealous, and a bit mad, that I left home."

"That's how good friends act. I find it so hard to keep in contact with people."

I notice her lips turn downward and suggest, "I haven't really got anyone to hang out with at the moment. Do you wanna show me around? You've visited this city before?"

Her face brightens. "Sure, I can play tour guide."

Yesterday, our school group was in Paris. I followed some kids around, but I didn't make any friendships. It's the same at school. I live in the dormitory and share classes with my hallmates, yet it seems like I block myself when trying to get close to anyone. Sometimes, I'm annoyed at myself for this, but I try not to think about it too much. Maybe it's because of all the shit that went down last year. I met new people and hanging out with them seemed to mess stuff up. Every relationship I tried to hold onto seemed to crumble.

I'm overseas for a fresh start and I thought keeping to myself would help, but that's dumb. I should make friends. I see myself travelling when I finish high school. I can make contacts now for when I need places to crash or a local guide. Maja seems like a perfectly lovely person to start with.

"Which do you prefer, France or Italy?" I ask to keep the conversation flowing.

"Oh, Italy by far," Maja says. "The food wins me over every time. What do you think?"

"I thought it would be Italy, but France truly stole my heart," I say clasping my hands and reminisce about the view from the Eiffel Tower, ambling through The Louvre, and gazing at the romantic curves in the architecture. "I thought that 'city of love' stuff was Hollywood nonsense, but I'm telling you, I truly felt it."

Maja snorts. "Don't tell me you are one of those hopeless romantics?"

I shake my head and sigh. "I would never have called myself one. My sister has always wanted to go to Paris. She was so jealous when I called her yesterday."

"Oh, you have a sister?" Maja asks. "That is nice. I always wanted a sister, but I'm an only child. Thanks, Mum and Dad."

I laugh. "Be careful what you wish for. We do fight a lot."

"Who is older?"

"She is. By twelve minutes. We are twins."

Maja's jaw drops and she stops dead. "You kid me. That is very, very cool."

"I guess it is if you're not one."

"Stop it. It is cool," she insists. "And it means there is another girl out there as pretty as you are."

"*Ha*! Whatever." My mind drifts to Brittany. "She is a good sister. It's hard being away from her."

"Why didn't she come too? Don't twins do everything together?"

"Maybe in the movies," I smirk. "We have very different interests. She said she wasn't brave enough to come. I think it was down to the fact she didn't want to be away from her boyfriend."

Maja *tsks*. "Ah. It makes sense. What about you? No boyfriend? Girlfriend?"

I wrap my arms around my waist, creasing my forehead to block out thoughts of Sanford boys. Just the thought of Travis, Preston or

Reece gives me a headache. "Let's just say, I'm glad to be away from boy problems."

Maja raises her hands. "Enough said."

"Are you dating anyone?" I ask as we gaze at the beautifully sculpted buildings in a market square.

"No. I broke up with my girlfriend a few months ago."

"Oh, I'm sorry."

"It's ok. We had it coming. Distance is hard."

"Yeah, I get that. But sometimes distance is good."

Maja's smile curves to the right. "Sometimes."

"It's still so crazy that I'm here."

"Hey, you like gelato?"

"Is the Pope Catholic?"

"Hmm, we go to the Vatican tomorrow, so you must educate me," she teases.

I laugh. "Please, I love gelato. You know a good place?"

Maja wraps her arm around mine. "The best. I'll take you."

Maja whisks me through a cobblestone alley, her cheeks lifted by the most enthusiastic of smiles. "Here it is!"

"Is this special gelato or something," I snigger.

"Special?"

"You seem very excited."

She grasps my shoulders. "Charli, you have no idea. Expect to have your socks blown off."

"Wow, way to talk it up."

She pushes the door and nods. "After you. Be ready to have a *foodgasm*."

My mouth drops open as she presses on my back. We walk into a decent line of people.

Maja points to the glass casing. "They put the gelato in separate pots, so they are at the perfect temperature depending on the ingredients. Everything is good."

"You've tried every flavour?"

She shrugs. "Sometimes I sample my parents' choice. And one time I came here and there was no one inside. It was like heaven. I took my time taste testing several flavours."

"Wow, having an ice-cream shop to yourself would be a dream."

"Gelato," she corrects me.

I nod. "Gelato. So, what do you recommend? One has to be the best."

She rubs her chin, considering the choices carefully. "Tiramisu is fabulous. Pistachio is divine. Oh, and last time I had a caramel fudge. So good!"

"Oh, pistachio sounds good."

Her arm nestles on my low back. "Good choice."

When we reach the counter, Maja samples three flavours before settling on the strawberry swirl. She buys my double-scooped pistachio after beating my pathetic attempt to pay. We leave the crowded store and move outside.

Maja leads us to a fountain, and we perch on the edge.

"Happy with your choice?" she asks, digging in her spoon.

"Yes, thank you," I say, lifting my cup in salute.

She nods, sliding the spoon over her tongue. "Welcome."

"What's thank you in Swedish."

"*Tack.*"

"Tack?"

"*Varsagod,*" she says, digging her spoon into gelato. She fills my silence with, "You're welcome."

"Oh, *tack.*" It'd be ironic if I picked up Swedish quicker than my poor attempt at Spanish.

She giggles, nudging my side. "You're cute."

My cheeks flush and I'm quick to eat another spoonful of green gelato. Damn, it's so good.

Curves of romance,
Rays of sunlight dance,
A heart that can't take,
The beauty and ache,
In a city of wonder,
As my thoughts fall under.

In a quiet corner of the hotel foyer, I slide my notebook to my side and hit video chat on Brittany's contact page. My heart pitter-patters as I wait for her to answer. Finally, her smiling face fills the screen.

"Hi!" her bubbly voice rings through as she waves madly.

"Hey Brit. How are you?"

"I'm good, but more importantly, how are you? I thought you'd have the colosseum in the background."

"Sorry," I laugh. "There was a lot to take in today. I'm at the hotel for a rest."

"*Aw*, poor baby got it so hard with all the sight-seeing," she jokes.

"Don't be like that," I say, holding back my laugh. "Anyway, just thought I'd check in."

"Are the Italian guys as hot as they say?"

"And why would you like to know, Miss In-A-Committed-Relationship?"

"*Geez*, mild curiosity."

"To be honest, I haven't really looked."

"*Ugh*, that'd be right. Well, when you see one, send me a *Snap*."

This time I can't hold onto the laugh. I hold my stomach and nod.

"Ok, Brit, you got it."

"Stay safe, love you."

"Love you too."

My smile stays planted on my face as she vanishes into her contact photo. We're acting like sisters. We were chatting once a week, but during this trip it's increased to almost daily. Who knew moving to the other side of the world would bring you closer to your sister? I hope it stays this easy when I get home.

When I lower my phone, Maja skips over and pounces on the couch. "Have you heard about the Greek Islands trip?"

"No, when is that?"

"Next school break. In July," Maja says. "When we get back to school, you should sign up."

"I have to ask my parents, but I'm sure they will say yes."

Maja swats a hand. "Ah, they'd be crazy not to let you go. Who were you talking to?"

"My sister."

"Oh, that's nice. See, you two are close."

"We're working on it."

"I hope we can go to Greece together," Maja says intertwining her fingers with mine.

The pressure on my hand intensifies. "Ah, yeah. Me too."

Her face edges closer to mine and the scent of coconut wafts from her hair as it dances by my shoulder. A tingle runs up my arm as she wets her lips.

"I..." I begin, but then her lips are on mine. It's a delicate kiss. A kiss no boy could ever deliver. There's this perfect little suction on my bottom lip and she tastes of strawberry.

She pulls away, smiling, her freckles highlighted against her rosy cheeks. "Sorry, did I not give enough warning?"

"I... ah... I..."

Her hand brushes against my thigh, but there's this tingly feeling in the pit of my stomach.

I place my hand on hers and lift it. "Sorry, I... I'm just not—"

"Oh no." Her hand rushes to her mouth. "You're not... You're not into girls?"

"No, I... I didn't, I mean, I've never thought about it."

Maja covers her face. "I'm so embarrassed."

"Don't be." I take her wrist. "It was one helluva kiss."

Maja lowers her hands. "Really?"

"I've never been kissed like that."

"Oh my." Her smile resurfaces. "That's a good thing, yes?"

I nod. "Terrific thing."

"So, friends?"

"Absolutely. Just lay low on the kissing."

"For now?" she teases.

My heart *ba-booms*. "Maybe." She really is beautiful.

"I hope you still want to go to Greece."

"More than ever."

Her cheeks brighten. "*Aw*, I'm glad."

2

Brittany

I scrape at my nail polish and the flakes fall onto the desk. Slumped in my chair, I glance at the clock on the classroom wall, which is taking its sweet time.

I hear tapping on my desk and glance to the right.

Fiona leans over and whispers, "We're voting for captain after this."

"In the gym?" I whisper.

She nods with a happy grin.

I sigh. "Do you think it'll take long?"

She shrugs, tossing her fair hair over a shoulder.

"I hope not. I want to spend lunch with Bryce."

"*Naw*, cute," Fiona says, playing with a strand of hair against her porcelain-like skin.

Madison turns in the seat ahead of me and pretends to pick up a pen. "I heard Chloe pushed for a vote because Ms Harvey wouldn't pick her as captain this year."

I spy the ground for the phantom pen. "Yeah, I heard that too."

Madison leans closer to the ground, her sleek, cocoa-coloured hair fanning over her face. "It's just a vote. Should be over quick. You'll have plenty of time to see your boy."

As she sits up, I give her a thankful smile.

The bell rings and I leave the classroom with Madi and Fi on either side. When we reach the gym, Kimberley greets us, and hands out slips of paper.

"Write a name down and dump it in the hat over there on the floor," Kimberley says, her dark brown hair in a bun, accentuating her toffee-coloured complexion.

Chloe crosses her arms and stands too close to the hat for comfort. Her product-heavy face is etched with a frown and I can't help noticing the dirty-blonde roots of her platinum hair.

I move further into the gym, away from the other girls, and tap a pen on the blank sheet of paper. Meah struts into the gym, flipping her *doesn't-suit-her* blonde hair, and squawking at Kimberley. I tune her out the best I can and focus on the paper.

Can I write my own name?

No one would know I wrote it...

I'd have to disguise my handwriting.

I eye Chloe. She'd write her own name.

I look across to Kimmy. Would she write her own name? Nah, too far up Chloe's butt.

Back to the paper.

It'd be too weird to write my own name.

What if I'm the only one who writes my name? They'd all know I did it. It'd be a total loser move.

"It's just a name," Chloe grizzles. "C'mon, girls. It's not rocket science."

In a panic move, I scribble the first name that comes to mind. I refuse to write *Chloe*. Without a confident reason, I write *Fiona* and fold the paper.

I drop the paper in the hat and give Chloe my most charming smile.

Once all the votes are in, Kimberley picks up the hat and draws names. "Chloe, Chloe, Brittany." Wait, she called out my name? "Chloe, Brittany, Brittany, Fiona." Fiona squeals with surprise, clapping her hands. "Brittany, Brittany, Brittany."

"Holy shit," Madison says, doing quick maths. "Brit won."

Chloe grabs a fist full of slips from Kimberley and shuffles through them.

"*Ohmigawd*, Brit," Meah squeals, jumping beside me. "Congrats."

I slide a hand over my heart as my brain hurries to keep up. "Sorry? I won?"

Chloe drops the paper to the ground and her eyes slit. "Think you can run my squad?"

I bite my lip and gaze at everyone huddling around me. "No," I say. "I think I can run *our* squad."

Fiona pulls on my arm. "Are you going to bring in a heap of new moves for us to learn?"

"Can we ditch the pompoms?" Madison asks.

"Can I do more twists and less shouting?" Fiona adds.

Meah pulls me away from the girls. "*Oi*. Back off. Give our captain some room to breathe."

I stumble backwards as a wash of happiness makes me feel lighter than a feather. Holy crap. I won. I fan my face and move away from the group. "Well, thanks, guys, but I seriously need to get going."

Chloe slams her hands onto her hips and *tsks*. "She's already pulling a runner.”

“We’ll have a practice really soon,” I say, making my way out of the gym.

Meah chases me, linking arms as we hit the corridor. “You’re, like, total queen bee now.”

“Oh, I dunno.”

“Do you think Fi voted for herself?”

“No. That was me.”

“What? Why?”

“I dunno. I felt weird voting for myself, so I wrote the first name that popped into my head.”

Meah scoffs. “How was my name not the first one you thought of?”

My jaw clenches and I keep eyes front, hoping to skirt past the question. “I can’t believe they voted me in.”

“I can. Everyone’s nuts about you. Plus, you and your boyfy are, like, the *it* couple now.”

“Speaking of,” I say, tapping her vice grip arm. “When we get to mess, I need to spend time with him.”

She lets me go, giggles and flips her hair. “*Duh*, I get it.” Meah skips ahead and into the mess hall. She approaches our table and sings, “BK, you’re now dating the head cheerleader.”

Bryce turns around and frowns at Meah. He looks past her, and when we lock eyes, he smiles. “Huh?”

I bite my bottom lip to stop blushing.

Meah sits on top of the table and snags chips from Will’s food tray. “We just voted.”

Bryce clutches my hand and kisses my cheek. “Congrats, Britty.”

“Head cheerleader for your birthday,” Will jokes.

“Um,” I say, lifting Bryce’s arm to show off the new watch on his wrist. "I got him a kickass birthday present, thank you very much."

Jace laughs from the other side of the table. "So, she branded you, BK?"

I roll my eyes, but I can't shake my smile.

Bryce kisses my forehead and pulls me in close. "I don't mind."

Naveen throws a balled-up napkin at us. "You two are sickening."

Kellie gets up from beside Will and squeezes his shoulder. "From inferring some information, I gather Chloe will be pissed because Brittany won. Seeing as she's not my biggest fan, I think I'll make myself scarce."

Will throws his arms around Kellie's waist. "Nup, you're not going anywhere, Kelarino."

Kellie yanks on his arms. "Let me go. I gotta go check on Reece anyways."

Will lets her go and stands. "I'm coming with. I don't wanna be around Chloe either. That's a death wish."

I whisper to Bryce, "You wanna get out of here too?"

Bryce's lips crook left, and he nods.

As we pivot towards the door, I stop him and ask, "Oh, have you eaten?"

"Enough."

I raise an eyebrow and stare into his eyes.

He laughs and bunches his shoulders. "Have you eaten?"

"I don't care if I eat. I care if you eat."

"Well, that's just dumb."

We both snort a laugh. I pull him towards the food line to get something to take away. I hug him tight and ask, "Are you having a good birthday?"

"Yeah, it's pretty good."

"Better than keeping it a secret?"

"I dunno," he says, staring off to the side. "Last year's birthday was pretty damn good."

I hook a finger under his chin and kiss him softly.

"While you're liking me, I should tell you," he says, "Will asked me if we'd hang out with him and Kellie this weekend."

A groan reverberates out of me, slouching my body.

"Sorry," he winces. "It was too awkward to say no. She was right there."

"He manipulates you when I'm not around. I mean, I don't mind hanging out with them, but you two always go off and do something and leave me to make lame small talk with Kellie. We have nothing in common."

"Hey, there has to be something. She's your sister's best friend. Surely, you two can find something to talk about. Will is dying to show off his new car."

"Speaking of cars," I say. "Are you driving us tonight?"

"Hell yeah."

"I can try to get out of going to my dance class tonight."

"No, it's fine. Our reservation isn't until eight. We will have plenty of time."

"It's another hour with Chloe. She was totally giving me daggers in the gym."

Bryce looks over my shoulder. "Looks like she's cooled down."

I turn to our table as a grinning Chloe slides onto Jace's lap. My stomach knots. I know her too well... it's not over yet.

"Brit," our instructor Tiffany calls out when I enter the dance studio. "Come over here."

I dump my gym bag and walk over. I ease out a slow breath as

Chloe stands by Tiffany.

"I wanted to talk to the two of you away from the group." Tiffany shows us a flyer. "I want you both to audition for the *L'Amour Dance Company*. They are holding auditions for a professional troupe. If you get in, you'll get paid to dance."

"*Whoah*," I gasp. "That's the dream."

Chloe twists her hair around a finger. "Tiff, I already know about *L'Amour*. Is that all you've got for us?"

"Oh," Tiffany says, taken aback. "Do you have a routine in mind?"

Chloe eyes me and screws up her face. She spins on her heels and walks the edge of the dancefloor, stretching her arms over her head.

"She all right?" Tiffany asks.

"Don't worry about her. She got some bad news at school."

Tiffany holds the flyer up. "Are you excited, Brit?"

"Yes, of course. When's the audition?"

"You have a few months. We can do one-on-one classes to get you prepped."

"I'm so down."

"Excellent."

Tiffany greets the rest of the group and I walk towards the wall of mirrors and strike a strong pose. I sway my hips to the beat in my head. My arms rock to the side and I walk out my steps. My moves morph into light, ballet-inspired spins and lifts. Whenever we freestyle, I love experimenting with my old ballet moves and my new contemporary moves.

"I remember a time when you were too frightened to freestyle," Tiffany says, walking towards the stereo.

I giggle and spin on the spot. "It's taken some time, huh?"

"But you have a great, unique style now. You'll be a shoo-in for

L'Amour."

Chloe groans as her reflection approaches mine. "Are we going to start or not?"

"Yep. Girls, huddle up," Tiff calls out.

Our group takes up the dancefloor. Chloe stands by me as we count out the beats. I eye her reflection as we make our moves. She keeps in time with me, but she's not as sharp as usual. She's rattled.

I rattled her.

A smile creeps on my face and I focus on my reflection. There's more power in my moves and an easiness takes over my body.

I got this.

In my foyer later that evening, Bryce says, "Happy anniversary."

"Anniversary?"

"Yeah. Of our first kiss."

I giggle. "That's true, but today is your day. I want to celebrate you."

"No," he says with the cheekiest of grins. "It's my birthday and I want to celebrate our anniversary."

"Ok then. You're the boss."

"Since when?" he jokes.

I nudge him playfully. "Whatever."

He smiles and traces the purple beads around my neck. "I'm glad you wore this necklace."

"It was weird taking off the crystal heart because I wear it every day, but I felt like tonight called for this one."

He takes my hand. "Ready to go?"

"Yes."

"Happy birthday, Bryce," Mum says, walking down the staircase.

"Thanks, Ms Matthews."

I whip out my phone from my clutch. "Mum, can you take a photo of us?"

"Certainly," she says, landing in the foyer and taking my phone.

We bunch up, sliding our arms around each other, nestling our faces together. *One, two, three, cheese.*

"Thanks Mum," I say, taking my phone.

"You two be careful tonight," Mum says.

My back stiffens. "Careful?" What does she think we are doing tonight?

"You have your licence, Bryce," she says, "but that doesn't automatically make you a safe driver. Take it easy on the road."

"Will do," he nods.

"Ok, Mum, we gotta go." I kiss her cheek and wave goodbye.

I know Mum would hate it, but I hold Bryce's hand as he drives. My thumb draws circles on his palm, and I fixate on his rosy lips. I'm so gonna attack them when the car is parked.

Our reservation is at *Le Petit*. It's the kind of fancy place where my parents schmooze clients. Mum made the reservation, got us the best table, and asked the maître'd to send her the bill. I feel so grown up sitting across from Bryce, who's in a dress shirt and tie. Maybe we can convince a waiter to leave champagne on our table? I could tell Mum it was an error on the bill.

After the waiter places two kid-friendly lemonades on our table, Bryce takes my hands and looks deep into my eyes, snagging my soul. "I really love you, Britty."

The urge to launch across this table is so strong. "I love you so much."

When the waiter brings our meals, I can't help thinking about how much we've overcome. My heart warms as he eats without prompting. We've grown miles closer because of how much time we spent together this past summer. With Mr Kerry in terrible grief over the loss of his wife and his heavy guilt over ignoring Bryce's illness, he let us have run of the house. Not that we want the entire house. Bryce's bedroom is always enough.

We've taken things slow, and I've loved every minute. Seeing him without a shirt was a huge deal. His body issues kept him guarded for so long that it was a huge leap in trust for us. Once, he had recoiled if I touched his stomach. Now I've seen every inch of this boy.

Outside the restaurant after dinner, I stroke my hands over his tie and gently kiss the nape of his neck. I whisper, "Want to detour at your place before you drive me home?"

"Anything to spend more time with you."

And now I lie on his bed, unravelling his tie, and teasing his bottom lip.

His hands slide along my thighs and creep inside my dress. We've been naked together three times. The first time, I shook like a leaf. One time, things really heated up, but Bryce's antidepressants slowed our pace. In a way, I'm glad. It's giving us a chance to ease into things. But tonight, I think I might be ready.

As I undo his last button, Bryce lifts my dress up. I sit up and raise my arms as the material glides over my head. He drops my dress to the floor along with his shirt and I run my hands down his torso. He scoops me into his arms and I wrap my legs around him. I lie back as he hovers above me. The warmth of his kisses against my collarbone makes me shut my eyes and I let out a breathy moan.

"Remember how we talked about taking things to the next step?" I whisper.

He pulls back to look at my face.

"I'm ready." I bite my lip as I take in his sweet face. "If you're not, that's ok. But I'm ready when you are."

Apprehension crosses his face but it's quickly replaced with a crooked smile. He leans down and kisses my lips. He pulls away and whispers, "I don't know."

"That's ok, B." I stroke his cheek with the back of my hand. "I'm in no rush. I love you."

"I love you. Let's ease in and see where it takes us."

"Whatever you want to do, Baby."

His fingers play with my bra straps and he kisses my collarbone. I close my eyes, taking in the sandalwood on his skin, and run my hands down the length of his back. His lips meet mine and our passion intensifies as he moves deeper between my legs.

He unzips his trousers and my heart hastens as he pulls them down.

"You all right?" he whispers, brushing back my hair.

I nod with a closed-mouth smile. I want to. I do. The magnitude of *it* is sinking in and I need a moment.

"You don't have to say you're ready just because it's my birthday."

"No," I blurt. "I want to. I do."

"You look worried."

"I'm nervous."

His thumb slides against my bottom lip. "I love it when you bite your lip like that."

I shut my eyes. "Am I doing it again?"

"It's cute."

I open my eyes to the most adorable smile. The light blue shades of his eyes hypnotise me.

I grin. "Hurry up and take off my bra."

He laughs. "Yes, ma'am."

I love his arms locked behind my back. He's strong. I love running my bare legs against his. I love the way he moans as we rock against the bed. They didn't lie. It hurts. It hurts but being with him makes it better. Being closer to him than anyone else has ever been.

He's mine.

And I love him.

3

Charli

On the edge of my seat, chin in palms and elbows rocking on the desk, I decode every Spanish word spoken. I take advantage of Spanish-speaking classes as most are in English at our international school.

"Are you keeping up?" Maja asks beside me.

I relax in my seat. "I'm trying. I'm still struggling, and it's almost been five months."

"I'm glad I was taught English at an early age," she says. "Otherwise I'd be translating two languages."

When the bell rings, Maja and I pack up our things and leave the classroom.

"Got any weekend plans?" Maja asks.

"I'm exploring Old Town. Did you want to join me?"

"No, my mother is coming to town. Apparently, we are having a spa day."

"That sounds nice."

Her nose wrinkles. "You don't know me well, do you?"

I can't help but laugh as we meander through the corridor.

"*¡Hola Charli!*" Miguel calls out, jogging towards us. "*Buenas tardes. ¿Cómo estás?*"

"*Buenas tardes. Estoy bien, gracias,*" I reply. "Are you well?"

"Very much so," he replies, smiling. He turns to Maja. "*Hola.*"

She waves. "*Hola.*"

Miguel turns his attention to me. "My parents have invited you to dinner tonight."

"Really? Me? Dinner?"

He takes a step back and lifts an eyebrow. "I didn't mess up my English again, did I?"

I laugh. "No, no. You did perfectly. I'm surprised, that's all."

Miguel's full lips form a smile. "This is good. You will come tonight?"

"*Si,* I'll be there. *Muchas gracias.*"

"*De nada, hermosa.*" He kisses my cheek. "I will come to your room at five to collect you."

Miguel leaves for his next class and my heart pitter-patters. A real-deal Spanish meal, with a real-deal Spanish family. This is exactly what I needed.

"Oh my," Maja says. "Looks like your weekend plans fired up."

"I won't lie, I'm excited."

"So, you two are an item?"

I hug my books. "Miguel and me? No, we're just friends."

Maja chuckles to herself, walking ahead. "Aha."

My cheeks flush as I keep up with her. "I'm serious. We are friends and nothing more."

"Sure, sure," she says, with a smile that won't quit. "Or is this why you asked me to join you this weekend?"

My lips quirk and heat rises up my collar. "You know I like spending time with you."

Maja winks. "Next weekend, I'm all yours."

Every moment in Madrid is eye-opening. At first, I was out of my mind with nerves. Thank goodness, someone from the school greeted me at the airport because being alone in a foreign country is a huge undertaking.

Miguel was my assigned guide on my first day of school. Despite the accent, his humour easily translates. He's fun to be around and I'm grateful he's stuck by my side.

When classes finish, I go to my dorm room to decide what to wear. My hands tremble as I fish through my wardrobe. I shake it off. Why am I nervous? It's just dinner. I think about a table full of native Spanish speakers with broken English and swallow uncomfortably. There are the nerves. With my broken Spanish, this will be one hell of an experience.

From my desk, my laptop sings the *Skype* ringtone. I walk over, hoping Brittany's calling. **_Incoming call: Kellie._**

My lips twist as I consider answering. Yes, Kellie is my best friend, but her calls bring me down. She reminds me of home. Dating Will has made her focus on schoolyard politics. I don't want to hear the latest *John Thomas High* rumour. What I need is to keep Sanford, and its residents, out of my mind. I lower my laptop screen until it clicks shut.

I edge towards my wardrobe, swallowing the guilt. I'll find time over the weekend to call her back.

I spend longer getting ready for dinner than a school formal. The only time I cared more about how I looked was for my dad's wedding. Let's quickly shove that memory to the back where it belongs.

The knock at my door sends my heart aflutter. I take a sharp breath in and open the door. My smile hurts my cheeks. His olive skin and dark, mesmerising eyes take me in, and I forget I should say words after answering the door.

"You look *magnífica*," he says, looking me up and down.

"*Gracias*." I clasp my hands behind my back and jut out a hip to show off my ensemble: a black, faux-leather jacket over a navy chiffon blouse, accessorised with a gold, blue-beaded necklace. Below, I wear black skinny jeans and black knee-length boots.

"Ready to go?"

I nod and follow him into the hall.

The first time I rode on the back of Miguel's vespa, I shook like a leaf. The narrow laneways don't leave room for error. I freaked out, imagining us running into pedestrians. After no accidents occurred, I began trusting Miguel. And now it's fun!

He's asked me a few times to drive but I trust him more than myself. I can just hear my parents if I had called home saying I'd skidded off a vespa *and* I was the driver. They'd probably boil over melting point and bring me home. Not an option.

"How far away is your home?" I ask, throwing a leg over the vespa and buckling up my helmet.

"One hour," he says, starting the engine. "Will you be ok on the back for that long?"

"I'll hold on tight."

He chuckles. "*Bueno*."

Riding over the cobblestones is the worst part. You have to be careful not to grit your teeth too tight. Although, I long for the cobblestones once we're on the open road. It's a tad scarier than riding in the city.

As cars whoosh past, I squeeze Miguel's waist. He asks if I'm ok, and I nod, digging my chin into the nape of his neck. I feel him laugh and it eases my tension.

Once I was used to the speed, the hour passed quickly. I admired the landscape of rolling green hills, bobbing with shrubbery and waves of grapevines. The afternoon sky is an ombre of royal blue and baby blue, broken by three straggly clouds. Sights like this make me so thankful to be here.

"This is my village," Miguel says as our speed slows.

The square stone houses huddle together. A green leafy vine travels up a two-storey building. The streets wind around buildings, like in Madrid, yet the village's pace is slower. Children laugh and play in the laneways. Women sweep their front steps and tend to pot plants. Men hang by open-topped trucks, dirty, sweaty, and smiling, recounting the day's events.

We park outside Miguel's family villa and he takes my hand, leading me to the front door. He turns the doorknob and I slip my hand away. We aren't a couple and I'm worried the family will get the wrong idea.

Miguel grins and takes my hand back. I exhale and smile. He's my friend. I'm such a goof.

An older, stout woman rushes towards me and grabs my shoulders. "*Hola, Carli. La chica bella.*"

"*Buena tardes*," I say as she kisses my cheeks and squeezes me in a hug.

"*Esta es mi madre*," Miguel says, introducing his mother.

"*Mucho gusto*," I say, smiling at the *more-than-welcoming* woman.

"*Hola, Carli*," the rest of the family says in unison.

My heart warms at the mispronunciation of my name and I wave. "*Hola.*"

"My English not so good," Miguel's mother says, rubbing my arms. "*Excusas.*"

"It's ok. My Spanish not so good."

His mother laughs boisterously and beckons me further into the house. "Come. Come."

Miguel shows me to a sofa and introduces me to his younger brother and older sister.

"*Me llamo Rosa,*" his sister says. Her smile grows cheeky. "I speak English."

A quick breath of relief escapes me.

"How is your Spanish?" Rosa asks through full mauve lips.

"It's broken; I speak half English, half *español.*"

"*Me llamo Dom.* You miss Australia?" Miguel's brother tries his best English pronunciation.

"*Un poco. Pero la diversión aquí.*"

Dom smiles, appreciating my poor attempt at Spanish.

I snort a laugh and gather my curls to the side. "That was probably terrible," I say to Rosa. "I feel bad my Spanish is still broken. We speak so much English at school, it's hard to practice. I need more time with locals."

Rosa pats Miguel's thigh. "We should take a trip to Madrid. Go to all our favourite places. Carli will be a true Spaniard after that."

"*Si, Charli* will," Miguel teases.

Rosa continues grinning, seeming not to hear the difference.

Miguel's mother and aunts strut from the kitchen, holding dishes and announcing in Spanish, dinner is ready. They say some other sentences I don't catch. We move to the long table surrounded by Miguel's cousins. There is an array of meals, but I stock up on paella. I'd eat it for breakfast, lunch and dinner if the dorm dining room provided it.

One aunt pours white wine in my glass and I try my best Spanish to tell her, I'm only sixteen.

Eyes ogle me and Miguel explains a little wine at dinner is customary in their family.

I nod at the wine. I want to live like a local. I raise the glass as the others raise theirs and we say, "*Salud*."

I taste alcohol for the first time and it's a mixture of sweet and bitter. My lips pucker as I decide if I like it. It tingles and fizzes on my tongue. I take another sip and start balancing the flavour with the paella.

Ok, I could start living my life this way.

"You like?" Miguel asks.

I nod. "I like."

Saturday is a *me day*. I grab my backpack, tie-up my sneakers, and cover up with a baseball cap and aviator sunglasses.

Outside, the sun bounces off the stone and I'm now sure-footed, unlike the cobblestone-klutz I was a few months ago. This place made me grow up fast. The freedom is intoxicating. I still make good grades (it's a must or my butt gets kicked back to Sanford), but I get to choose when and where I do things. Immersing myself in a new culture is thrilling. The world seems so big now I'm on the other side of the planet. There is so much to see during my lifespan. My goal is to check off every single country.

In the town square I deviate down a side alley. Today, it calls to me. The freer I feel, the better an idea it becomes.

I walk into a tattoo parlour.

"*Buena días*," I say.

A girl with bright pink plaits, piercing along her ears, and tattoos down her neck and arms greets me with a smile. *"Buena días. ¿Cómo estás?"*

"Estoy bien. ¿Estás libre?"

"Si..."

She speaks so fast that I'm lost in translation.

I ask, "Sorry. *¿Hablas inglés?"*

She giggles. *"Si.* I heard your accent and wondered if you would ask. How can I help you?"

I blush at how terrible I must sound.

I slip a piece of paper from my pocket and place it on the counter. "I wanted to get this tattooed on my hip. Do you have any time today?"

"Ah, cool. Luka should be free in an hour."

"Wow, ok." My body tingles, and I feel slightly sick, but in a good way. *"Magnífica."*

I'd heard horror stories about tattoos, but they must be lies to scare kids from getting them. Yeah, the buzzing is annoying, but the needles merely feel like a hot scratch. Getting a filling or period pain is more intense.

The buzzing stops and Luka puts down the tattoo machine. "Finished, *señorita."*

"Wow, really?"

I jump up from the seat despite my tender hip. I skid in front of the mirror to study the artwork on my body.

My hands rush over my mouth. It's more awesome than I imagined. I pivot, taking in the greens and purples of the peace sign hugging my hip.

"You like?" Luka asks.

"Muchísimo."

Leaving the tattoo parlour, a morsel of guilt surfaces. Kellie and I planned to get our first tattoos together when we turned eighteen. Will she see my new ink as a betrayal? My stomach swirls and a pain pings between my eyebrows.

I'll surprise her with it when I'm back in Sanford. She won't get mad if I show her in person. Right?

4

Brittany

The car swerves as Will speeds along the climbing road of the forest.

We fly around the bends and I sink into the plush, leather backseat. Clutching Bryce's hand and smiling at him almost makes Will and Kellie disappear.

Will parks the car at a barbeque area at the top of the mountain.

"Ain't she a beaut!" Will boasts as we get out of the car.

"It's awesome," Bryce replies, studying the sporty car with Will.

"D'you get this whole car thing?" Kellie asks me as she pulls the picnic basket out of the boot.

Pulling out a blanket, I reply, "It's a pretty sweet ride."

"I dunno," she says as we find a grassy spot to set up. "Maybe I'll never understand the fascination with cars."

"At least its freedom, right?" I say, laying out the blanket. "We can go wherever we want without the parentals."

Kellie smiles, impressed. "That's an excellent point."

As we spread out the food, I note the boys talking, laughing and circling the car. "I guess one flaw of the car is it makes us invisible to our boyfriends."

Kellie snorts. "Will is too much sometimes. I'm happy for him to have a new toy to obsess over."

"You two still ok?"

"Yeah, we're great. You and Bryce?"

"We're solid." I bite my lip, blushing. More than solid. I still can't believe we did it. I wonder if Will and Kellie have done it yet. I tilt my head, staring at her. Should I ask? That'd be weird. We hardly ever speak and then I ask about her virginity.

Ohmigawd, I actually lost it. *Eep*!

Awkward silence hovers over us. I glance at the boys. How can I tell them to get their butts over here without being hella obvious?

"So," Kellie fills the air and I cringe at the impending small talk. "Did you watch '*The Bachelorette*' last night?"

My eyebrows raise. "'*The Bachelorette*'? I didn't think you watched that kinda stuff."

Kellie exhales. "Ok, so usually I don't. But I knew we would hang out. You like that show, right? And... although it pains me to admit this, I found the show addictive."

I fall back, laughing. "Oh, that's too good." I pull myself up and ask, "What do you think of Marcus?"

"*Ugh*, he's such an arse. How has he not been kicked off already?"

"I know. He's the worst. But what about Georgie?"

"Girl, I'd marry him in a heartbeat."

I grab her hands and hush, "*Ohmigawd*, me too."

"Well, well, well," Will says as he and Bryce walk over. "Are you two finally besties?"

I move away from Kellie and pat the space beside me for Bryce to sit.

"Just girl stuff," Kellie says as Will cuddles up to her.

Conversation always flows easily with the boys around. Kellie and I are just so freakin awkward without them. But, I guess, she made an effort today. Is that what I should do? Watch something for her? Not one of those weird Japanese cartoons she watches with my sister. No, thank you.

I need to try something. With the boys able to drive now, there will be tons of adventures. What will I do between '*Bachelor*' seasons? There must be something else we have in common. What does she like? Science? Do I get her to teach me science stuff? *Eww*, no. Why would I even suggest that?

Maybe I can teach her fashion. The ripped jeans and baggy t-shirts are so 1998 that I could scream. Yeah, we should go on a shopping spree. I'll suggest it in the next awkward silence after our boyfriends inevitably ditch us again.

"So, I went to therapy today," Bryce says, his voice low.

"Yeah?"

His smile curves to the left. "Dr Vernon thinks I can ease off the antidepressants."

"Baby, that's so great," I whisper. I plant a hand on his cheek and kiss his lips.

"I want off them so bad."

"I know. You've been doing so well."

"It's just a lower dosage for now."

"But it's a start."

I take in the twinkling happiness in his eyes. He's worked so hard all summer to feel better. He's loosened up so much and genuinely has fun when we hang out with our friends. In a lot of ways, he's morphed into someone else the last few months, yet he's still the boy I fell for.

"Have you heard from Charli lately?" Kellie asks me.

"Yeah, we text every other day. Why?"

Kellie fidgets and gives me a see-through smile. "Oh, good. I just hadn't heard from her in a while and wondered what she's up to."

Will slings an arm across Kellie's shoulders. "Wasn't she just in Italy?"

"And France," I say. "I'm beyond jealous."

"So, she's doing ok?" Kellie asks in a small voice.

I nod. "Yeah. Doesn't she video chat with you on the weekends? We do, so I assumed you still did?"

Kellie shrugs, pushing for a bigger smile. "Maybe she runs out of time?"

"Well, the latest thing is she wants to go to Greece. I can't believe how adventurous she's being."

"It's very cool," Kellie says. "I'm really happy for her."

"You should call her tonight," I say. "I'm sure she's got lots to gush to you about."

Kellie eases into a genuine smile. "Yeah, I will."

"Bryce, you can sit up front if you want," Kellie offers as we walk to Will's car.

"No, that's ok. I'm happy next to Brit," Bryce replies.

"Hey, no funny business back there," Will says as we get into the car. "Kellie and I haven't broken in the backseat yet."

Kellie scoffs and whacks Will's arm. "Shuddup."

Will leans over and kisses the top of Kellie's head. "Now, now. You know I need my main squeeze up front with me."

"Main squeeze? Boy, I'd better be your only squeeze," Kellie teases.

"Of course, you are," I say to Kellie. "Who else would take him?"

"*Har-har.*" Will starts the engine. "C'mon, let's see what this baby can really do."

Kellie's shoulders jiggle in the seat ahead of me. Only she could love a guy like Will.

The car hugs the mountain as we make our descent. Will takes the curves as sharply as before, but this time I'm swung side-to-side on my seat.

"Will, man, you're not invincible," Bryce says, leaning forward. "What's ya mum gonna say if you scratch up this car."

Will laughs, looking back at us. "Oh, Imma be a dead man."

I hold my breath until he looks at the road. I try to distract myself with looking out the window, but the palms and eucalyptus move by so fast I get motion sickness.

The car veers to the other side of traffic and my heartbeat pulses in my ears as air clogs my throat.

"Will! Look out!" Kellie screams.

The car swerves hard. We move back to our lane and then skid off the road. I scream as we fall over the side. The car jerks against the unlevel terrain and flies into a bank of trees. The car bounces on the ground and flurries of dirt attack the windows.

A haunting bang cracks as the car smashes into something. The car bends and flattens over me. Shooting pain runs up my leg. Everything grows hazy. My body and brain stop connecting as if I'm drunk. A flat, ear-piercing tone mutes all other noise. My eyes fall heavy. Everything goes white.

5

Charli

I scream myself awake. A shooting pain runs the length of my left leg and my hip rages like I'm on fire.

I switch on my lamp and fly towards the mirror. I reef up my shirt and pull down my shorts, expecting the tattoo to be infected and poisoning my leg. It's tender as I rub my fingers over it, but most of the redness and peeling disappeared days ago.

With a swig from my water bottle, I gulp two ibuprofens. Every step sends pulses of pain up and down my leg. Did I sleep wrong? Like an extreme case of pins and needles?

I hobble back to bed, hoping to fall asleep quickly.

My phone buzzes angrily on the table by my bed, jolting me awake. Grimacing, I reach for it. The screen illuminates **Incoming Call: Mum.**

"No, thanks," I mutter, lying the phone down.

When the call ends, I hear the ping of several notifications. I lift the phone and check the lock screen. My eyes bulge. Five missed calls from Mum. Something must be up.

I pull the bedsheet around me and put the phone to my ear, calling Mum back.

Mum abruptly answers. "Charli. Where have you been?"

I immediately regret the call. "Asleep. What's up?"

"There's been an accident."

My heart leaps into my throat.

"Brittany is hurt."

I sit up, hand trembling around the phone.

"Your dad is on the phone with the travel agent getting you a flight home. Can you start packing?"

"What? Holy shit." I pant heavily into the phone. "What happened? Is Brittany ok?"

"She's in surgery. We will tell you everything when you get here. Start packing and we will email you the flight details."

"Ok." My throat is Sahara dry. "Ok, I'll get ready."

"Be safe. We will see you soon. I love you, Charlotte."

"I love you, too."

My stomach triple knots. I slide off the bed and crawl towards my suitcase. I'm so dizzy I could puke.

What do I pack? How long will I be in Sanford? What happened to Brittany? A broken arm? A head injury? She's in surgery?

I'm gonna hurl.

I breathe in deep and long.

Ok, just pack.

I lay the suitcase open and chuck my clothes inside. I pile in books and question what I'm doing. My hands tremor as I stare at the floor.

Why am I going back to Sanford?

I jump at a knock on the door. I clutch my heart and creep towards the door.

It's Miguel. "*Buenos dias*, ready for class?" He looks in the room, then back at me and frowns. "What is going on? You look white as ghost."

"I have to go home," I whisper. My eyes fog, but I'm too confused to cry.

"Why? You have home sickness?"

I shake my head and sniff. "My sister."

"Something is wrong?"

"Yes. But I don't know what. She's hurt."

He holds my shoulders and asks, "You need to go to airport?"

"Yes, my dad is booking a flight."

"Get your things and I will take you."

The taxi to the airport was a blur. Miguel wanted to escort me in, but I made him get back in the car and go to school. Something about him comforting me made me sick. Nothing he did was wrong, but hugging me, stroking my hair, and telling me everything would be ok, was weird. Weird because I didn't know what the hell was going on.

"Miss Matthews, your plane is boarding soon," says the woman checking me in. "We are aware of your circumstances and will have a cart ready for you once you pass through security. They'll take you to your gate." She slides my boarding pass to me. "Have a safe flight."

Dumbfounded, I trudge my way towards security. Once cleared, I find the cart and climb aboard. It zips through the airport as my head threatens to tear in two.

At my gate, I'm ushered through the boarding line and rushed on the plane. Everyone seems to know I'm in a hurry but they're not saying why. I feel like I'm being sling-shotted everywhere.

"Welcome aboard, Miss Matthews," a cabin crew member greets me. "We hope you enjoy your stay in business class. Your seat is second on the right."

As I take my seat, crew members smile at me like they know more about why I'm onboard than I do. I spend twenty-three hours sitting, my stomach twisting and my imagination running wild with the hideous situations my sister could be in.

"Charli! Charli!" my step brother Nick calls out. He waves as I enter the arrivals lounge.

I wheel my bag around to him and watch his forced smile.

"How was your flight?"

"I was sick to my stomach the entire time."

He takes my bag. "I'm sorry you had to come back."

"What happened?"

Nick grows pale. "Your mum and dad should be the ones to tell you."

"*Nicholas*," I shriek. "I've been on a long-arse flight with no answers. Tell me something!"

"Car accident," he blurts.

I stumble backwards.

Nick takes my hand and shakes his head. "I'm sorry, I don't want to be the one to tell you."

My eyes become wet and I whisper, "How bad is Brittany?"

"She was out of surgery when I left, but I don't know much."

My poor Brit. I swallow the vile thing leaping up my throat.

I promise Nick I won't ask any more questions as we take the hour-long drive to Sanford. I'm so zonked, I spend the trip with my eyes shut, wishing to wake up in Spain.

#

I burst into the hospital waiting room. "Mum!"

"Charli." Mum pulls me into her arms. "I'm so glad you're here."

Hugging her causes panic to surge through my veins. "Mum. What's going on?"

Mum squeezes my hand and leads me to a row of seats. "Sit down. Rob, Charli's here."

My dad walks around the corner. Dark bags hang under his eyes.

I push back tears. "Hi, Dad."

"Pumpkin," he says and rushes to me. He kisses the top of my head and my limbs tremble with trepidation. My parents sit either side of me, cradling my hands.

My voice warbles when I ask, "What's going on?"

"There was an accident—" Mum starts.

"Brittany is ok," Dad is quick to add. "She came out of surgery and the doctors say she's stable."

I gulp hard. "Surgery? What happened?"

"It was a car crash," Mum says, steadying her composure. My hands leave my parents' grip and rise to my face. "The car bent around a tree. Brittany was crushed."

"Brit... no..."

"One of her legs was severely injured," Dad says. "We're waiting for the doctors to tell us more."

"Can I see her?" I whimper.

"She's in recovery," Mum says. "They haven't let us in yet."

My forehead scrunches as I try to make sense of this. "Who was driving?"

Mum and Dad tense up and a coldness shifts the air.

40

"Will," Dad says flatly.

"Bryce, Will, and Kellie were in the car," Mum says.

My hand slides over my heart. "Kellie's here? Is she ok?"

My parents exchange looks.

"Seriously, are they all here? Is everyone ok?"

Dad clears his throat and shifts his weight. "Bryce is sore but only has a few scratches and cuts. He was the one to call the ambulance."

"We are so grateful that he's okay," Mum adds, eyes watering.

Dad continues, "Will hit his head pretty hard on impact. Penny said he's in for a few nights with a neckbrace, but it's all precautionary."

I quickly breathe out. "That's good to hear. And Kel? Is she all clear or did she need surgery too?"

Mum squeezes my hand too tightly. "Charli." Her face creases and tears slip to her cheeks.

My eyes well as fear cloaks my body. "Mum?"

Dad rubs my back and says, "Kellie didn't make it."

A sick, torturous stab twists my abdomen and cuts off my air.

"The impact... it was sudden..." Dad continues but his voice is a garble.

"She, what?" is all I can manage.

"Charli," Mum pleads.

A sob croaks out of me with such a mighty force that my chest and throat hurt. "She's dead?" I collapse to my knees. Kellie's face clouds my mind. I won't see her again?

NO.

She's gone?

NO.

How can she be dead?

My head feels like it's caving in. The pain pulses through my body and I let out a soul-crushing moan.

Dad sits on the floor next to me and holds me close. For a moment I'm calm, but his weight sends me back to Earth and I don't want him near me.

I wriggle away and run out of the waiting room.

I run with no end goal.

A bathroom appears off to the side and I bolt in and screech to a stop at a toilet. My entire insides torpedo into the bowl.

I wipe my mouth, crouch to the floor, and gasp for air.

I drag my feet to my family. My head hangs low with the weight of an anvil. My eyes are red raw with a mixture of jet lag and death.

Dad's wife Tara sits by his side with her youngest daughter, Alyssa, on her lap. Dad and Tara's heads nuzzle together and I turn away.

Mum is further up the hall, speaking in hushed tones with Bryce. I edge closer to listen.

Bryce shakes as he talks. "The police were asking me questions about the accident. There was something I didn't tell them... I just... I'm not sure what I should do."

Mum grips his shoulders, her face serious like she's in lawyer mode. "It's ok. We will sit and talk first."

Bryce turns toward me, and his eyes widen. One side of his face shines with purple blotches. Two red cuts lay under his right eye. I swallow a sob.

He runs to me and wraps his arms me. My eyes clamp shut as a tsunami of tears threatens to break through. I hold him tight. So tight. I clench my jaw and bury my face in the nape of his neck.

He rubs my back and whispers, "I'm sorry."

"What happened?"

His hug gets stronger, but he doesn't say anything.

I hold onto him, my eyes stay closed, and I hope I wake up soon.

"Mr and Ms Matthews?" a voice says behind me.

Bryce and I break apart as my mum and dad rush toward a doctor.

"You can see her now," the doctor says.

"Oh, thank you," Mum says breathlessly.

Bryce and I walk towards the doctor, and he responds by putting his hand up and saying, "Just the parents."

He has whacked a baseball bat into my chest. I cough for air and stamp my feet. "No! You let me see my sister. It took so long to get here. LET ME SEE MY SISTER."

Bryce holds my hand. "Charli."

"No, Doctor," Dad says. "Charli and Brittany are twin sisters. She is coming in too."

The doctor nods, expressionless. "Of course."

Bryce lets go and my body quakes. My poor sister. Surgery. Alone. Hurt.

She needs me.

I'm on my parents' heels all the way to Brittany's room.

A nurse meets us at the door. "She's not awake yet, but she's doing well. You'll only have a few minutes."

"Thank you," Mum replies.

The nurse opens the door and we scramble inside. A sharp bleach smell attacks my nostrils. Machine beeps fill the silence and LED lighting plays against the overhead lights.

Attached to tubes and monitors, my sister lays on her back in a hospital bed. Blankets cover her body and bandages cover the left side of her face. Her hair is greasy and falls back into misshapen curls.

It doesn't look like her.

It's not her.

It can't be her.

This cannot happen to my sister.

My Brittany.

Mum and Dad crowd her and whisper sweet sentiments in her ear. I edge to the foot of the bed and ask my nerves to settle. My breathing is off. My nose snots and a lump forms in my throat.

"Brittany," I manage, but it's followed by two grotesque sobs.

I cup my mouth, clawing at my cheeks. My nails dig into my skin, trying to distract myself from the breaking of my heart.

"Brittany," I sob harder.

Brittany's eyes flicker, but she doesn't wake.

I find her hand and stroke it. *Please, wake up.*

The worst experience of my life is putting on this black dress. Today, I'm expected to say goodbye to my best friend.

She's dead.

She can't be dead.

I'm terribly lacking sleep. The jetlag is insane, but I get up every day to visit Brittany. Most days I've blocked thoughts of Kellie, but today it's impossible. Getting out of bed this morning was agony. How can I face this?

I collapse to my bedroom floor and pan the walls I had escaped from. Being home is nightmarish. My bedroom is four times larger than my dorm room, plus a balcony overlooking the beach. Idyllic, right? My sister's bedroom is next door... but my sister is not at home.

This bedroom feels far from home.

Tears blur my vision and the image of my bookcase. An entire shelf is dedicated to photos of Kellie and me being goofballs. And now... we will never take another one of these shots?

No. It can't be true.

There's a knock at my bedroom door and Sophia, our housekeeper, pops her head in. "Charli, you ready to go?"

My stomach wobbles with sickness. "No."

Sophia frowns and embraces me with a hug. She rubs my back and hushes, "I know."

I swallow with every step down the staircase and towards the car, so nothing escapes my stomach and covers my dress. When the car approaches the church, a pain pings between my eyebrows. I lower my head toward my knees and gently massage my forehead.

"Charli?" Mum whispers.

I look up.

"We're here," she says.

I swallow and breathe deeply. From the car, I follow Mum and Sophia to the church. I'm five paces behind them with no rush to go in.

A rustling in the bushes by the church draws my attention. It's accompanied by unmistakable vomiting.

Will Maclean stumbles out of the bushes.

"William, you ok?" his mum calls.

Will wipes his mouth and sees me. We stare at each other in silence.

He was the driver.

I race into the church.

I search for Mum and Sophia and choke upon seeing them on the same pew as Dad and Tara. Can my life become any more upside-down? I slide in next to Sophia, but Mum and Dad tap the space between them. With a gulp, I sit in the middle.

"Are you ok, hunny?" Tara whispers to me.

I raise an eyebrow and shrug.

"Nick and Shae are sitting with Brittany," she continues. "So, she won't be alone while we are all here."

Mum taps my thigh. "The Watkins are a few pews ahead."

My stomach threatens to erupt again as I peer ahead to find Reece. His parents and three brothers sit tall and strong. A solemn head hangs next to Steven. Reece is hunched, but I'd recognise that mop of hair anywhere. Between sitting at the hospital and wrapping my head around the accident, I haven't contacted him yet. I hope he's doing ok. We're both Kellie's best friends. He must be as confused as me.

His head bobs up and down and I realise he's crying.

Reece.

Crying.

Reece isn't one for openly displaying emotions, and now he's in a crowd of people, crying?

The sickness reaches the back of my mouth and I gag. I swallow and avert my eyes from Reece.

At the front of the church, Kellie's parents huddle together. Kellie's younger brother Bailey eyes the crowd with gloomy apprehension. A look I recognise from the mirror.

The minister starts the service and my heart begs me not to listen. Every heartstring tugs. How can I say goodbye to Kellie? Watch her lowered into the ground. To move on. To forget her.

NO.

NO.

I pick at a jagged nail to zone out. Dad plants a hand over mine, a cue to stop. With a huff, I lay my hands flat on my lap and hang my head low.

Kellie's uncle reads the eulogy, which is heavy on Kellie's scientific endeavours and her high academic record. My heart pounds as I wait to hear about her love of anime, the music of Joni Mitchell, her OTT obsession with superheroes and the length she would take an argument.

Nothing.

They remember her as a brainiac. I've lost my funny and loving friend, and they gloss over the parts of her life that made her *her*.

I shift in my seat and whisper to Mum, "I have to go."

She forces all her weight on my thigh. "No, you don't."

"I can't listen to this."

"I'm not having you look rude in front of Commander and Mrs Saunders."

"They're not even talking about her. Not the real her."

Dad clears his throat. Another sign to stop.

I slam my back against the pew in protest. They stare ahead, ignoring my needs.

A slow but muffled cry comes from the back. Over my shoulder I spot Will with his face in his hands, shoulders shaking. My jaw clenches and I face front. The minister says more words meant for comfort, but I shut down for the rest of the service.

When '*Ave Maria*' plays, we stand as the pallbearers move forward to take the coffin out. Reece's eldest brother, Eric, moves from his pew to the front. Steven wraps his arms wrapped around Reece and taps their brother, Jeremy, mouthing, Go up for me.

Steven holds Reece snuggly, as Reece buries his face in his brother's jacket. My head spins. I hold onto a pew with fear of fainting.

They walk the coffin up the aisle, but I don't watch. People from the front follow it, and we wait until it's our turn.

"We should go to the wake," Will says to his mother as we approach their pew.

"It's not a good idea," she replies.

"But she was my girlfriend."

"The family isn't ready to see you."

Will's face is long and devastated. I hold my breath as we pass them.

"Chaz," Will says, reaching out for my arm.

Mum slides his hand away from me. "Don't touch her."

"Julie," Mrs Maclean gasps.

"Sorry, Penny," Mum says. "He almost took one of my daughters away from me. I don't want him near either of them."

Mum takes my shoulders and leads me out of the church. Dad and Tara are quick behind, keeping distance between us and the Macleans.

I don't want to be here. Sitting on a couch in Kellie's living room. A couch where we binged old-school '*Dragon Ball Z*' and bitched about our families. How can we never do that again?

People eat from a buffet while my stomach swishes like it's a sailboat on open waters. We just witnessed Kellie lowered into the ground. How could anyone possibly eat?

"Hi Charli," Steven says, edging towards me.

"Hi," I say, unable to meet his eyes.

He sits beside me. "How are you doing?"

I bite inside my cheek and shrug. What does he expect me to answer? *Pretty good, bummer about the funeral, though.*

"When did you get back?" he asks.

"A few days ago. You?"

His hands fall into his lap. "Same. Look, I know this is a hard time and all, but I wanted to talk to you about my brother. You know Kellie looked out for Reece once we all moved away, and now that she's... Well, we need someone to check he remembers to eat and goes to the right classes, as he can get preoccupied with books. I know with your sister..."

"Are you serious right now?" I blurt out. "I can't listen to this."

I leap off the couch and storm out of the living room.

Mrs Saunders takes my arm as I pass her. "Oh, Charli. I'm so glad you could come back."

My eyes well at the sight of her. I hug her and say, "I'm so sorry. I'm so, so sorry."

Her hands gently touch my back and she whispers, "Having you here is like having a piece of her with us."

We pull out of the hug and I wipe my eyes. "Would it be ok if I go inside her room?"

Mrs Saunders' red-rimmed eyes droop. Her cheeks sink and she sniffs loudly. She nods, eyeing the stairs.

I thank her and race up to Kellie's bedroom.

I shut the door behind me and slide to the carpet. The murmurings from downstairs seep in, but I'm safe. Like every time I came to this house when I was sad or confused, I am safe. I am with Kellie.

I pan the room and it is a mess. It's like she never left. I stand up and walk through the piles of clothes and books and sit on the unmade bed.

They can't tidy this room. Then she would truly be gone.

A pair of glasses sit on the bedside table. Her old, damaged pair. She hated the idea of getting new glasses, but her parents forced her, saying she looked like she had no home.

I put the glasses on, and everything zooms closer and distorts.

I pull them off. "*Whoah*, she is blind."

My face crumples as I look down at the glasses. *Was.*

I put the glasses on the bed and hug my waist. A painful groan rolls out of me. "Uh, I can't do this."

My insides shatter. I slam pressure against the sharp shards of my heart. I turn to her bedside table and focus on the bottom drawer. I scuttle towards it and reef it open. I toss the notebooks and pens until I get to the bottom.

I sigh with relief and smile at the ceiling. *Thanks, Kel.*

I pull out the bag of weed, and it's surprisingly heavy. Kellie knew how to stock up. I shove it inside one of Kellie's satchel bags, along with the pencil case she kept the papers and lighter in. I swing the bag over my shoulder like it's always been there.

A knock at the door and Mrs Saunders walks in. "Everything ok?"

My face flushes. "Yes, I'm ok."

Mrs Saunders clasps her elbows, looking around the room. "We couldn't bear to change it."

I eye the floor. "This is Kellie."

We stand together in eerie silence. Mrs Saunders' chin quivers and I avert my eyes.

I pick up the glasses from the bed. "Mrs Saunders, you can say no, but... would it be ok if I had these?"

"I hated those things." Tears pool at her eyes, but she smiles. "Yes, you can take them. They'd only remind me of arguments."

"Thank you. Um, I'm gonna go."

She nods, not looking at me, and I leave her alone in the room, holding herself.

I hurry downstairs and am met with my mother. "We are going to see Brittany."

"Ok," I say, sliding the bag around my back.

"What's that?" Mum asks.

"A bag I'd left here," I cover.

"Your dad is saying goodbye to the Commander. Is Mrs Saunders upstairs?"

I look upstairs and frown. "Yes, but I think she wants to be alone."

"Sophia is getting the car ready." Mum squeezes my shoulder as she moves to the stairs. "Go on. We will be right out."

As we approach Brittany's hospital room, I halt. I rub the back of my neck and tilt my head, wincing.

"Coming, Pumpkin?" Dad asks, approaching Brittany's door.

My eyes are glued to the linoleum floor as I follow my parents, and only lift once I pass through the doorway.

My sister.

She looks so helpless. So beaten.

Nick and Shae move from their armchairs and stand by their mother.

"How was it?" Shae says to me.

I frown at her. "The funeral?"

Her face grows pale and she shifts her weight. "I just wanted to check you are ok."

I shrug. "No, I'm not." I turn towards Brittany and edge towards the bed.

"Did she wake up at all?" Dad asks Nick and Shae.

"Only for a moment," Nick says. "I don't think she registered we were here. She fell asleep pretty quick."

Dad strokes Brittany's hair. "She needs all the rest she can get."

Mum traces her finger along Brittany's jaw and lifts it away before touching the bandage on the side of her face. I shudder at the dark, purple and blue bruises under her eye and down her cheek.

"This isn't fair," I whisper, clutching Brittany's hand.

Mum whimpers as she runs a hand across my shoulders. I wriggle away from her touch.

"Charli?" Mum says mid-whimper.

"I can't just stand here while she's stuck in this bed," I say, backing away. "It's bullshit. Kellie's in the ground and Brittany's not waking up. I can't do this."

"Brittany?" Dad says, almost excited.

I stop and pivot to look at Brittany's face. Her eyes flutter open.

I rush to her side. "Brit?"

Mum takes Brittany's hand and part of me wants to yank it away from her.

Brittany's eyes lazily open and she rubs her chapped lips together. She squints at the ceiling.

"It's ok, Sweetheart," Mum whispers.

Brittany shifts her shoulders and Dad plants a hand beside her. "Don't try to move. Save your energy."

She pivots her head down and glances between us all as her brow furrows.

"Where..." she manages in a rough, croaky voice.

"You're ok, Sweetheart," Dad says.

Brittany sinks her head into the pillow. Her eyes fall shut. She's asleep again.

Tears pool in my eyes as I say, "Is she ever going to stay awake?"

"Charli," Mum hisses at me.

"You're not helping," Dad whispers harshly.

"She's been asleep for days," I persist.

"It takes as long as it takes," Mum replies.

Without realising it, I'm backing away. When I reach the hallway, I spin towards the exit and move away in a brisk walk. I can't take it anymore. Brittany stays asleep and Kellie's never waking again.

I burst out of the hospital, crunching fallen leaves beneath my feet as I veer off the cement path. I dive behind a hedge and open the bag before my bum hits the ground. I fish inside the pencil case and find a pre-rolled joint. I hold it between two fingers and gulp. If only Kellie knew what she had prepared this for. I place the joint between my lips and flick at the lighter. I inhale deeply and feel like I'm breathing for the first time in days.

I take two more drags and butt it out to save it getting on my clothes. I drop it into the pencil case and sit on the grass, finding the courage to go back inside.

The knots in my back dissipate and I get up. The throbbing in my head numbs and I walk into the hospital. As I pass through the waiting room, Tara and her kids walk away from Brittany's room.

"You ok, hun?" Tara asks, her tall and skinny frame curving with concern.

"Mhmm."

"Your mum and dad are talking to Brittany's doctor," Tara says. "They'll be out in a minute."

I look up the hall. "Should I go in there?"

"Why don't you have a seat with us," Tara says, sitting on a plastic waiting room chair. "They want to speak with you once they come out."

I glance at the three of them. "You don't have to wait with me."

"We're family," Shae says.

"She's my twin."

The three of them exchange looks. Tara nudges her head towards the exit. "Why don't you kids wait in the car? I'll be out when Rob's ready."

As Shae and Nick scuff their feet out of the waiting room, I eye Tara. "Are you part of the conversation with my parents? Cause, if not, you can go too."

Tara purses her lips and shakes her head. "Sit down, Charli. I know you're hurting and I'm not leaving you alone."

I don't sit. I clutch my elbows and pace the waiting room, keeping an eye on Brittany's door.

My parents walk out, thanking a doctor. Tara gets up and pats my back—which makes me flinch—and exits the waiting room.

"Good, you're back," Mum says as she and Dad walk towards me.

"What did the doctor say?" I ask. It meant to sound urgent, but I'm getting lightheaded.

"She's doing well after surgery," Dad says. "He's a little concerned she's taking so long to come around, but considering her trauma, he's optimistic."

"Optimistic?" I want to feel more concerned, but my insides are mellow.

"Charli take a seat," Mum says, moving to a row of chairs.

"Everyone's so concerned with me sitting."

"No, Pumpkin," Dad says, moving by Mum. "We need to talk to you."

I move to the seats and they insist I sit between them.

"We think it's best you stay here," Mum says.

I point around the waiting room. "Here?"

"In Sanford," Dad says.

"Of course, I'll stay until Brittany's better, but I have to go back and finish my exchange."

Mum clears her throat. "You're not going back to Spain."

"What? Yes I am."

"We don't want you girls apart. We can't send you over there," Dad says.

"No, you have to let me finish the semester."

"Brittany is in a bad way," Mum says, a tear streaking her cheek. "I'm too scared to let you go. I need to keep you here."

"You'll stay here. That's final," Dad says firmly.

Mum pulls me into a hug, and I eye my dad. It's been years since he had my mum's back. And keeping me here brings them together?

55

6

Brittany

My throat is on fire. Beeping sounds beside me. I scrunch my eyes closed, wishing it would stop. I open my eyes, and everything is a blur.

I swallow and it's like broken glass. I try to readjust on the bed, but my body is a heavy lump. I huff and sink into the bed, letting my eyelids fall shut.

When I open my eyes again, daylight shines through the window and my head bangs with the need for more sleep.

"Oh, Sweetheart, you're awake."

My head seems to move in slow-motion as I inch it to the side and my mum and dad grin ear-to-ear.

My eyes close. Why are they together? Is this a fight?

I hear the beeping again and squint my eyes. I pivot my head as my dad says, "You're in the hospital, Brit."

The thumping in my head gets stronger. Past and present are mushed together. What day is it? What was I doing before I went to sleep?

"Why?" I croak.

Mum strokes my hair. "It's ok, Sweetheart. You're ok. Just get some rest."

My eyes are so heavy I have no strength to agree or disagree. I stare at the doorway as my eyelids give in. Just before they close, someone walks into the room. With all my might, I keep them open as I recognise Charli.

I manage, "You're back?"

Charli turns to our parents with fearful eyes. She creeps closer and nears my bed. Her lip quivers and her eyes are glossy.

"Charli," Dad mutters. "Don't."

"We're letting her rest," Mum adds.

Charli takes my hand and sniffs. "I'm glad you're ok."

My forehead creases as her sad face looks away from me. In the silence, the beeping comes to the forefront. What is that? Where am I again?

"C'mon, Charli," Dad says, clutching Charli's shoulders. "Let's give her more time to rest."

Dad veers Charli out of the room as my eyes lazily fall shut.

I open my eyes and it's dark. Blue light emits from a machine, but no beeping.

No beeping.

Heaven.

My eyes fall shut again.

I tilt my head from side-to-side as I wake up. I'm lying on my back. I never sleep on my back. I wriggle my arms and notice they are on top of pillows wedged against my sides. I pan across the stark white room and watch the rays of sunlight dance through the window blinds. Where the heck am I?

I'm really groggy. Crap, I'm hungover. Whose house did I crash at?

"How's the patient?" a man asks, walking into the room and landing at the foot of my bed.

Is he talking to me?

He's in a white coat and has a stethoscope around his neck. I take in the room's decor. Holy crap. Am I in hospital? *Ohmigawd*. How embarrassing. I partied too hard and fell over drunk. Did I hit my head or something? *Ohmigawd*. My parents are gonna be so mad.

"Miss Matthews, can you hear me?" the man asks.

I nod. "Yes." Did that raspy voice come from me?

"I'm Dr Patel," he says. "Do you remember what happened to you?"

I shrink into the bed as my body flushes.

Dr Patel tucks a clipboard under his arm and moves around the bed. "You're in *Saint Andrews Hospital*. You were brought in after a car accident and emitted for emergency surgery."

He must be speaking a foreign language. I understand nothing he just said.

He flicks on a mini torch and shines it in my eyes. "Follow the light for me."

It's weirdly difficult.

"You've had a few days of recovery," he continues, "I'm hoping your alertness increases now."

Did he say... "Surgery?"

"On your leg." He gestures to my left leg. "You had a fracture in your femur and tibia. There is also a break in your hip, so we need to book you in for another surgery."

My throat is inflamed, but I say, "Another?"

Dr Patel pats my shoulder. "Please, try to rest. I'll be back in an hour or two to check in."

I stare at the ceiling and rush my breaths. I try to reef my hands from under the covers, but something snags my right hand against the blanket. Panicked, I pull up my arm until it's released.

I exhale loudly when my hand is finally free. A needle thingy pokes into the back of my hand, connected to a tube that runs away from the bed.

"Don't think about yanking that out," says a short, stocky woman in scrubs, waddling into the room. "That's your IV. You'd be feeling a heck of a lot of pain without that lil beauty."

I drop my hand and the woman squirts hand sanitiser from a wall-mount bottle.

"You feel more alive today, girly? Haven't been getting much out of you lately."

"Who?" is all I can manage.

She rubs her hands together and approaches the bed. "I'm Sue, a nurse on this floor."

I'm in the hospital? What did that doctor say?

The nurse ambles to the bed. "Lemme check your incisions aren't infected."

She slaps on gloves and pulls my blanket below my stomach. She reefs up my gown and inspects my body. I want to wriggle away, but my body doesn't respond.

She pulls the gown down and blanket up. She takes off her gloves and says, "Ok, all looks good there."

"Oh, Brittany, I'm sorry I wasn't here when you woke up," Mum says, rushing into the room. "Are you ok?"

"Yes," I croak.

"Just checking she's healing ok," Sue says, waddling away from the bed. "No problems in that area."

"Thank you so much," Mum says.

"I'll be back in an hour or so," Sue says, leaving the room.

Mum stands by my bed, smiling and stroking my hair. There's an eerie look in her eyes. I gulp, it hurts, and I ask, "I'm in hospital?"

"Yes, Brit. You were in an accident," Mum replies. "Do you remember it?"

My mind is blank. I'm having trouble remembering what the doctor said. "No."

"It's ok," Mum says. "Don't push yourself. Dr Patel said it might take a while to come back to you. All the pain meds aren't helping, they're keeping you groggy. You've been out for a few days."

"Days?"

Mum rubs my arm. "It's ok. You're ok. Just rest."

I want to ask what happened, but my throat is so sore I can't bear to make another sound.

Mum brings an armchair close to the bed and sits. "Your dad will be here soon. We have a meeting with your doctor regarding a decision on your next surgery."

My eyes bulge. "Surgery?"

She squeezes my shoulder. "You've hurt your leg and your hip. We need to decide how best to get you up and moving again."

Mum's phone buzzes and she reads the screen. She smiles and looks up at me. "Are you feeling awake?"

I shrug a kinda yes motion.

"Do you want a visitor? He's busting in the waiting room to see you."

"Dad?"

Mum laughs. "No, Bryce."

I suck in so much air I cough. My chest aches like a train hit it, but I nod as I cough.

Mum gives me a concerned look. "Perhaps we should hold off his visit."

I shake my head, struggling to get air as I talk. "No, no. Bring him."

Mum smiles and nods. "I'll get him."

She leaves and my heart ping-pongs in my chest. I breathe deeply and notice there are tubes at my nose.

"Hey, Matty."

I draw my attention from my nose to the doorway. Will stands in the doorframe, hunched and sad.

As he walks into the room, I look over the shiny bruise on his face. "You're hurt."

"Don't worry about me. I'm ok," he says, standing at the foot of the bed. "I heard you don't remember what happened?"

I look down at my body covered in heaped blankets. I reply in a harsh whisper, "I did something stupid?"

"No, Matty. You didn't. You did nothing wrong."

"You look bad."

"Good. I look how I feel."

"What happened?"

"Just remember we're friends, right?"

"Yeah..."

"William," Mum snaps from the doorway.

Will hunches more. "Hi, Ms Matthews."

Mum marches into the room. "It's time for you to go."

"He's ok," I croak.

"William," Mum continues, daggers in her eyes. "Out."

"Bye, Brit," he whispers and turns to leave.

"Bye," I say, watching Mum glare at him.

My heart rate picks up again as I glimpse Bryce by the door. The boys lock eyes for a moment and Will leaves down the hall.

Bryce rubs his temples as he walks into the rooms. He drops his hand and smiles when he sees me. He moves to the bed. "Britty."

I want to grab him and kiss him but moving my shoulders an inch from the bed feels like a massive workout. I resort to smiling, which hurts my muscles just as much. He touches the side of my face and his eyes shine with tears. His face is bruised and cut, and I shiver. "Your face?"

He shakes it off. "It's ok."

"You and Will."

He smiles. "Don't worry about it." His hand moves up my face and I feel something between my skin and his hand. I tense as I try to work out what it is.

"You feel that?" he whispers.

My forehead crinkles.

"A bandage," he answers without me needing to use words.

"I hurt my head?"

"A lot of you is hurt. Do you remember being in the car?"

I shake my head.

"Will's new car."

"I was?"

"Bryce," Mum says sternly.

He leans toward me, and his breath warms my cheek. He kisses me and stays close as he says, "It'll all be ok."

"I dreamt Charli was here."

He squeezes my hand. "No, Britty, she's here."

"Why?"

His eyebrows lift. "For you."

"That's enough for today," Dad says from the doorway.

Bryce steps away from me and says, "I'll be back to visit."

I don't want him to go.

"Bye, Britty."

My eyes prick. "Bye."

He walks to the door and I miss him already.

"I'm so glad to see you awake," Dad says, moving to the opposite side of the bed to Mum.

"Maybe we should tell her what happened," Mum says to Dad.

"Do you think she's ready?" Dad asks.

Why are they talking like I'm not in the room?

"It will never be easy to have this conversation," Mum says.

My eyes widen, waiting for them to say something to me.

Dad sits by my side with a soft sigh. "Brit, you were in a bad accident."

"A car accident," Mum says.

"I was?"

"Do you have any memories of it?" Dad asks.

"No."

"Will was driving," Mum says, her voice warbling. "He swerved off the road... the car smashed into a bank of trees."

"The car crushed you," Dad says, his face drooping. "You had surgery on your leg." His hand runs over my leg, but I can't feel it. "It's a cast."

"Broken?" I croak.

Dad frowns, holding back tears, and nods.

"Ah, good, Mr and Ms Matthews," a man says in the doorway, "you're here. Are you ready to come to my office?"

Mum wipes under her eyes and turns to the man. "We are just explaining to Brittany what happened."

The man walks into the room with a kind smile. "We had that talk earlier."

I squint at him.

"I'm Dr Patel," the man says. "Do you remember me?"

I look to Mum, wondering whether I should.

Dr Patel chuckles. "No harm. It was when you woke up. I won't hold it against you."

"It was this morning and she doesn't remember?" Dad says with concern.

"Don't be alarmed, Mr Matthews," Dr Patel says. "The morphine can account for that. Do you need me to help explain anything to Brittany?"

Mum strokes my hair and asks, "Brit, did you understand what Dad and I told you?"

I blink at her.

"Perhaps Brittany could do with more sleep," Dr Patel suggests. "Mr and Ms Matthews, let's go to my office and then we can return and talk to Brittany about our new plan."

I glance at Dad. "Plan?"

Dad pats my shoulder. "Get some rest, Sweetheart. We will be back soon."

Mum and Dad plant kisses on me and then leave with Dr Patel.

I look up at the ceiling and try to make the conversation sink in. I'm in hospital? My eyes grow heavy. When I open my eyes after who knows how long, Charli is sitting by me.

She gasps, "You're awake?"

I blink my eyes a few times as my vision clears. "You're home?"

She clasps my hand. "I'm here to help you get better."

"What happened?"

"You don't remember?"

I take her in, and my mind clears. "Car accident."

Her eyes gleam with tears. She nods with pursed lips, busting to break out in sobs. Her hand tightens around mine and she says, "I don't know what I would have done if I lost you."

"It was bad?"

"The car was smashed," she whimpers. "And poor Kellie."

"She's hurt?"

Charli's chin drops. "You don't know about Kellie?"

I shake my head.

Tears streak Charli's cheeks and she swiftly looks away. Her shoulders shake, but her cries are silent. She wipes her face and stares at me. "She's dead."

For a moment, everything inside my body stops working. "What?"

"Shit." Charli hushes as her hands rush to her face.

Kellie's face forms in my mind. Fragments of the last time I saw her come to mind. "We were on a picnic."

Charli lowers her hands. "What?"

"Picnic," I repeat, my voice disappearing. "She can't be dead."

Charli nods, her eyes reddening. "I know. She can't be."

"Everything ok in here?" Dad asks as he and Mum walk into the room.

"She didn't know about Kellie," Charli says softly.

Mum gasps. "Charli, you told her?"

"She should know," Charli says, eyes on me.

Mum rushes to my side and blocks view of Charli. She squeezes my hand and says, "Sweetheart, are you ok? We didn't want to overload you with too much."

I blink at Mum as Dad nears the bed. My throat is a vortex of fire, and a weight presses on my chest. I try to smile to say I'm ok, but instead, I close my eyes.

"What did the doctor say?" Charli asks.

"We'll talk about it later," Dad says.

Charli huffs. "Talk about it in front of her. She should know."

"We booked the next surgery," Dad says, and I open my eyes. Mum's eyes well as Dad says, "They're going to put the metal plate on her hip."

I shut my eyes, certain I'm in a weird dream, as nothing happening makes any sense.

"The doctor was called away to another patient," Mum says. "But he'll be back to talk you through it, Brit."

I open my eyes and turn to Charli. Her hand weaves between flowers in a vase by my bed.

Mum moves closer to the table and gestures to the many bouquets with teddy bears scattered between them. "Your friends have been coming quite regularly to visit you. I've tried to convince them to give you some time, as you've been asleep so much, but they are very keen. I caught Chloe trying to bribe a nurse to get in here."

I let out a faint laugh, but my chest hurts too much to feel good about it. I scan the wall beside my bedhead and notice a few balloons dancing by the ceiling. I can't believe I've been asleep through all their visits. I hope they come back soon.

Dad sits beside me. His face longer than usual. "Dr Patel booked you in for surgery in a few days. Do you feel ready?"

"Why do I need another surgery?" I ask him.

The bags under his eyes enlarge as he sighs. "There's a crack in your hip. He doesn't think it will heal with what they did last surgery. He wants to add a metal plate."

I shrink away from him. "Like something an old man would have?"

Mum comes closer. "He thinks you'll always walk with a limp if you don't get the metal plate."

"And one day you might get it removed," Dad adds.

Mum squeezes my hand. "Once you get this surgery, you can start physical therapy and relearn to walk."

"Relearn to walk?" I question her. "I know what walking is."

"You'll be in the cast for six weeks," Dad says looking down at my leg. "It'll take some time to heal. You'll have a lot to get used to."

"No," is all I can think to say.

Charli makes a weird whimper noise and jolts off her chair. She's out of the room before anyone can say something to stop her.

Mum sniffs and hugs her mid-section. "Dr Patel will be in soon. He can explain this better than us."

I huff and push back on the pillow wall behind me. I doubt he can because this is all one big mess of words. How can I wake up to so much change?

A cold sweat outlines the surrounding sheets. My second surgery happened a few days ago, and my mind is still in a fog. The surgery was supposed to make everything better, but I'm still a numb lump on a bed.

As the fluorescent lights make bouncing shapes above, I recount the last choreography sequence I learnt in dance class. They say it's an eight-week recovery. Eight weeks away from dance are too many. And I have metal on my hip. What will that mean for dance?

"*Ohmigawd*, she's actually awake."

I turn to the doorway and Chloe stares at me with circular eyes.

She twirls a piece of hair around her finger as she struts into the room, followed by Jace, Kimmy and Sean.

"Hey," I say in a croaky voice.

"*Whoah*," Sean says, looking at me sideways. "You look like hell."

Kimmy whacks his stomach, a smirk to her lips.

"How you feeling?" Chloe asks, sitting on the edge of my bed.

"You just had a surgery, right?" Jace adds.

I nod. "Yeah. I still feel kinda out of it."

Kimmy's hands stay on her hips as she pans my bed. "You'll be outta school for a while, huh?"

"I guess."

"Don't worry," Chloe whispers. "I took over as captain. You don't need that stress."

I fake a smile. "Thanks."

The boys linger by the door, ready to leave, and the girls discuss the next cheer practice. My teeth grit as they talk like I'm not here. They mention things from school that I don't know the backstory of and don't bother filling me in. What was the point of the visit? Desperation for a location change?

"How are we today?" Nurse Sue says, waddling towards my bed.

"*Um*," Chloe says with an eye roll, "we're, like, in here."

Sue chuckles, snapping on gloves. "And you can shove off."

Chloe stands from my bed and huffs. "Excuse me?"

"I'm on my rounds," Sue says, gesturing for them to move. "You can come back later."

"Do you know who my father is?" Chloe argues.

"Do you really want me to skip your friend?" Sue replies.

Chloe huffs and pulls Kimberley to the door. "Fine, whatever. We'll see you at school, Brittany."

At school? "You can come back," I call out.

Chloe shoots daggers at Sue. "*Ha*! Like we're welcome to come back."

The foursome leaves the room and Sue waddles closer. "Finally," she huffs. "Time to get down to business."

I eye her but don't reply. Is she really this rude? Even if I was out of the conversation, it was still nice to have a reminder of school. And Sue shattered it within minutes.

"Don't mind me," she says, fussing by the bed. "I'm just here to drain your catheter."

My what?

Eww. Is that pee in that bag? My pee?

I push my head back on the pillow and turn my attention to the overhead lighting. Now I'm glad she made them leave. Embarrassment city.

"You need to be sitting up," Sue says as she makes her way to the bathroom.

I ignore her as the contents of the bag drains into the toilet bowl.

She waddles to the bed with a now empty bag and reattaches it. "You know what Dr Patel said. You need to be sitting upright at ninety-degrees after your hip surgery. If it weren't for that damn cast, I'd have you sitting in an armchair."

I want to tell her to give me a break because I just woke up, but I can't be bothered with Sue. She's grumpy and I don't like her. Sitting up takes it out of me. So much effort because of the bruised ribs. They say the bruising will go away, but I've been told so many things.

"C'mon, girly," she says, pushing me up and stacking pillows behind me. My blood boils every time she calls me girly. "And I think it's time to get you into a new gown."

She unties the gown behind my back, and I flinch. "What are you doing?"

"You don't want to get bed sores from being in this thing too long."

I pull at my hospital gown and it's damp with sweat. I nod. A change would be nice.

Sue pulls apart my gown at the back and it falls down my front. My cheeks flush and I push the gown against my chest.

"Seen it all before," Sue says, tugging at the gown.

I let her take it. Not that I had much choice. I shiver from the exposure. Sue leaves my side and I pull my blanket as far up my front as I can. Sue returns with a bucket and a new gown slung over her arm. She drops the gown onto an armchair and retrieves a sponge. She reefs my blankets down and I'm left with nothing covering my body. I grow ghostly white and shiver again. As Sue brushed the sponge against my skin, I tap into my bravery and look down at my body. I wince at the dark purple bruise under my ribs. My hip is illuminated in yellow and grotesque stitches hold pieces of me together.

My stomach quivers and I look away as my eyes blur with tears. I shut my eyes tightly as Sue continues to run the sponge over my body. I recount the steps in my choreography for the *L'Amour* audition, trying to remove myself far from this situation.

When I'm in a fresh gown with damp hair running down my back, Sue leaves. My head falls forward and my hands are limp in my lap. A tired sob whispers out of me. That was humiliating. I was naked and she prodded at me like I was nothing. Another thing on her to-do list. Those horrible stitches and bruises... I shudder the thought away.

Another sob croaks out of me and shakes my body. Wails reverberate from my gut and clog my throat. I don't want to be here. I wrap my forearms around my face and cry louder. It's not fair.

I gasp for air.

It's not fair I'm in here. It's not fair I can't do anything for myself.

Mum walks into the room holding a tray. "Wanna try eating something?"

As she places the tray onto a moveable table with her back to me, I quickly wipe my eyes. The skin under my eyes is so puffy, and I probably look crap twenty-four-seven.

Mum wheels the table to fit over my bed and smiles at my damp hair. "Oh wow, you've had a shower. Feel better?"

I chew on my bottom lip and shrug. I don't want to talk about how it was nothing like a shower. I want to forget it. I look down at the *greenish-brown-smooth-something* in a bowl and my mouth waters in a bad way. With a sealed-shut mouth, I shake my head.

"It's just apple. I tried it," she says, filling a spoon. "It's sweet. You'll like it."

I frown at the incoming spoon. "I don't want it."

Mum drops the spoon into the bowl and huffs. "Fine, we'll leave it till later."

My chin dimples. "You're mad at me?"

"No. No, I'm not mad at you. I just want the best for you."

I wriggle against the pillows stacked behind me. Despite how much I want her gone, I am craving something sweet. "I'll try some."

"You sure?" Mum asks, already picking up the spoon.

I lift my arm to take the spoon, but it's such an effort.

I can't even feed myself. What is the point? I feel like a loser.

I drop my arm and nod at Mum. She holds the spoon to my mouth, and I open. It's soft and cool, and in some small way, I feel better.

"Ms Matthews," Dr Patel says from the doorway. Mum turns and he says, "We have the physio lined up."

"Marvellous," Mum beams.

"What does that mean?" I ask as a glimmer of hope warms me.

Mum turns to me, grinning. "You can start physical therapy soon. We'll get you out of this bed."

A surge of relief pours out of me. Out of this bed? That's a sentence I desperately needed to hear.

7

Charli

Before leaving for Spain, I hadn't spent any time at Dad's house.
Between the rush of him getting married and the ticking timer to leave
for exchange, I got out of it. But now I'm stuck. I'm forced to shift my
time between my home and this place. Here, I spend nights grimacing
at my dad and Tara snuggled on a couch as the family watches a movie.
Like everything is fine? Like we're one big happy family? Like this
wasn't one of the biggest reasons I left Sanford?

The only person I give attention to is my seven-year-old step
sister Alyssa. When I'm forced to spend time with *the family,* I sit at the
coffee table and draw with her. It's mind-numbing in the right way. We
talk about which animals we'd want to morph into. Her choices are cute
and fluffy. Mine, something that can fly.

When my step brother seeks advice from my dad like it's his own
dad, my skin crawls. It's not fair. They shouldn't get this much time
with him. Dad shouldn't want to spend all his time with another family.

Almost losing Brittany should have drilled this realisation into him.

I spend most of my time alone in my bedroom at Dad's. Tara driving me to school is beyond weird—her insistence squashed my protest. Thankfully, she drops me off first before going to West Sanford for Nick's school. But that relief quickly disappears as I stare at the front of *John Thomas High*. I've spent a lot of time at home, but now my parents are forcing me back to school. I'm not ready.

My head hangs low as I trudge through the corridors. People whisper by the lockers I pass, muttering Brittany's name, but I drown them out.

In history class, the gossip gets louder and changes direction.

"Shouldn't he be in prison?"

"Like father, like son."

"Except he's a murderer."

"Had to out-do his dad in the crime department."

I slouch in my seat as talk of Will grows nastier. Mr Hughes hushes the students, but the words are already repeating in my head. I rub the pain in my forehead and shoot my hand in the air. I ask Mr Hughes if I can be excused, and I'm up before he answers.

Murmurings are directed at me as I leave the classroom. In the corridor, I take a deep breath like I've been without oxygen all class. I lean against a wall and everything in front of me becomes cloaked in grey. I peer down the corridor that leads to the science labs. The labs I coaxed Kellie from so many times.

I look to my shoes and sniff back runny mucus. I can't deal with these memories. I need to be thousands of kilometres away.

The bell rings and I power through the corridor before students burst through the classroom doors.

"Charli."

I halt at Reece's voice, but I can't talk to him right now. I keep moving.

"Charli," he calls out again.

My jaw clenches as I stop and hug my waist. Over my shoulder, Reece catches up to me.

His eyes round with sadness. "Hi," he says in a raspy voice.

I turn to face him. "Hi."

He looks beside me, his forehead creasing, finding the right words. "How are you?"

"How do you think?" it rushes out of me and much too harsh.

He takes a half-step back. "You're back for good now?" There's a tinge of hope to his words.

My stomach twists. The glassiness of his eyes flashes my mind to the shattered mess he was at Kellie's funeral. Are we really going to act like that didn't happen? Like we didn't lose the most important person in the world?

"I've gotta go," I mumble, sliding my feet backward.

"What?"

"Sorry, I can't do this." My hands are out like stop signs and my feet twist me away from him.

I bolt from Reece. I don't listen for him to call out. My surroundings blur until I'm outside. I don't stop running until I make it to the grassy slope beyond the football field. I collapse to the ground, my chest rising and falling through rapid pants.

My fingers twitch. The way they yearn for a pen so I can scrawl the mess in my head onto paper. Poetry is the key that unlocks my thoughts.

But I don't want that. I don't want to think about how messed up everything is. I want to freeze my brain and forget everything going on around me.

I don't want to be at school.

I can't be here.

My fingers twitch again. I need a smoke.

I pull out my phone, contemplating which parent to text to take me out of school. No-brainer. Sophia would be here in a heartbeat.

I sit up and take some deep breaths before calling her. I thumb through my phone and land on my text chain with Kellie. My neck twinges at the sight of her many texts I never answered. She needed to talk to me about something.

My insides twist.

It must have been Will.

I drop the phone.

She wanted to break things off with him and needed my help. That must be it.

Why didn't I reply?

She'd still be alive.

I could have saved her. Saved her from him.

I run my palms across my eyes and call Sophia. She picks up within two rings and immediately asks me if I need to come home.

I reply with a warbled, "Mhmm."

Sophia signs me out of school and suggests taking me to Dad's, where I'm supposed to be living this week. I'm too forlorn to put up a fight, but Sophia sees something in my eyes and changes her mind. She drives me home.

At home, I tell Sophia I'm tired and bound up the stairs to my bedroom. Closing myself off in there is instant relief. I pull out the bag I stuffed under my bed and fish inside for a joint. I twirl it between my fingers and eye my balcony. I shouldn't smoke it at the house.

A vision of Brittany banged up in hospital takes over my mind. My ribs ache for hers. My breathing becomes laboured and my head swirls with dizziness. Pain radiates down my back and buzzes at my feet. I scrunch my hair, clawing at my scalp until Brittany vanishes from my mind.

My body tightens and I move towards my balcony. I sit on the chair by the railing and flick the lighter. The whoosh of the tide beyond the backyard, and the swirling, salty air drifts my thoughts into nothingness.

I put the joint to my lips and flop onto the chair. I gaze at the strolling clouds and smile at tweeting birds. My legs creep forward, and I recline in a deep slouch. I take my time exhaling the next drag.

I pull out my phone and mindlessly scroll. I tap the text message from Miguel I'm ignoring and push the email from Maja I'm yet to open from my mind. They need to leave me alone. *Forget me.*

My phone buzzes and I almost drop my joint. **New text: Travis.** My hands shake. I tap open the message.

> *(Travis)* **Hey. I'm so sorry. I wanted to get in touch sooner. But this is such a shit way to get back in contact. I just want you to know**

Before I can scan the rest of the message, I hurl my phone over the balcony, and it smashes against the garden rockwall.

Can everyone just forget I exist!

Two knocks tap on my bedroom door. "Charli?"

My heart leaps into my throat with an anxious pounding. I jump off the chair and stamp on the joint. I turn to my bedroom and slide the glass door open as Sophia opens my bedroom door.

"Do you want to visit Brittany with me?" Sophia asks. "I'm meeting your mother there."

I slide the door somewhat closed, hoping the smell won't enter. "I'm kinda tired. I think I might sleep."

"You sure?" Sophia says, stepping into the room.

"Yes." I put my hand out as my blood rushes through my veins and my pores explode with sweat. "I might cycle over later to meet you, but I think I'll sleep for a while."

She replies with a kind smile and retreats out of the room. "Ok. You rest, don't push yourself." She shuts the door behind her, and I collapse forward gratefully.

With the house empty, I creep downstairs to await my delivery. On my laptop via *Facebook*, I asked Kellie's former supplier Veronica to hook me up with a weekly supply. Easy to organise when you have parents with money and they don't pay attention to how you spend it.

I sit on the bottom stair, mellowing out after finishing a joint in the empty house. A deafening succession of knocks makes the front door quake. My heartbeat goes from zero to one hundred. I jolt to standing, reefing the door open.

"Heya," Veronica says, with a wink. Her jet-black hair frames her pale face and her stick-like frame slouches as she holds two brown cardboard boxes.

"D'you have to make so much noise?" I mutter.

"It's what you get for a last-minute delivery," Veronica says, pushing her way inside.

I slide an arm out in front of her. "*Whoah.* What do you think you're doing?"

"Ah, coming inside."

"No, you're not. I'll give you the cash now and you can leave."

"Give me five minutes," Veronica says, slipping past me and into the living room. "I got stuff to show you."

"I don't need you and this stuff in my house," I say, my heartbeat blasting in my ears as I try to recall if Sophia said when she'd be home.

"My mum could be home any minute."

"Chill, would ya?" Veronica groans. She opens a box and I spy a bag. "This is what you ordered." She closes the box and opens the other. "This is something I think will take your fancy."

I scan the box. "Cookies?"

"Some *edible* delights," Veronica says with a grin. "Pot cookies."

I lower to inspect them. "Oh. They don't even look suspect."

"Exactly. You could eat these in front of your mother and she'd never know."

A lightbulb illuminates my brain. *School.* "I'll take them all."

Veronica closes the box. "Glad to be doing business with you."

"Are you feeling better?" Sophia asks, running a hand over my head and kissing my forehead when they get home.

"A little." I shrug. "I've got a bit of a headache."

Mum pats my back and turns to leave. "Have a lie down. That's what I'm doing."

"I have been lying down," I say, walking to the back door. "I'm going for a walk along the beach."

"Don't be too long," Sophia says. "It's getting cold out there."

I look back for Mum, but she's already on the stairs. "I broke my phone," I tell Sophia. "Can you ask Mum to get me a new one?"

"Oh, sure, darling. No problem."

Once I hit the sand at the back gate, I pull the joint and lighter from the pocket of my jeans. I light up as I cross the sand, cupping the flame tightly as the ferocious winter winds approach.

Charcoal clouds rumble over the ocean, brewing a storm to attack our house. It's far enough out, I gamble I can finish the joint before it closes in. I sit on a rock and watch the waves leapfrog each other.

The wind plays at my hair as I inhale. My cardigan billows out as the wind surrounds me. I smile, thankful the wind will take the smell away.

"Hi, Charli," a voice says.

I look to my left and butt the joint on a rock to my right.

Will.

My jaw clenches and I want to be mad, but in the haze, my head grows woozy. "What do you want?"

"My mum is at the house, talking with your mum," he says walking closer. "She told me to stay in the car, but I've been wanting to talk to you. I came down here to work up the courage to walk into your house. Maybe this is a sign?"

"A sign?"

"How's Brittany doing?"

"What?"

"I want to visit her, but they won't let me."

I drop my gaze to the sand, wanting to focus on anything but him.

"I get you don't want to talk to me either. But I am sorry. I wish I could erase everything I did that day."

I cross my arms, digging my feet into the sand, hoping it swallows me whole.

"I'm not trying to make you mad. Do you want to talk about Kellie?"

"Talk about Kellie?" I splutter. "You're the reason I don't have Kellie."

Will's lips quiver and his gaze dips to the sand. "I know."

The wind whips around me, knocking me off balance and almost sending me to the sand.

"It's not his fault," the wind howls. My blood runs cold and I shiver with deadly chills. I gaze around the sky and to the crashing waves for the ghastly sinister voice. *"It's yours."*

"I wish I could take it all back," Will whimpers.

"How could you do it?" I whisper, and I'm not sure if the question is for him or me.

"Charli, I..." he starts, but I'm already off the rock. I push past him towards my backyard and ignore him calling my name.

I slide open the kitchen door and the sizzle of stir-fry and smell of delicious sweet and sour sauce drags me in.

"Hi gorgeous," Sophia says by the stovetop. "How was the beach? Not too cold?"

I squint one eye closed and push my busy hair flat. "Yeah. I'm pretty hungry."

"This will be ready soon," Sophia says, but I'm already at the fridge.

I pick out a slice of cheesecake with my fingers.

"Hunny, don't eat that. Have some actual food."

The cold cheesecake smears my lips and I chew with ballooned cheeks.

Sophia frowns and turns to the stove. "I'll put some aside for you."

My lips smack against my cakey fingers as I leave the kitchen.

"I already helped you by talking to the Saunders. I told you I wouldn't do anything else."

"Please, Julie," Mrs Maclean says to my mother in the foyer. Her hands clasp and shake towards my mother. Her face droops, aging her usually ageless, milky complexion. "He's getting death threats."

"It's not my problem," Mum says, her back stiffening as she crosses her arms.

"I need to send him to boarding school to keep him safe," Mrs Maclean continues. "I'm also scared for Daisy and me. I think we might have to move too. If only you and Rob could make statement to the community."

"*Pah!*" Mum smirks. "Like what? I forgive your son for almost killing my daughter?"

I drop what's left of the cake onto the tiled floor and Mum and Mrs Maclean turn to me, mouths ajar. I stare back until I shrink in size. I dash past them and hightail it upstairs to my bedroom, the thought of Brittany dying ripping my tainted heart in two.

Mum said it upset Dad that I didn't go back to his house, but she seemed to enjoy the fact she kept me over here. She didn't make me go to school today. She's still doing half days at work and picks me up at lunchtime to visit Brittany.

"Oh, Ms Matthews, do you have a moment?" Brittany's doctor says as he passes us in the hall.

"Sure. Is this about Brittany?" Mum says, her voice raising an octave of urgency.

 Dr Patel smiles and shows Mum to an office. "Yes, but nothing alarming. Just need a minute of your time to catch up."

"Ok." She turns to me and says, "Go keep your sister company."

They walk into the office and I shuffle my way towards Brittany's room. My stomach plummets with dread. The sterile bleakness of the hospital sends shivers down my spine every time I'm here. And yet, this fate is better than the one afforded to Kellie. I stop before Brittany's door and lean against the wall. I scrunch my eyes closed and hold my breath. I think about the cookie in my bag and open my eyes.

It's there if I need it.

As I edge my way to the doorframe, the sound of muffled crying became distinct.

"Brit?" I turn into the room to see Brittany slumped over a

tabletop, sobbing in wrapped arms. "Brit? You ok?"

Brittany sniffs a glob of mucus, wipes her eyes, and glances up at me. "Come to join the party?" Her voice is a broken imitation of her once bubbly persona. Her frown wilts her face, making it almost unrecognisable.

"Whaddaya mean?"

"Weren't you going back to Spain?" she grumbles, swiping at her dripping nose and eyes.

"They won't let me." As soon as I say it, I know it was a mistake. I don't know what I'm doing. How can I possibly help?

My sister stares at me with a hollow expression and I know I should have said I stayed for her. To be by her side as she gets well. But as I think this, I feel my feet sliding backwards.

"At least you're up and walking," she mutters under her hand. Her eyes shift to the window as she huffs. "You have no idea how humiliating it is to not be able to wash yourself."

"What?" It stammers out of me. Every second I look at my battered sister tears at my heart. I clutch my bag like a security blanket.

She falls on her pillow and keeps eyes on the window "Was it even worth surviving the crash?"

I stop shuffling backwards. "What are you saying? Don't say that."

She looks at me and there's no lively shine to her eyes. "They said I have to relearn to walk. No dance. No cheer. It's all taken from me."

My heart thumps. It hurts my chest as it thwacks my ribcage. *Who is she?* She's not my sister. I'm hollow inside as I take in her damaged shell. My knees tremble and the sterile stench of bleach makes my lips pucker. I don't want her gone. Not ever. I need her. I need her alive.

If she's taken from me, I have no purpose. I can't see her broken. It cripples my brain. Every fibre inside me decays as she lies there in grim despair.

As Brittany's eyes close, I spin and move to the door. Quick yet quiet.

I hurry down the hall, head low as I pass the office Mum and Dr Patel are in. Pain jolts down my left leg. I will my brain to remember it's not my pain and to leave it in that room.

I leave the hospital and break off a piece of cookie from inside my bag. I keep walking, eyes almost closed, but my feet determined to get where they're going.

I veer through the parkland and walk through the cemetery gates. I swallow the unpleasant feeling rolling around in my stomach. *I left her, but I had to leave her.* I eat more cookie and my body eases. I'm lighter as I make it to the grave. I kneel before the tombstone and run a finger across the engraved *Kellie Margaret Saunders.*

I fish inside my bag and retrieve her glasses. I sit them atop the tombstone and rest a cheek against the stone. "I need you."

My hand brushes against the grass sprouting over her. I imagine where she lies and slide down onto the earth to snuggle beside her, like all the times we talked through our problems. I rub my heart. But maybe it was a lot more one-sided than I realised.

"I'm sorry I didn't listen," I whisper to her. "I'm sorry I didn't help you get away from him. You'd still be here with me."

A tear threatens to break free and I lunge for my bag. I ransack it for a joint. A quick scan of the area and then I light up. I smile, knowing Kellie is looking down on me.

I lift the joint to the sky. "This is how you'd want me to get through this, right? You left these for me."

I inhale again. As I exhale white smoke towards the clouds, I tilt my head to the side, knowing I should confess what I did.

"Kel, I'm sorry, I know we always said we'd get our first ones together..." I run my hand under the waistband of my jeans. "But I was so caught up in being on my own, I couldn't help myself." I pull down my jeans and lift my shirt, revealing the colourful peace sign on my hip. "Do you like it, Kel?" I smile up at the clouds and take another drag. "The one we found on *Pinterest*."

An icy breeze runs the length of my body and sends me into a shiver. My chin drops as I eye the darkening clouds. "You're that mad, huh?"

The wind whirs around me and a haunting whisper swirls along with it. *"Why don't you kill yourself?"*

"What?" I gasp. I sit up, my stomach launching into my throat. Chills prick my back and I swallow hard.

"Leave me," the wind hisses.

Kellie?

"I'm sorry," I whimper. The wind thrashes with cruel intent and my eyes well.

She hates me.

My stomach knots and I snatch the glasses from atop the tombstone. The joint sits between my lips as I sling the bag over my shoulder and make a getaway from the cemetery.

I didn't mean to hurt you, Kellie.

8

Brittany

"Bryce, Bryce," my mother whispers.

I blink my eyes open as Mum gently nudges Bryce, who's slumped in a chair.

Bryce stirs from sleep and rubs his face.

"Bryce, hunny, you should go home," Mum says, leaning over him. "She sleeps most of the day. I'll tell her you were here."

"No, I'm ok," he mutters, sitting up.

"You need to look after yourself too. Go home and get some rest."

Bryce's face falls and he nods. He stands to leave and looks over to me. He smiles and rushes to my side. "Hey, you're awake."

My throat is dry and my tongue sticks to the roof of my mouth, so I reply with a smile.

"Good morning, Brittany," Mum whispers.

Bryce turns to Mum. "Is it ok if I stay for a bit?"

Mum smiles at Bryce and nods. She moves to the corner of the room and sits on an armchair.

"Did you sleep ok?" Bryce asks, bringing his chair closer to the bed.

"I guess."

Every time I wake up, I feel as if I'm coming out of a blackout and all my days are blurring together.

The back of his hand caresses my face. There's no bandage between us, but my skin feels bulged and tender. "It's gone."

"What's gone?"

"The bandage."

He smiles. "Yeah. It's looking a lot better. You have a bruise, but you won't have any scars."

The cuts on his face have healed, but the fact they were there in the first place makes me sad. I reach towards him and he catches my hand and kisses it. I relax and sink into the bed.

I tilt my head and spy Mum in the corner. Could she be any more awkward? "Mum."

She smiles like she doesn't realise she's the worst right now. "Yes, Sweetheart?"

"Could you, like, go... or something?"

She smirks. "Excuse me?"

"Can we have a minute alone?"

Bryce squirms beside me and I can tell he's uncomfortable by the way his hand tightens around mine.

"Alone?" Mum questions but gets up anyway. She glances at Bryce, then at me. "Five minutes."

Bryce's releases my hand and sighs in relief as Mum leaves the room.

"Sorry about her," I whisper.

"I don't mind your Mum."

"Maybe because she's not yours," I say to the empty doorway. I then hear what I said and gasp. I turn to him, my mouth ajar, and rush to take it back. "I didn't... I didn't mean... I'm sorry I said..."

He brushes my hair and smiles. "It's ok, don't freak. I know what you meant."

I pinch the bridge of my nose and shake my head. "I wasn't thinking."

"Your mum has been really good about letting me visit," Bryce says, and I drop my hand. "But she's starting to get worried. Everyone is worried about me."

"Why? What's wrong?"

"Because I want to be here all the time."

"I like that you're here."

"Me too, Brit." He kisses my hand again. "But everyone thinks I'll fixate on you and get sick again."

I gulp hard. "I don't want to make you sick."

Bryce slowly and very gently places his lips on mine. The wetness of his lips shows how chapped mine are.

"You aren't going to make me sick," Bryce says. "I love you and I'm not going anywhere."

"I'm glad you didn't have to be in hospital."

"I'm angry that you have to be. I want to make it all better for you."

"Maybe you can help me escape."

Bryce looks down at my legs. "I don't think we'd get very far."

"I can't wait to get out of here. What's been happening at school? What have I missed out on?"

"It's weird there without you. It's weird in general."

"Why?"

"Will. There was this big rift between our friends because of what he did and how people blame him."

"What are people saying about him?"

"It got so bad, Brit." Bryce's face falls. "Did you hear he left for boarding school?"

"No. When?"

"Recently. He was getting bullied, and it got so brutal he was getting death threats at home."

"Death threats?" My mind whirs to keep up. "I don't understand..."

"I don't have all the facts. I didn't talk to him directly. It's just what I heard at school."

"What do you mean? You didn't talk to him?"

"I couldn't, Brit. I couldn't look at him after what happened."

My forehead scrunches. "Because he crashed?"

Bryce's eyes widen and his hand tenses around mine. "He was out of control. He's the reason you're here and Kellie is dead."

It's like something slammed into my chest. I choke as I inhale my next breath. Processing anything negative about Will is hard. It's a foreign concept. He can be dumb, but he has the biggest heart.

Bryce winces and sits back. He rubs the heel of his palms into his eyes and sighs. "I'm sorry. There's been a really weird vibe going around school."

I steady my heart. "There's so much to take in. This is all so crazy."

"I know." He drops his hands and tries to smile. "Madi says hi, by the way."

"That's nice. I haven't seen anyone in ages."

"She said she wants to come by but wanted to make sure you were doing well first."

"I'm fine." I huff. "All I do is lay here. It'd be nice to have some company. It's like they all wanted to see me when I was first admitted and now the novelty has worn off."

He takes my hands. "You know you've always got me."

"I know." We kiss, soft and sweet. "I love you."

"Hey, I got it fixed," Bryce says, lifting and twisting his wrist to show off the watch I brought for his birthday.

"Fixed?"

"The glass was cracked," he says, tapping the face of the watch.

"In the car crash?" I croak.

He kisses me quickly. "But it's all fixed now."

I try a smile. "That's good."

"Knock, knock," sings a voice. Over Bryce's shoulder, a girl pushing a wheelchair enters the room. Mum follows her.

I pull myself up to sitting. "Is that for me?"

The girl laughs, setting the wheelchair by my bed. "Always love it when my equipment gets more attention than me. Hey, Brittany, I'm Aisha. I'll be your physical therapist."

Aisha smiles at Bryce as he anchors pillows behind me. "Hey, there."

"Hi," Bryce replies.

"Bryce," I tell Aisha, "my boyfriend."

"Hi, boyfriend," Aisha says with a giggle. "Are you going to be helping Brittany today?"

"Any way I can," he replies.

Aisha says to me, "You're a lucky girl."

I blush. "I know."

Mum moves around the other side of my bed and plants her hand on my shoulder. "Bryce, you should get home. Your dad will be waiting."

"I can..." Bryce begins, but Mum gives him the look and he

changes his mind. He brushes my hair and says, "I'll come back soon."

I nod. "Ok."

He kisses my cheek and whispers goodbye. I frown as he leaves.

"Cute boy," Aisha says, moving beside me. "How does it feel when you sit up?"

"Sore, but I reckon that's from lying down all the time."

"Good answer," she nods. "Have the nurses been making sure you sit up for a couple of hours every day? That's very important after hip surgery."

"Yes, we make sure," Mum answers for me.

"I wanna try getting you to sit on the edge of the bed before we try the wheelchair. Up for it?"

My heart patters. "Definitely."

Aisha pulls the covers off me and lifts my cast as she helps swing my other leg off the bed. Mum's hands press against my back, as one leg dangles in the crisp air and Aisha holds onto the long cast covering my left leg. Pivoting my legs to the side is exhausting, but it feels oddly freeing to be *almost* off the bed.

"How are you feeling?" Aisha asks, propping my leg up against her body.

"Ok," I puff.

"We'll just sit you here for a minute," Aisha says.

Mum rubs my back. "You doing ok, Brit? You can lie down if it's too much."

My jaw tenses. "No, it's fine. I don't want to stay in bed anymore."

"Are you in any pain?" Aisha asks.

"Not pain. It was just harder than I thought."

"It's ok. You're doing it. That's a big success."

I take a few lengthy breaths as I swing my right leg in the breeze.

Aisha smiles. "Ready for the chair?"

I smile. "Yes, please."

I gradually slide across. A horrible stretching sensation pulls around my hip and pelvis. *Eww.*

"You doing ok?" Aisha asks as I put my weight on her.

I hold my breath until I land in the chair.

"Brittany?" Mum asks with an undercurrent of panic.

I exhale and nod.

"Ok, take a rest and then we'll take this baby for a spin," Aisha says.

I collapse my shoulders and sink into the chair. It supports my back, so I don't sink far. I look over to the bed and my eyes pop. I'm out of it. I'M OUT OF IT.

I grin eagerly and say, "I'm ready."

"Aisha said to take a break," Mum scolds, looming behind me.

"Just get a feel for the chair," Aisha says as she props my leg on a support at the front of the wheelchair.

I do as I'm told and Aisha teaches me how to use all the wheelchair gadgets, including how to brake and how to steer. She plants my right foot on a footrest and explains how the prop she strapped my left leg to is removable. It's a reminder that the cast is temporary, and this chair is a step to getting better.

Aisha pushes me out of the room, taking a wide berth so my leg doesn't hit anything.

The physical therapy area has gym equipment and a wide-open space. I'm nervous to take control of the steering. This is the first time I've left my hospital room for something other than surgery. And now I can move myself around? A slick sweat runs down my arms as I grip the hand-rims.

There's an abundance of space in this room and I take up only a fraction. It's like I have absolutely no muscle in my arms. I'm weak. I'm useless. My core burns and it doesn't contract like it used to. Did I lose my abs?

My arms become jelly and I let go of the wheels. "I'm pathetic."

"Don't be so harsh on yourself," Aisha says, moving behind me. "It's your first go."

"Brittany, you're doing well," Mum says, pacing towards us.

"You don't get it," I frown. "I'm a dancer and a cheerleader. I'm strong. I should be able to do this."

Aisha kneels by the chair. She eyes me and whispers, "You were in a car accident. You've undergone two surgeries. Your hip cracked and your leg broke in two places. You are rebuilding. You will be strong again. You need time."

I gulp and my throat quivers. My eyes water, but I blink it away.

"Wanna try some more?" Aisha asks.

I shake my head. "I'm tired."

Mum strokes my hair. "You did so well. I'm proud of you."

I flash her a fake smile.

I didn't do well.

This is nothing to be proud of.

When we get to my room, Aisha has me lean all my weight on her as she lifts me. I land on the bed, and she smiles and wipes her brow. "Good first session, Brittany. You'll be walking between the balance beams in no time."

I grit my teeth and eye her, trying not to let my annoyance show. My tension leaves when she leaves. Mum fusses beside me, but I stare at the wheelchair.

I smile at it. *Finally*. A way out.

"I'll see where Charli is," Mum says, tapping her phone and putting it to her ear. "She should be down here."

Tension tightens my jaw at the memory of Charli disappearing when she saw me crying. That was days ago, and I haven't seen her since. "Is Charli going back to Spain?"

"Of course not. She's staying here with her family where she belongs." Mum lowers her phone and frowns at the screen. "She didn't pick up."

"She wants to go back."

"No, she doesn't," Mum replies quickly.

I think over Bryce's words about what Will did. "Will's at a new school?"

Mum's body locks and her eyes focus on a spot on the wall. "Don't worry, you'll never have to see him again."

"He's the reason I'm in here?"

"Yes. It's all because of him."

An unsettling shudder flips my insides. "Did Kellie have a funeral?"

Mum forces a smile. She pats my hand and says, "Yes, she did."

"Is it bad that I wasn't there?"

"Sweetheart, not at all. Kellie's family know how lucky we are that you lived. No one holds anything against you. They are all hoping you recover very soon."

I cross my arms against my waist. "They haven't visited though."

"They are doing it very tough. They aren't seeing anyone right now."

My eyes prick with hot tears. "They're mad I survived when Kellie didn't."

"Brittany, no, they're not."

"Maybe that's why Charli stopped visiting," I sniffle. "She'd prefer Kellie than me."

Mum grasps my shoulder. "Why would you say that? What did

Charli say?"

"Nothing. She just walked out on me."

Mum lets go of me and dials Charli's phone again.

As she puts the phone to her ear, I shake my head and say, "Don't bother. I don't want to see her."

"No, I'm making sure she's here," Mum says.

Charli doesn't answer.

She didn't visit.

#

"Hello, hello," a familiar voice chirps into the room. Meah struts her way towards my bed. "How's the patient?"

I wriggle against the pillows to sit as upright as possible. "Meah, you're here."

"In the flesh, baby." She shuffles some items she's cradling. "I got you all the essentials. Tim Tams, Oreos, and Rocky Road." She tosses them on the bed, and I flinch out of instinct. "Oh shit, was that your bad leg?"

I tap the blankets over my cast. "No, it's this one."

Meah circles the bed to the left side. "You have a cast. Should I sign it?"

I wince, not wanting her to uncover the cast. I hate the sight of it. "If you want."

"What's that face?"

"What face?"

"Your face is all screwed up. Brittany, I know you. What's up?"

I huff. "I just don't want to see the cast."

"Why not?"

"Because it's scary."

"It's a broken leg. At least you're alive," Meah says, moving to the right side of the bed. "You know, we had this big talk at school about Kellie. The counsellor has been holding all these sessions for people who need to talk. It's a good way to get out of classes. You know Will left school?"

I smooth over my blankets, keeping my head down. "I heard."

"He wasn't really in the group anymore."

"Whaddaya mean?"

"Chloe said we had to cut ties with him. Her dad stopped supporting Will's dad's case and told Chloe to follow suit with Will."

"Were there rumours going around about the accident?"

"Rumours?" Meah's voice goes up an octave like she's on defence. "I dunno. Information has been passed around."

"Were you spreading stuff?"

Her eyebrows raise and her lips purse. "I only say what's needed to be heard by other people."

I want to ask what she's been saying about me, but on the other hand, I don't want to know. My gut swirls with thoughts of what she could spread after seeing me today.

"I can't stay long," Meah blurts out, scrolling through her phone. "I'm meeting Fi at the mall to find a dress for the formal."

My head tilts. "It's not time for that already, is it?"

Meah nods with a bored expression. "In two weeks, but you know how you never find the perfect dress in the first shop."

My hand slips under the blankets and runs over the hard and bumpy cast. "I wonder if I can go to that."

"You totally have to," Meah says, taking more interest in the phone than me. "When are you coming back to school anyway?"

"I don't know. I don't even know when I can go home." I think about my time with Aisha and smile. "But it must be soon. I actually got to get out of bed and out of this room."

Meah's "Mhmm" dashes my excitement and her huffs make me want to kick her out. She must see something in my eyes when she looks up from the phone because she quickly says she has to call Fi.

"Bye," I say as she backs her way to the door.

"Feel better," she says with a wave, and then she's gone.

Feel better? It's not the flu.

I look down at the array of chocolate by my side and sigh. The first visit from a friend in ages and it lasted five minutes. No one is visiting me. It's like I'm a leper.

If I can't dance and I can't be a cheerleader, will that mean I won't have any friends? Are they already phasing me out because I'm in hospital? It's only a few more weeks until the cast comes off. I can't go back to being a loner. I just can't.

When Dr Patel makes his rounds the next morning, he asks me the usual questions, which I answer the same way. *Yes, no, no, yes.*

"Good," he beams. "Now, I need to talk you through your last scans. Looks like everything is healing but the impact of the crash, where your hip cracked, has caused some damage to your pelvis. We did all we could in your last surgery, however, the way it's sitting around your uterus might mean the need for further treatment down the line."

"Another surgery?"

"Yes, perhaps. Nothing I would suggest right now. I want you to heal from these surgeries and get your physical therapy underway. But as things stand, you may have trouble carrying a child to full term."

I squirm away from him. "As in, getting pregnant? I don't want to be pregnant."

"This is the furthest thing from your mind at sixteen, but it is important to note when considering the future."

I shift away again, shaking my head. "I don't want to talk about this."

"Are you sexually active, Brittany?"

I scoff. "What?"

"It's ok to be," he says. "But I would suggest not engaging in sexual intercourse for a few months to avoid any further damage to the area."

"Ok, got it," I blurt, looking away from him so he gets the hint to leave.

"Do you have any questions for me?"

The colour drains from my face. I keep my eyes averted and shake my head.

"All right. Please let me know if you do." He moves away from my bed. "I'll see you on my next rounds."

I exhale when he leaves the room. I block out the conversation... another thing I don't want to think about.

When my parents visit, I blurt out, "I want to go home."

Mum sits beside me and strokes my hand. "We want that too, Sweetheart."

I pull my hand away. "No. I want to go home now."

"Brit," Dad rounds the other side of the bed. "You're in recovery."

"I lie in bed," I protest. "I can do that at home."

Mum shoots Dad a look and whispers, "That's true."

Dad stiffens. "When you get the all clear."

I eye him. "Make them give the all clear."

My parents look across at each other.

"I know you can," I push.

Dad holds his head high and smiles. "We will take you to my house."

"What?" Mum squeaks.

"It makes more sense," Dad says. "She'll be on one floor, no stairs to combat with. The halls are wide, and the rooms have ample space to move the wheelchair around."

My bedroom forms in my mind. The one I grew up in. That has all my stuff in it. My eyes prick and my voice warbles as I say, "I can't go back to my home?"

Mum and Dad fidget and stare at me like they have no response.

I wipe under my eyes and sniff, "I want to go home to my bedroom. I want it to be like it was before. I want to feel normal."

Dad moves over to me and wraps his arms around me. He whispers, "I'll give you whatever you need."

"She needs to come home with me, Rob," Mum says.

"Brittany, you want to go home to your mum's, then you'll go home with your mum," Dad says. "I'll even pay to install a stairlift."

Mum stamps a foot. "Rob, you don't have–"

"Oh, Dad," I hug him tight. My wet face rubs on his coat as he strokes my hair.

"I'll talk to Dr Patel now," Dad replies.

"*We'll* talk to Dr Patel," Mum huffs.

Mum is dead on Dad's heels and I fall back on the pillows, catching my breath.

I scroll through Netflix with little interest before sliding my laptop away. I think I've gone through the entire rom-com section twice while in here.

"Hey, you want a visitor?" Nick asks, leaning into my room.

Warmth radiates from his grin and his hand sweeps through his neatly cropped brunette hair.

I beckon him in. "Yeah, come in. Besides Bryce, seems like the only visitors I get are my parents, and that's not cool."

Nick walks in, a guitar case strapped to his back and a smaller case under his arm. "How is that possible? Aren't you Miss Popularity?"

I shrug. "Must only count at school."

"Well, I got you something to distract you from boredom," he says, taking off his guitar case and putting the smaller one on my table. "If you're up for it, that is."

"Sure, what is it?"

"Not as lame as Sudoku," Nick smirks. "Mum told me she tried to get you into that."

"I appreciated the visit," I say, "but, yeah, it was way boring."

Nick opens the smaller case and pulls out a hot pink ukulele.

"*Ohmigawd*, that's so cute."

Nick laughs. "Oh good, you like it. I thought if you had something to practice, it might make the time in here go quicker. Well, that's what music does for me."

"I'm willing to give it a go."

"Take this one and I'll get my guitar."

Nick pulls out his guitar and shows me how to hold the ukulele. With the guitar on his lap, he presses my fingers against the cords and shows me how to strum.

With open chords, he gets me to strum up and down. I smile as it sounds like a song. When I've got the rhythm, he strums along with his guitar, and for a few beats, we sound good until I lose it and drop the uke, laughing.

Nick smiles and moves his guitar away. "You're getting it."

He takes my laptop and saves a few YouTube tutorials he says are the best for learning ukulele chords.

"Thanks. I'm sure I will use up a lot of time getting frustrated at the ukulele."

"Glad I can help. So, Rob was saying you're coming home soon."

"Yeah, he put the hard word on my doctor. Should be out very soon. Dad wanted me to stay at your house."

"My house," he mutters.

"You like it better in The Heights than West Sanford, right?"

Nick slouches in the chair and sighs. "I dunno. Like, the view is nice and all, but I'm gettin heaps of shit at school."

I snort. "What, for living in a nicer house?"

"Just a lot of shoving about for being 'the rich kid.'"

"Why don't you transfer to *John Thomas*?"

He shudders. "Nah. Not that desperate. Besides, I got my band at *West Sanford High*."

"*John Thomas* has a good music program."

"*Geez*, you sound like your dad."

I throw my hands up in surrender. "Ok, I'll totally shut up."

Nick relaxes into an easy smile. "It'll be good to have you home."

"I can't wait."

"I hope you have fun with the uke."

"Yeah, hopefully I'll have a song for you next time you visit."

"I look forward to it."

"Thanks for visiting. You have no idea how much I appreciate it."

He rubs my arm. "I'm glad I could make you smile."

9

Charli

I'm only mild relieved that Will left for boarding school, though it doesn't magically make being at *John Thomas* any easier. I loved the distance from this place, and now I'm back without the person who made it bearable.

I made it through two classes today. I call that an accomplishment. I never realised how easy it was to skip classes. Or do the teachers realise I'm gone and cut me some slack because my sister is in the hospital? Either way, I don't care. School is the last place I want to be.

The beach is my new best friend. The wind can be harsh and force me to relight the joint, but overall, the gusts off the ocean are a saving grace. It whips around me, disallowing the smell to linger on my clothes. The more I smoke, the less I hear the echoing voice reminding me of death. On the sand, I sit on my winter coat so when I leave the beach, I can wrap myself in it and cover any signs lingering on my uniform.

I trudge to the house at four in the afternoon. A believable time for walking home from school. When I slide the back door open, muffled voices and laughter seep out from the front of the house. With everyone visiting Brittany, I usually come home to empty silence.

I scuff my way through the kitchen to the dining room and peer into the living room. I gasp, losing my balance, as I spy the back of Brittany's head over the couch.

Shit.

She's home.

Mum and Sophia hover around Brittany, and Dad sits next to her. Wait... Dad? Dad is in our living room. Dad is in the house and he and Mum aren't screaming at each other? Mum beams at him, her eyes shining with life.

"Charli!" Mum cheers. "Look who's home."

Dad turns and smiles at me over the couch. "Pumpkin. You must be so relieved to have your sister home."

I edge my way toward the couch. "Yeah. Hi, Brit."

Brittany looks over her shoulder, lips pursed. "Hey."

Dad claps his hands together and stands. "Before I head home, I'll go to the store. What do you need, Julie? Brit, any requests?"

"No, Mr Matthews, it's ok," Sophia says. "I have a list. I'll go to the store in the morning."

"No, no, I insist," Dad says. "Please, Sophia, bring me your list."

Sophia blushes and leaves for the kitchen.

"Brit, want anything?" Dad repeats.

She shrugs and shakes her head.

"Tim Tams?" he offers.

She cracks a smile and nods.

Mum places her hands on Brittany's cheeks and kisses her

forehead. "I'm so glad to have you home."

When Dad leaves for groceries, Sophia prepares vegetables in the kitchen, and Mum apologises a million times to Brittany for leaving to make three work calls.

We are alone.

Her hair is shaggy and dull, but she is more fresh-faced than last time I saw her. A wheelchair sits by the couch and I shudder.

"I didn't see much of you when I was in hospital," Brittany says.

"Ah, yeah," I reply, backing away. "Well... it's been, like, hard being back."

"It was hard for me not being home. I was in there for over a month." She drops her head and exhales loudly. "You ditched me and couldn't even text me."

I bite hard inside my cheek. "I didn't know you wanted me to."

Brittany's eyes widen. "Are you serious? When you were away, we started talking like normal sisters. You didn't think I'd want that when I was in hospital?"

"I... I," I stutter and don't finish the thought.

Brittany waves me off. "Forget it. I'm tired anyway. Can you help me get my legs on the couch so I can go to sleep?"

I suck in my lips as I take in her full-length leg cast, which is propped on the coffee table.

"How... How do I...?" I barely move an inch closer to her.

Brittany huffs and looks away from me. "Just leave then. I'll wait for Mum."

Prickles irritate my eyes. I edge closer to her cast and slip a hand beneath it, ready to turn her, but she slaps my hand away.

"I said leave," Brittany snaps.

I jolt away.

Hurt burns Brittany's eyes.

"I'm sorry," I whimper and back out of the living room.

Upstairs, I face the bookshelf in my bedroom and trace a finger around the edges of the photo frames. Kellie's energetic laughter caught in a still moment. Another captures her squeezing me in a hug.

The wind bashes on the glass door to my balcony. I shiver at the gloom outside the glass and my heart drops to my stomach from the fear that the hollow voice will return.

I pan the pictures of Kellie. *She wants me dead?* I slide a finger across her face. We'd be together then. My stomach somersaults and threatens to burst. That would mean I wouldn't have Brittany.

With intensity, I slam the photo frames down so Kellie can't stare at me. *Stay away from me.*

I crawl under the covers of my bedding and squeeze myself into a ball. Flashes of Brittany, bruised and covered in tubes in the hospital bed, batter my mind. She was sweaty in the sheets and constantly asleep or sitting up and moaning ugly tears. I couldn't see her like that for one more moment. I can't see her downstairs and unable to move on her own. I can't do it. I can't do it.

My heavy eyes drain away the power of my mind and I surrender to darkness.

"Charli. Charli."

I wake to my mother calling my name. My eyes wearily open as I grumble noises. For the last few weeks, I could nap any time I pleased while Mum visited Brittany between her meetings. I frown at a growing headache. Mum will be home a lot more now.

"Charli," Mum says again, knocking on my door.

I reply with a groan as the doorknob turns.

Mum steps into my room and gasps. "Charli, this place is a pigsty."

"It's fine," I mumble, sitting up and rubbing my eyes. "Whaddaya want?"

"Come downstairs to eat with us," Mum says, skirting between the piles of clothes and books strewn across my floor. "You need to be with Brittany. I know she's been napping, but you shouldn't be timid around her. Treat her like nothing went wrong."

My eyes slit. "Like nothing went wrong?"

"She feels bad enough being stuck with that wheelchair. Don't make her feel inferior. Now, get yourself presentable and meet us at the dining table." Mum walks to my doorframe. "Move it. *Pronto.*"

When Mum disappears across the landing, I hurl myself backward. *"Like nothing happened."* But something did happen. If nothing had happened, I'd still be in Spain. If nothing had happened, I would call Kellie right now. If nothing had happened, Brittany would be coming home from dance class.

Mum has always acted like this. Before she and Dad split, she swept everything under the rug, hoping her marriage would magically fix itself. The mentality of, 'If I don't acknowledge the problem, the problem doesn't exist.' It must kill her that she can't hide Brittany's injury.

Dad's an avoider. He told Mum there was nothing to save, and he walked out. His reaction to problems is to find a way to look the best. Be the best lawyer in town, have the best kids in the school, and have the best woman by his side. Brittany quitting ballet annoyed him because of how it reflected on him. We must be the best at something. He only allowed me to go to Spain because I promised to keep high grades. I'd probably still be doing that if I were back there. If he noticed me not paying attention to my schoolwork, he'd flip out.

But is it really this easy to get stoned? Are my parents really oblivious to it? Are they so fixated on rectifying one child's problem, they'll let the other go totally unnoticed? How far would I have to go to draw their attention?

My parents are too alike. Maybe they never should have been together. Maybe Brittany and I should never have been born. Or maybe the egg should have never split in two. They could have had Brittany only. Without me, she would never have been hurt. Without me, Kellie and Will would never have been together. I was the reason he showed up at that party where they first kissed. If GiGi Larkin never hated me for being with Travis, she never would have targeted Kellie's party.

I cause everyone's misery.

I slip off my bed and break off a piece of cookie from the container in my bag. I munch on the cookie, smooth my curls into a high bun and swipe my puffy eyes. *Ugh.* Perhaps tying my hair back is only accentuating my enlarged, blood-stricken eyes. I swallow the last of the cookie, hoping I take the path of mellowing out instead of *panicking-the-fuck* out.

In the dining room, Brittany is seated at the table in her wheelchair. Under the table her white cast is propped up and stretching the width of the table. I used to sit directly across from my sister, but that cast gives me a nice excuse to take a seat further down.

"Sleep well?" Sophia asks Brittany, placing a plate in front of her.

Brittany shakes her head. "Not really."

Sophia looks across at me. "You don't look like you slept either."

I catch Brittany's stare. Her eyebrows raise as she takes me in. Her nose crinkles and her lips downturn; her sign of disgust.

"I'm fine," I say at my empty place-setting.

Mum sits and takes in her food. "Sophia, when you get Charli's plate, can you please bring one for yourself and eat with us?"

I instantly lift my head. Sophia's face is a mix of confusion and happiness. "Are you sure, Ms Matthews?"

Mum nods. "You've been exceptional through this tough situation with Brittany. Constantly at the hospital and running this household as if a horrendous incident hadn't occurred. Please join us."

Sophia smiles and nods. "My pleasure. Thank you, Ms Matthews."

Dinner is silent, except for the pockets Mum fills with work stories. Brittany twirls her hair as she chews, and I try to keep myself from faceplanting the dinner plate.

At the end of dinner, Brittany fidgets with the neckline and sleeves of her top.

"What is it, Brit?" Mum asks.

Brittany huffs, slumping in her chair. "I feel gross."

"How so?"

"I need a shower," Brittany says. "I think my last one was two days ago."

Mum drops her fork and sucks in a breath, irritation glowing in her eyes. "They didn't shower you for two days?"

Brittany shrugs, face falling. "I didn't want to. I wanted to wait to get home. I hated showering there. They didn't let me do it alone and the nurses were rough."

Mum lowers her voice. "They hurt you?"

She shakes her head. "No, it was just like they were rushing to move onto the next person. I didn't like it. It made me feel crappy."

Mum pats her hand. "It's ok. You're home now. But I don't like the idea of you in the bathroom alone."

I watch the revulsion morph Brittany's face.

"It's slippery and the tiles would be a hard landing if you fell," Mum adds.

"You put a chair in the shower?" Brittany counters.

"We will help you in and out of the shower," Mum replies.

She tenses. "*We?*"

Sophia clears her throat. "Your mother has asked me to help."

Brittany exhales. "Will you help instead?"

I gaze around the table and then realise she's talking to me. I lean in with a finger pointed at my chest. "Who? Me?"

She nods.

I part my lips to respond when Mum interjects, "You'd prefer Charli's help?"

"It might help to not feel so useless with my sister there, instead of you two," Brittany says. She finds my eyes. "Can you?"

I gulp and take in Mum and Sophia watching from either end of the table. I shrug a response, careful not to nod.

As Sophia clears the table, Mum wheels Brittany towards the stairs. I linger as Mum helps Brittany out of the wheelchair and onto the stairlift. Mum pulls a board out from inside the seat and props Brittany's legs on to it.

"Are you paying attention, Charli?" Mum asks as she presses buttons on the side of the stairlift.

I clutch my elbows as the stairlift hums. I swing my body away as Brittany slowly ascends the staircase.

"Comfortable, Brit?" Mum asks.

I swing back as Brittany winces. "Not really. But glad it's moving, I guess."

Mum compacts the wheelchair and gets me to help her carry it as we follow Brittany.

When Brittany's back in the wheelchair, Mum gestures for me to push Brittany into the bathroom. My hands tremor as I grip the handles. I push Brittany into the bathroom as Mum walks down the stairs.

An unsteady lump tingles my throat as I close the bathroom door behind us.

"Thanks, Charli," Brittany says, pulling her arms out of her sleeves.

"It's ok," I whisper, pulling her shirt over her head.

"This is elastic," she says, pulling at her skirt. "You just have to help me off the chair so I can pull it down."

I walk around the chair to face her. A sharp gasp escapes me as I see the scars wrapping around the left side of her lower torso. I lower and swing an arm around her. She hugs my neck and I lift her, but she squeaks as the chair pushes away.

She lets out a soft laugh. "You need to lock the chair first."

I sit her down and round the chair. "Where's the lock?"

Before Brittany replies, there's a knock at the door. "Ok if I come in?" Sophia asks behind the door.

I lunge for the door and open it with relief.

Sophia holds up a large black garbage bag. "I brought this so your cast doesn't get wet."

"Thanks," Brittany says, covering her chest.

Sophia places the bag on the vanity top and stops by me. "Looking for the lock?" she asks, clicking in the locks by each wheel.

I smile my thanks at her.

I move around to Brittany and help her up. Sophia helps remove the rest of her clothes and I look over my shoulder at the shower. "Do we just," I whisper to Sophia, "carry her over?"

Sophia smiles and almost laughs. She holds Brittany's sides and guides me to lower Brittany into the chair. "We wheel her over so it's less of a strain on us. That's all your mother needs, to find us on a heap on the floor."

Sophia gets behind the wheelchair before me and I let her push it.

Once she's in the shower, Brittany eyes me and puts a hand on the shower seat. My stomach flips and I move over to her. As Sophia keeps the shower seat steady, I use all my strength to help Brittany on to it. The cookie dulled my senses and yet the loom of panic becomes overwhelming.

Sophia pulls the garbage bag over Brittany's leg and I take in the heaped slump of my sister. It doesn't look like her. Helpless. I become aware that I'm backtracking.

Sophia moves out of the way when she turns on the water.

"I'll call you back when I'm done," Brittany says, loofah in hand.

Sophia squeezes my shoulder and says to Brittany, "We'll be close by."

I reach behind for the doorknob and slip out of the bathroom. I keep moving until I get to my bedroom door.

"I can help you get her out of the shower," Sophia whispers.

I shake my head. "I can't do it."

"I know it's hard, but–"

"No, I can't," I urge. "I can't be around her."

I open my door and pull it shut behind me. I exhale painfully and slide down the door. Sophia's footsteps sound near my door, but then turn and move towards the bathroom.

My face collapses in my hands.

I can't do it.

This week was a blur. I spaced through my classes, only knowing a week has passed because I overhear Sophia say Brittany's been home that long. I avoid the front half of the house like the plague as Brittany's always on the couch.

I was almost tempted to spend this weekend in the forest. It was my favourite place in Sanford. *Before*. Mine and Kellie's favourite... I just can't. Picturing the memories is too heartbreaking.

The beach will remain my sanctuary, but the risk is increasing. It was easier when Mum and Sophia spent the bulk of their time at the hospital. *Ugh*, and now Dad randomly pops in.

As I exit our back gate and scuff over the sand, barking steals my attention. I pan the wind-ravished beach to find a dog running around in happy nonsensical squiggles. Sammy. Reece's golden retriever. I suck in a breath and eye the house three down on the left. Reece and Steven stand by their gate watching Sammy disperse his energy. Steven notices me and nudges his brother as he waves. Reece turns to me, expressionless. He pulls his sweater sleeves over his hands and looks for Sammy, saying something to Steven. Before Steven can return his attention to me, I spin the opposite direction and rush against the sand and chilling wind.

I keep moving until I get to the cluster of rocks. It's quiet as I sit on a rock, and the wind subsides just enough for my lighter to work its magic. I let the greying navy waves hypnotise me as I take a long drag.

I want to stay numb.

I want to travel along the clouds rolling above and leave everything behind.

As I deeply inhale, the crashing of waves bangs like angry drums. I stand on the rock with a need to listen to metal music, like right now. I rub my forehead and giggle. Maybe I'll sleep instead.

With lazy eyes, I watch the sand soar in the wind and follow its dance. Tiptoeing across the rocks, I slip and scuttle downward, grazing my leg. I giggle at the missing skin and blood oozing down my calf. I swipe at the blood and roll backwards in a fit of laughter. My belly jiggles and the laughs scratch my throat.

NACHOS.

I stop laughing and sit up. I, like, need nachos right now. I pull a perfume bottle from my bag and douse myself in its sweet scent.

Barrelling across the sand, I zigzag towards the house. As I slip in through the back door, I stop. What was I getting again? I meander through the kitchen towards the staircase. Rounding the stairs, my ears prick at a buzzing noise. My vision distorts at Brittany on the stairlift... or off the stairlift? I creep up the stairs, squinting to work out what the hell she's doing.

"Help me get up, will ya?" she moans.

I stumble on the stairs and giggle at my feet. Man, shoes are weird. Like, I've never thought about how weird it is we cover up our feet to walk around. I keel over and splutter with laughter.

"Charli, why are you laughing? Help me."

I gasp and hiccup for air, laughing.

"What's going on?" Mum shouts, racing up the stairs and pushes me out of the way.

I hang onto the banister, giggling at my elbow.

Mum squeezes my cheeks, reefing my face forward. She stares into my eyes. "What is wrong with you?"

I snort and blow out my cheeks.

"Oh, good lord. Go sit on the couch and wait for me." She pushes me away. I blink at her until she bellows at me, "MOVE."

I meander down the stairs as Mum picks up my sister.

Collapsing on a couch, I ponder the world's best pizza toppings. I rub my eyes. Hang on, what just happened? I claw the couch and crawl into a ball. *Holy shit.* Does Mum know I smoked? I curl over the arm of the couch. *Fuck.* What do I do? I gotta run. I gotta get outta here, right?

My head spins and I flop on the couch. Maybe after a nap. What the fuck is on my pants leg? Oh, it's blood. Cool.

My lips are dry and stick together after I'm shaken awake. My eyes are red raw.

"Have you sobered up now?"

"What?" I croak, sitting up. I blink my eyes open and Mum stands over me, arms folded.

"Where is it, Charli?"

"Where is what?"

She leans over, glaring at me. "The weed."

I suddenly feel wide awake. "What weed?"

"The one you smoked so you were too high to help your sister," she snaps.

My breathing accelerates. "I... I..."

"I don't want to hear it, Charli! You give it to me. Now."

"But–"

"NOW."

I gulp and leap off the couch. Mum is on my heels all the way to my bedroom. I open a drawer and pull out one joint. She deadpans me, expecting more. I try to stare her down, but her determination is fierce. I sigh and pull out the stash.

Mum snatches it from me and paces to the bathroom.

"What are you doing?" I ask, hurrying behind.

My insides shatter as she pours the contents of the bag over the toilet and hits flush.

"Was that all of it?" she asks.

I nod.

She cups my face. "Never again, ok. No more."

I gulp. "Yes, Mum."

"Your sister needs us. We can't have anything like this going on."

"Ok."

"Where did you get it from?"

I avert my eyes. "School."

Mum lets me go and gasps. "There are drugs at *John Thomas*

High?"

My gaze falls to the toilet and dread climbs my back.

"Get cleaned up before dinner," Mum says and walks out of the bathroom. "Are you bleeding?"

"It's nothing."

My body trembles. Is that it? She knows... and it's done?

I slink to my bedroom, close the door and slide to the floor. My heart thuds. I look to my open drawer.

Shit.

It's gone.

I crawl to my desk and rummage through the drawers, hoping I stowed something in a drawer in one of my mellow hazes. I slip a hand behind some papers and feel a plastic bottle. I pull it out and almost laugh.

The focus pills.

Totally not what I need right now. I need to escape this mess, not be ultra-focused on it.

Wide-eyed, I pat down my body. Where's my bag? There are cookies and a few joints in it. I plant a palm on the door. Is it on the couch? *Shit.* What if Mum goes through my bag?

I open the door a crack. The hall is empty. I hold my breath and slip out of my room, trying not to make a sound as I walk down the stairs and quicken my steps into the living room. I spot my bag near the couch and a smile dares to cross my lips.

Sophia picks up my bag.

"NO." I slap a hand over my mouth to stop another outburst.

Sophia stares at me like a deer in headlights.

"What's in the bag?" Mum says, stepping into view.

"What?" I say breathlessly. "Nothing."

Mum holds her hand out. "Sophia. I'll take that."

"Mum," I whimper.

Mum fishes around in the bag and my gut twists in agony. She pulls out two joints and eyes me. "You lied to me."

I bite my lip, shifting my weight. "I'm sorry."

"Do I have to search all your bags?" she asks.

I shake my head. "No, that's all of it."

She chucks the bag at me. "Get to your room. I don't want to see you for the rest of the night."

I hug the bag and race upstairs. I slam the door behind me as hot tears streak my face. The bag holds three crushed cookies. I sigh and shove a piece of cookie in my mouth. As my eyes close, I wish I could sleep all of this away.

The next morning, sitting in the breakfast nook, I get the silent treatment from Sophia. First time in history she hasn't wished me good morning with a bright smile. My insides contort. Sophia is disappointed in me? I didn't know that was possible. She slides a plate in front of me and promptly leaves the kitchen.

I rub my forehead as a monster headache pulsates around my skull. I have half a cookie left, but I'm trying to keep it for school. It was a mistake to eat the other two last night, but what's done is done.

I lift my head and pan the benches. Something in here that might help. With a quick inhale, I move past the island bench and peer around the kitchen, trying to remember where I saw them last. I shuffle through the mess of papers on the bench before moving to the cabinets. *Eureka.* The orange container sits near the coffee cups. I pick it up and read the label; *Miss Brittany May Matthews, Take 1-2 Tablets Every 3 Hours, Do Not Exceed 18 A Day.* I twist open the lid and jiggle out a handful of pills and shove them in my pocket.

"Sophia? Is that you?" Brittany calls from the living room.

I chuck the pill bottle on the counter and race out of the kitchen to the back deck. I make my way through the yard and shove two pills in my mouth. I retch as it's hard to swallow with a dry, sticky mouth, but I force them down. My chest rises and falls, and I keep moving toward school.

I ate the remaining cookie after first period. My fingers twitch as I pace the east wing. The barrage of voices in the corridor usually pound my temples, but Brittany's pills help soften the blow. I know I can't handle school sober. I can't handle anyone asking me how I'm coping. Losing Kellie… Almost losing Brittany… How can they think that asking me how I'm coping is ok? I don't want to keep that on my brain. I need to forget.

I head to the lawns by the footy field to find Veronica.

"I need my next supply early," I say, crouching by her on the grass.

Her eyes narrow. "How did you get through it already?"

I groan and flick my eyes up. "My mum found it."

"Well that's too bad for you, ain't it?" Veronica smirks and reclines on the grass.

"What?"

"Believe me, Charli, I'd love to take more of your money." She picks at a jagged fingernail. "My supplier got busted. I'm out."

My heart plummets. "Out?"

"I gotta look out for number one," she says. "I can't give my stuff away when I don't know where the next amount is coming from."

I stand up, mouth ajar. "Are you freaking serious?"

What am I supposed to do now?

Shellshocked after not getting what I wanted, I couldn't function while playing hooky. Getting weed from Veronica was the sole reason I went to school. I can't be sober. I can't see Brittany like this.

"Charli," Bryce calls out, jogging towards me. "You want a ride home? I'm going to visit Brittany."

I shrug. "Yeah, sure."

We're silent through the carpark, the only noise is the scuffing of our shoes against the gravel.

"Hey, BK," Jace calls from his car. "Come over here a sec."

"I'll be right back," Bryce says, unlocking his car. "You can wait inside if ya want."

I plonk myself on the front passenger seat and watch Bryce approach Jace and Naveen. My gaze drops and wanders the interior of the car with little interest. I rest my cheek against the seat and thumb through the contents of the centre console. My eyes widen as I spot a small rectangular box. The label includes two long words, a description of the contents, and *Bryce Liam Kerry; one a day with food*.

I rub my lips together.

His antidepressants.

I look up and he's still with the boys. I open the box and see two aluminium sheets with two lines of pills running the length. I don't know what they will do if I take them, but it has to be better than how I'm feeling. No more hesitation. I whip out one sheet and close the box. I shove the pill packet in my bag as Bryce approaches the car.

"Sorry about that," Bryce says, starting the ignition.

I smile. "Not a problem."

10

At Dad's, I spend most of my time in my room. It's easier. When Dad's at work and Nick's at school, I'm on my own to ward off Tara's fussing. She's sweet and she means well, but I wish she hadn't taken time off work.

I agreed to three days here, but I've relented to a week. Whenever Charli goes back to Mum's, it upsets Dad, so I didn't want to make it worse. Any time I have away from Charli is a perk. She barely looks me in the eye these days and we haven't spoken since she laughed at me on the stairs. What is wrong with that girl? I get she misses her friend, but *I* was in the accident and I'm better adjusted than her.

Moving houses exhausts me. Well, the comments and concerns are exhausting, and they overdo the niceties. It stops once I'm settled and everyone is familiar with my presence. When I move to Mum's, it'll reset to zero, and the same thing will happen when I eventually come back here.

Tara holds my dining chair steady as I move from my wheelchair and I let her push me in closer to the table. She wheels my chair away as the rest of the family take their seats. Tara serves our delicious smelling meal and my stomach gurgles with anticipation.

"Can I have a go of your chair?" Alyssa pipes up.

"Alyssa!" Tara snaps. "How many times do I have to tell you no."

I smile. "It's ok. You can have a go."

Alyssa pushes off her chair but is road-blocked by Tara. "Not now, Lyss. Eat your dinner."

Alyssa climbs onto her chair and pouts at her overloaded plate.

"Are you excited to go back to school?" Tara asks.

"For a change of scenery, yes." I smile. "Being stuck at home is boring. The most exciting thing is all the homework sent home to get me prepared."

"I bet you never thought you'd say that about homework. All your friends must miss you." Tara looks to Charli and says, "You must be excited to have your sister at school with you."

Charli doesn't look up. She slides back on her chair and stands, saying, "I have a headache. I have to lie down."

I roll my eyes as she leaves before anyone utters a response. It's now her default to leave me stranded. Like the humiliation of when she left me in the bathroom. How could she? Why didn't she say she was uncomfortable?

She never thought about how uncomfortable it was for me.

She misses Kellie, but I'm still here. I can't wait for her to escape to Mum's again.

"Ok, Pumpkin," Dad says as Charli trails down the hall. "Hope you feel better soon."

Between bites, everyone keeps an eye on me. Their brows crease and they chew slowly like they want me kept centre of attention but don't know how. It's annoying.

"You guys can stop staring."

"We're not," Dad, Tara and Nick reply, dropping cutlery.

I smirk as an easiness washes over the table, and everyone relaxes into laughter. Finally. Maybe they'll be normal now?

After dinner I ask to go to my room, but the hurt is clear in each pair of eyes. I change my mind and sink on the couch to watch TV.

Dad is the embodiment of awkward. He's thinking about work and torn between that and wanting to spend time with me.

"You don't have to sit with me."

"No, no I want to," Dad insists.

"You want to watch the news or something?"

He eyes me suspiciously. "*You* want to watch the news?"

I smile. "No. But it's, like, the only thing I've seen you watch. Besides documentaries and those black-and-white movies with Charli."

"How is Charli? She's very quiet."

"She's always quiet."

Dad nods. "She misses Kellie. She'll come around."

My jaw tightens at the comment and I quickly push it aside and hand Dad the remote.

He pushes it back. "No, it's fine. Watch whatever you want."

"I'll be asleep in ten minutes. It doesn't matter."

And like that, I am watching headline news with my father.

It's peaceful on Sunday morning. Tara and her kids are at church, and Dad is upstairs in his office. Charli got up late and left via the back door. Maybe to see Reece? It's nice having some time alone. It seems like everyone thinks I'll break in half if they are not by my side.

Watching TV gets boring, so I crash on my bed. Lately, I've been feeling better so I'm trying to cut out the painkillers. I'm sick of taking them and I doubt I still need them.

I drift in and out of sleep and the family must be home because Nick's guitar strums in the neighbouring bedroom. An easy smile lifts my face and my eyes close as he sings. His soulful, yet delicate voice lullabies me to sleep.

A sharp pain jolts me awake. I massage my hip, but the pain intensifies to the point I want to scream. I look for my pills. Moving to the dresser is too stressful.

I squeeze my torso, hoping to crush the pain away, but it persists. Nick plays in his bedroom and I will Tara to pop her head in. I can't take it anymore and call out Nick's name.

On the third 'Nick' the strumming stops, and his door opens and then mine.

"Brit? Are you ok?"

I send my arm out, pointing to the pills. In a croaky voice, I ask, "Can you get them, please?"

He rushes over to me with them and hands me the glass of water by my bed. It takes all my strength to sit up. Nick sits on the floor, holding my hand. When I lay down, I squeeze his hand, probably harder than he was expecting. But he doesn't flinch. He stays seated. Quiet. Waiting.

I wish Bryce was here. I want the comfort of a warm body beside me. I look down at Nick and frown. "Would you stay with me?"

"Of course."

"Up here?"

"Ok." He moves onto the bed and wraps me up like he's a proper big spoon.

I rub the muscle by my hip and whisper, "Thank you."

A falling sensation jolts me awake.

"*Whoops*. Didn't mean to wake you," Nick says, pulling his arm out from under me. "My arm was falling asleep."

I sit against the pillows, rubbing my eyes. "That's ok. I should probably stay awake now anyway."

"Are you feeling better?"

"Yes. Thanks for staying with me. I always feel better when someone's around. I don't know why."

"Probably from all that time you spent alone in hospital."

"Yeah, that could be it."

"Besides, I didn't mind at all. I'm glad I could help you feel better." He looks at his watch. "I promised my nan I'd visit today. D'you mind if I go?"

"Not at all."

He smiles and slides off the bed. "D'you wanna come?"

"To your nan's?"

He runs a hand through his thick brown hair and grins. "I know it's not the most exciting thing to do. Just offering in case you wanted out of the house."

I shrug. "Could be nice."

"She's at a nursing home and I play the piano for her and her friends." He shrugs. "They seem to like it."

"A nursing home?" I giggle. "That could totally be my speed. I might be faster than some of the residents."

"I dunno, some of them have those motorised scooters," Nick teases.

I grin. "Way to show me up."

I hate this wheelchair, but no one at the nursing home bats an eye. We enter a common room and the female residents fawn over Nick, pulling at his cheeks and telling him he's handsome. Watching him squirm is fun.

Nick slips out of the grip of two grandmas and suggests, "How about I start playing?"

There are some disappointed awes, but the group takes their seats. Nick rushes over to one lady, who is already seated, and kisses her cheek. "Hi, Nanna. How are you doing?"

"I'm well, dear," she says sweetly. "How are you?"

"I'm good. Nan, this is Brittany."

I wave to her.

Her eyes shine eagerly. "Your girlfriend?"

Nick laughs. "No, Nan. Brittany is my step sister. You know, Rob's daughter."

"Oh, that's right, nice to see you again dear," she says.

"Nice to see you too."

She pats Nick's shoulder and says, "He's a good boy, our Nicholas. We are very proud of him."

I nod. "Yeah, he's a great guy."

"He is a very talented musician. His grandad and I made sure they put him into lessons as young as possible."

Nick blushes and says, "Ok, Nan, I'm gonna start playing."

"Ok, dear."

Nick moves towards the piano and says to me, "Wanna sit next to me?"

I push myself towards the piano. He plays easy-listening, crooner music. His wrists hover with masculine strength, yet his fingers move along the keys with an elegant softness. His voice is more mature when he sings, and I can imagine him in a 1940s piano lounge.

After playing two songs, he nudges me. "Wanna play something?"

"I don't know how to play the piano."

"I'll show you."

"No, no. I'm happy to watch."

Nick turns to the residents and asks, "You wanna hear Brittany play something, right?"

They answer with applause and I shrink in my chair.

"C'mon, it'll be fun," Nick urges. "Put your fingers here."

Nick places my fingers on the keys and tells me to follow his lead. My timing is off, and I miss a few of the keys, but after five attempts, we have rhythm. We stay on the same loop for a few bars until Nick uses his other hand to play something more intricate. It's hard to remember my timing, but my dance training kicks in and I listen for cues in music. Somehow, it sounds like a real song.

"Big finish," Nick whispers, and we end on the last note together.

The residents, those that are awake, respond with claps.

Nick kisses his grandmother goodbye and we get ready to go home. Nick helps me in the back of his mum's van and packs away my wheelchair. As he reverses the car out of the space, he thanks me for joining him.

"No problem. It was fun."

"Seeing all my adoring fans," he jokes.

"They were very handsy."

"I definitely take any opportunity to see her. I feel bad that she is there without my granddad."

"How long has he been gone?"

"I was eight-years-old when he died," Nick says, focusing on the road. "It sucked. We moved to West Sanford to live with Granddad and

Nan after my parents split up. I never saw my dad, but my granddad made up for it. He taught me music and convinced Mum I needed singing and piano lessons.

"Alyssa's dad kept saying they couldn't afford them, but Mum said they were worth it. Or, I was worth it, I guess. I want to make it big to repay my mum. I want to honour my granddad's memory too. I hate that he died before he could see how I turned out."

"I'm sure he's watching."

Nick's face softens. "Yeah, I like to think so."

"Your mum spent her money well. You are very talented."

"Thanks, Brit." He blushes. "Thanks for trusting me earlier, at the house. I've never played the older sibling role before. Shae's always looked after everyone, and Alyssa has, like, three parents. Being needed by someone is nice."

I rub a hand over my chest. "Don't thank me, I'm the one that's grateful."

He smiles, looking back at me. "Maybe we can look out for each other."

I nod. "I'd like that."

"Brittany, you're catching up very well," Mr Palmer says, closing his book and binder folder. "I see no problem with you re-joining my class. I'm sure you'll keep up with the other students."

I smile, relieved. "Thanks. I guess it's easy to get work done when you're not actually at school."

Mr Palmer smiles, holding back a laugh. "Yes. Free from distractions. *John Thomas* can be filled with those, especially in the corridors."

I eye my cast. "Yeah, kinda not looking forward to that part."

Mr Palmer pats my shoulder. "You'll be fine. From what I've heard, the majority of people are excited to have you back. You're missed, Miss Matthews."

"Thanks, Mr Palmer."

As Mr Palmer stands, Mum walks into the living room. "How's it going in here?"

"We're finished," Mr Palmer says. He steals a look at me and then to Mum. "Brittany's essay was brilliant. She'll have no problem returning to class."

Mum clasps her hands, grinning eagerly. "That's excellent. She got the all clear for maths and history yesterday. Brit, this is so wonderful. Well done."

"Thanks." My heart pitter-patters. This is pretty darn cool.

"Good luck with tomorrow," Mr Palmer says, nodding at my cast. "You won't know yourself."

I smile and nod in response.

Mum asks Sophia to show Mr Palmer out, and then she practically skips toward me. "Are you excited about tomorrow?"

I push out my palms like stop signs. "Yes. But stop going on about it or you'll make me nervous."

Mum sits on the couch, patting her thighs. "Oh, Brit, there's nothing to be nervous about. It's fantastic that you are getting the cast off. You'll be on the mend in no time. Have you done the exercises Aisha recommended? You know, just because the cast is coming off that doesn't mean you can skip them."

"I know, I know, Mum." I wave a hand at her. "I'll do them. Can you give me some space?"

She huffs. "All right, all right." She gets off the couch and moves toward the foyer. "I'll be in my study. Holler if you need me."

"Sure, whatever. Can you also refill my prescription?"

Mum stops dead. "Already?"

"Yeah, they're low."

Mum's eyebrow arches and she circles back to me. "It shouldn't be. Have you been taking too many?"

"No, I take less now."

"Brittany, you can't overdo them. It can lead to an addiction that will bring on more prob–"

"*Mum.* Just forget it, I won't take them anymore."

She sighs. "It's ok. I'll refill it for you. Make sure you tell me if the pain gets worse."

"Fine."

As Mum leaves, I pull out my phone and scroll *Instagram*. I sink into the couch, happy and accomplished with my tutoring session, but the high quickly disappears. My feed is littered with videos of my dance group practicing. I find Chloe stepping out my solo and watch other routines I haven't learnt yet.

I lock my phone and chuck it onto the coffee table. My groan reverberates throughout my body. I should be in that dance studio. It's my solo. I should be learning those new moves.

What am I without dance? I need to practice for my *L'Amour* audition. I knock on the cast. At least it's coming off tomorrow. Finally.

There's a knock at the door and through the foyer, I spy the doorknob turning. Bryce slides through the door.

Magically, my mood lifts. "Hey, what are you doing here?"

"Hey, Sophia," Bryce says towards the hall. He walks into the living room. "I came to see the prettiest girl in town. Have you seen her?"

"*Har-har.*"

Bryce sits beside me with a pack of Tim Tams. "I know the drill."

I giggle and take them as he plants a kiss on my cheek. "I'll look like a Tim Tam soon."

"I didn't think it was possible for you to look any sweeter."

"*Ehck.*" I retch, giggling. "Stop it,"

"How was your tutoring session?"

"So good. Mr Palmer gave me the tick of approval."

Bryce hugs me. "Brit, that's awesome. Can't wait until you're back in class."

"Me too. I never thought I'd miss school this much."

Bryce runs a hand over my cast. "Would suck to be out of school so long."

I nod. "Yeah."

"You wanna watch a movie or something?"

I yawn and nod.

Bryce puffs a laugh. "Or sleep?"

I shrug, leaning into him. "Put something on. I don't care what."

"So, I can put on a *car-chase-blow-everything-up* movie and you won't make a fuss?" Bryce asks sceptically.

I rub my heavy eyes. "Yeah, whatever."

Bryce laughs. "Wow. You must be tired."

We snuggle closely as Bryce scrolls through *Netflix*. The opening credits roll and my eyelids droop. I fight to keep them open and, after a hard blink, a hip-hop track blasts through the speakers with the closing credits.

"Did you skip to the end?"

Bryce laughs. "I think you slept through it."

"No way," I lie with a smile.

"Don't worry, you didn't miss the best movie of the year."

"Good." I stretch out before yelping in pain. I fell asleep in the wrong position and now my hip is paying for it.

"Brit? Shit. Are you ok?" Bryce asks frantically, sitting upright. "What can I do? How can I help you?"

I use my dismal strength to sit firmly on both butt cheeks. Through gritted cheek, I say, "I'll be ok,"

"I'm sorry," he says, helping me sit tall. "I shouldn't have let you sleep like that."

I try to smile. "I dunno. It was nice at the time."

He smiles and his breath tickles my neck. "Yeah. It was."

"I think I might need to go to bed," I whisper.

"Oh, ok."

"Will you help me upstairs?"

He grins. "Of course."

Though I now get myself into the stairlift, I enjoy letting him strap me in. He's so gentle and careful. He's adorable.

He helps me to my room and to my bed. In moments I'm a starfish. Bryce snuggles beside me and I'm glad Mum's stopped caring if he's in here. Maybe it's the fact that the cast and my surgery limits what we can do. The first time he was in bed with me, I was super embarrassed that I fell asleep, but now we laugh it off.

As my head rests on his chest, Bryce catches me up on the latest gossip at school. Listening to the soft beats of his heart, I wished he never had to leave. I almost want to ask Mum to let him stay overnight. With him, I'm safe.

But I shouldn't push it. She's just become cool with the door being closed. And I don't want Bryce to dwell on the things we can't do. Spending so much time in a bed with a girl who's told she can't have sex could be difficult.

"What you thinking about?" Bryce asks.

I kiss him soft and slow. "How much I love you."

"Funny, me too," he whispers, his fingertips dancing down my back.

A shiver runs down my spine and I flinch.

"You ok?"

A queasiness shrinks my stomach and I pull away.

"Brit?"

I sniff and look away. "Are you mad we can't have sex?"

"What?"

I eye him, scared he is mad.

"Why would I be mad about that?"

I bite my lip. "Because we're in a bed and we just started..."

He brushes my cheek and rests his forehead against mine. "Britty, I love you. I'm so happy you're home and I get to be with you. I don't care about sex. I'm glad you're still in my life. We spent all summer in bed without having sex."

My eyes fog with tears. I wrap my arms tightly around his neck and bury my face into his chest. I need him. I won't let go. I need him so much.

"Ready for it to come off?" Dr Patel says, sitting by my foot the next day.

He spent what felt like an eternity cutting my cast with an electrical saw. I was so terrified he would cut my flesh.

Cast free at last! "Yes, I am so ready."

"I didn't miss it, did I?" Aisha calls out, hurrying into the room with a walking frame in front of her.

"Just in time," Mum says, grinning ear-to-ear.

Aisha puts the frame down and slinks behind Dad and Tara, giving me a giddy wave. I smile and wave back.

The cast makes a suction sound as Dr Patel and the nurse pull it apart. I grimace at my exposed leg. It is sickly pale, lacking toned muscle, and the hairs are darker than my usual soft blonde hair. There are ugly surgery scars above and below my knee sealed with stitches the nurse will remove.

As Dr Patel pulls the cast away, I no longer care how different my leg looks. It's free. I have two free legs. No more stupid wheelchair. Refreshingly cool air dances around my skin.

"How does it feel, Sweetheart?" Dad asks.

"So far, so good."

Dr Patel talks to Mum and Dad about aftercare and he and Aisha agree on a minimum three school days in the wheelchair. Mum halts my protest as soon as I open my mouth. More time in the wheelchair? *C'mon.* This isn't fair. I don't want to go to school in the chair. Aisha tries to lighten my mood by saying my leg won't be on a prop like with the cast, but I'm less than thrilled.

After they remove my stitches, Aisha helps me walk with the frame. I squeeze the rubber handles like there's no tomorrow, praying I won't fall. I move two metres before taking a break. Aisha says I'm doing well, but it's such a slow pace I have trouble believing her.

My hip radiates in pain and I try not to show it on my face. I'm determined to get further, no matter how much my body screams at me.

"Hey! You're doing so well," Bryce's voice rejoices behind me.

I gladly stop and peer over my shoulder, blushing and smiling.

"She's kicking booty," Aisha says as Bryce kisses my forehead. "You think you can walk a bit more before we call it quits for the day?"

I steady myself on the frame and push it forward. My steps are small but I so badly want to show Bryce how much I've improvement.

"Britty, I can't believe you're walking," he gushes. "You look so good."

I snort. "Shuddup. I do not."

"No way, you look *hawt*," he says.

I stop moving when the giggles pang at my belly.

Aisha smirks. "Ok, let's call it."

I'm good at steering myself in the wheelchair but my arms are like jelly after physio. I'm happy that Bryce pushes me along.

"I'm so glad I made it," Bryce says. "I need to get to training soon, but I'll be around to see you this afternoon."

"Ok, cool."

"I can't believe we'll be able to walk around together."

I sigh in relief. "I know. I can't believe it."

I wake up on the couch in the afternoon sun and stretch out until it hurts. I check my phone: 5.16pm. I frown and listen for any surrounding voices.

Mum walks in. "Have a good sleep?"

"I didn't mean to fall asleep. Is Bryce here?"

"No, Sweetheart, he's not."

"He said he'd be over after footy training."

Mum sits on the armrest, face plastered with concern. "Bryce needs to take care of himself too."

I sit up. "What do you mean?"

"His dad and I have been talking. We are worried he's focusing too much on you."

Blood pumps loudly in my ears. "What? No, he's not."

"No one wants him to relapse. After what happened last year..." She takes a moment to regroup. "We don't want to allow the same patterns to occur."

"But Bryce and I talked about this and—"

Mum squeezes my hand. "Nothing is your fault. We just think it will be healthy for you to spend some time apart. Plus, you'll be at school on Monday. The time will pass sooner than you think."

I roll my eyes and Mum catches her cue to leave. I click his number and press the phone to my ear.

He answers and says, "Sorry, I'm not there."

"I was asleep, and Mum just told me."

"Dad is being way strict about it. I tried to ignore him and visit you anyway, but your mum turned me away. I didn't realise she was in on it too."

"I miss you already."

"I miss your face like crazy."

"I miss your hugs."

"Not as much as I miss yours."

I frown, forcing the tears away. "So, how was training?"

"It was ok. The guys were stupid, but it's easier without Will. No one's awkward anymore."

"It'll be good to start school without him around. I wouldn't know what to say to him."

"You'd be like me and not talk to him. Oh, the girls wanted to know if you wanted to do something this weekend?"

My heart pounds. "Which girls?"

"You know, Chloe and Kimmy and that. They were talking about visiting you. Did they text you?"

"I didn't check my phone. I'll see."

"It'd be good. If I can't be with you, at least someone can be."

I smile. "Yeah, I'll text them."

Friday night Chloe, Kimmy and Meah hang at my house. I barely remember their early hospital visits and then they stopped coming. It's good to hear gossip again, though it's hard to keep up. I forgot how fast everyone talks.

"It's so good to see you guys. I've been going crazy in this house." I pull at my frizzy hair. "And I feel like a mess. I haven't done anything nice for myself, like straightening my hair or having a facial, in months."

"We can fix that," Chloe says, standing up and rounding my chair. She plays with my hair and says, "We can totally have a pamper night."

"Yeah," Kimmy cheers, waggling her fingers. "How about a manicure? Meah, you can do the pedicure."

I giggle. "*Ohmigawd*, that sounds *ah-may-zing*."

As the girls make me over, I feel a rush of tingles. It's like my wheelchair isn't a big deal. Maybe going back to school will be easier than I thought? I figured being wheelchair-bound will make me an outcast. But maybe the girls will have my back?

As Chloe steams my hair through the flat-iron and Meah and Kimmy paint my nails, I contemplate leaving the house for an adventure.

"I'm so sick of being cooped up in here. What fun stuff have you guys been doing?"

"Too much cheer and gymnastics practice," Kimmy huffs.

"We had the formal and the after-party at Fi's," Meah says.

Chloe scoffs. "That was weeks ago. We should have another party. But, like, I so don't wanna host."

"Me either," Kimmy and Meah reply.

"We'll make one of the boys do it," Chloe suggests.

"I don't know how long I'd last at a party," I say, "but getting outta the house would be nice."

Chloe puts the flat-iron down and moves in front of me. "I've got my car. Why don't we do that now?"

"Whaddaya mean?"

"We can go for a joy-ride. Go up to the lookout and hang with some wine coolers," Chloe says. "You wanna leave the house, right?"

I grin and nod. "Let's do it."

It doesn't take much to convince Mum to let me out of the house. I give her the sad-puppy eyes and the girls back me up with the *giving-me-a-social-life* talk. We hurl my walking frame in the back of Chloe's car and pile in.

It's so good to be out. It doesn't matter where. I'm with my friends on a weekend adventure.

Chloe takes a corner sharply and I white-knuckle the door handle. My heart jumps in my throat and I close my eyes, trying to relax. The car continues to swerve towards the lookout. My mind whooshes with memories of the accident. Wrong side of the road. Hurtling past trees.

SMASH.

WHITE.

NOTHING.

I squeak a quiet scream and cup my mouth. Meah glances but ignores me to yell her way into the conversation. My heart works overtime and it's hard to breathe. My nostrils flare, and the car finally parks.

The girls leap from the car and my heavy breathing mutes their *woohoos*. I open the door and swing my legs out as Chloe leaves the walking frame by the car. I tell her I'll be a minute and she skips away with the other girls to squeal at the view.

My hands shake and the need to cry constricts my throat. My eyes fog and my ears ring, just like they did after impact. A haze of brown dust and branches stabbing through glass crashes into my mind and tears roll down my cheeks. I hold back my sobs as best I can, pushing call on Bryce's number.

"Hey, what's happening? How's girls' night?" he answers.

My eyes flood with tears and a throat-scratching sob bursts out of me.

"*Whoah*, Brit, what's wrong?"

"I just got scared and..." my voice wavers. "The car was going fast and it was like..." I sniff hard. "I don't want to be here... Can you..." Talking is too hard. I pant with shaky breaths and the threat of more sobs.

"Brit, Brit, calm down. Where are you? I'll come to get you."

I bury my head, hoping the girls don't look for me. Air clogs in my chest and my panic intensifies.

"Brittany, what's going on?"

I wipe my face and sit up. "We're at the lookout. I don't want her to drive me again. Can you take me home?"

"I'm getting in my car now."

I can't bear to get out of the car. The girls climb rocks and fling insults back and forth. I don't want them to catch how scared I am.

After what seems like forever, Bryce's car pulls up and relief trembles through my body. I stand and hold onto the walking frame, but in an instant, he moves away the frame and I'm in his arms.

"Hey, Bryce is here," Meah says.

"Oh hi, what are you doing here, gorgeous?" Chloe says as they approach us.

My head stays buried in his chest as Bryce says, "Oh, you know, there's only so long I can stay away from this one."

I put on my bravest face and turn to the girls. "Thanks for bringing me out, but I'm way tired."

Chloe scoffs, hand on hips. "You serious?"

Kimmy whacks Chloe's arm. "*Duh*, like, they wanna be alone."

The girls giggle and we say our goodbyes, making our way to Bryce's car. Bryce drives downhill and then parks the car. His hand slides on my thigh and he asks if I'm ok. Everything I was holding in busts out. I cradle my face in my hands and wail as I hunch over my knees. Bryce leans over me, his arms protecting me. He repeats he's sorry but it doesn't stop me crying because he did nothing wrong. I lay my head against him, trying to stop the images flashing in my mind.

"I see it too," he whispers.

I run a hand over his heart and open my eyes.

"I see it all the time," he says. "I wish I didn't, but I can't forget the crash."

"I'm sorry," I whisper.

"Why are you sorry?"

"Why are you?"

We wrap each other tighter and sit in silence. The fact that he remembers it all hurts. It hurts that he was awake for it all. I want to talk to him about it. Just... not right now.

11

Charli

I stagger down the staircase for breakfast. As I round the foyer, an odd clop-and-slide sounds ahead. As I make my way to the kitchen, I catch up with Brittany who's ambling with her walking frame. A shudder-worthy sight.

"Brittany, you're doing so well," Sophia says, kissing Brittany's cheek. "Ready for today?"

"As much as I can be," she replies as I push past her.

My head throbs like I've got a hangover. I don't like how every thought bubbles to the surface and I can't make them go away. I collapse into the breakfast nook and let my hair hang over my eyes.

Brittany sits opposite me. "You look like a mess. You're not going to go to school like that, are you?"

By mistake, I look up at her. I make eye contact as her face turns to horror.

"Charli. Your eyes are bloodshot. What's wrong?"

My throat closes in and I scramble out of the nook and lunge for the back door.

"Charli? Where are you going?" Mum calls.

I freeze with my hand gripped around the door handle.

"Sit and have breakfast," Mum says. "We should have breakfast as a family to celebrate Brit's first day back at school."

My gulp is so loud it echoes. "Back at school?"

"Yes, now sit," Mum huffs, sitting opposite Brittany.

I stammer awkward sounds, searching for an excuse. "Ah... I forgot an assignment upstairs. Gimme a minute."

Mum drives us to school. Mum has never driven us to school. Brittany's first day back is turning out to be an *uber* deal.

I'm frozen when Mum parks the car and helps Brittany with her wheelchair.

"You're sure I can't take you in on your first day?" Mum asks.

"Mum, no," Brittany grumbles. "We've spent too much time together already. Besides, Charli's here."

Mum eyes me. "You'll take your sister in?"

My inside swirl but I nod.

"Bye, Mum," Brittany pushes.

"Ok, ok," Mum says, backing off. "Remember to call me if you need anything."

"Yeah, sure, whatever," Brittany says, beckoning me over.

I'm two seconds from fainting. I push the chair, leaning in with all my weight. We take the south entrance for the ramp.

We are only past one row of lockers before Brittany's friends swarm her. A pair of hands take over my position and shove me aside. *Phew.* That chair makes me sick to my stomach.

I look at Brittany, staring wide-eyed at her friends and my heart rips in two. Man, I need Veronica to find a new supplier ASAP. I slip into an alcove and scoff a couple of Brittany's pain meds. Should I bother with today? Maybe I should forget school and head to the beach.

Ugh.

No weed.

What's the point?

I daze through my classes until the final bell rings and I can hibernate at home. I curl up in the sheets of my bed and escape into an anthology of Keats' poetry. I dog-ear a page and swipe my hand across my bedside table for a pen to make an annotation. A smash of random things fall to the ground and I grumble, reefing myself up. I swing my feet off the bed and land on the floor.

CRUNCH.

Something snaps under my foot. I lift my foot and look down.

Oh fuck, shit, no, no, no.

I drop to the ground and gather the mangled pieces. The frame and lens of Kellie's glasses are bent and broken. A gut-wrenching shriek pours out of me. *I broke her.*

Mallets smash the remaining shards of my heart. That's it.

I storm out of my room and hang over the landing. Brittany's voice is amongst Mum and Sophia's below, so I continue into her bedroom. I tear open every drawer of her desk and dresser until I find her fake ID. I yank something tight and low-cut from her wardrobe and bolt to my room.

When the dark of night blankets the sky I leave the house unnoticed. The taxi I ordered waits a few houses up from mine. As I walk towards it, the wind rushes from the beach to attack me.

"No one will miss you," it growls. *"Don't come back."*

I dash into the taxi, my pulse racing. I give the driver the name of a seedy bar in West Sanford and smooth my hand over my high ponytail. I check my makeup with my phone's camera and barely recognise myself.

Good.

Who cares if no one will miss me? I'm not me anymore.

I leave the taxi and flash my ID at the security guard, who waves me inside. A dub beat thunders through the speakers, and I rub my temples, not ready for something quite so loud.

I need a drink immediately. I pull out Mum's plastic and ask the bartender for the strongest drink he can make.

When he puts it on the bar, I hand over the card, but a guy to my left hands over cash. "This one's on me."

"Thanks," I say, taking the drink.

He clings his glass against mine. "No problem. You alone?"

"Constantly."

"Wanna change that?" he asks, stepping in too close.

I take a large sip and my head spins. I lower the glass and ask, "Does it come with more of these?"

He chuckles and says, "You betcha."

His hand slips behind my back and he edges me towards the dancefloor. I stumble backwards, tipping the drink down my throat. He takes the empty glass and slides it on a nearby table. His hand cups my bum and before I can smack it away, his mouth attacks mine.

I pull away, ready to tell him to go to hell, when a new drink appears. I reach for the floating drink and realise it's a different guy. He's holding one for me and one for the guy grabbing my arse.

We both take a drink and he says, "Thanks for looking out for us, mate." He clinks my glass. "Stick with me and you'll be drinkin all night."

I shrug. Ok, he grabs my arse, but the booze is flowing. I can handle that.

Two more drinks in and we're still standing on the dancefloor, our bodies pressed together. I wish I was tucked in a dark corner, but his arm around me helps me to stand as I'm so lightheaded.

"You wanna try something else?" he asks.

He opens his hand and two blue pills lay in his palm. I take one without questioning what it is. I wash it back with my Jack and Coca-Cola and close my eyes. His tongue fishes around my mouth, like he's trying to retrieve my drink. I tip backwards and throw my arms around his neck for stability. His hands move under my skin-tight shirt and I do not give a damn.

Whatever he's saying is distorted and I'm dizzy.

My eyes grow heavy and I'm ready to sleep standing up. My head bobs as I drift off but I'm suddenly jolted awake. I blink hard at the table in front of me. I feel the spongy material beneath me. When did I sit in this booth?

"Ready for a hit?" he yells into my ear.

"Huh?"

His hand waves over a white line on the table. "It's ready for you."

The harder I stare at it, the more my brain refuses to work.

His head lowers and he snorts the white line in front of him.

He hands me some kind of straw thing. Instinctively, I put it to my lips and he promptly moves it to my nostril. In a nano-second, I lower my head and sniff hard.

It's like a bolt of lightning shooting up to my brain and awakening my senses. My body tingles and I have an almighty urge to dance on this table.

He laughs at me and says, "Looks like you could do with another Jack."

I stand up to make my way out of the booth.

"Hey, where do you think you're going?"

I fling his arms off me and shuffle out of the booth.

"Hey, hey!" he shouts, sliding in front of me. "Ain't no free ride, Toots. You don't get to leave."

"I need to move." I push him away and for the first time look him in the eye. What is he, like, thirty? I don't feel drunk anymore. I'm energised. I need to run, or dance, or spin in a circle. I jump in place. "I need to do something."

He slides a hand along my lower black and grins. "Oh, you wanna do something? I got something you can do." Someone hands him a drink and he waggles it in front of me. "You want?"

I reach for it and he pulls it away.

"*Nah-uh*! I wanna feel your tongue wrapped around mine first."

I squint at him. He's expectant. My mind is clearing, and I don't like it. I need that drink.

I grab his face, jam my tongue down his throat and suck at his lips. It is the most un-passionate kiss, but he grabs my arse as if satisfied.

I trip as he leads me across the room. He pushes me against a wall as our lips mash together. His hand cups my breast and I wanna hurl.

"Come with me," he whispers. "I've got more stuff."

I want another one of those pills. I take his hand and we slip out a door. Icy water drops on my head and I almost slip on the slick cement. He corners me against the dumpsters. His lips run down my neck and his hands paw at the front of my pants.

"What have you got?" I ask, pleading.

He grabs a chunk of my hair and holds it violently. My heart races. I hear a zip lower.

"All for you, baby." His hand pushes my head down and the

weight of his grip sends me to my knees.

I collide with his crotch and his dick whacks my forehead. I plant my hands on his thighs and pull away. He's stronger than me and pushes me forward.

"No. I don't want to."

"C'mon, baby. You've been hanging about me all night. You want this."

I fight him but it grazes my lips.

"Drugs don't come free, ya know?"

"I've got money," I squeak. "My parents are lawyers."

He yanks my hair so I'm forced to look up. "WHAT?"

Terror rushes down my body. "No, no, I didn't mean—"

"Little cock tease," he grunts and his knee rams into my face.

The pain sears hot as I tumble back. He grabs me and throws me against the wall.

BLACK.

"Can you hear us? Can you wake up?"

Someone opens my eyes. Torchlight shines into my face and I fight to close my eyes. When someone pulls my eyelids up again everything comes in threes and my head aches.

BLACK.

"You knew she was doing drugs?"

"I thought I had taken care of it."

"You should have told me the minute you found out."

"*Dammit*, Rob. And what exactly would you have done about it?"

"I would have kept an eye on her. Something you obviously can't do."

"She's your daughter too. You should already be watching her."

I rub my eyes and they notice I'm awake. I scan the room. I look down at the single bed with white linen and pull at the gown I'm wearing. I'm in the hospital? A needle and IV is hooked up to my arm. I follow the tube and hope there's something strong pumping into me.

"What the hell were you thinking?" Mum yells at me.

A raging headache pounds my brain and I shudder in response.

"Charli, I can't comprehend my disappointment in you," Dad says, rubbing his temples.

"Whaddaya mean?"

They look at me, stunned.

"What do we mean?" Mum says.

"Charli," Dad continues, "they read us the toxicology report."

"The, what?"

"Five different drugs in your system," Mum wails. Her eyes flood with tears and her expression becomes unfamiliar.

"How could you be this reckless?" Dad shouts.

"What are you talking about?"

Mum's tears flow. "Charli. You're not coming home."

"What?"

"You are going away for treatment," Dad says, turning his back on me.

"What? Treatment? I'm not sick. I'm not going anywhere."

"And a tattoo?" Mum wails, shaking her head.

I look between Mum and Dad, scrunching the sheet close. They know about that?

"The nurse checked your bruises and we saw it," Dad says. "How long have you had it?"

My heart throbs and I swallow hard.

Mum walks up to me and, in a low voice, says, "You took Brittany's pain medication, didn't you?"

My eyes bulge and I stop breathing.

She gasps and moves away. "I can't even look at you. Rob, I have to go."

Mum walks out and Dad follows, saying, "I don't know who you have become, Charlotte."

They leave the room and my heart jackhammers. "You can't leave me!"

I reef off the sheet, ready to jump when two nurses rush into the room. They hold me down and I scream, scratching my throat and thrashing my limbs.

"*No*! Mum! Dad!"

"Charlotte, you need to cooperate," a nurse talks over me. "We don't want to restrain you, but we will if it's necessary."

I fight against them, swivelling my shoulders and kicking my legs.

"Ok, get the straps," the other nurse says.

"*No!*"

The nurses hold me down and I wriggle and push with all my might. They yell at me to stop, but I won't let them hold me captive. I scream until my throat is red raw.

"All the commotion," a voice travels over us. "Nurses, let her be for a minute."

The nurses back away from me, and I pant like I've run a mile as I scamper to the top of the bed.

A man in a pressed white coat and shamefully wide smile steps towards me. "She's frightened, and rightly so. Charlotte, I'm Dr McMahon. I facilitate at *Lyndon House Youth Drug and Alcohol Rehabilitation Centre*. Have you been told about our work?"

My gown sticks to me from my sweat, my heart is ready to burst out of my body, and my eyes are bulging to the point of explosion.

"Your parents have enrolled you in a rehabilitation course to combat your addiction," Dr McMahon says. He may as well be speaking Chinese to me. I look around the room for an escape route and the doctor notices my eyes land on the IV. "It's fluids. You're severely dehydrated. You've been putting your body through the wringer."

"Look," my voice is oddly shaky, "it might look bad, but I'm not a drug addict. I've never gone out to a bar like that before."

Dr McMahon tilts his head and there's an unmistakable smirk on his face. "We'll keep you here overnight to get your strength up, and then I'll travel with you to *Lyndon House*. Get some rest and be kind to the nurses. Being strapped to a bed for twenty-four hours won't be a nice way to go about things."

Rehab?

Rehab is for junkies.

Weed is not a big enough deal to send me to rehab. It's been ages since I've had it. They're over-reacting. Sending me away so they don't have to deal with my problems is such a Mum and Dad move. They like to make out that nothing's wrong. I wonder if they'll tell people where I am.

They kept the lights on all night in my hospital room. I sleep on and off, but I keep quiet. I believe the doctor. Being strapped down would be the worst way to go.

Dr McMahon pushes me out of hospital in a wheelchair. I wriggle my toes. I'm not broken. I'm in a wheelchair? Because they think I'm fragile? I take in my surroundings, realising this is the view my sister had for months. The thought makes me sick and I shut my eyes.

Through a side entrance, we arrive at a black sedan with tinted windows. I'm told to get into the backseat. I'm not helped out of the chair, so they are aware I'm not broken.

The tinted windows are a welcomed relief, bringing darkness inside the car. My eyelids fall until the doctor sits beside me.

"We've got about forty minutes of travel time," Dr McMahon says, tapping a pen against a clipboard. "I will use this time to ask you some questions, ok?"

I shrug my answer and stare out the window.

"In your own words, what would you say triggered your addiction to drugs?"

I *tsk* as my eyes roll.

"Would you say it was the death of your friend?"

I shoot him a look as pain stings the back of my eyes.

"Did it start then or was it an earlier habit that was not picked up on?" He looks down at his clipboard and flips a page. "Your parents stated you spent some time in Spain. Did you experiment over there?"

I hug my waist and move my gaze to the window.

"Charlotte, I'm trying to figure out whether this was a build-up of experimentation over an extended period or it happened within the last few months or weeks. Did it escalate over a short amount of time? Because you took a lot of drugs at once."

My eyes want to roll on a loop at these stupid questions. I only went out once.

"They found amphetamines, codeine, and citalopram in your bedroom. Did you experiment with all concurrently?"

My heart rate speeds up. They were in my bedroom?

"Your night at a pub is not the main issue here," Dr McMahon says. "We have proof this is a long-standing issue."

I rest a hand over my mouth and swallow hard to counter my

gagging. They know about the *focus pills* I took last year.

"It's easier if you cooperate," he whispers.

"What I did isn't a big deal."

"Even if you were legally an adult," Dr McMahon says, "abusing a substance of any kind is dangerous and irresponsible. If a doctor prescribed you pain medication and you took more than the daily dosage, they could send you to *Lyndon House* for the same addiction management." He scrutinises his clipboard. "It was your sister's pain meds you used. Correct?"

Whatever.

"You need to reflect on how your addiction has altered your behaviour," he says, "and what it has done to the relationships with those closest to you."

I keep my eyes on the window. "I have a headache."

Dr McMahon's pen is deafening as he writes on his clipboard. I know he's making assumptions about me. I couldn't care less.

Dr McMahon didn't talk to me for the rest of the trip. He wrote on his clipboard or typed on his phone. Maybe I pissed him off?

Good.

The car stops by a tall, wrought-iron gate, which opens by itself. The car winds along a gravel driveway surrounded by lush green grass. A large, white building with walls of glass at each corner looms ahead.

"We're here," Dr McMahon says, opening his door. "Out you get."

I open the car door and get a waft of freshly cut grass. I'm wobbly when I stand, so I keep hold of the door for balance. Dr McMahon beckons me to follow and the driver stares me down like he assumes I'll make a run for it.

I follow the doctor toward the house and stamp my way up the steps to the massive dual front doors. Everything inside the building is blindingly white. The urge to find a heavy blanket to hide under is rampant inside me. I keep my gaze low, but the tiles are so shiny and bleached that I recoil, shutting my eyes.

"This way, Charlotte," Dr McMahon says, pushing my shoulder.

I shrug him off and open my eyes.

"Hello and welcome," a man wearing a phoney smile and an extremely pressed, button-down shirt and chinos says. "My name is David. I am a therapist here and I'll show you around and run you through your schedule."

Dr McMahon lifts his clipboard. "I have some notes to go over with you. Meet you in your office in an hour?"

David nods. "Sounds good."

"I'll see you later, Charlotte," Dr McMahon says.

I bite the inside of my cheek and reply with a deadpan look.

As Dr McMahon walks up the hall, David steps in closer. "You prefer to be called Charli, right?"

"Whatever."

"I'd like you to feel comfortable. Personally, my skin crawls any time someone calls me Dave."

Noted.

"We believe a schedule and repetitive daily routine is the key to a successful recovery," David says, and we walk into a large communal area. "Wake up time is always seven am," he chuckles, "some of our residents find it a rude shock their first week here."

I shrug and mutter, "I get up for school every morning."

He gestures to some long wooden tables. "This is where we serve meals. After breakfast, we conduct individual counselling and group therapy sessions. You will do both. The individual sessions are great for getting to the root of the issue and group is fantastic for showing you that you're not alone in the fight."

Fight? Fight to get out of here.

"After lunch, we have free time and room for alternative therapy. You can read and meditate. We have art workshops to clear the mind and express any abstract feelings you might be having."

The mention of arts and crafts makes me want to stop listening. What am I doing here?

"And there are fitness classes. Exercise is a big part of recovery. Running, yoga, weight training."

Recovery. I'm not an addict!

"Dinner is at seven pm and we always end the day with a group discussion, highlighting the best and worst parts of our day and using encouragement to build excitement and enthusiasm for the next day. It's hard to see the positives some days, so we like to add in personal mantras. We also have movie nights and relaxing activities before lights out at ten pm."

I've shifted so much my back is to him.

"How does that all sound, Charli?"

I *humph*.

"I'll show you to your room and the other facilities." He touches my shoulder. "It'll all be ok."

I knock his hand away.

"Come now."

My room is narrow with two white linen single beds and grey tiles. It's also equipped with an ultra-sullen roommate. David introduced her as Diane, otherwise I wouldn't know her name. Any attempt for me to make nice fell on deaf ears. I wouldn't normally mind except for that steely look in her eyes. The kind which makes you think she has a knife.

I'm not discounting it.

I go to breakfast the next morning after a sleepless night. Diane made grotesque noises throughout the night. She's withdrawing hard. Her sunken eyes and ghostly pale skin tells me she's a junkie. She's made for this place, not me.

A worker dressed in white shows me to the food. I take a bowl of cereal and sit at a table. A few people are chatty, like they've been here for a while, but everyone is quiet at my end. Good. If someone wanted to chat with me, I'd throw this bowl of cereal over my head.

I take a mouthful and mistakenly lock eyes with my stony-faced roommate. I shudder, remembering her screams as she curled in the foetal position at the foot of the bed. The goosebumps haven't left my arms since. She's fucking scary.

"Good morning, Charli."

I roll my eyes and look off at a window as David sits beside me.

"After breakfast you'll be my first therapy patient. Once you've brushed your teeth, I'll show you to my office."

My jaw clenches. "Can I finish my breakfast first?"

He chuckles. "Of course."

David's office is compact. He sits on a chair and asks me to take the couch. I pull my knees to my chest and stare at his bookcase, hoping to tune him out.

"We will have a quick, forty-five minute session today," he says. "To start off, tell me in your own words, why you're here."

My fingers run through my hair and I will the clock to wind forward.

He clears his throat and shifts. "How do you feel at school? Do you have any friends to lean on or particular classes you enjoy?"

I scrunch my brow and rest my cheek on my knee. I hug my legs as he pushes for my response.

"Would you prefer to speak about home? Or your time in Spain?" David asks, remaining calm. "I don't mind where we start. I want you to be comfortable with me as we start a dialogue."

It's been so long since I've had a smoke. Man, I miss it. I want that slow drag and the feeling of mellowing out. Maybe it could make this guy interesting.

David's unmistakably disappointed when our session ends. I stared at those book spines like my life depended on it, not saying a word for the entire forty-five minutes.

Next, is my group session. Everyone sitting in the circle is young and sad. I sit with my arms crossed and focus on a mark on the vinyl floor, hoping to make a repeat of my last session.

"Hi everyone," a woman of about forty joins our circle. "For those of you who are new, I'm Cindy, a therapist here at *Lyndon House*. We always start with introductions. Arnold, care to start us off?"

A boy with a mixture or acne and fight scars to her left, huffs and slouches. "Hey, I'm Arnold. I've been addicted to meth for two years. This is my fourth week here and it sucks balls."

"How is recovery, Arnold?" Cindy asks.

"I hate it. Every fibre of my being screams for a hit," he pauses, "I guess that doesn't happen as much anymore."

"You're well past the twenty-eighth day line. You're on the road to recovery." Cindy claps. "Everyone, a round of applause for Arnold."

A few mediocre claps break out. My arms stay folded.

"Hilary, tell us how you're doing," Cindy says to a girl sitting opposite her.

Hilary's hair is white blonde hair and her figure is frail. Her face is as pretty as a porcelain doll and she could easily be a student at my school.

"Hi, I'm Hilary. Apparently, I drink too much, and it made people mad. Mostly my parents and my friends, I guess. Well, I don't think I have friends anymore."

"Do you think that will change when you go home?" Cindy asks.

Hilary shrugs. "We drifted apart long ago. I spent all my time at the uni dorms, getting drunk with the guys there. My friends totally ditched me. I don't even want to go to school, they all call me a skank and a whore."

That's not me. I wasn't isolating anyone or causing fights. I just want to be on my own. Fuck, why am I here?

"And you," Cindy says. I look up, and she's smiling and nodding to me. "Hi, you're new. Want to introduce yourself?"

I take a big breath in and hold it. My shoulders bunch to my ears, and I shrink as small as possible.

Cindy looks over her clipboard and says, "Charlotte, isn't it?"

I roll my eyes and look at the black mark on the off-white floor.

"It's ok, this is a safe place. No judgement."

Shifts of uncomfortableness round the circle and my stomach flips. I hold my breath tight. I will not speak a word.

"Ok," Cindy says slowly. "We can come back to you."

I take in a rush of air and close my eyes. I try to teleport somewhere else. Anywhere else.

I really like alcohol. I didn't think about anything and everything blurred. I want more of it.

12

Brittany

I'm so glad my parents didn't force me to see Charli in hospital.

I'm so mad at her.

She is so selfish. How could she make the car crash all about her? She's forever been a drama queen, but to stoop this low? Mum said she's the reason my medication ran low. She was stealing my pills? My brain wants to implode. She's been spacey, but I didn't think it meant drugs. Apparently, they found all different kinds of drugs in her bedroom.

She's a disgrace.

I'm at Dad's. My leg is flaring up. I had to miss school and double the dose of my painkillers. My head is filled with heavy fog and I blame the mess in Charli's head for my pounding headache. We've always had this weird thing where we feel each other's pain. I'd rather forget her. I'm in bed when Bryce visits.

"Your step mum let me in," he hushes. "She told me I can't stay long because your dad will be home soon."

I take the collar of his shirt and pull him closer. "Yeah, whatever."

Bryce lies next to me. "Do you want to go to sleep?"

"I do. I don't know if I will. My hip feels on fire."

He massages my shoulders. "I won't leave until you're asleep."

His warmth always helps, but I'm so uncomfortable. I close my eyes tightly and press my palms against his torso. I slow my breathing and try to clear my mind. It doesn't work when the house fills with the noise of incoming people.

I squirm in place, wishing the painkillers would hurry up and numb everything.

"You ok? D'you want me to close the door?"

I hold him tight and nod.

He hugs me and lets me go, moving off the bed to shut the door. The living room sounds muffle.

I huff and roll onto my back. "I'm not gonna get to sleep."

"I got something for you," he says, sitting on the edge of the bed. "Maybe it'll distract you."

"I'm up for that."

Bryce fumbles in his pocket and then holds out a jewellery box. He opens it to reveal a beautiful, glimmering emerald ring. I gasp and he says, "It's a promise ring. A promise that I'll always be here for you. Always and forever." He takes the ring out of the box and slips it over my fluttering finger. "Even though I might not be physically with you, you can look at this ring and know I'm always be by your side. You are my best friend and my one true love. I don't want you to ever be scared. You're not alone."

The happiest tears streak down my cheeks. My arms rush around his neck, lowering him, and I press my lips firmly against his.

"I love you so damn much," I whisper. "You have the most

beautiful soul."

"I love you." He rests his forehead against mine. "Maybe I should get going. I don't wanna get either of us into trouble."

My grip tightens. "How can you think I'd let you go?"

His breathy laugh patters against my neck. "I don't know how I thought I'd pull myself away."

"This looks expensive," I say, looking at the light dancing in the stones. "How did you get this?"

"Mum left me some money."

I wince. "Oh, *she'd love* that you used it to buy me something."

He puffs out an uncomfortable laugh. "Don't worry, I didn't spend all of it."

Bryce lies down and I stretch out. My calf muscles cramp and I squeak in pain. I cup my mouth, kicking out my legs.

Bryce leaps and sits at the foot of the bed. He rests my feet in his lap and runs a hand up my leg. He hushes me to rest but my arms lock around my face to hide my pain.

The cramps subside and Bryce massages my feet. I exhale and lower my arms. I wipe away tears and unapologetically wipe my sleeve under my dripping nose.

I blink hard at him as he tries a smile. A sob lingers in my throat as my mind clutters with thoughts that I don't deserve him. I fight so hard not to cry, but the sob breaks and more tears flood my eyes.

He continues rubbing my feet and asks, "Is it helping?"

I cough to clear my throat and stop the sobs. I nod and push for a smile.

"It's ok to cry," he says.

My chest relaxes and I sink into the bed. Somehow, that helps me to stop crying.

"Thanks for being here," I whisper.

He smiles and rubs his thumbs against the arch of my foot.

I giggle. "*Ohmigawd*, that feels amazing."

"Did you expect anything less from me?" he teases.

The bedroom door swings open and Dad busts in. My foot slips from Bryce's hands and we both stare at him.

"What's happening in here?" Dad asks, eyes bugging.

"Her feet hurt," Bryce replies in a small voice.

Dad's head pivots between us like he's watching a tennis match. His face transforms from ultra-serious to slightly foolish. He clears his throat and says, "Just make sure the door stays open, ok?"

"Ok," we reply.

He backs out of the room, clearly jumping from conclusion to conclusion. I laugh at Bryce as his shoulders droop and he stares at the empty doorway.

"That was a tad intense," he whispers.

"We have it better at Mum's."

"She's just used to us. He'll come around."

"Have you just met my dad?"

He laughs and picks my foot up. "Well, maybe I'm the optimist of the duo."

"Just make sure you do that thing with your thumbs again."

"Your wish is my command, beautiful."

I twist my lips and think about the question I don't want to ask him. "When you got sent away last year..."

He eyes me.

"You know, to that wellness centre..."

"You thinking about Charli?"

I suck in a breath. "What will it be like for her?"

He sighs and rubs a circle on the ball of my foot. "I dunno. At mine they put me on drugs, at Charli's they are taking her off them."

"Will they be mean to her?"

He shakes his head. "She'll be ok. She just has to listen to them and open up."

"She stole my pills."

He nods, frowning. "Mine too."

"What?"

"I drove her home from school and a day or so after, I noticed a whole tray of pills were missing. I didn't suspect her at the time, but now..."

"*Ugh*. She makes me sick." I rub my stomach. "Have you told anyone?"

"No, I don't want to. I mean, she's already in there getting the help she needs. I don't want to make it worse for when she comes home."

"It's already as bad as it can be. How could she do those things? I don't think I can look her in the eye."

"You'll get through this. I'm here for you."

"You're the one thing I know I can count on."

"Do you think you'll make Sean's party?" He rubs my calf. "Will you be up for it?"

"There's no way I'm missing this party. I'm dying for a social life."

He smiles. "I'm glad. Having you at school has been so good, almost back to normal."

"Except for the fact that I'm holding up traffic with my walking frame or taking the long way round with my wheelchair."

"Bright side is you're back."

I giggle. "You are the optimist, aren't you?"

"I need the party too," he says, looking down. "It's a year since Mum passed."

"Already?"

He nods, head hanging low. "We'll spend Saturday morning by her grave."

"Are you going to be up for the party?"

"It's not something I want to dwell on. I'll welcome the distraction."

"Hey guys," Tara says, knocking on the doorframe. "Bryce, hun, you want to stay for dinner?"

"Oh, no thanks. I gotta get home."

Tara smiles and backs away. "Ok, no problem. Brit, it's pasta carbonara tonight."

"*Delish*. Thanks," I reply.

Bryce moves up the bed and finds my lips with a passionate kiss. I brush my hands through his butterscotch hair and want to pause this moment.

"Get some rest, beautiful," he whispers. "I'll see you Saturday night."

I nod. "I'm going to Mum's for the weekend."

"Ok, I'll pick you up from there."

"You want me to go with you to the cemetery?"

"No, it'll just be the three of us."

I nod and he blows me a kiss as he leaves my room.

Phew. I'd be there with him if he needed me, but cemeteries freak me out. This pang of guilt hits my stomach as I wonder if I should visit Kellie's grave. I don't want to remember her as buried. I'd rather snigger at the goofy girl trying to love *'The Bachelorette.'*

"Mum, Rob," Nick begins as we sit at the table for dinner. He takes a deep breath. "With Charli gone, I don't want Brittany to struggle at school on her own. I'd be ok with changing schools."

"Nicky, are you sure?" Tara asks.

Nick holds a breath and nods.

Dad pats Nick's hand and smiles. "Excellent decision, Nick. I'm proud of you. I'll have the transfer papers drawn up."

Nick exhales and smiles at Dad.

I whisper to Nick, "You don't have to change schools for my sake."

Nick turns to me and cups a hand around his mouth. "It's ok. All the *rich kid* remarks and other stuff are getting outta control. I don't mind leaving. Plus, I like this whole big brother thing."

"I'm happy you'll be at *John Thomas*."

He smiles. "Hopefully, it'll be a smooth transition."

I knew today would be a lot for Bryce to handle. I'd be surprised if he turned up at the party. He's adamant he's coming but said he will be late so he asked if someone else could drive me. I'd have happily waited for him, but Meah said o*k*. I heard she's a lead-foot behind the wheel so, thankfully, it's a short drive. I must remember the good part. A party. Finally, I'm going to a party.

All afternoon, Mum pestered me to take the wheelchair. Good thing Meah has no patience and we left the house before Mum left her study. It's my first time outside of a physio session with my crutch. The walking frame is way easier to balance with, but I'm hoping this walking cane will draw less attention.

"Did you hear about Sean and Kimmy?" Meah asks on the drive.

"No, what?"

"They broke up."

"Shuddup."

"I kid you not. He's been cheating on her with Fi since the formal after-party."

My mouth hangs open from shock and the thrill of gossip. "Fi never said anything?" I manage to spit out.

"Apparently, Chloe knew. Kimmy was pissed."

"Wait, did this all happen the day I missed school?"

"Not a good day to play hooky," Meah teases.

"*Whoah.* I'm guessing Kimmy won't be at the party."

"I'm not sure."

My mind is buzzing as we park outside Sean's house. I can't believe Fi did that to Kimmy.

"Hey Brit," Madison says as I follow Meah through Sean's house. "You look almost back to normal."

I blush. "Hopefully, I don't stack tonight."

Meah links arms with me. "So, we gonna dance tonight?"

"Yes, I miss that so much."

"*Aw*, Brittany, what a cute outfit," Chloe says, tilting her head and pouting like I'm a puppy in a pet store window. She's been giving me extra pity ever since her recent *L'Amour Dance Company* audition.

I smooth down my pale pink dress. "Thanks."

"You totally look short in those flats though," Chloe adds.

Instagram showed me the *L'Amour* finalists had been selected. I didn't see Chloe's picture. She's making me out to be the sad case so no one fixates on her failure.

"Yeah, what's up with that?" Fiona asks, frowning at me.

I shrug, reddening. "Um, I can't wear heels."

"*Ohmigawd*, you bitches," Madison grumbles. "She's up and walking and all you care about is the fact she's not wearing stilettos. Give me a break. C'mon, Brit, let's dance."

Madi takes my hand and leads me away from the girls. I try my hardest to swallow my giggles. That rocked.

The girls join us in the centre of the living room as our bodies bounce with the beat. My knuckles whiten as I hang on to the cane for dear life. Every sway of my hip brings on a jab of pain. I keep moving, hoping it will go away, but it niggles deeper and deeper.

Naveen pulls Madi away as the other girls gather around me.

"You don't need that," Meah says, grabbing the crutch and the grip above my elbow slides off my skin.

Fiona grabs my other arm. "Yeah, we got you."

"*Ohmigawd*," Chloe says, smiling. "Now you, like, do look normal."

I smile, liking the fact I'm standing without a cane or frame, but I know I'll crumble the moment they let go. My balance is shaky, and the girls are distracted by boys. The blood pumps loudly in my ears as I brace for an impending fall.

Meah calls out to Sean and lets me go to chase him. Fiona grizzles and follows Meah. Panic-stricken, I latch onto Chloe's shoulder.

She shakes me off. "What are you doing?"

"Chloe, I can't stand."

She huffs, annoyed that I'm ruining her moment of boys ogling her. It's not my fault *L'Amour* didn't like your dance moves.

She leaves me and my stomach flips. I'm half a second off faceplanting until I'm scooped into two arms. My head rests against Bryce and I let out a heavy yet relieved breath.

He strokes my hair and whispers, "You ok?"

"I can't keep up."

He holds me tight as his lips graze my forehead. "I'm happy to slow dance with you."

I clasp my hands around his waist and my heart slows its pace. We move in a small, slow circle, but we're dancing, nonetheless. I am at a party, dancing with my boyfriend, and it feels right.

"Where's your walking frame?" he whispers.

I lift my head from his shoulder and look to the side. "I brought my cane, but I don't know where it is. Meah took it."

"What? Why?"

I wince. "So, I'd look normal."

He huffs. "She's a bitch. So, she ditched you?"

"I dunno. I guess."

"Don't stick up for her, she's not a good friend."

I press my hands into his back and whisper, "How was today?"

He nods. "It was ok. It played out as expected."

"I'm surprised you're here. D'you think you'll wanna go home early?"

"No," he answers quickly. "No, I need a party."

My gut drops. I could have done with using him as an excuse tonight. The girls have already deserted me. Were they always like this? Did I not notice before because I could move quickly behind them?

At least I have Bryce.

Bryce rubs my back and then gestures to the side. "You wanna take a seat on a sofa and I'll find your cane?"

"Ok." I am so ready to sit down. Who knew standing could be so exhausting?

After Bryce helps me to a sofa, he brushes my hair off my face and asks, "I'll get us a drink too. What would you like?"

I shrug. "Just a Coke or something."

"You sure?"

"I took some pain pills and I can't mix them with alcohol "

He nods and says he will be back soon.

I breathe out and slide back on the sofa, trying to sit as upright as possible. The more upright I sit, the less pain I experience. The couple next to me furiously make out. The guy's back rubs against me. *Ehck.* I do not want to be involved in this, thanks.

"Brittany."

Jace walks toward me, twirling my cane.

"This yours?" he asks, smiling. His smile drops as he sees the couple. He smacks his hands together close to their faces. "*Oi.* Get moving. Can't you see Brittany sitting here?"

The guy scoffs at Jace, but when Jace looms over them with his broad Fijian build, the couple scampers off the couch and find another make-out area.

I smirk at their getaway. "Thanks for that."

Jace sits beside me, handing me the crutch. "No problem. You taking a breather?"

I nod. "Yep."

Jace lifts a leg and rotates his ankle. "I broke my ankle a few years back during a footy game. It still flares up now and then, but I remember how painful it was to stand after getting the cast off. Are Chloe and that giving you a hard time?"

I shake my head quickly. "No, what makes you say that?"

Jace laughs. "Because even though I try to ignore my girlfriend, her squawking still breaks through."

I squint at him. "What's she been saying about me?"

"Not so much about you, just how you being down for the count affected her cheer squad and dance classes."

"I bet she was loving me out of the picture."

"Let's just say she acted like it was a big-time deal."

The girls return to the centre of the living room with bottles of hot pink liquid. Chloe slams a hand on her hip when she spots Jace with me. She shouts at him to come and dance with her.

Jace pats my shoulder. "Have fun tonight."

I smile as he moves to Chloe. Chloe eyes me as she wraps her arms around Jace. My smile drops and I pretend my phone is more interesting.

With my phone in hand, I notice the time ticking over. I'm surprised Bryce isn't back when the girls are on their next round of drinks.

I take a deep breath in and stand up, putting all my weight on the cane. *Geez*, I wish I'd brought the walking frame. As I make my way through the crowd, it's obvious a walking frame would be too awkward. But me, a crutch, and this environment is a bad mix.

I edge my way through the house and find Bryce by the back door, a drink in hand, laughing and talking with a group of people.

Sweat builds in my palm as my grip intensifies on the handle. I shake off my nerves and walk closer to the group.

Madison notices me as she leans on Naveen and fixes her brunette ponytail. "Hey, Brit. Where ya been?"

Bryce pulls himself off the wall and rushes to me. "Sorry," he says, taking my free hand. "I forgot to go back."

"Forgot?" I look at the half-empty bottle in his hand. "I thought you couldn't drink alcohol with your medication."

"Oh, I was just trying it."

"Are you not driving tonight?"

"No, not tonight. Oh damn, you were counting on me to drive you home?"

"You seem so scattered tonight. Are you sure you're ok? You know, after today with your mum?"

He shakes his head. "I don't want to talk about it. I just want to have a fun night."

"Ok. I can get behind that."

Bryce squeezes my hand and helps me closer to the group.

"How's it going, Brittany?" Naveen shouts and lifts his bottle. "Want a drink?"

"Oh, no, I'm ok."

"Oh, shit," Bryce gasps. "I had a drink for you somewhere."

"It's ok."

"Sorry," he says, his shoulders bunching high. He slides his drink onto a nearby table and wraps his arms around my waist. This close, I'd forgive him for anything.

"Are you having a good time?" Madi asks.

"Yeah, I'm happy to be at a party again."

Madi flicks my cane. "This thing has to suck though."

I nod. "It does."

"*Meah*," Naveen shouts, throwing his hands in the air. "Meah's at the party."

Meah shimmies her way over with a cutesy squeal. "Hey, guys." Her eyes all over Naveen. "What's happening?"

"Need another drink?" Naveen asks, slinging his arm around Meah's shoulders.

"Sure," Meah says, letting Naveen swerve her in another direction.

As the two slink away, I ask Madi, "What's going on with those two?"

Madi laughs under her breath. "Nothing worth worrying about."

My eyebrows stay raised. I know Meah too well to think it's nothing.

Bryce's arms unravel me as he turns to Sean. Fiona pulls Madi away to talk and I balance awkwardly between groups. *Geez*, I just want to sit again. This is pathetic.

I scout the nearest seating and spy Chloe with her hands all over Jace. Would Chloe turn it into a scene if she caught me sitting down all party? I've never noted how much I sit at parties. I guess it's cool if I'm curled up with Bryce? But sitting on my own... *Ohmigawd.* Total Loserville.

But I can't do this much more. I'm losing strength. I can't keep up with everyone moving around. It's uncomfortable to dance. I can't drink.

Shit.

What's the point?

I tap Bryce's shoulder.

He turns, expressionless.

"I think I'm gonna go home."

He clutches my shoulders. "What? No, you can't. Stay a little longer."

"Maybe, but I don't think I can last much longer."

"What's wrong?"

"I can't stand this long."

He takes my hand and gestures ahead. "That's ok, we'll sit."

"You sure?"

His lips crook left. "*Duh.* Spending time with you is my number one past time."

I laugh and pinch his cheek. "You goof."

"C'mon," he says, nodding behind me. "Let's snag one of the comfy couches."

"Now you're speaking my language."

My balance wobbles as he leads me to a couch. As he asks someone to move over for me, I take in his profile. The irony of it all. Last year I had to beg him to stay longer at a party. His phone was always pulling us apart. Now, as my mind drifts to my bed, he clings to my hand and pleads with me to stay.

Really, who could be mad when they're snuggled up to this guy?

On Saturday morning, Mum and Sophia won't stop hovering around me. They're so scared I will fall because I'm refusing to use anything other than my cane. I've worked so hard with Aisha. She's cleared me for three days of school with no wheelchair. I need the all clear pass. I can't wait!

I've parked it on the couch to do my homework. "Seriously, Mum, I'm sure you have work to do."

What is this topsy-turvy world that I'm pushing my Mum to do *her* homework?

The doorbell rings and Sophia moves to the foyer to answer it.

"Oh, hi Reece," Sophia beams. "Come in, come in."

"Hi Reece," I say as he edges into the room, hands clasped in front of him.

"*Um*, hi," he says quietly.

Mum steps closer to him. "Reece, how are you? Haven't seen you in a while."

"I'm good," he replies. "I wanted to see if I could help?"

"Help?" Mum says.

"Yeah, if Brittany needs any help. I couldn't help Charli... it's like I lost her, and I lost..." he stops and stares at the carpet, mouth half-open.

"I know how you can help," I blurt out. I pat the seat beside me. "You can keep me company."

Reece's eyes brighten.

Mum nods. "Sounds like a great idea."

Mum and Sophia leave the room and Reece sits on the edge of the couch.

"Nice to have some company, other than Mum and Sophia."

Reece nods with a closed-mouth smile.

My chest tightens, hoping this doesn't stay awkward. Like, you came over here, you can't be mute.

"Like, I remember last year when Mum was never home and I wish I saw her more," I say, desperate to fill the silence. "And now she's everywhere I turn."

"So, it's ok that I'm here?" he asks, staring at the curtains.

"Sure, it is."

"Good, because I don't know what to do with myself."

"What do you mean?"

"I don't know why Charli didn't talk to me. Kellie was *our* friend and I thought we'd talk about it."

"You didn't talk at all?"

He shakes his head.

"She didn't talk to me either."

He looks at me. "But she came back for you."

"No, they forced her to come back."

"But she always said she wanted to protect you."

My back straightens with tension. "All talk, I think."

He turns to the curtains. "I miss Kellie."

"I'm sorry. She was your best friend, right?"

"She was my person."

We sit in silence; however, it is easier this time.

"I kinda thought Charli would..." he stops and shakes his head. "Bryce is your person, right?"

"My person?"

"The one that's always there for you. That looks out for you."

I sigh in that dreamy way. "Yes. Bryce is most definitely my person."

He smiles. "That's nice."

"Are you doing ok?"

His smile disappears and he shrugs. "Ok. My parents send me to my therapist more often. I think it helps."

"You have a therapist?"

"I've always had therapists," he says. "Because I'm a weirdo."

I laugh by mistake. "You're not a weirdo."

He grins. "Yes I am."

I sink into the couch. "Wanna watch some TV."

"Ok."

"Let's find something weird."

On his first day at *John Thomas*, Nick pushes my wheelchair into school. I don't need the help but I want him close because he's nervous. Busying himself with the chair can only help.

"Why, hello," Chloe says, leaning against her locker. "Who's this hanging all over Brittany? You know she has a boyfriend, right, new boy?"

My stomach flips. "This is my step—"

"*Eww*, it's her brother," Fiona squeals by Chloe.

Eww?

Sean drapes an arm over Fiona's shoulder. "What? Are you saying her brother wants to nail her?"

Chloe smirks, opening her locker. "You know they're all twisted over at West Sanford. His mum and dad are probably cousins."

"Better than this sibling grossness," Fiona squeaks, shaking her head and wincing.

Fiona is lead away by Sean, exaggerating some gagging noises, and my stomach contracts and my face reddens.

I look up at Nick. His eyes are wide and his jaw is dropped.

"Are you ok?"

He shakes his head, watching Chloe as she struts away. "What was that?"

"My friends?" Repulsive.

"What? Those are your friends? Good lord, what are your enemies like?"

Same people.

"I'm just trying to help. Why did they lash out like that?"

"I'm sorry," I whisper. "Forget them. All they do all day is look for new targets. I've seen it way too many times."

We move further down the corridor and I'm embarrassed. Nick left his school because of bullies and finds new ones ten steps into *John Thomas*.

"Hi Brittany," Reece says, shutting his locker and lowering his headphones. "How are you?"

"I'm good. And you?"

"Yes, good." He shies away as he notices Nick.

"Reece, have you met my step brother Nick?"

"Um, hi," Reece says quietly.

I look up at Nick. "This is Reece."

"Hi Reece," Nick says, moving around my chair and extending his hand.

Reece looks at Nick's hand and freezes. *Gah*. Awkward. In my living room we sat in silence on separate couches. But the feeling was good. His company was good.

Nick drops his hand. "You all right?"

"Yes," Reece says, arms slinking behind him.

"Nick just transferred," I say. "Do you want to walk to class with us?"

Reece nods and starts us walking. Nick pushes me but I wave him off. I like them walking beside me.

Dad got Nick assigned to many of my classes. I'm thankful because his presence will make it bearable.

No one pestered Nick in our first few classes, and they left me alone too. They don't harass me, they just give me too much overdone pity.

In history class, a tapping pulls me out of my daydream. At the front, Mrs Lewis has stopped writing on the blackboard, so it's not her. To my right, Nick's fingers tap against his desk. His fingers dance to a tune I can't place, flurrying one after the other until he taps his index finger three times.

His hand stops in mid-air and he sucks in a breath. "Sorry, was that annoying?"

"No, not annoying."

He slides a hand along his neck. "I didn't realise I was doing it. I have a piano exam coming up. I've developed a habit of practicing without the keys."

"Well, it was good. Whatever it was."

"Thanks, Brit."

"Miss Matthews," Mrs Lewis calls out.

Geez, why do I always get picked on for talking in class?

"The bell will ring in a few minutes," Mrs Lewis continues. "Would you like to take this opportunity to get down the hall?"

"Oh yeah, thank you." Chair perk: *get-out-of-class-early* card. "Can my brother come with me?"

Mrs Lewis nods. "Sure. You two pack up your things and get a move on."

Some groans reverberate around the classroom and I catch myself smiling.

As we make our way down the corridor, I ask, "How are you

finding *John Thomas* compared to your old school?"

He plays with his tie and taps his blazer. "The uniform takes a bit of getting used to."

"Yeah, it's a few more layers than *West Sanford High*'s uniform."

"They didn't care if we wore the uniform or not. Other than this morning, this school's not bad but I have that *fish-outta-water* vibe."

"I'm sure that'll go away," I say with transparent hope.

The bell rings and the corridor floods with students that are ready to trample us. I suggest we take the door out of the west wing and head outside where it's less hectic.

Nick helps me manoeuvre the cement path by the quad towards the grassy gumtree area.

"Isn't that your friend?" Nicks says and I spot Reece ahead.

"He's reading, I dunno if he'll want us to join."

"Sure, he will. He's alone." He pushes the wheelchair with more vigour on our way to Reece.

"What are you reading?" Nick asks, sitting by Reece on the grass.

Reece looks at my chair. "Should we move to a bench for you?"

I tap Nick's shoulder. "Help me to the ground?"

"You sure?" Nick asks, moving closer.

"Yep. I'll just need help getting up."

Nick helps me to the grass and we lock the chair so I can sit upright against it.

"So, what's the book?" Nick asks again.

"'*The Picture of Dorian Gray*'," Reece says, lifting the cover. "You should read it."

"Looks hella old," Nick smirks. "What's it about?"

"This guy wants to stay young forever so he makes a deal with the devil," Reece replies. "I'm up to the part where he descends into darkness."

Nick reclines on the grass and stares at the clouds. "Eh. I'm more of a writer than a reader."

"What do you write?"

"Song lyrics. You know, kinda like poetry."

Reece looks in my direction, but we ignore the thought of who poetry reminds us of.

Nick taps the book in Reece's lap. "Do you always read old books?"

"Classics."

"What?"

"It's classic fiction, not old."

Nick smiles and holds his hands up. "*Oops*, sorry."

"I mostly read classics, but I read a lot. I like to analyse literature. It helps to figure out people."

Nick lies on his back and says, "Yeah, I think I use lyrics to do that." He tilts his head to me and says, "Do you use dance to do that?"

I puff out a laugh. "Um, no. It's terrifying on stage. Doesn't help me with people at all."

Reece picks up his book and nods at it. "She has Bryce to help with that."

My heart drops. He misses his person. He misses Kellie.

"Hey Reece," Lenny says, dropping to the ground. "I just got the new *'Night Crawler'* game. You wanna come over today and check it out."

"Sure," Reece says to his book.

"Hi Brittany," Lenny says. "How are you doing?"

"Good," I smile.

Lenny's girlfriend, Tayla, joins us and snuggles into Lenny. "Hey, guys!"

"You guys probably haven't met my step brother," I say, pointing to Nick, who sits up. "Lenny and Tayla, this is Nick. Nick, this is Lenny and Tayla."

"No way, you go here now?" Lenny says to Nick.

Nick nods. "First day."

"You play video games?"

Nick smiles and shakes his head. "Not really."

"He plays music though," I offer.

"Serious?"

"Guitar and piano," Nick replies.

"I play guitar too," Lenny says. "I was in a band before our drummer left for boarding school last year."

"My mate Zach and I are looking to start our band up again, if you're interested."

"I'm cool to see if we gel. What kind of music?"

"Classic and alt rock."

Lenny nods, grinning. "I think we'll do just fine."

"Was Zach sad you switched schools?" I ask Nick.

Nick shrugs. "Sucks we're not at the same school, but he always blended in more than me. Zach was like Rob, telling me to go for the music program and better opportunities. Plus, he saw how things changed for me at school."

Tayla touches my shoulder and I almost jump. "So, Brit. If the boys are playing video games, do you wanna do something after school? Go to the mall or watch trashy TV?"

"Um, maybe."

"No pressure. I used to drag Rikki along, but since she left for boarding school, I've felt a little lost."

"Something girly sounds fun, but maybe another time?"

"Sure. Text me when you're free." She smiles.

My phone buzzes. **New Text: Bryce.**

(Bryce) Hey. Where are you?

(Me) Outside with Nick and Reece.

(Bryce) Why? You stuck? Want me to help you inside?

(Me) I'm not stuck. I'm just sitting with them.

(Bryce) Are you shitty with me?

(Me) No. Why?

(Bryce) Why are you not in mess?

(Me) I don't really wanna be around Chloe and Fi right now.

(Bryce) Why? What happened?

(Me) Just being themselves, I guess.

(Bryce) What happened? Is it the Sean thing?

(Me) As if I care about that. Come outside or stay inside with them.

(Bryce) Sounds like you are shitty with me.

I sigh, long and loud. My hands shake around the phone, so I don't type a response.

Nick touches my arm and I flinch. "*Whoah*, you ok?"

I shake my head and drop my phone on my lap. "Just thinking about the girls this morning."

"Oh yeah, the welcome wagon," Nick smirks.

"What this?" Lenny asks.

"These girls," Nick begins, then looks at me. "What were their names?"

I shake my head, cheeks reddening. "Oh, nothing. We don't need to say anything."

"*Bull*," Nick replies. "They were bitches. Two blonde dye-jobs."

Tayla bursts into laughter. "Chloe and Fiona?"

As I drop my face into my hands, Lenny says, "Sounds about right."

Nick nudges me. "Was that them?"

I keep my palms pressed to my face and nod.

"Tay cheerleads with them," Lenny says, I lower my hands as he puts an arm around Tayla. "I always try to convince her to quit because of the shit they say to her."

"What do they say to you?" Nick asks Tayla.

Tayla giggles and leans against her boyfriend. "Nothing original. Just that I'm a loser, or made for the special class, or that I'm only kept around because I'm from a mafia family."

"Mafia?" Nick questions.

Tayla giggles, shaking her head. "I just have a big family."

Nick reclines against the bluegum. "They're jealous. I'd be jealous of a big family."

Tayla grins. "Your family got bigger with Brittany in it. She's bubbly enough to fill a room."

Nick tilts his head and meets my eyes. "You ok?"

I nod. "I'm fine." I show them the lock screen of my phone. "But I took it out on Bryce."

"Whaddaya mean?" Tayla asks, sliding closer.

I huff. "I didn't want to sit in mess hall because I don't want them to say anything nasty about Nick and, I dunno, it was like I expected Bryce to already know. We had a text fight. I can't be bothered to explain it to him."

Tayla holds her hand out. "Want me to fix it?"

"What?"

"Tay is good at it," Lenny says. "She stops all our fights before they happen."

I slip my phone into my pocket. "We'll work it out later."

Tayla drops her hand to her lap. "No worries."

"Thanks anyway."

She smiles and nods.

When the bell sounds, everyone jumps up to head for class. As Tayla and Lenny walk away, Bryce approaches. He throws his arms out wide, questioning.

As Nick helps me into the wheelchair, Bryce stops by us and asks, "Was that you texting me?"

I rub my chest, breathing out slowly.

"You ok?" Nick asks, holding onto my wheelchair.

"I'll help her," Bryce says, waving Nick off.

Nick mutters a response, but I say, "It's ok. Are you all right to get to class?"

"Ah, yeah," he stammers. "If you're ok?"

I smile and laugh like I'm being ridiculous. "Yeah, totally."

Nick nods and catches up to Reece, patting his back. "Walk with you?"

Reece, sliding on his overhead headphones, nods and keeps walking.

"What was with the hostility?" Bryce asks, sitting beside me.

"You know how it's hard to get tone across in a text."

"*Nah-uh.* Your tone was clear."

"I didn't mean it."

He leans in. "What did you mean?"

I look down. "Nothing."

He hooks a finger under my chin. "Britty. What happened?"

"They were being bitchy to Nick because he was helping me, and they are constantly bitchy to me because I'm in this chair."

"But you're almost out of the chair for good."

I eye him. "Are you defending them?"

"No."

"It sounds like you're saying it's all ok because soon I'll be outta the chair, so it doesn't matter what they've already said."

He huffs. "Why are *we* fighting about this?"

"You won't defend me?"

"What? Yes, I will. I already asked Chloe what happened."

I sit back. "What did she say?"

"She wanted to know what I was talking about because she didn't know." He shrugs. "I couldn't tell her because I wasn't there."

I groan so hard it hurts my throat. "You let her off the hook."

"What hook? I don't know what happened."

I shake my head and reverse the chair. "It doesn't matter. We're late for class."

He takes the hand grips and pulls me close.

"Don't."

"Stop. We don't need to go to class. Let's talk about this. You're obviously upset."

I push his hands away. "Forget it."

"You just accused me of not caring enough. Talk to me."

"Stop. I need to get to class"

"Brittany."

"You don't see it." I almost spit the words.

"What?"

"The way they all look at me now. They couldn't wait to get away from me at Sean's party."

His arms pull around me before I can push them away. "I'm sorry. I'm sorry."

"Why are you sorry?"

"I'll pay more attention. I promise. I don't want us fighting when something special is coming up."

13

Charli

Showering regularly isn't important anymore. At home, I'd go days without it. At *Lyndon House*, they enforce it every morning. Something about being under water quiets everything and brings my thoughts to the forefront. I hate that. I turn the cold on full blast. The water is icy. It numbs me from head to toe. My skin dulls to blue. I tremble and my teeth chatter under the cascading water.

A hand reaches in and shuts off the water before a towel hits my chest.

"Out. Now," Cindy orders. Our shower cubicles are open, just another way they show that they don't trust us. "Charlotte, don't make me assign someone to watch you during shower time. Get dressed and don't do that again."

I wrap the towel around me, chattering and shaking, and shuffle towards my clothes.

I robotically eat my breakfast of sad muesli, wash my bowl, and find my way to David's office.

David says things, but I cling to the numbness under my skin and drown him out, running my eyes up and down the spines on his bookshelf.

David walks me to group therapy. I don't blame him for not trusting me to get there on my own. I'd rather walk to my room and get some comfortable sleep while Diane's not there.

I slouch in my chair, tap my feet, and play with the hem of my t-shirt. Sitting next to me, Kevin talks about his time in boarding school and I close my eyes, moments off sleep. A faint voice calls a name. Is it my name? I dunno. Who cares?

"*Charlotte.*" One gets through and I open my eyes. Cindy stares at me, mouth ajar.

"Huh?"

Cindy sits back on her chair and crosses her legs. "Charlotte, do you have anything you want to add to today's session? Anything you want to get off your chest. Anything you want to work through?"

I dig my fingers into the fabric of my shirt until my nails pierce my stomach. I latch onto the pain and keep my face stony.

"Are you sure you don't have anything to add today of all days?"

I bite inside my cheek, unsure of what she's getting at.

"How do you feel about being away from your family on your birthday?"

I blink hard. "My, what?"

"You are a twin," Cindy continues, "does that make the situation worse? Is being away from your sister hard?"

My chin dips and I look at the people next to me, stunned. I shake my head at Cindy. What is she saying? Why is she embarrassing me in front of everyone? And... what?

"What?" I stammer.

"Do you miss your sister? Did you act out this morning because it is your birthday?"

I try to make words come out for what feels like an eternity. Finally, I get it out. "It's my birthday?"

"You didn't talk it through with David?"

I pull at my hair. "Why are you saying this?"

Cindy uncrosses her legs and leans forward. "What's hurting you the most?"

I pull my hair over my eyes. "Stop. Stop it."

"Charlotte, talk to us."

"*Stop.*"

I jump off my seat and race out of the room. Cindy calls after me, but I don't stop.

My birthday?

My family didn't call?

No Brittany?

Our birthday?

Fuck. I need air.

I skid at a glass door and jiggle the handle, hard. It's locked. I groan and move along the window wall until I reach another door. I reef on the handle and it flies open.

Did I forget my own birthday?

No. No, it's not my birthday. It can't be. My parents can't hate me so much that they would leave me in here today.

Fuck.

My nostrils flare at a distinct smell. I tiptoe along the cement path and halt when I come face-to-face with Hilary. She drags on a cigarette, eyeing me.

"Where did you get that?"

She shrugs and removes the cigarette from her lips. "I'm eighteen. It's a legal addiction."

The smoke from the cigarette twirls and plumes and I bite hard inside my cheek.

Hilary's eyebrow raises. She lifts the cigarette and asks, "You want?"

I take it from her and put it between my lips. I inhale and wince. I've never had tobacco before. Fuck, it's gross. An ashtray swirls in my mouth. Weed might not be the nicest thing in the world, but how can anyone have a cigarette twice?

I take it from my lips and look at it between my fingers. What am I doing? I can't have weed, so I go to this? Is that all I'm going to do now? Go from one drug to the next. Man, I did those things at that bar, didn't I. Random drugs with a random guy. I get a flash of being with him in the alley and shudder.

I push the cigarette at Hilary and brush myself off.

I can do better than this.

I rub the back of my neck and sigh. I don't want to be here. I don't want to get out just to be sent back. What do I want?

I look around at the bright green lawns.

Brittany.

I want to see Brittany.

It's like magnets draw me inside and I walk to David's office. He's in the middle of a session so I pace the space by his door.

After I've left sufficient scuff marks on the tiles, the door opens and a girl walks out, followed by David.

David's eyes widen. "Charli. What are you doing here?"

"David, I think I'm ready to talk."

"That's excellent. I look forward to our session tomorrow."

"Can we talk now?"

"I have my afternoon sessions to prepare for. We will talk in the morning."

I frown. I've been good at keeping a stony face, but I can't hide this frown.

David turns and beckons me. "Come in."

He walks to his desk and turns around with a notebook and a pen. "Write down what you are feeling. You can write pages. Write in sentences, dot points, or draw it. We will evaluate in the morning."

I nod, chin dimpling. "Ok."

"Do you want me to wish you a happy birthday?"

My eyes drop to his shoes. "No."

David walks me out. "Perhaps you should join yoga during free time."

"Ok."

I go into my bedroom and sit on the bed. I open the notebook and I'm as blank as the page. It's my birthday. I scratch a giant *hate* across the page. My heart tears. I don't want to be angry anymore. I scrawl *love* underneath it. Brittany comes to mind and a tear drops onto the page. I write *sad* next to *love*. I hunch over the book and moan ugly cries. I toss the notebook and Diane walks into the room. I swipe at my wet face and she kicks my bed until my whimpering stops. Diane hurls herself onto her bed, back turned, and I hiccup sobs. She grunts under the covers, but I can't stop myself.

Kellie's beautiful face forms in my mind. My stomach contorts and my eyes burn. *I'm sorry, Kellie, I'm so sorry.* I should have been there for you. Why didn't I answer the phone? I'm sorry.

The image changes to Brittany in that hospital bed and my sobs disappear. I choke and cough and my tears dry up. I can't. I can't see Brittany right now. It's too hard. I'm not ready.

#

"Did your birthday create this turn around?" David asks in his office the next morning.

I cross my arms tight. "No one told me what day it was."

"We discussed it."

"What?"

David smiles. "Well, I did. You stared at book spines."

I stare at him like he's upside down.

"You haven't been marking off the calendar in your room to track your progress?" He sighs. "I asked you how you felt about being here on your birthday, away from family. You zoned out."

I push back against the couch, rub my stomach, and swallow uneasily. "Can we not talk about this?"

"Why? How does it make you feel?"

I cover my face and hunch. "Stop it."

"Fine, Charli. What do you want to discuss?"

I lower my hands and sigh. I don't know.

David lets me sit in silence for a few moments, then asks, "Why do you think you're here?"

I throw my arms up and look at him wearily. "Because I did drugs."

He shakes his head. "No. *Why*? Why did you do those things? What was the reason you started taking drugs?"

I sink lower. "I found them."

"Found them where?"

I fidget in the seat. "In Kellie's room."

"And who is Kellie?"

A lump bulges my throat and I suck in my bottom lip. My eyes tingle at the edges.

"Is this the friend that died?"

My insides deflate and I deadpan him.

He leans over his armrest and says, "We were given a brief by your parents when you were admitted."

"So, what? This is some sick game to get me to spill my guts?"

"I just want you to explain your story in your own words. I want you out of here and I want you to be well when you are home."

I curl my feet up and trace the divots in the couch fabric.

"Take your time," he says. "You have forty-five days in here and you're only through seven of them. We have a long way to go. Perhaps I'll recommend you extend your stay."

"*What.*"

"Or we can discuss why you're here. It's up to you."

"I didn't know blackmail was a therapist tactic."

"We need progress. I need you to respond."

"Forty-five days?"

He nods.

"Yes. My friend Kellie died. I found her weed at the wake."

"Is that when you started smoking?"

I gather my hair to the side, turning away. "Kinda."

"Kind of?"

"I did it a few times with her."

"When was that?"

"My dad's wedding day. Once before then and a few times after."

"How did you feel about him getting married?"

"Hurt."

"Why was that?"

"Because he was picking another family over ours."

"Did he stop seeing you?"

I sigh and rub my temples. "No. We saw him... But he was

supposed to come home."

"When did your parents get divorced?"

"Couple of years ago."

"And was that hard to cope with?"

I straighten as breathing becomes hard. "Yes."

"You're close with your dad?"

I shrug. "Thought I was."

He waits for me to continue.

I play with a knot in my curls. "I don't think we are any more."

"And what about your mum?"

"What does it matter? They hate me."

"Why do you think that?"

"They threw me in here and they didn't call me yesterday."

"That's because we didn't allow them to."

I choke. "What did you say?"

"We have a twenty-eight day no contact policy. Cindy would have discussed this with you."

"Oh."

"Your mother was quite persistent on the phone. Threatened legal action."

"What?"

"I reminded her of the program she put you in and she ended our conversation."

My heartbeat speeds up. "My mum tried to talk to me?"

"I believe your dad was there too."

"Together?"

He nods, smiling.

I stare at the bookcase as my mind catches up.

"Don't you want to get on the track of wellness so you can see them?"

I keep my sight on the books and nod. "Yes."

"So, tell me, did you turn to cannabis to hide?"

Yes. "I think so."

"Have you ever felt the need to hide before Kellie's death?"

"I guess so."

"Did you have a way of dealing with things before cannabis?"

I scratch behind my ear. "Poetry, I guess."

"You wrote poetry?"

I nod.

"And why didn't it work this time?"

"I used poetry to work out my feelings. I didn't want to feel any of my feelings. It was too scary."

"And what were you scared of?"

My body closes in and I clench my jaw. I work hard to make my mind blank. I shiver like the punishing wind has thrashed its way in here. *"Why didn't you die?"* The reminder of death jolts my eyes open and I note the room isn't destroyed by the tornado in my head.

"Charli?"

I sit tall. "I'm not scared."

David sits back in his chair, his clipboard resting in his lap and his hands are clasped together.

Arrogant jerk. My blood boils and without thinking I blurt out, "I didn't want to lose my sister, ok!" I collapse forward, tears streaming from my eyes and an ugly moan hurls out. I choke on cries as I settle my breath. I sit up and cover my face.

"It's ok, take your time," he says.

I press my hands firmly over my eyes and shake my head. "I don't want to talk about it."

"Can you write about it?"

I rub my eyes. "Not Brittany."

"What about something for Kellie?"

Maybe. I say nothing. I'm exhausted like I've run a mile.

"Try," David says. "During your free time this afternoon, try to write something. Charli, you have done really well today. A huge step forward. I'm proud of you."

My chest heaves. I'm glad to get out of this room.

"Take some time to reflect before going to group."

I leave his office and dawdle to the bathroom. I splash icy water on my face and the heat disappears.

"So, Charli, I hear you had a good session with David," Cindy says. "Are there any new feelings you want to share with us? You might find a connection with others."

I grow rigid. "David told you what we talked about?"

Cindy almost laughs. "No, your individual counselling is completely confidential. He told me you've made positive progress."

My pulse slows. It's nice to hear I'm seen as positive.

"So, is there anything you want to discuss? You have been quiet in all other sessions."

I fold my arms. "I'm not sure."

"Remember, Charli, this is a safe place."

Something about her calling me Charli puts me at ease. "What should I say?"

"Anything," Cindy says, her eyes shining with excitement. "It can be about your addiction, or your family and friends, or something from your past you want help to deal with?"

"Like anything from my past?"

She nods, holding her smile and trying to keep her eagerness in check.

I shift in my chair, feeling eyes on me. I scan the circle and a lot of kids are staring at the ground. My heart thumps and my stomach swirls. I want to talk about it. It would be nice to talk about it. No one ever understood me before... and I miss him.

I play with my curls and say, "No, I'm ok."

"It's ok. If you have something on your mind, it's ok."

I bite the inside of my cheek and pull at my hair so hard a few strands snap. Ever since reliving the moment in the alley with the random dude, it's brought up a lot of memories. Memories of a guy I had thought of as my most special person.

Toby, a boy next to me raises his hand. "I've got something." He looks to me and says, "Maybe you'll feel better after I talk. Give ya a breather."

I nod at him and lower my head.

"Ok, Toby," Cindy says, "please share with the group."

Toby shares a story about spending a month on the streets, eating out of rubbish bins and drinking water pooled in the gutter. Sickening. I've never had such a horrendous experience.

"I'm sorry," I whisper to him.

He pushes for a smile and then stares at the floor.

"I can't share after that."

"We all have pain," Cindy says. "We can't judge others for their personal anguish. If it matters to you, it's valid."

I blurt out, "I really missed my boyfriend after we broke up."

Heads turn my way and my heart plummets. I must sound like a whiny brat.

"I was so in love with him and I told him all my secrets. But there was this party and he got drunk..." I pause, expecting someone to interrupt. Everyone, especially Cindy, stays quiet. It's ok? It's ok to continue. "I dunno. He said everyone was peer pressuring him to have sex but I thought he knew I wasn't ready. He was so much stronger

than me and I thought he would force me into it. But he was so drunk…
so drunk he lost his balance and I got away." I stop because I'm
panting. My chest is heaving. My pulse accelerates. "Everyone told me
I had to break up with him. But I loved him. I couldn't forgive him. I
couldn't be with him. But I loved him." Tears fog my eyes and I sigh.
"I miss him."

"Did you stay broken up after it?" Toby asks.

I swallow the lump in my throat and nod.

"Do you think your addiction happened because you didn't have
him to tell your secrets too?" Cindy asks.

I sigh again. "I don't know. Maybe. I don't have him, I don't have
Kellie," I groan at myself and cup my face, "and I threw away my
relationship with Reece. I'm such a fucking idiot."

"No, Charli, you're not," Cindy says. "Addiction happens when
we feel weak, alone and frightened. When we have fears we can't
confront and no one to turn too. Did you feel abandoned?"

"Not at first."

I expect another question, but she waits for me to elaborate.

"I didn't want to be involved. I was away for school and came
home because my sister was hurt. Seeing her banged up in that bed was
the hardest thing I've had to experience." I blow out a hard breath and
massage my hip. "We're twins and sometimes I take on her pain. With
hers and mine, it was too much to take. I didn't want to go back to the
hospital. I hid as much as I could. But then it felt like I was invisible. It
was what I wanted, but I didn't think I would go unnoticed. No one
cared until I did something majorly stupid."

"Did you feel unnoticed by your sister?"

I freeze. "No. I don't want to talk about her."

"Ok. What do you want to share about your boyfriend? What did
you want others to understand?"

"I don't know. I hated that no one *ever* understood us. From day one, people said we should break up. But I liked that it was the two of us against everyone else. I liked confiding in him and having his protection." Fuck, I love him. "I believed he still loved me. He was taken away from me."

"Did your parents stop you from seeing him?"

"I didn't tell them about what happened, but my dad never liked us together." I rub my temples. "I hate that I love him still."

Everyone is quiet.

"I shouldn't, right?"

Everyone is still quiet.

"I couldn't forgive him, so I shouldn't love him?"

Everyone is silent.

"Hello?" Anyone? "Cindy?"

Cindy shifts in her chair. "Why do you love him?"

I slouch in my chair and gaze up at the ceiling. Because he's Travis. My Travis.

I look at her and shake my head. "I'm done for today."

She smiles and nods. "Thank you for sharing."

I get claps from a few group members and then Harriet takes over the discussion.

14

Brittany

"Happy birthday to you, happy birthday to you, happy birthday dear Brittany, happy birthday to you."

It's kinda nice having only Bryce, Mum, Sophia and Dad at the house for my birthday. I can't believe Dad is here and everything is fine. Mum and Dad were so nice to each other after I came home from the hospital, but the Charli thing got them arguing again. Today, they are playing nice. I'm having a separate cake at Dad's house with the step family but he wanted to be here on the actual day.

Everyone still looks at me with thankful eyes. Thankful I'm alive. Every other day, I wish I didn't get those eyes, but today it's nice.

My mind drifts to Charli. How can she not be here? We have never had a birthday apart, and now she's gone and done something so stupid that I can't see my twin sister on our birthday.

I blow out the candles and hesitate on the wish. I think of her, but then I wish to dance again.

Sophia cuts the cake and I pivot between Mum and Dad. "Can we call her?"

Mum and Dad look at each other.

"Charli. Can we call her?"

Dad lays a hand on mine. "I wish we could. The centre has a strict twenty-eight day, no contact policy. It's bad timing."

"But it's our birthday."

Mum whimpers and cups her mouth. She takes a deep breath, lowers her hands and shakes her head. "Sorry."

Uncomfortableness shakes the room and I focus on the cake.

After Sophia clears the plates and Mum and Dad whisper in a corner, I slide my arms around Bryce and ask, "What is it really like?"

His eyebrows raise.

"In rehab. Will they celebrate her birthday?"

He plays with my hair. "I would think so. They are trying to help her."

I rest my head on his shoulder and play with his watchband. "I'm so mad at her. But I hope she's ok."

Dad loudly clears his throat behind us.

I lift my head and turn to him.

"Picked a movie, Brit?" Dad asks.

"'*Save the Last Dance*'," I say. "Classic."

"You're seriously not going to have a party?" Chloe stares me down like I told her she'd gained weight.

Everyone circles in on me with a mix of disappointment and confusion.

"I dunno, I thought I'd skip seventeen and have a big eighteenth."

My voice is so small.

"Why not have both?" Kimmy questions. She's been trying to act brave and cool lately, but the whole Sean and Fiona thing has rattled her. There's this sadness to her eyes I've never seen before. It's crazy feeling sympathy for Kimberley Jones.

My brain goes into overdrive, searching for the perfect excuse. Sean's party totally wiped me out. I know I'm not ready to host a party. And my parents would never go for it. Mum is constantly over my shoulder. Everyone would probably think the stairlift was a ride. *Ohmigawd*, imagine how much they'd complain about how slow it is.

There's a tap on my shoulder and relief takes over at the sight of Bryce.

"Just wanted to let you know I'm headed to practice," he says.

"Bryce," Kimmy begins, "talk some sense into your girlfriend and make her have a birthday party."

Bryce eyes me and holds a laugh. He says to the girls, "Like I'm the one to do that? I never have parties."

Oh, I love him.

The girls groan at him.

Chloe presses her hands on her hips. "Yeah, BK, don't think we're still not pissed at you for that."

Bryce kisses my cheek. "I'll catch you later."

I nod, brushing his jaw.

"All right, are we heading to the gym?" Madison asks the group.

"Last cheer practice," Chloe says, "let's make it count."

They move away. I used to go to practices and watch. It was painful to see the girls out of time and being unable to step in and show them how to fix their moves. They fussed over me when I first came back to school. Like it was some great honour to push my wheelchair. They used to ask if I was ok with them leaving. Now they just leave.

They don't want to be stuck with me.

Maybe I don't care anymore? I'm out of the wheelchair for good, but I'm still trailing behind them. I'm deserted at Chloe's table in mess, the best place to be in the school, and feel like an outcast. I decide on a more private location. If I can't cheer, I may as well do something with my time. I head to the library to study. I've gotten weirdly good at it. Plus, I'm all for a predominantly seated activity.

The quiet of the library is welcoming after listening to gaggling gossip. There are a few random kids at desks. Some watch me suspiciously, eyeing me like the girl I was pre-accident. My heart flutters. Maybe I am still someone.

Reece is ahead, typing on a laptop.

"Mind if I sit?"

He looks up and almost makes eye contact. "Sure."

School is almost over but going into grade twelve doesn't give us the normal blow-off last few weeks of school. I was thinking about working on my textiles design, but that class has become kinda a bummer. Even when Meah and I started drifting apart, we'd still talk about fashion and bounce ideas off each other about our designs. Now, she acts like I'm invisible. Sitting with her cousin makes me want to put distance between me and Meah Watkins.

"Have you finished the Shakespeare essay?" I ask Reece.

"Yeah. You need help?"

"You'd do that?"

He shuffles the notes beside him and slides a paper towards me. "Sure."

I push it back. "I don't want to steal your work."

A faint laugh escapes him. "It's not my essay. They are notes from class."

"Oh." I grin. "I have those. I actually make notes now. I need help with some quotes."

Reece digs through his bag for his copy of *'Macbeth'*. "Oh, I can do that."

"I really dig Lady Macbeth."

He nods. "She's badass. *"But screw your courage to the sticking place"*."

"What?"

"Lady Macbeth. She wears the pants. She orchestrates the entire plan but then her guilt takes over and drives her mad. *"Out damn spot"*."

"When she thinks she always has blood on her hands?"

"Exactly."

"I like her. I just have trouble with the language."

"*'Macbeth'* is one of the easier plays because it has a lot of action."

I nod. "I do like it. For Shakespeare."

He smiles as he taps on his keyboard. "Watch it."

Studying is fun. Who am I? Hanging with Reece is fun. Who knew? The sound of pages turning is oddly soothing. I enjoy marking up paragraphs and forming answers in my head.

I'm good at this. Maybe I'll ace this essay?

That evening, I kick back on the couch and open my phone to the text chain with Bryce.

> *(Me)* **Hey what you doing?**

It takes fifteen minutes to get a response.

> *(Bryce)* **Hey. Just at the mall with the guys. What you doing?**

(Me) **Just bored and was wondering whether you wanted to come over.**

(Bryce) **We are going to Chloe's. Want to meet us there?**

Chloe's? I hold my stomach. That's the last place I want to be. The thought of my boyfriend around her makes me want to scream.

(Bryce) **I can ask Jace to swing past and get you. You at your dad's?**

His dad is still being way strict about Bryce spending evenings with me. In a group setting it's allowed, but our parents are freaked that if we spend too much time alone, Bryce will get obsessive and worry about me more than himself.

(Me) **Don't worry about it. We'll be having dinner soon.
See you at school.**

(Bryce) **Ok. Love you.**

I never complained about having a boyfriend who cared so much about me. Thanks for driving the wedge, Mr Kerry.

(Me) **Love you too.**

I drop my phone and scrunch my eyes closed.
This freakin sucks.

At school the next day, I pass the music room and sneak inside. My sneak is more of a hobble with my cane, but when you walk like this, you barely get into trouble.

"Hey, what's up?" Nick asks, leaning on the piano.

"Not much. How's rehearsal?"

"The sheet music is super easy. I'm just here as accompaniment." He rolls his eyes. "It's tedious."

I giggle and take in the voice singing. Madison is behind the microphone. I never knew she could sing. When it comes to music, I'd only heard her talk about playing the cello and hating it.

We watch her sing and then Nick winces, "*Oof*, she's flat."

Nick slides onto the piano stool and starts playing the accompanying music.

Madison stops singing, taken aback.

Nick stands as he hits the keys and calls out, "Keep going."

Madison shakes it off, her high ponytail swishing behind her, and sings. Nick braces through gritted teeth. He then sings the lyrics with Madison. Madison turns to him and they maintain eye contact as they sing. Her body relaxes and her voice grows stronger. I shiver with goosebumps as their voices blend.

Nick stops playing. "That was better."

The music teacher Mrs Bartholomew applauds. She reaches her hands towards Nick. "Perhaps this should be a duet."

"What?" Nick shakes his head and arms. "No."

"Oh, yes," Mrs Bartholomew beams. "You two together are gold."

Nick plops onto the stool, eyes wide.

"You're really good," I say. "Why wouldn't you sing when you're already classically trained?"

Madison skips towards us. "Hey, thanks for the help."

"Ah, no problem," Nicks says.

"So, a duet?"

"I didn't mean to steal your thunder," Nick rushes.

"Mrs Bartholomew has made her mind up. And I don't mind the company."

"Really?"

Madison leans in close and pinches his cheek. "It's a good thing you're so darn cute."

Nick gulps as Madison's eye contact intensifies and I totally get the feeling like I should leave the room.

Madison lets go of Nick and giggles. She eyes me and says, "Brit, why didn't you tell me your step brother was so attractive."

"*Arhhh...*"

She turns to Nick. "I'll have to come over to your place for extra rehearsals."

She's so bold. I could never be like that with a boy I liked. I was so timid around Bryce at first and couldn't stop shaking. Madison's in total control.

She blows a kiss at Nick. "I'll see ya next rehearsal."

"*Whoah,*" Nick whispers as Madison saunters away.

"Madison seems to know what she wants."

"She is amazingly scary," Nick says, his lips curving like he's impressed.

I lean against the piano to shift my weight. "I just wanted to let you know that Bryce is driving me home today. Did you want to come with us?"

"No, I'm good. Zach is picking me up to practice for our gig at *Gina's.*"

I nod. "Ok, I'll catch you later."

"For sure."

I leave the music room and walk down the corridor with my cane. I can't stop smiling. I'm walking at school. This is awesome.

I move past the boys' bathroom and hear laughter inside. I recognise some voices and slow down to eavesdrop.

"I used to be so fucking jealous of BK," Sean says. "Because he's with Brittany and she was so friggin hot."

I bite my lip and blush.

"But now it's like dodging a bullet, right," Sean continues as others laugh. "It would fuckin suck to have to dump a cripple."

'*Yeahs*' and laughter responds, and I'm stabbed and gutted. I turn and move fast, but almost trip on my cane. The tears pool as my anger at my inability to move faster intensifies. I hobble away, hoping they don't come into the hall.

I hope they don't say anything to Bryce. But what if they already have? What if he's talked to them about it?

I duck into an alcove and slide to the floor. I sit on the hard tiles gasping for air.

Everyone is talking about me.

The cripple girl.

The girl who *used* to be hot.

The ex-cheerleader *nobody*.

I pat my eyes dry. I need to get outta here. I push on the ground and my core feels inflamed.

What was I thinking? Why did I go to the floor? I can't push myself up. EVER.

My face collapses to my hands and I whimper sobs. I'm so friggin pathetic.

"Heya, you ok?"

I lower my hands and see Tayla Martinez bent over and staring at me, her long chestnut hair falling by her tanned arms.

I nod slowly.

Her eyes round.

I shake my head.

She holds her arms out. "Lean on me to get up."

I bite my lip, worried how uncoordinated I'll look.

"Don't worry, it's cool," Tayla whispers.

I have no choice. I grab onto her forearms and push my weight onto her. I puff. It's a bigger workout than physio.

"You good?" she asks as I wobble to standing.

I nod and rest with relief when she hands me my cane.

"Did you fall?"

I bite my lip. "Can we just forget about it?"

"Sure. I've missed you at practice," Tayla says. "I liked your routines, and you were always so nice when teaching us the moves. It's been *different* without you."

"I'd love to be back on the squad."

"D'you think you can come back next year?"

"I hope so."

"Are you heading to lunch?"

"Yeah, I think Bryce is in the mess hall."

"I'll walk with you."

"You don't have to, I'm kinda slow."

She shrugs. "It don't bother me."

My knee hurts from hitting the ground, but I don't think my limp is any more obvious than usual. My eyes prick and my smile hurts when I see Bryce. He moves away from their table in mess and walks towards me. I rest against his body and let his arms hold me up.

"Is everything ok?" he whispers.

I nod against his chest. I run a finger under my eyes and lift my head. His crystal eyes warm me with comfort. I run my hands along his back and look over his shoulder.

My stomach flips as Meah comes into view. She struts around the table and flicks her hair too many times. My jaw drops when she slides onto Naveen's lap.

Meah and Naveen? When did that happen?

I get the sense everyone at the table is cool with her presence. Meah is in. Meah is in without me.

My eyes tear up, and I want to shrink into nothing. What kinds of things would she be saying about me? Would she have put those words into the boys' heads?

A sob breaks and I cover my mouth.

Bryce runs a hand over my hair. "Britty? What's wrong?"

I put both hands over my face and rock my head.

He holds my wrist and I know he wants me to show my face. "Brit?"

"I heard something... people are just mean sometimes, that's all."

"What was it? Who was it?"

I shake my head. "Nothing."

"Britty."

I lower my hands and make the mistake of peering over his shoulder. Meah and Naveen are making out. I squeak and put my hands back.

Bryce spins us in a one-eighty and holds me close. "What is it? Was it Meah? Did she say something?"

I lower my hands and rest them on his chest. "Is she looking at me?"

He smirks. "Nah, she's kinda busy right now."

His heart beats fast as I try to slow mine down. My breaths are heavy, and I keep my eyes closed. I reach up to caress his cheek and find his lips with mine.

"I'm ok, I promise."

"You need to tell me if something is wrong," he whispers. "I wanna make it right."

"I know. Thank you, but I just want to forget it."

"Have you eaten?"

"I'm not hungry."

"Wanna get out of here?"

"Yes, please."

I turn towards the exit as Chloe walks towards us, giggling behind a cupped hand beside Sean.

"Hey BK," Chloe says mid-giggle. Her fingers dancing up my boyfriend's arm. Her smile drops when she looks at me. "Hey, Brit."

"Hey," I say bluntly.

Sean looks me up and down with a smirk.

"You ok?" Bryce asks him.

Sean shrugs. "Sure, bro."

I clasp Bryce's hand. "Please, let's go."

"BK, can you come here a minute?" Chloe says, walking to the table.

Bryce pivots towards the table, but I tug on his arm. "Bryce?"

"What?" Bryce calls to Chloe.

Chloe *tsks*, hands on hips. "Like, I'm not gonna yell it. Come over here, would ya."

"Nah," Bryce says, shaking his head at Chloe. "You can tell me later. We're on our way out."

My heart *ba-booms* in my chest as Bryce's hand curls around mine. The look in Chloe's eyes burns a hole in my stomach, but the feeling disappears when my beautiful boy walks me out of mess hall.

15

Charli

"Do you think you have come to terms with Kellie's death?" David asks. "It seems it took a long time for you to comprehend that she is no longer with us."

I hug a pillow and squirm on the couch.

"Besides being overseas, what made the news so hard to take?"

I squint at him like he's stupid. "She's my best friend."

He waits for me to continue.

My gut grumbles and I clench, not wanting to think about it. I sigh and blurt out, "It was my fault, ok?"

"Your fault?"

"She died because I didn't help her."

"Charli, you were in another country."

"She was calling and texting me." I hunch over my legs to stop the stabbing pains in my gut. "I kept ignoring her. She had something important to say. I didn't want to hear it. I wanted to be away from

Sanford. I wanted her to wait. I wanted her to let me be away and not drag me down." I sniff back a sob and my voice cracks. "I was so fucking selfish. She needed me and I blocked her out. She wanted to talk about her boyfriend. She must have wanted to break up with him and needed help. *Fuck.* If I had taken those calls, we could have talked through it. They could have broken up before the crash and she would still be alive."

"Why do you say this?"

My chest heaves. "He was the one driving."

"You are putting the blame on yourself instead of the driver?"

"Yes. She needed my help and I failed."

"This is the same accident your sister was in, yes?"

I fidget and turn to the bookcase.

"Why don't you want to talk about Brittany?"

Acid shoots up my throat and hits the back of my mouth.

"Something happened between the two of you?"

"No."

"What's blocking you?"

"*Nothing!*" I snap. "Nothing. I did nothing."

David studies me like I'm fascinating.

"I'm supposed to protect her and I let her down. I wasn't there for her, and I am supposed to always be there for her."

"Do you feel guilty for going overseas without her?"

"No."

He taps a pen to his lips.

"I couldn't cope with the thought of losing her. If she had been the one that died, I don't know what I would have done. I don't want to think about it, but I might have hurt myself." Goosebumps shiver my body. That horrible voice and what it wanted me to do. "Now she's in a wheelchair. She's an amazing dancer who can't walk." I pat my eyes dry. "I wish I could trade places with her. She deserves to walk. I want to take away her pain. I want her to be happy. I love her so much, and I'm so sorry I abandoned her."

"You can still make it up to her. It's not too late. She's alive and has more life to live," David says. "As do you."

I nod. "That's true."

"If you could see her today, what would you say to her?"

My hand lays over my heart. "I don't know. I have so much to make up for."

"Is there something you share? Just the two of you?"

My lip quivers. "Our birthday."

"I'm sorry you missed that."

I shrug. "Don't be. It's my fault."

"Anything else?"

"We drifted apart so much. There wasn't much we shared."

"There has to be something."

"Sometimes I would let her do my makeup. I don't really like it, but she does. We would talk about random stuff and laugh together. Those times were always good. She's good at makeup, so I never minded in the end."

David smiles. "That sounds like a wonderful time. So, that's something she does for you. What's something you do for her?"

My heart pounds in my ears. "I don't know. I feel like I never did the right thing. I was trying to look out for her last year, but she always pushed me away. I didn't like who she was friends with, but she didn't listen."

"Were you jealous?"

"No."

"So why did you not like her friends?"

"Because they are vapid and mean. She's better than that."

"You want to be her friend?"

"Of course," I rush. "She found her boyfriend who is perfect for her. I guess I like that she found friends, even if it pushed us further apart."

"You feel you two butt heads?"

"All the time."

"Why is that?"

I shrug. "We are different?"

"Your opposites could pull you together. You could tackle problems together using your different strengths. I think you'll find you will be stronger together. Is that something you want to work on when you get home?"

I clasp my hands. "Desperately."

David smiles. "I think that is a great goal to come out of your time here."

I look down at the open notebook beside me, at words I poured my heart into.

We are still broken,
Our words unspoken,
Our blood-bound connection,
No more than a shattered reflection,
The haze in the mirror,
Is not any clearer,
I am hurt without you,
And wish, my love, you knew,
I am destruction and I am fire,
Wishing our sisterhood was one of desire,
I want to be your hand,
And strong enough to help you stand.

"So, what do you want out of life?" David asks.

My chest clenches. "That's a loaded question."

"If you could go out into the world on your own, what would you want to be doing?"

"Being on my own would be major."

"How so?"

"I loved being in Spain. I loved the independence away from my parents."

"Is that why you rebelled with substance abuse? You wanted to be further away from your parents?"

"I didn't need to hear that I'm not good enough."

"Would you go back to Spain?"

"I'd go anywhere. I want to travel."

"For holidays?"

"For anything. For all the time. I want to see everything. Being over there made me realise how big the world is. Life is more than the crap going on in Sanford. Kellie is dead and never got to leave. She never got to pursue her dreams. I want more out of life. I don't give a shit about school; I just want to make a difference. I want to go to places that are not as well off and make a difference."

"Like developing countries?"

"Yeah, maybe."

"Humanitarian work?"

"Perhaps. I haven't really thought it through. I want more out of life. I don't want to be like everyone else at school who follow in their parents footsteps. That was my plan. I wanted to become a lawyer, but I don't care anymore. They clearly care less about me, so why should I bother?"

"You think your parents care more about your sister than you?"

"I think it depends on the situation. They hounded Brittany worse than me, but after the accident, they wrapped her up in cotton wool."

"So, you say you don't care about school. Is it classes or interacting with classmates?"

"I don't care about them. I've always tuned people out. I don't know, I guess its expectations I don't want to deal with."

"Do you want to care about certain classes that will help you achieve your goals after graduation?"

"Yeah... if I decide what that is."

"Maybe that will be your next step."

I nod. "Maybe."

"Have you had more cravings?"

"No. I certainly haven't. I promise I will never touch the stuff again."

"Charli, you are doing really well. Good to see that you are so strong."

"Thank you, David."

I am shit scared. I am passed the twenty-eighth day mark and feeling great, health-wise. But today is family day. I've vomited twice.

"Doing ok?" Cindy asks, walking past me.

"Ok."

She stops and tilts her head. "Looks like you're holding onto the wall pretty tight there."

"I might pass out if I don't."

"Get some water and sit down. We don't leave you alone with your family, it's all mediated," Cindy says, prying me away from the wall. "You'll do great. You're acing the program. Everything will be ok."

"You don't know my family," I mutter.

"Hunny, I've seen it all. A rich family is nothing compared to a junkie family."

Whoah. What are the other families going to be like? Will they be violent? I hope it doesn't send anyone to relapse when they get out.

Cindy places a cup of water on the table and I sit. In group, we played out scenarios of family day. It's brought a million pictures to my mind. From an ambush and yelled abuse, to embracing, to crying and them telling me how much they love and miss me. The scales tip in scenario one's favour.

"Charli?" David calls behind me.

I turn, and he's with my parents and Brittany. My stomach flips. Brittany is walking. She puts her wait onto a crutch, but she's walking,.

I'm breathless. "Brit, you're walking." My smile pulls at my cheeks.

Her face scrunches with disgust. "I was walking before you left."

You were?

David shows them to my table. Mum sits, then Dad sits opposite her with Tara next to him.

"What's she doing here?" I blurt out.

"*Charli,*" Dad snaps.

David sits beside me and reaches his hand out. "Ok, there's some hostility here we need to work through."

"Charli, Tara is your step mother, she has a right to be here," Dad continues.

"Mr Matthews," David insists. "Please, we need to remain calm."

Brittany moves around to sit next to Mum and I instinctively get up. My urge to help her is strong.

"I got it," she grunts, pulling at her seat.

I sit as Mum helps her with her cane.

"Today, we are here for Charli," David says to my family. "There are problems to deal with and goals to strive for. Namely, a hopeful and positive return home. Should we start with the step family issues? Charli has discussed that it's been a problem."

"Maybe the lines of communication weren't open when my relationship with Tara began," Dad says, waving a hand across the air.

"Were you aware she dabbled with substances at the beginning of your marriage?"

"What?" Dad shouts.

"How long has this been going on for?" Mum asks me. "I thought this was only since Kellie passed."

"It was," I say, shrinking in my seat.

David holds a hand up in front of me. "Ms Matthews, please try to refrain from accusations."

"You want us to coddle her while she's in rehab?" my dad asks, reddening from the neck up.

"No, I want a calm and rational discussion," David says, not taking any shit.

"Charli, please know I'm here for you," Tara says in a quiet voice. "I'm sorry if our relationship has been hard on you. I'm sorry we haven't had a proper discussion about this before, but I'm happy and willing to do this. I love and care about you."

"Thank you, Mrs Matthews," David says. "Charli, do you have anything to say to your step mother?"

I squirm in my seat. For some reason, I never thought that Tara would be here. Her eyes are kind as she looks at me. I gulp and shake my head.

"That's ok, we will work up to that," David says. "The goal today is to work through the conflicts at home and find the best outpatient care for Charli. This includes rules set by you, as parents, to ensure home life is as harmonious as possible."

I can't help staring at Brittany. She looks so well. Shiny hair, no bags under her eyes, and a plump, acne-free face. My heart pitter-patters and warms my body.

She catches me staring and glares. "What?"

"You look fantastic. I'm so happy to see you up and about."

"Maybe you would have noticed things when you were home if you weren't so drugged up all the time."

I gasp and my heart stops for one beat too long. It starts again, booming in my ears.

"Ok, not as productive as we would like, but opens us up for discussion," David says. "I want you all to tell Charli how you feel about her substance abuse. How you felt when you found out, and how having her away from home has felt. Brittany, would you like to begin?"

"Hell, no," she blurts out.

Ouch.

David address Mum. "Ms Matthews?"

Mum sits tall and slowly exhales. "Hurt. Disappointed. Charli, I hate that you couldn't talk to me about what was happening," she pauses as her eyes well. "But the longer you were away, the more I blamed myself. I wasn't there for you. I'm sorry. I let you down. Brittany needed so much care and it was all I could focus on. I didn't see you needed help. We snatched you home and told you your best friend died and expected you to cope with it in an instant. I'm sorry. I'm so, so, sorry."

A tear streaks my cheek. "Oh, Mum."

Dad reaches across the table and takes Mum's hand. "Julie, we both did that."

My chest heaves as my parents hold hands.

"Charli," David says, "Anything you want to say to your mother?"

"I can't believe you're apologising," I say.

Mum leaves Dad's hand and takes mine. "Pumpkin, I don't condone what you did. It was wrong. So very, very wrong. But I understand you felt helpless. We need to work as a family more. I'm willing if you're willing."

I nod. "I'm willing."

"Great start," David says, smiling.

Our hands let go and I sheepishly turn to Dad.

"I'm sorry I wasn't more open about Tara in the beginning," Dad says. "I had in my head you girls would get on board. I didn't think it would have such a great impact. It was selfish, but at the time I wanted to be selfish. I hadn't been happy in a long time, and with Tara, everything felt better."

"Better than being with us?" my voice squeaks.

"Pumpkin." Dad takes my hands. "You and Brittany are always top of my list. I will put you two before everything. I've been bad at expressing myself and I wanted to go off on my own to reflect. I went MIA on the dad front and I think that's where my responsibility in all this mess comes from. I also think Tara being here can help us move on. Do you agree?"

I slide back in my chair.

David pushes my chair forward. "How about we take another approach on that point? Charli, how do you feel about Tara being here?"

I shrug. "I've never really talked to Tara."

"How can you say that?" Dad snaps. "We've had countless–"

"Mr Matthews," David interrupts. "Let Charli explain herself."

Silence sweeps the table and I shy from all the eyes on me. "Yeah, we've been in the same place at the same time, but I know nothing about her. I don't know what her deal is or why you two got together."

"That's fair," Tara says, patting Dad's hand. "Charli and I have never found it easy to talk. I can give you my bio. I grew up in West Sanford, dirt poor. I moved away with my high school sweetheart and thought marriage would stop him hitting me."

I flinch. "What?"

"And then I thought kids would lower his temper. I didn't mind him hitting me if it meant he never touched the kids, but when he hit Nicky, that was the last straw. We moved in with my parents." Tara squeezes Dad's hand and her eyes shine. "Your dad is a prince and I'm so in love with him. He loves you and Brittany so much."

Beads of sweat line my forehead and I'm panting as she continues her story.

"I wish I'd met you sooner than we did. I was so nervous and talking too much and too fast. I want to try harder. I want us to be a family. Your dad makes me laugh and makes me feel like a better person, and I hope I do the same for him. That's why we are together."

I'm breathless and my thoughts scatter.

"Sounds like there are open communication lines for you with Tara, if you want to take it," David says. "How do you feel about that?"

I bite inside my cheek. "It's better."

"Good." Tara smiles and nods.

"And what about your dad," David asks. "Do you have a response for him?"

"I hate that you left for all those months," I tell Dad. "It felt like you abandoned us. Well, me. It felt like you were abandoning me. I was selfish too, but I hated you didn't call as often. I hated we had to share you when you came back. You never felt like my dad after that. I was always fighting for your attention and losing."

"Charli," Dad says, his eyes fogging. "I'm sorry. I never meant for that. Do you promise not to do drugs again?"

"Like your love is conditional?" I fight back.

"That's not what I'm saying," he argues.

"Ok, take a breather," David says. "Remember, we want calm, not hostility. Charli is past the halfway mark and told me she has no cravings. She will need support and I want to focus on family relationships during this meeting."

"So, you're going to stop?" Dad asks me.

I clamp my hands on my head and groan. "Dad, stop."

"What?"

"It's like you want to be a trigger."

"So, you will smoke again?"

I slide my seat and walk away from the table with my hands up. "I don't want to go home."

"Charli," Mum says, standing.

"Charli come back to the table," David says. "Please."

"I can't do this. I don't want to go home to be interrogated every day."

"Please," David insists.

My breathing quickens as I hold my stomach and hope the remaining contents don't unload.

Brittany plants her hands on the table and says, "Why don't you come back so we can talk."

It's like magnets drawing me back. As I sit, David thanks Brittany for her effort and asks her for her thoughts.

"I tried to talk to you," she says to me. "You couldn't even look me in the eye."

I pull at my hair. "I don't really remember it."

She groans and rolls her eyes.

"What do you remember?" David urges me.

"Being sad. Overwhelmingly sad that Brittany was hurt. I wished it were me instead."

Brittany looks at me again.

"I couldn't handle it, Brit. I was monumentally selfish. It hurt so much to see you in pain and stuck in bed. It physically hurt me. The thought of losing you was too much. I'm so, so sorry I didn't support you. All I want to do is help you and make sure everything is ok, but I didn't do that."

"I was scared," Brittany says, voice feeble. "And alone. It would have been nice to have you by my side."

"I know. I'm sorry. I didn't want to be home and I was thrown into all this chaos."

Her eyes water. "It's not good enough."

"I'm sorry."

She purses her lips as her tears fall, and she shakes her head.

"Really, I am."

She wipes her face and looks away.

"Brittany, do you have any thoughts on Charli coming home?" David asks, but Brittany puts a hand up.

"It's ok," I whisper to David.

Mum rubs Brittany's back and I know I have so much to make up for. It will be a colossal task when I get home.

David moves discussions onto rules for when I get home. Mum, Dad and Tara chime in with things they expect for me. I agree with everything to move the conversation along because I can't stop watching Brittany. Her puffy eyes and drooped face. My heart tears. I want to hug her but I know she doesn't want me near. All I want is to make her happy.

"And when you go back to school, you'll be repeating grade eleven."

I blink hard. "What?"

Mum fidgets in her seat. "You were failing your classes. You can't move onto twelfth grade."

"Pumpkin," Dad says, "they wanted to expel you."

I shrink. "Expel?"

"You'll start over fresh in the new year," Mum says, patting my hand.

Pumpkins grow on trestles,
Climbing from Earth to light,
Fine green leaves,
To show everything is alright,
A shiny dimpled surface,
Many to sneer at,
Or abandon without burden.

Pumpkins, sweet or spiced,
Someone else's choice,
No tender love and care,
Shrivelled, no rejoice,
Decay within unseen,
Perfection you want,
But your Pumpkin I will no longer be.

16

Brittany

Charli will be home soon. The thought makes my back knot. I don't want her home. She's drama and trouble. I'm getting back to normal and my pain is now minor. No matter how hopeful our last meeting was, I don't need her here making things worse.

"How could you say that?" Madison squeals, punching Nick's arm as we crash in Dad's living room.

"What? You'd prefer me to lie and say you *weren't* off key?" Nick teases.

"What are you two fighting about?" I ask as Reece sits next to me.

"Madi can't sing for shit," Nick says, laughing.

Madison shoves him. "*Bitch.*"

"Don't be mean to her," I say. "She has a beautiful voice."

"Thanks, Brit," Madi says. "At least *you're* a true friend."

"I'm being a friend by telling you the truth," Nick argues, grinning.

Madison *tsks*. "After all I'm doing to help your music."

"Joining his band, you mean?" I ask.

"More than that." Madison whips out her phone and opens YouTube. "I've started a channel for him. The world needs to see his music."

I peer over her phone. "That's so cool."

"It's not cool," Nick whines. "It's weird."

"It's not weird," Madi sighs. She scrolls through the thumbnails and says, "Look, this one got fifty-thousand views. Someone with a following must have shared it." Madi turns to Nick and whacks his arm. "This way people in the biz can see you. Don't you want to be out on a stage somewhere?"

"I already do that."

She rolls her eyes. "Other than lame, coffee shop gigs."

Nick shrugs. "At least it's something. You don't have to come tonight if it's gonna be so lame."

"I'm just giving you options," Madi says. "Wider options. And you know I'll be there tonight. You need me, Baby."

As the two continue to bicker, Reece thumbs through his book and whispers, "So, is Charli coming home?"

I bite my lip and nod.

His face droops.

"Are you ok with that?"

"I'm not the one living with her."

"Hmm." Subject change, stat. I turn to Madi. "Besides the arguing, how are rehearsals going? You feel ready for tonight?"

"Hells yes. The band is pumping with me in it."

"Nick, is she overshadowing you?"

Nick grins. "She's all right, she just needs to be nicer to the guys."

Madi blows a raspberry. "Zach and Lenny love me."

We all laugh in response, even Reece.

Nick leans over the couch and taps Reece's book. "Are you onto a new book?"

"Yeah. *'The Colour Purple.'* Have you started *'Dorian Gray'*?"

"I tried."

"It's a quick read. Well, it is for an eighteenth-century book. Where is it?"

"By my bed."

Reece holds out his hand. "Givit and I'll mark up the pages you should read."

Nick gets up and beckons Reece to follow.

As the boys leave, Madi waggles her phone at me. "You think the YouTube thing is a good idea?"

"Yeah, sure."

"Me too." She smiles, pleased with herself as she scrolls through her phone. "Hey, where's Bryce?"

I purse my lips. "I dunno."

She looks up from her phone. "Chloe?"

Shudder. "I don't wanna think about it."

"You'd better. You know what the vulture is like." Madison taps her phone. "Her plaything Lucas isn't in town anymore."

"Why aren't you with Chloe & Co?"

Madi exhales and slides her phone in her pocket. "I guess I prefer to hang with fun people."

I giggle, side-eyeing my cane. "Yeah, it's a riot over here."

"Over here, we can talk about actual fun things rather than fill the air with bullying or stupid rumours." Madison plays with her glossy, high ponytail. "It's summer holidays and I could use some time away from schoolyard bullshit."

"It's good to get away from the noise."

Madi's eyes drift to the hall. "Need my eye candy to come back."

"Are you and Nick...?"

She laughs. "No."

"What, I dunno?" I shrug with a laugh.

She bites her lip and grows a cheeky smile. "Actually, me and Zach are..."

"You and Nick's best mate?"

"Nick and I aren't a thing. We're friends. He's bitchy to me and I like it."

"So, you and Zach... since when?"

"Like, second practice after I joined the band."

"Does Nick know?"

She nods. "It's nothing serious, that's why I asked him not to tell."

"Ok, I'm happy for you." I cross my arms and ask, "D'you think Chloe will come tonight?"

"To the gig at *Gina's*? I doubt it. I tried talking to Fi about it and she blew me off." Madison frowns at her chipped manicure. "I thought Nav would be a safer bet, but he's somehow tied up with Meah."

I blow out a breath. "Yeah, that happened."

She nods. "Somehow. Is Bryce taking you? Maybe he could encourage the others?"

I unintentionally make fists. "I haven't asked him to go."

"What? Why not?"

I throw my arms out wide. "The four of us have been hanging out here since school finished, yet Bryce is never around. Didn't make me too confident that he'd come to West Sanford with us."

"Does he have a problem with Nick and Reece?"

"Not that he's told me, and I don't see why he would."

"You guys have a fight?"

"Only about me not hanging with Chloe & Co. I don't think he likes I've made other friends."

"Typical boy. Want me to talk to him?"

I smile. "No. No, it's cool."

"Why don't you text Bryce?"

"To get Nav at the gig tonight?"

Madi rolls her eyes and smiles. "No, to come over here. You two are drifting apart and I don't like it."

"Oh, um, I dunno."

Madi leaps, gripping my hip pocket. "I'll do it for you."

I squeal and bat her away. "Stop, I'll do it."

Madi smooths her clothes, looking pleased. "Fantastic."

I decide to play it cool and blame Madi.

(Me) Hey. Madi said you have to get your butt over here.

"Talk some sense into Reece," Nick says, walking into the living room with Reece tailing him.

"What's wrong?" I ask, monitoring my phone for the incoming *dot dot dot.*

"He doesn't want to come tonight," Nick says.

"What?" Madi shouts.

I whack her arm. "Don't yell at him."

Reece's head hangs low, tilted toward the front door.

I pat the space beside me. "Reece, why don't ya sit down?"

He doesn't lift his head but shuffles over.

As he sits, I say to Nick, "It was probably hard for him to tell you that."

"I know," Nick hushes. He sits on the armrest by Reece. "I get it if you don't wanna go. I'd just like you to come."

Reece's shoulders bunch as his fingers lace together.

"I guess you can't exactly wear those big headphones at the gig," Madison jokes.

Nick slides off the armrest and sits on the coffee table. "Decide later. It's ok either way."

A smile curls Reece's lips. "Yeah, right."

"Has he replied?" Madi asks.

I look at the text chain. "Nope."

"The worst," Madi winces, taking out her phone.

"Don't text him," I whine. My phone buzzes. "Ah, he replied." I hurriedly tell him to come over to Dad's, autocorrect struggling to keep up.

He's not over immediately. We are in the kitchen when Madi says, "Here comes your boy-wonder now."

I move towards the entryway to spy Bryce's car through a front window.

"Was he with Chloe?" Madi whispers.

I shake my head. "I dunno. I didn't ask. He didn't say."

Madi opens the door when Bryce lands on the porch. "Hey, nice of you to show up."

My stomach quivers in a weird way.

"Hi," he says, eyes narrowing.

Is he annoyed I made him come over here?

"Hey, gorgeous," he says, grinning at me, and moving in to kiss my cheek.

His lips send me into tingles, pushing the weirdness away.

He gasps and holds onto my arms. "No cane?"

I giggle. "I'm trying to go without it at home."

His grin grows. "That's awesome. Does it hurt?"

I shrug. "A little, but there's enough furniture to lean on if I need it."

The three of us move into the living room where Nick and Reece are. I sit by Reece on the three-seater couch and spy something weird in Bryce's eye before he sits on my other side.

As the boys continue to talk, Bryce's hand sits on top of mine, but he's turned toward Madi. He scrolls through his phone like he wants to be anywhere but here.

He lifts his head and I flinch. He tilts his phone screen and says to Madi, "Did you get the text about Mermaid Cove?"

"Mermaid Cove?" I ask, peering at his phone.

"What?" Madi glares at her phone. "They planned it for tonight? After I already invited them to the gig? *Bitches.*"

My gut pangs for Madi. "I can't believe they'd do that."

She deadpans me and I purse my lips and nod. Yes, I can.

"You wanna come with me?" Bryce asks.

"Ah," I stammer. "You're going to Mermaid Cove tonight?"

His brow furrows as he tilts the phone screen more toward my direction.

"I was going to ask you to go to West Sanford with me tonight."

"Why?"

"*Hello,*" Madi says, throwing her arms out wide. "We're playing a gig tonight."

"Oh," Bryce says, tucking his phone in his pocket.

Oh?

Nick blows out a breath, swivelling away, and Reece slides further away from me as the hostile awkwardness takes hold of the room.

Madi stands and snaps her fingers at Nick. "C'mon, let's get some practice in."

Nick stands and says to Reece, "You wanna come with us."

Reece slings his backpack over his shoulder, shaking his head.

"I'll head home."

"You want me to drive you?" Nick asks.

"No, I'll board."

"Be safe," I say as he waves goodbye, leaving for the front door.

Madi follows Nick to his bedroom and Bryce pats my thigh, saying, "Are you going to come to the beach tonight?"

I show him my phone. "Not invited."

He *tsks*. "You're my girlfriend, your invite is implied."

I roll my eyes. "I'm hardly in the group anymore."

"You keep hanging out with other people."

I nod at the cane. "People who don't make a big deal outta that thing."

Bryce sighs. "No one cares that you're walking with a cane."

My jaw clenches and my eyes sting. They do. I heard them.

They called me a cripple.

I suck back the tears. He knows they make a big deal about it.

"You'd prefer us to go to West Sanford?"

I lean my forehead against his shoulder. "I feel like I don't see you as much."

He rubs my back. "I don't think I should have to give up my friends to be with you."

"But I don't get why you won't hang out with these guys."

He sighs and pulls away.

"You're mad at me."

He shakes his head and brushes my cheek. "Never. I just don't want to argue."

I bite my lip as my jaw clenches. I stare into his ice blue eyes and wish he'd just want to be with me all the time.

He squeezes my hand. "You know I wanna spend my time with you no matter the location. I just didn't know the location had changed."

"Sorry, I don't know why I was assuming you could read my mind."

He laughs. "I know, I am Superman. I must have been off my game."

I giggle. "Goof."

"Your dad or Tara home?" Bryce asks, twisting a lock of my hair around his finger.

I rub my leg against his thigh and shake my head.

Bryce eyes the hall leading to my bedroom and then back at me, wriggling his eyebrows with a ridiculously adorable smile.

I giggle, blushing.

He hugs me tighter and whispers. "Although, I guess we can make ourselves at home on this couch."

I squeak as he pinches my bum. I playfully hit his arm. "Stop it. Nick and Madi are in his bedroom."

Bryce smirks. "Then we definitely got time up our sleeves."

"Whaddaya mean?"

"C'mon, they're all over each other."

"Nah-uh, they haven't hooked up."

"And what d'you think they're up to now?"

"*Duh*," I say, flinging an arm towards the hall. "Listen to them. They're rehearsing."

His hands run through my hair. "They are distracted enough to leave us alone?"

A nervously excited giggle pours out of me. "Sounds that way."

Bryce pulls me close and slides backwards on the couch. I'm anchored between his thighs as I lay on top of him and kiss his lips. His hands run down my back and press into my low back. I move my lips below his jaw and suck at the soft skin of his neck. A soft, breathy moan escapes him and makes me want to explore him more.

His hands cup my bum and I giggle and move my lips to his. I run my hands under his shirt as his phone rings in the pocket of his jeans. He pulls his lips away and *humphs*.

When he reaches for his pocket, I latch onto his wrist. "Nah-uh."

He laughs and puts his hand on my hip and kisses the spot under my earlobe. When he makes me moan in the best way, his phone rings again.

"*Ugh*. Just let me get it so they'll stop interrupting," he whispers. He pulls out the phone and places it at his ear as he hits answer. "Hello?"

I push on his chest to move off him, but he hooks me with his arm. I land on his chest as he shakes his head with a cheeky smile. I giggle and then slap a hand over my mouth as I realise how close I am to the phone.

Bryce places a finger over his lips, eyeing me like I'm naughty. Another giggle spills out of me.

"Yeah, I got the text," he says.

I tilt my head. Is it Chloe?

"I'm currently convincing Brittany to go," he says, smiling and winking at me.

I suddenly feel very uncomfortable on his lap.

Bryce laughs into the phone. "I am *not* saying that."

My stomach drops as I imagine Chloe telling my boyfriend to ditch me.

Bryce shakes his head, grinning. "If you promise to be nice." Bryce laughs and lowers his phone, hitting speaker. The screen illuminates with **Naveen**.

I breathe out a rush of air.

"Brittany, can you come and be fun," Naveen sniggers through the speaker.

I pull away, my forehead scrunching.

Bryce rubs my back. "I said be nice."

"I am nice," Naveen argues. "All I mean is, she was fun. She should come hang out and be fun again."

"Is she going to come?" Meah's voice whispers in the background of Naveen's call.

"I will," I reply and hit the *end call* button.

Bryce drops his phone on the couch cushion and smiles. "You will?"

I slide my hands up the sides of his face and kiss his lips. Meah's voice squawks in my head. *"She's not fun. Why even bother inviting her."* I kiss Bryce harder as *"cripple"* repeats in my mind.

He pulls his lips away and rests his forehead against mine. "You ok?"

"Mhmm." I push my lips closer to his, but he pulls away again. "What are you doing?"

"You don't seem ok," he says.

"I just wanna make out and not talk."

Bryce blows out a breath and runs a hand down my back. "Well, be in a position that won't hurt you."

He slides me off his lap and I move to the end of the couch, cradling myself between the armrest and backrest. Bryce rests his palms on either side of me. He leans over and gently kisses my lips. I hold onto his waist and pull him down, but he doesn't budge. I frown and push my lips against his.

When I pull him down again, he takes his lips away and says, "I don't wanna hurt you."

"You won't."

"You got hurt just sleeping next to me."

I huff and turn my head from him.

He hooks his finger under my chin and turns me back. "I'm sorry. I'm scared."

I gulp and my stomach swirls. "Of what?"

"Losing you." His eyes grow glassy.

My arms creep over my stomach. "I'm not going anywhere."

"I feel like we're not close anymore," his voice wavers. "You talk to other people more than me."

"You're not here."

He sits back, his chin dropping and eyes rounding. "So, you're saying it's true? We're drifting apart?"

The sorrow across his face makes my eyes water and a tickle threatens my throat. "I just want you here more."

"And I want you to hang out with our friends. You know I love spending time with just you, but I also want my friends."

"They cut me out."

"No, they didn't. They just get tired of you ditching."

"I wasn't ditching. I couldn't keep up."

"So, they don't know how to act around you now. Talk to them."

I huff and tighten my arms around my mid-section. "I don't want to."

Bryce tightens his jaw and falls back on the couch.

"You're angry with me?"

He rubs his brow and shakes his head.

"Looks like it," I mutter.

He drops his hand and exhales, frown ironclad. "Brittany, I love you, but I had to adjust to school without you. Our parents forced us apart. What did you expect me to do? Sit alone?"

My eyes water and I blink it away.

"I'm sorry I enjoyed hanging out with people, and you got scared when you were out with the girls," he says, a hard edge to his whisper. "I dunno, being social helped me feel better. It feels like you want to punish me for it."

The sob tickling my throat breaks. I cup my mouth as tears streak my cheeks. I wipe my face and say, "I didn't mean to make you feel this bad. I didn't know."

Bryce moves towards me and digs his arms around me to hug. "I don't want to blame you," he whispers. "I liked when we had the same friends. I'm happy for you to have new people to fit in with, but I don't feel like I fit in with them."

"Sure, you do."

"With Madi maybe, but not the others."

"You haven't tried."

"You haven't told me why you stopped hanging out with *our* friends."

I pull my arms around him. "I don't care that you hang with them, I hate what they say about me."

"They just ask where you are."

"To your face. Behind your back—" I can't let the word hit my tongue. "They say nasty stuff."

He kisses the top of my head. "What stuff? I get you feel weird because you stopped cheerleading, but you can still hang."

"Kiss me?" I blurt for a subject change.

"But you didn't—" he begins, but I interrupt him by sliding my hands up to his face.

His body relaxes and he tries a smile. He leans in and kisses me softly.

His hands move down my body and he asks, "Will you come to Mermaid Cove with me? I think it will pull us back together."

I close my eyes and rest my forehead against his. I let out a slow breath and nod. "Ok."

His thumbs move in circles above my hips. "It'll be fun. I promise." He takes my right hand and rubs the emerald on my ring finger. "Just like this is still a promise."

I smile. "I know. I know you're still with me."

"Are you still with me?"

I kiss him. "I'm still with you."

His smile brightens his face. "I'm so glad. I love you, Britty."

"I love you, B."

He kisses me, this time with passion. I sink into the couch and hold the back of his head as he sinks lower. I want to make him happy. The last thing I would ever want to do is undo all the hard work he's done to get better. I love him. I love him so much and don't want to hurt him.

His hands move down my body and all I want is to be close to him. My fingers dance down his back as his hand plays at the hem of my pants. When his hand moves under my shirt, I flinch. His fingers run over a scar and my stomach instantly churns.

"Are you ok?" he asks, kissing my earlobe. When I don't answer, he adds, "Can I see it?"

I suck in a breath. "What?"

"The scar."

The contents of my stomach threaten to erupt. I push his hand away.

"I don't care about your scars," he whispers.

I sit up. "I do."

"You're beautiful, no matter what," he says and moves his hand over my skin, but I slap it away. He lifts himself off me and sits at the other end of the couch. "I can't do anything right."

"It's not like that."

"I would get it if you didn't want me to touch you, but you initiated that."

I shake my head and swing my legs off the couch. "I need the bathroom."

He moves closer. "I'll help you."

I push myself to stand. "I got it, just wait here."

I make my way up the hall, staggering as I plant my palm on the wall, trying not to show any signs of struggle. On my way to the bathroom, I stop by Nick's door. It's ajar and the sounds of Nick and Madison singing over Nick's guitar clears away my thoughts.

When they finish their song, Madison clicks a button on top of a camera, propped on a tripod to record the pair.

"Hey Brit," Madi says, staring at the gap in the doorway. "What ya think?"

"Sorry, I didn't mean to be nosy or anything," I apologise, blushing. "It was beautiful."

Nick gestures to the camera. "This is weird but."

Madi pulls the door open to fully see me. "Nick would ya get over it. When you're famous, you'll have stacks of music videos. I'm just getting you ready."

"It is one of your originals?" I ask Nick.

He smiles and nods.

"He's crazy talented, right," Madi says, hugging herself, eyes all over Nick.

"You guys going to perform it tonight?" I ask.

Madi nods at Nick. "We totally should."

"If Zach and Lenny are ok with it," Nick replies, a sparkle in his eyes shows that he really wants to.

I excuse myself and go to the bathroom. The energy in Nick's bedroom was warm and comfortable. I unzip my fly and run my hand over the scars on my hip. My stomach is no longer flat like it used to be. My eyelids crinkle at the thought of being in a bikini. My skin dimples where the bone misformed and the raised scars make me quiver. I think about the metal plate that gives me a dull ache now and then and zip up my pants. I can't go to Mermaid Cove.

"Cripple."

Bryce will say it doesn't matter if I don't wear a bikini, but I'm reminded of the big deal the girls made when I wore flats to Sean's party. They will make a big deal out of me wearing jeans to the beach.

Chloe's disgusted face appears in my mind, looking me up and down like I'm an invader.

It's not just my hip, I have scars on my thigh and shin from surgery. I was told they would fade, but for now, I hate the idea of having them on display. Tights and stocking help when I wear a dress or school skirt, but they can't help at the beach.

Bryce is scrolling through his phone when I walk into the living room. "I don't think I can go."

He drops his phone and looks up at me. "Huh?"

"Mermaid Cove, I can't go."

He sits up straighter. "Why? What's happened?"

I pull at my hair and lie. "It's the beach. I can't walk very well on the sand."

"I'll be there with you." He stands and smiles. "I'll piggy-back you."

I hug myself. That would be so cute. I wish it were that easy. I'd love to be there with him. But I can't. I can't be there with *her* around.

"Why are you chewing on your lip like that," he asks, running his hands up my arms. "You're worried."

"Chloe." It's all I could get out.

"She's called you?"

I shake my head. "I don't want to be around her."

"You two were friends."

"Not really," I wince. "She kept me around when it was convenient. Now I'm an inconvenience."

He lets me go and takes a big step back. "Brittany, stop talking about yourself like that, I can't stand it anymore."

"Then maybe we should just take a break for a while." My eyes brim with tears, surprised at what came out of my mouth.

Hurt changes his expression. A look I'd given him once before and swore I'd never do again. "What are you saying?"

"Just be honest," my voice breaks, "you want her more than me."

He throws his arms in the air. "When did I ever say anything like that?"

"You want me to be like Chloe."

His face screws up. "I don't want Chloe. How can you think that after everything we've been through?"

I look away from him as my tears fall. "I can't do this right now."

He steps closer. "Are you breaking up with me?"

My fingers dig into my sides. "We just need some time apart."

"This is crazy. Why?"

He moves closer, and I turn away. "Please."

"Brittany?"

"I can't. Can you please go?"

"No. I need you."

I keep my face turned from him, holding my trembling body, words clogged in my throat.

"There's something you're not telling me," he pleads. "Tell me. Tell me how to fix it."

I can't bring myself to bring up the nasty stuff said about me. I don't want to put it in his head. It'll make him want to end things first.

He picks up his phone and moves towards the front of the house. I eye him as he turns back.

"I don't want to leave," he whispers.

I swipe my face as my heart thuds. "Bye."

He is a miserable shell as he leaves the house.

Feels weird to be in my Beetle. I've never driven it solo. Aisha thinks I could drive, but it's been so long that I'm too nervous. Plus, the white smoke I see every time I get in a car makes me think I'd be a danger on the road, like Will. I'll stick with letting Nick drive. I trust him.

We walk into *Gina's Coffee House* and Nick sits his guitar by an amp on the small stage framed by old rock band posters. Something about the décor in this place screams 'second-hand.' Nothing like my favourite place *Shakes*, where everything is super slick and modern.

"Make sure you bring it tonight, Cooper," Madi says, dragging her bass guitar behind her.

Nick throws his arms out wide. "Like I wouldn't?"

Zach spins his drumsticks around his fingers, walking in behind Madi.

Nick tilts his head. "You two getting along?"

Zach slings an arm around Madi. "Yes, sir."

"How do you feel about bandmates dating?" I whisper to Nick.

Nick splutters a laugh. "It's a terrible idea." He shrugs and adds, "Maybe he'll be a good distraction for her. Zach doesn't party and Madi parties too much on her own. You've seen the crazy setup at her house, right? No wonder she hides vodka in her bedroom."

"You saw that?" He's been in her bedroom?

He smooths over his neatly styled brunette hair and whispers, "I feel bad for her. She doesn't know what she wants, and her parents pressure her. At least I wanted to learn music before I was put into lessons."

"True," I say, looking around the café. "Is Reece here?"

Nick looks over each shoulder. "I don't think so. I don't think he'll like the noise."

"You two became good friends, huh?"

Nick smiles. "Yeah, I think so."

"I hope he comes."

Nick pats my thigh and stands up. "Me too."

Nick moves to the stage as the rest of the band members set up. Madi slings the strap of her bass over her shoulder and waves madly at me. I giggle and wave as Tayla sits beside me.

"This is gonna be so fun," Tayla cheers.

"I can't believe Lenny and Madi are getting on," I reply looking at the pair talking onstage.

Tayla giggles. "I know, right? I put in a good word for her. Told Lenny she always tried to be nice to me at cheer practice."

"You'd say you two are friends now?"

"Heck yeah!" She grins. "We're all friends." She pulls me into a giant hug that sends me into giggles. "Where's Bryce?"

My stomach flips. I'd spent the evening in my bedroom until Nick said it was time to leave. I avoided Madi when leaving our house as I knew she'd get it out of me. I didn't want to ruin everyone's night with my problems. I also can't quite get my head around what I said.

And that look on his face.

It won't get out of my head.

"He's not coming."

"Why not?"

I shake my head violently. "We're just not hanging out tonight."

Tayla pouts and nods. "Ok."

"I didn't mean to snap, I just don't wanna talk about it. Ok?"

"Ok."

"Hey everyone," Nick says into the microphone and I'm glad for the distraction from my tragic love life. "We're *Drops of Water* and we'd like to play you a few songs."

As Zach counts them in with his drumsticks, the crowd applauds, but no one is louder than Tayla, who adds in a standing ovation. She sits as the guitars start. Nick's voice is soulful and strong, sending chills down my arms. My cheeks hurt as I smile at him on stage. He looks blissful, like he can't be hurt when he's on stage.

Lenny backs him up on vocals, and something about his electric guitar sounds better than Nick's. Like he's faster and crisper. Tayla squeals beside me and I now totally get the appeal of dating Lenny.

Madi swings her hips as she plays. She flips her long ponytail off her shoulder and dips her knees. She looks badass. She adds vocals and the shivers return as her voice blends beautifully with Nick's, and Lenny's harmony flows between them. My eyes water in awe of them.

After their set, the band joins us at the table. Well, Lenny and Nick do. Madi slides onto Zach's lap before he can leave his drum set.

"How'd we do?" Nick asks.

"Wow, so good," I gush.

Nick grins. "Glad to hear it."

"Did you get this from Watkins?" Lenny says, showing Nick his phone screen. "Apologising for not showing up."

Nick rushes to pull his phone from the pocket of his jeans. "Oh, he suggested hanging at the skatepark." He pans around to all of our faces. "Can we go?"

Madi sniggers as she approaches the table. "Wanna rush to tell your bestie about the gig?"

Lenny laughs. "Jealous, Madi?"

Zach follows, fixing the flat-brimmed cap on his head. "Coop, *you* wanna go to a skatepark?"

Nick stands, rolling his eyes. "Don't look so surprised."

Madi plants a hand on Zach's shoulder. "It's his new bestie. You're out, son."

Nick blushes and tickles Madi's stomach. She gasps and giggles, batting his hands away.

Nick slides away from her and retrieves his electric guitar from the stage. "C'mon, let's go."

We pile into cars and drive to the skatepark. I wave Nick off when he goes to help me out of the car. The smile is instant on his face as he hurries to meet Reece, who boards in the rink with his friend Simon.

Madi eyes me as I dawdle my way towards the rink. "You ok?"

I rub my arms. "Yeah, I'm fine. Just goosebumps."

"I see it in your eyes. You wanna see Bryce? I don't mind driving you over to the cove." She laughs to herself. "I wouldn't mind giving Fiona a piece of my mind."

My throat throbs and I accidentally let a sob break through.

"Brit? *Ohmigawd*," Madi says, rushing to my side. "What's happened?"

I back away, shaking my head. "I'm ok."

"No, you're not." She turns to the rink and calls, "Nick."

I whisper 'no' harshly as Nick replies, "Yeah?"

"Your sister's upset," Madi calls out.

I slap my hands over my face. "I'm ok."

Nick jogs over. "What's happened?"

I can't look at him. Two more sobs tumble out of me and my knees tremble.

Nick's arms loop around me. "Tell me what's happened. Bryce?"

His name floods my cheeks in tears.

Nick briskly rubs my back as Madi steps in closer and asks, "Did you two fight about tonight?"

I bury my head against Nick's t-shirt and soak it with tears. "We broke up."

"What?" Nick and Madi gasp.

"Why didn't you tell us?" Madi asks.

I wipe my face and sniff back mucus. "I didn't want to ruin your night."

"Oh Brit," Nick says, brushing back my hair. "This is the kinda thing we want to know right away."

"One hundred percent," Madi agrees.

"Hey, what's going on?" Tayla asks, skipping towards us.

Madi throws her palm out. "Give us some space."

Tayla stops dead and spins around, making her way back to the rink.

"I can't believe I told him we should have a break," I whisper to my shoes. "I don't want to be without him. I... I just..."

"Maybe a break will do you good?" Nick suggests.

Madi clasps my hand. "I can stay over tonight if you wanna talk it out. Maybe it'll feel clearer after a night's sleep."

I smile at her, a tear fogging my view. "Thanks, Madi. I'd like that."

"You wanna go now?" she whispers.

I lean against Nick as his arms anchor around me. "No, I'd like to stay out here. I like how dark the night sky is. I'll just watch the stars and stay quiet."

Nick kisses the top of my head. "If you're sure."

I hug him back. "Yes. Thank you. You are the *best* big brother."

We walk toward the rink and I lean into Nick, who props me up.

"You guys good?" Lenny asks, the skateboard he'd retrieved from the boot of his car under his arm.

Nick rubs my arm. "Yeah, we're good."

Zach perches on the edge of the rink, tapping his drumsticks against the cement. "Awesome acoustics, man. We should jam."

"Your acoustic is in the back of the car, right?" Madi suggests to Nick.

"Oh, I dunno," Nick mutters, pulling me close.

I pat his stomach and push for a smile. "I'd love to hear you play."

"Sure?"

I meet his eyes. Eyes that are so dark in the moonlight and comfort me like a security blanket. "Yeah." I pull out from his arms. "Go get it."

Nick retreats to the car and Madi sidles up to me, linking our arms. "Tell me if you need to go early."

I pat her hand and smile. "Thanks."

Tayla stands by the rink, a pout to her lips.

"She's ok, Tay," Madi says, trying to stop Tayla's prying questions.

I stop, jerking Madi forward as the suddenness forces her to stumble.

I blink hard at Tayla, knowing I won't be able to control my tears all night and she'll want to get it out of me.

"Me and Bryce," I say, coated with a sob.

Tayla rushes to my side. "*Ohmigawd*, you broke up?"

"I... I..." We didn't break up... Did we? I want a break. *We* need a break. But to end everything? No. I don't want that.

"Don't try to force the words," Tayla whispers, rubbing a circle on my back. "It's a shock, right?"

I hiccup a sob and nod.

"Is everything ok?" Nick asks, his tone showing he thought the question was beyond lame.

Tayla nudges him. "Serenade us, would ya?"

Nick smiles, moving to a bench by the rink. "Happy to."

"You get into this skating stuff, Tay?" Madi asks and we start off walking.

"Nah, I just watch."

"Thought you might if your boy always drags you here."

"Nup. You gonna if Zach keeps coming here?"

Madi's eyebrows bounce. "I might."

Tayla giggles and it eases me. Like tonight might be the great distraction I needed.

We settle on the cement, shoulder-bopping as Nick strums his guitar. I fidget in place, searching for a comfy position, but stop when concern coats the girls' faces. I lean my arms behind me and flash a smile to make out I'm relaxed.

Uncontrollably, the girls' eyes keep finding their boyfriends. They stick to me like glue out of solidarity and support, but I don't know what will make me feel worse, watching them pine, or seeing cuddled-up couples.

"Just go," I say.

"Huh?" they both respond.

I smirk. "You're two love-sick puppies. Go see your boys. I'm fine."

"No. No, that wouldn't be cool," Madi says.

Tayla swats a hand. "Yeah, we can see them any old time."

"We've been here half an hour," I say, "and I haven't been a sobbing mess. I'll be fine."

"You sure?" Madi asks, shifting like she could leap up at any moment.

I nod. "Totally."

"I'll only be a minute," Tayla says, standing. As she brushes herself off, I hold onto a laugh. You only need to know Tayla five minutes to know that's a lie. It's crazy she's already spent this long off Lenny's lap.

"Same," Madi says, making her way to Zach.

And... it's worse. The boys look at the girls like they are the only girl in the world. My heart explodes as Bryce's face from earlier appears in my mind. He didn't want to leave.

I huff and lean backwards until I'm laying down on the concrete. I shut my eyes before they well.

This sucks.

Nick's guitar stops and footsteps sound by my ear.

"Brit? You ok?"

I open my eyes to Nick standing over me. "Yeah."

"You ok lying down like that?" he asks.

"Totally comfy." It weirdly is. "I'll just need a hand getting up."

He smiles and nods. He then nudges ahead. "I'm just going over here. I haven't talked to Reece yet."

"Ok, I'll be here."

Nick walks away and I breathe out. Relieved and stressed at being alone.

I take in all the surrounding voices. They are happy and soothing. Listening keeps my thoughts at bay. I don't want to think about Bryce. I don't want to think about Bryce at Mermaid Cove. Will he announce he's *single and ready to mingle*?

The shudder radiates through my entire body.

"*Woo*! Check out the party!" a drunken slur shouts across the parkland between us and the beach.

I lift my head to see four swaying figures heading our way in the darkness.

"Madi!" a male voice calls and I can tell right away it's Naveen.

The foursome comes into the overhead lighting of the skatepark and its Meah and Naveen with their arms around each other, and Sean and Fiona with their arms around each other.

My stomach twists.

Great.

I turn my head until I find Madi. Her body is tense.

"*Aw*, will someone teach me how to skateboard," Fiona says in a whiney-baby tone, skipping towards Lenny's board which leans against a bench.

Tayla snatches the board before Fiona takes hold. Fiona reacts by poking her tongue out, to which Tayla rolls her eyes.

"Heya," Meah says, stepping over me so her feet are on either side of my body.

Her fake grin makes my frown ironclad. "Hi."

"Where's Bryce?" Meah asks.

I frown. "Whaddaya mean?"

"When neither of you showed and he didn't reply to any of Naveen's texts we assumed you two were off getting busy somewhere."

Part of the tightness in my chest unravels. He didn't go to Mermaid Cove. I lie my head down. *Phew.*

Meah throws her hand out to help me up. My frown doesn't budge and neither does my body. *Just get away from me.*

Meah drops her hand. "Fine." She steps away from me and spins towards Naveen.

"Whadda we have ere," Sean says, walking by Nick's guitar and picking it up.

"Hey," Nick calls out. "Put it down."

"Why?" Sean smirks. "Afraid I'll be too awesome and steal your thunder?"

Sean spins the guitar with a flick of his wrist and loses grip, throwing the guitar and sending it scuttling into the bowl, crashing at the bottom. The guitar cracks on the side and busts open.

"*Whoops*," Sean laughs.

Nick's eyes widen with shock. His mouth hangs open and his skin grows ghostly pale.

Zach shoves Sean. "What is wrong with you?"

Sean shoves him back, balling a fist by his ear. "Come at me again and you'll be sorry."

Reece steps forward and Sean turns toward him until Fiona tugs on his shirt.

"Don't, he's a Watkins," she warns in a low voice.

Lenny skids down the rink, having faith his shoes will grip the slick surface. He carefully picks up the broken guitar.

Nick steps on the edge of the rink and looks down at the guitar, shellshocked. He whips around and darts behind the benches, leans over and vomits.

"*Whoah*," Naveen laughs. "He must have had more to drink than you, Sean."

Madi groans, which then morphs into a scream when she stomps her foot. "Would you guys just fuck off!"

"So touchy, Madi," Fiona says, screwing up her face.

"Get out of my face, you Albino bitch," Madi snaps.

"What did you say?" Fiona screeches, lunging at Madi.

Sean leans in and scoops Fiona up into his arms, spinning her away as her white-blonde hair whips her pale face.

Zach takes Madi's wrist as she tries to lunge at Fiona again. "That's right! You'd better run!"

Naveen beckons Meah as he walks away from the cement of the

skatepark. "Let's go."

I labour my breaths as my eyes land on Nick. Panicked, I call out, "Someone help me up."

Tayla runs by my side and helps me stand.

"*Nicky.*" I move as fast as my body will let me. Zach gets to Nick first, but he moves aside. I wrap my arms around my brother's waist. "I'm sorry."

Nick pinches the bridge of his nose, his eyes scrunched closed. He blows out a breath and his voice shakes as he whispers, "That was my granddad's."

My heart shatters. He misses his grandfather so much.

I've said it before but...

I hate Sean Hastings so much.

He wipes his face and turns around to everyone else. "Sorry, guys, I think I wanna go home."

Zach pats his shoulder. "I don't blame ya. Want me to stay over?"

Nick looks to the ground and nods.

I look to Madi. "Are you still coming over?"

Awkward energy passes between Madison and Zach.

"I'll be staying in Brittany's room," Madi is quick to say.

"Yeah, of course," Zach is just as quick, anxiety playing with his normally cool exterior.

"Sorry," Nick says to Reece.

Reece shakes his head. "Don't be. That's the same dickhead who humiliated Kellie."

I agree. "He's an animal."

Lenny and Tayla drive Reece and Simon home and Nick, Madi, Zach, and I head to Dad's.

The boys retreat to Nick's room. Nick was exhausted on the drive home. The broken remains of his granddad's guitar lay in its case on the boot of my car.

Madi takes a pair of my PJs and we snuggle into my bed. I don't notice how tightly I'm hugging a pillow until Madi points it out.

"Oh, I guess I'm a little wound up."

"That was intense," Madi whispers. "I can't believe they showed up. What jerks." She rubs her temples. "If I were at home, I'd pull out a bottle of vodka. You got anything stashed?"

"You don't need to drink so much," I whisper. "You have all of us to talk to."

"*Now*, maybe. I've clung to it to drown my parents out for so long now."

"You hide behind the booze?"

"I don't do anything crazy like drink at school," she says defensively. She huffs and whispers, "I don't drink as much anymore. Meeting Nick made things easier. Hanging with him helped me like music for *my* benefit and not because my parents forced me into it." Madi groans again, shaking her head. "I still can't get over those guys at the skatepark. I used to be in on that shit. It's just so mean."

"You were never as mean as the rest of them."

"I dunno... I called Fiona an Albino. That's just offensive to people with albinism. It was so unnecessary." She holds a breath and then asks, "D'you think Chloe sent them?"

I turn onto my back and sigh. "Wouldn't surprise me. She was probably pissed Bryce didn't show up."

"How do you know he didn't go?"

"Meah asked where he was. They obviously don't know what happened between us."

"That's good. You don't need the rumour mill right now."

"It's only so long until Chloe finds out."

Madi smooths my hair. "Don't worry. I got your back. I'll punch her out for ya."

I laugh. "I totally believe that. You rocked tonight."

She groans. "I'm so over their bullshit. Friendship officially over."

I clutch her hands. "So glad the good one from the group is on my side."

"I'm sorry I didn't visit you in hospital," her voice is croaky. "Chloe was calling the shots and I was still under her thumb. Still stupidly scared of what rumour she'd spread if I didn't do what she said."

"You don't have to explain. I know what it's like."

"I'm so glad we're friends," she whispers. She eyes the door. "You think Nick's ok?"

I bite my lip and nod. "He will be ok. Plus, he has Zach. They've been friends since they were kids."

In the shadowy darkness, I look to the wardrobe where the hot pink ukulele sits, untouched since my hospital stay. Nick's precious guitar is in pieces, which shatters my heart.

Madi nods. "You're right. I spose it took your mind off Bryce?"

"Not really. It all freaking sucks."

17

Charli

Going home is weird. I'll be watched constantly because of all the rules that were set on family day. They don't trust me. My parents didn't seem to believe David when he mentioned my progress.

But I was honest. I'm done with weed. I'll never pick it up again.

I'll never pick it up again for Brittany. So we can be sisters again.

"Ready?" David asks, walking toward me in the foyer.

I glance at my suitcase and shrug with a timid smile. "I guess."

He pats my arm. "You'll do fine." He takes a folded piece of paper from his breast pocket. "I wanted to give you this."

I take it and unfold it. "What is it?"

"We talked about you trying to find a meaningful activity. I found some information on an environmental activism meet-up in your area. Perhaps it is something you want to try? You may find like-minded people to bond with?"

I push the paper into my pocket, a real smile on my face. "Thanks,

David."

"I wish you well, Charli. And don't take this the wrong way, but I never want to see you again." He lifts his head and his face brightens.

I laugh and nod. "I promise to not do anything that'll land me back here."

He nods. "Good to hear. I'm proud of you."

Dr McMahon walks through the front door. "Charlotte, your mother has arrived."

My stomach leaps into my throat and somersaults back down.

David leads me to the door. "You'll be fine."

I hug David and thank him for the hundredth time. I pick up my suitcase and follow Dr McMahon outside.

"Ms Matthews, welcome," Dr McMahon says like the receptionist at a beach resort.

Mum looks pale. She's rattled. *Geez*, this will make for an exciting car ride home. I look past her. *Phew*, no Dad in sight.

"Mr Matthews not here?" David asks.

"He couldn't leave work," Mum replies.

I hear David murmur "*hmm*."

I eye him and whisper, "It's a good thing."

Mum joins us on the veranda and stands tall with her hands clasped in front. "Hi, Charli."

"Hi, Mum." I look between her and David. It feels like I should hug her but everyone's so stiff. Maybe I missed the memo that states I'm not allowed to?

David nods to me, so I take a breath and move towards my mother. She opens her arms and we embrace. It's not the best mother-daughter hug, but it's better than nothing.

Mum signs the paperwork with Dr McMahon while I load my suitcase in the back of the car. The thought of going home makes me queasy, but David insists things will get easier.

The car ride is mostly silent. It's like she's not even my mum. We are so awkward that we may as well be strangers. It's like the big emotional discussion and apologises from family day didn't happen. Everything has been swept under the rug. That's how all this started. She can't just throw money at *Lyndon House* and expect everything to be magically cured. I don't want that.

"Dad working on a big case?" I ask to break the silence.

Her steely eyes stay on the road. "Something like that."

"Thank you for bringing me home."

"I couldn't very well have you walk home."

Ouch. She's being so distant. Cold. "Mum," I begin. "I really am sorry. I'm sorry for everything I did."

She rocks her jaw and nods. "I know."

"You don't seem like you do."

She sighs and wipes under her eye. "I'm still processing everything."

I decide not to push. She might lash out without meaning too. I went so off the handle the past few months. At least we are in the same car together. She could have sent a driver. It could have been worse.

Sophia rubs my shoulder when we say hello. Her smile isn't as big as usual, and her hug isn't as affectionate. I push on my stomach and grow woozy. Even the house feels different.

Unwelcoming.

I drag my bag upstairs and hover on the landing, staring at Brittany's bedroom. The hurt on her face at family day hasn't left my mind. I want to make things right, *badly*. I dump my bag in my bedroom and then knock on her door.

"Brit?" I knock again and turn the doorknob. There's no answer.

The door swings open and it's clear she's not home. I frown and trudge to my room.

"She's at Reece's," Mum says, walking up the stairs. She taps the stairlift, smiling. "She doesn't need this thing anymore."

"Oh, that's good." I then shake my head, squeezing my eyes closed. "I'm sorry, she's where? Are you talking about Brittany?"

Mum nods, turning toward her bedroom. "They became friends after you... went away."

I turn toward the stairs. "Can I go see them?"

Mum thinks on it. "Just to Reece's. Nowhere else."

"Thanks," I breathe as I jog down the staircase.

I have to make amends with Reece as much as I have to make things right with Brittany. It'll either be far easier with them together or an epic disaster. I'll risk it.

I throw my hair off my shoulders on the path to Reece's house. My face scrunches again. *Brittany and Reece?* I'm seriously not comprehending those two hanging out. *They're friends now?* Madness.

Brittany's red Beetle idles out the front of his house. I spy through the rear window and see two people chatting on the front seats. Nick and Madison? Am I seeing things? Why do they have Brittany's car?

Reece's front door opens, and my feet stop working. Brittany and Reece leave his house and make their way to her car. They take the backseat and the car moves away from the curb.

I rub my eyes as the car vanishes around the corner. The weirdest foursome I've ever seen.

My stomach flip-flops. I've been gone for two months. In the months prior, I was in a drug haze and before that I was on the other side of the planet. Sanford isn't home anymore. I can't comprehend anything that goes on here.

I turn away from the beachside to the incline that extends toward

The Heights. My heart throbs, blocking out the sounds of the surging waves behind me.

I can't put it off. I know Mum said I could only go to Reece's house, but she'll forgive me for this. I need to make things right.

Careful not to alert Mum or Sophia, I walk my bicycle out of the garage and cycle towards Kellie's house.

Confronting the house and acknowledging the fact that she's truly gone is scary, but I must do this. I reacted terribly to her passing. It's shameful.

I knock on the door and a housekeeper greets me.

I'm gonna puke. "Hi, is Mrs Saunders home?"

The housekeeper moves inside and a few moments later, Mrs Saunders comes to the door.

She doesn't frown or smile. "Charli."

"Hi, Mrs Saunders. I just wanted to... I wanted to say..."

This is so hard.

"How are you, Charli?" she says, jaw unclenching.

"Good and not good. I'm clean, but I have such a mess to clean up. Mrs Saunders, I'm sorry for how I acted after Kellie. I made it all about me. I forgot other people were hurting."

Mrs Saunders crosses her arms and looks down and away.

My nails dig into my palms. "I miss her so much."

"So do I," Mrs Saunders replies and her face softens.

"How have you been the past few months?"

She hugs herself and meets my eyes. "As well as could be expected. The house is too quiet." She lets out a laugh and her tear hits her cheek. "I miss arguing with her. This might sound strange, but it feels odd that our arguments are no longer part of my week."

I rub my lips together, searching for the right words.

"She was so passionate," Mrs Saunders adds. "Everything she

cared about she held high like it was life and death..." she pauses on her word choice before shaking her head. "I miss her. I'd do anything to give my life for hers. The world has been robbed of her."

I wipe under my eyes before they well up. "You're right about that. It's not fair."

She rubs my shoulder. "Look after yourself, ok? That's all I can ask. Do it in honour of Kellie. Live your life. It can be over so quickly."

"I will. For you and Kellie."

Mrs Saunders smiles and nods.

"Is Bailey here?" I ask. Something about seeing Kellie's little brother gives me hope.

"He's at a friend's house," she replies quickly.

"Oh. Ok, no worries."

"Goodbye, Charli. I'll be watching your journey with enthusiasm. I wish you the best."

She retreats inside and closes the door between us.

I move down the path and pick up my bike. As I sit on the saddle, I bunch my curls and realise I have no one. Brittany is with friends on the day she knew I was coming home. A group including my step brother and best friend. If I can even call Reece that.

Shit.

I wish I had someone.

My mind drifts to Kellie and a twisting stabbing pain rips at my abdomen. Travis then takes her place and the stabbing goes away. I don't think I want him. I want the idea of him. Someone in my corner. Someone to talk to. Someone to hug.

Shit.

Kellie's bone-crushing hugs. Somehow, I'd forgotten about them. Fuck. How did I forget about them? What's wrong with me?

I cycle home to the solitary confinement of my bedroom.

I'm in my first outpatient therapy session and I need this shit off my chest. I've been home for three days and haven't seen Brittany. Mum is forcing me to stay with her while Brittany stays at Dad's.

"Brittany needs space," is what she told me.

How does that help us? I'm stuck at home with no one to talk to. Sophia eyes are glassy with hurt, which makes being home worse than the hell of rehab. Mum is always looking over her shoulder at me. There's zero trust. I *must* be doing something sinister.

I tell my group about the isolation. How it's exactly like coming home after Spain. I have no one.

"How could they make me fend for myself *again*?"

Our counsellor, Mariah, crosses her legs and leans forward. "Do you feel a relapse coming on?"

I shake my head. "No, but I understand why it happens. When there's no support to come home to."

"What do you need from your family and friends?"

I throw my hands up, defeated. "I just want them to ask how I am. That would be a great start. It's like I'm a leper they're banned from talking to."

"Pan, do you feel comfortable telling Charli your story?" Mariah asks a boy two seats away from me.

The boy sits tall in his plastic chair and nods at me. "I relapsed twice after rehab visits. Sometimes, you need to forget your family and be your own support system."

"I totally disagree," a girl with short spikey hair and a cute button nose pipes up. "You can't get through recovery without support. Maybe you need to find a new support system?"

"We're not all that lucky," Pan says.

"It takes time," the girl replies. She smiles at me. "I'm Yasmine."

I smile back. "Hi."

Pan continues his story and shortly after, Mariah lets us know the session is up.

I make my way over to Yasmine, feeling drawn to her as I take in her soft features and olive complexion. "Hey, d'you mind if I ask you a question?"

"Shoot," she replies.

"How long has it been since you were in rehab?"

"Six months."

"And were your parents good to you when you got out?"

She sighs and crosses her arms over her chest. She whispers, "Look, I know not everyone is lucky enough to have a good relationship with their parents, but we have to understand that recovery is a two-way street."

"Whaddaya mean?"

"Your family are hurting too. You abusing substances was just the same as turning your back on them. In a way, we are lucky to have the time in rehab in order to reflect and find the road to recovery. No one counsels our family and friends for two months. They don't know what it will be like when we come home."

I bite the inside my cheek. I get her words are supposed to be comforting, but something about them makes me mad. I sidestep past her and head for the door.

I cycle across the boardwalk and feel the same uneasiness about the salty air as I do from my bedroom balcony. Countless times, I had used the smell to hide the smell of weed. Now I'm not sure how I'm supposed to feel about the beach.

Laughter pulls me out of my thoughts as I near a carpark. There's no missing Chloe Benson and Meah Watkins as they cackle, cuddled together and surrounded by boys.

Gross.

The grey clouds grow darker and thunder sounds above. I bunch my shoulders and cycle by, hoping to stay off their radar and get out of the impending rain. I look back when I hear, "BK, get over here. You gotta hear this."

Bryce locks his car and walks over to the group. He stops mid-step at the sight of me. I raise a hand in a slow wave. His jaw tenses and he folds his arms, moving towards me. My heart speeds up. Holy shit. Someone wants to talk to me? Is he Brittany's messenger? I look to the group and crane my neck. Is Brittany here?

"Hi," I say, climbing off the bike.

"Hey," he says, nervously.

"Is Brit here?"

His eyebrows raise.

I sigh. "I know, it's bad. We haven't really talked since I've got home, but I wanna fix that. Any chance you could put in a good word for me?"

"Charli," he says hesitantly. "You need to talk to your sister."

"I know, I—"

He takes another step closer. "You asked me to look after her while you were gone. You've been back a long time now, it's time for you to step up."

I rub my chest as a knot intensifies within.

"She needs you now more than ever," he says, and then turns around to walk over to his friends.

I leap on my bike. Ok. Ok, I'm heading straight home.

As my house approaches, Reece's house is in my sights first. My stomach jitters but I choose to ignore it. As rain taps against my helmet and soaks my t-shirt, I steer my bike into Reece's driveway. New plan:

talk to Reece and then Brittany.

I lean the bike against the front fence and my hand trembles toward the gate. I suck in a deep breath, walking over the garden path, and remind myself I have so very much to make up for. I barely spoke a word to Reece once I came back from Spain. And now he won't reply to any of my text messages. It's understandable that he was wary of me coming home. But he's my best friend. He just needed some time.

I step onto the veranda, wipe my wet arms, and shake my hair dry. My stomach flips in an un-ignorable way. I hold my stomach and turn away from the front door. Man, I don't think I can do this.

As I clutch my stomach, a car pulls up curbside. Reece steps out of the car and I find myself hiding behind a pillar. What are you doing, you idiot? You want to talk to him, don't you?

Reece pulls his backpack from the car's backseat and waves to the driver. The car pulls away and Reece walks toward the gate.

I step out from behind the pillar and swallow roughly as he steps onto the path. "Hi."

Reece stops dead and stares at my shoes.

"I just want to talk," I plead.

His side-swept hair sticks to his forehead as the rain pelts harder.

"Please, come out of the rain."

He hugs his bag and stands taller, sending his gaze to a row of plants.

"Reece, please, I want to apologise."

"Go away, Charli." He's just audible over the rain.

"No, I'm not going anywhere." I stamp my foot on the decking. "We need to talk."

"You need to leave."

"I'm not leaving. Come up here."

He takes a wide step back. "I'm not going up there while you're there."

"Reece, I'm sorry! I *need* you."

"Need me?" He drops his bag on to the wet cement path with a thud and splash. A sound croaks out of him and it takes me a moment to realise he's crying. He swipes his face and shouts, "You left me! I needed you and you left me!"

The front door opens and, with my mouth ajar from shock, I look over my shoulder to Reece's mother.

"What's going on out here?" she asks. She eyes me then finds Reece and beckons him in. "Reece, come inside before you catch a cold."

Reece lifts his bag and moves up the steps to the veranda.

My heart races a mile a minute as I plead, "Please, just a minute with Reece?"

Mrs Watkins pulls a drenched and emotional Reece into her arms, stroking his hair. "Go home, Charli." She pulls Reece inside and as I step close, the door shuts in my face.

I plant a hand on the door, my jaw jutting like I wanna say something, but I have nothing. I am lower than low. I am the worst friend. How could I do this to him? I squeeze my eyes closed. My heart throbs. I want to cry. I'm sad, but too exhausted.

I turn to go to my house.

After I lock my bike in the garage, I ring my clothes dry and head inside.

"You're home late," Mum says, arms crossed. "What exactly have you been doing?"

"I haven't broken curfew," I grumble.

As I round the stairs, she grabs my shoulder and jerks me back. "Charli, I want to know where you've been."

I reef myself out of her grip. "I haven't done anything wrong. You can't keep treating me like a criminal on trial."

"I'm trying to look out for you."

"Maybe you should have tried doing that months ago." I race up the stairs before she can grab me again.

"Did you go to therapy?" she shouts up the stairs.

"Yes, I did." I'm fine, by the way, Mum.

"Good, because Dr McMahon says it is paramount in your recovery."

"*Ugh*. Dr McMahon barely saw us at *Lyndon*. It was a once a week physical and that's it," I yell over the banister. "David is the one you should be listening to."

"Don't back chat me, Charli," Mum scowls. "Now, get in your room. I'm sure you have to study for bridging classes."

With pleasure. I trudge to my room and almost fall backwards when Brittany walks out of her bedroom.

"You're home," I gasp.

She rolls her eyes. "We have two homes you know. Why are you so soaked?"

"It's raining." I gulp. "How... How are you?"

She moves towards the bathroom. "Do you really care?"

"Of course, I do."

"It's been months since the accident. You've never asked before," she says and closes the bathroom door behind her.

I pant like I've been deprived oxygen. I wanted my parents to check in on me, yet all this time Brittany was waiting for me to do that for her.

Man, I am a bitch.

As I walk into my bedroom, a thought strikes me.

Did Brittany steal Reece in a revenge move?

No, Charli, don't go there.

It breaks my brain they are friends. Without me.

The bathroom door clicks open and I swing to the landing. "Brit. Please?"

Brittany leans against the doorway, annoyance coating her face. No crutch in sight.

I point to her unsupported leg. "You can walk on your own now?"

"Ahuh."

"I really am sorry I wasn't there for you."

Brittany blows out a tired breath. "Sure."

A knot tightens between my shoulder blades. "I am."

Her arms cross. "I know."

"So," I drag out the word. "Can we talk?" I take a step forward in hope.

Brittany takes a step into the bathroom. "I don't know."

"Can you at least tell me how I can make it up to you?"

"Just be a sister," she whispers, the hurt loud and clear. "Stop being an over-dramatic flake who cuts me out. Be present."

I nod, taking another step forward. "Ok, I can do that."

"I'm being serious, Charli."

My eyes widen as I tilt my gaze at her. "I know."

She steps out of the bathroom. "I know you, Charlotte Jane. You know the right words to say, but I don't think you know the right actions to take."

"I can be better," my voice quivers.

"Just don't take me down with you," she says, rounding to her bedroom.

"You and Reece," blurts out of my mouth. "How.. You're friends?"

Brittany pushes her door closed saying, "We missed you."

I lunge and press my palms against her closed door.

"Don't shut me out."

My whisper is not loud enough for her to hear.

I didn't feel like talking at group today. Thankfully, it's just a once-a-week thing, not an every-freaking-day thing like at *Lyndon House*. I've been home three weeks and still haven't made any progress with Brittany and Reece. Brittany talks to me at home, but in the way you talk to a school acquaintance who borrows a pen.

I spent a week at Dad's and I don't think he looked me in the eye. Tara was surprisingly affectionate, which was just weird. I feel like my step mum shouldn't be nicer than either of my parents. On the other hand, Nick hasn't been very friendly to me since I got back. He's very obviously Team Brittany.

Screw it. I'm not going home. Therapy is the only place my parents let me cycle too. It's the limit of their trust in me. But I need some time away from the house. Both houses.

I ride across town to West Sanford. An environmental protection group is having a meeting at *Gina's Coffee House*. David recommended for me to go, and he seems to be the only person truly looking out for me.

"Can I get a black coffee, please," a guy at the counter asks when I walk into *Gina's*. "Oh wait, where were the beans sourced?"

"We have Kenyan and Brazilian beans," the waitress says.

"Kenya," the guy replies. "I can't support Brazil right now with what's happening in the Amazon."

"Um, hi," I say to him. "Are you here as part of the meet-up?"

"Yes," he says eagerly, extending his hand. "I'm Harrison. Are you new?"

"Yes," I say, shaking his hand. "I'm Charli."

"Nice to meet you. This is my first meeting in a couple of months. I've just gotten back from a project in Nepal." He gestures to the counter. "Can I buy you a coffee?"

"Green tea would be perfect, but I can pay for it."

He winks. "First one's on me."

"Ok," I laugh. I check out his profile as he orders my tea. He's probably twenty-years-old with scruffy chestnut hair, an infectious smile, and the wardrobe of a nomadic hippy. "What were you doing in Nepal?"

"Rebuilding. We have the last twenty-five percent of homes left to rebuild after the earthquake Nepal experienced a few years back. We're getting there"

"Oh, yeah. We kinda stopped hearing about that."

He nods as the waitress slides our cups across the counter. Harrison picks both cups up and nods for me to follow. "That's exactly why we hold these meetings. It's education more than action, in some regards." Harrison places our cups on a table. "If something important happens but the media doesn't deem it sexy enough to report on, at least we can spread the message."

I lean on a chair. "Environmentalism is sexy?"

He laughs. "Damn straight."

It surprises me when my cheeks flush.

"Hey, Harrison," a girl with red pigtails squeals and throws her arms around Harrison's neck. "You're back!"

"Lorna," he says, wrapping her in his arms. "So good to see you."

I'm embarrassed for blushing. *Duh*, he has a girlfriend. How can I fan my face without being super awkward?

"This is Charli," Harrison says, letting Lorna go. "This is her first meet-up."

"Hello, sister," Lorna says, throwing her arms around me with the same enthusiasm she showed Harrison.

"Ah, hi?"

Lorna presses her hands into the sides of my face. "I'm super glad you are here."

I am so confused. "Have we met?"

"Probably hundreds of times on some cosmic level," Lorna says, staring far too intensely. She lets me go and spins around. "I gotta set up. Toodles."

Harrison laughs. "She is very passionate."

I plonk onto a seat. "I see that."

Harrison sits opposite me and people come up to hug him, shake his hand, high five him, and generally share their love and admiration of him.

After everyone takes their seats, I say, "You sure are popular."

He shrugs, grinning. "Just what happens after a long trip away."

I take a deep breath. *Not for everyone.*

Lorna claps excitedly next to a projector screen. "Ok, everyone. We have a super cool video sent in from Dannika, who is in Cambodia. She filmed it during her stay, where she was rebuilding a school that had been taken out in the monsoon floods. She interviewed locals during and after the project's completion. Spoiler alert; it's super heart-warming."

Harrison smiles and whispers, "She says *super* a lot."

I grin. "I've noticed."

"Also," Lorna chirps, holding up a flyer. "We have some info on the protest at the national park. This is another all-night rally, but we understand if some of you want to team up and take shifts like we did a couple of months ago. But if you can stay for the entire twelve hours that would really help make our point." Lorna gestures to another girl and adds, "Sierra will hand out the flyers and I'll start the film. Please stick around after to chat about the project and the protest, we'd love to collect volunteer names."

"You been to one of the all-nighters?" Harrison whispers as the film rolls.

"No. I've only done all-night study sessions."

Harrison laughs. "You should come. We are there for a good cause and we swap stories and have a great time. Some people say you shouldn't have fun whilst protesting, but I disagree. Happiness and fond memories encourage a person to continue doing it."

"So, what is the protest about?" I ask as Sierra places a flyer on the table.

"Deforestation," Harrison says. "We've organised a film crew to document our peaceful protest. We'll sit amongst the trees of the rainforest."

My heart palpitates. "The forest?"

Harrison grins. "No better setting. The film crew will show our beautiful slice of Earth that hasn't been touched *yet*. We are going to try to make sure it stays that way."

I nod, trying to keep the apprehension off my face.

The place Kellie and I used to discuss all our important issues. Where Kellie was my spiritual guide and the voice of reason and logic. They want me to go to the forest. Shit.

"You look deep in thought."

I shake my head and flash a smile. "Guess I was."

"You worried about going? We watch out for each other."

"It's not that." I meet his eyes and his smile is lovely as he waits for me to continue. "I think I want to go."

Harrison grins and his eyes dazzle. "Terrific."

When the film finishes, which lights a fire under me to travel and volunteer, I stand up and Harrison introduces me to people. I love listening to him speak. He talks about things with passion and doesn't waste time on the negative. He's like a handsome embodiment of positivity.

I check the time and figure I should get home for dinner. I tap Harrison's shoulder and tell him goodbye.

"Are you sure you have to go?" he asks, rubbing my arm. "We're heading to *Sal's* for pizza to talk supplies for the all-nighter."

My heart swells. "Oh, I'd love to but I have to go. Put my name down for any supplies you need. I'm happy to help in any way I can."

He pulls me in for a hug. "So glad to have met you."

I plant my hands firmly on his back. "Me too."

Since meeting Harrison last week, I haven't been able to keep the blush from my cheeks. With everyone shutting me out, I'm glad to have someone include me in a conversation and look me in the eyes when they talk to me. Group is good, but it's forced. Harrison is organic. Natural.

I told Tara I'm going to Mum's tonight. She's been trying especially hard to get in my good books. Like we'll have a massive emotional moment and I'll bear my soul. Nice try. But she's the easiest to get around. I told her before Dad came home from work and that made everything less stressful. Dad won't call Mum to ask about me. They've made their level of care crystal clear.

I ride my bike on the road and scroll through my contacts to find Lorna's number from the flyer. I steady the handlebars as I bring the ringing phone to my ear.

"Hello?"

"Hey, is this Lorna?" I reply.

"Yes," she says as bubbly as ever. "Who's this?"

I clear my throat. "Charli. We met at—"

"Oh, the curly-haired girl sitting next to Harrison."

I laugh with surprise. "Yes, wow, you have a great memory."

Lorna giggles. "One of my many talents. You calling about tonight?"

"Yeah, where do we meet? Oh man, do we have to bring anything because I—"

"Don't stress. We have enough supplies to equip an army. Well, an army that wanted blankets, water, plastic-free snacks, and to destroy their guns."

"Ok, good. I didn't want to seem like a flake or anything."

"Just bring your beautiful soul and we will be complete. We are at the picnic area near the entrance of the *Phillip Sanford Trail*. You know it?"

My stomach knots. I swallow hard. "Yep, I know it."

"Perfection. See you soon."

I push on the brakes and jump off my bike. It falls with a clang. I push back my hair, moist from sweat. My mouth waters as my stomach throbs with sickness. I crouch to the ground and squeeze my eyes closed. I don't know if I can do this.

Memories of sitting between tall, leafy trees, picking at the grass between my fingers, and searching for the sunlight dancing around us flash through my mind. Images of her smiling face and drooping glasses follow. Her copper hair wild in the breeze and a joint between her lips.

Going there without her… Going there while she'll never be able to go there again…

She died there.

I throw myself toward the gutter as bile surges up my throat and shoots out my mouth. I wipe my mouth as tears roll from my eyes.

I miss her so much.

I sit against the gutter, hugging my knees, and stare at my bicycle. My gaze shifts upward and I try for a smile as the clouds roll apart. The sun shines as bright as I remember Kellie's smile.

Should I go, Kel? Will it be ok?

When the sun warms my skin, I take it as a good sign. That hollow, cruel voice was never hers. It was my own fear attempting to paralyse me. And it had won. My hands tremble, my stomach still queasy, as I pick up my bike and I fling a leg over and peddle.

The breeze cools my face as I peddle up the incline and I take lengthy breaths, hoping I don't look like a total mess when I meet the group.

Bicycles are parked in a line near the timber fence at the trail entrance. As I park, I look at the dirt path towards the trail. It's bumpy with ridges made from wheel tracks. Memories of trips I used to take with my dad resurface. That tradition seems dead now.

"Welcome," says a guy with a shaved head and torn t-shirt. "I'm Keith."

I smile, nerves settling. "Charli."

"This is Raahi," Keith says, acknowledging the guy beside him. "This your first all-nighter?"

I nod. "First rally in general." I look to Raahi. "Hey, I know you."

Raahi smiles, smoothing his long, silky jet-black hair off his caramel face. "Oh, yeah?"

"I faced you in a debate at *West Sanford High*." I grin. "I whooped your butt."

Raahi and Keith laugh, holding their stomachs.

Raahi leans his elbow on Keith's shoulder. "I was off my game that day. Yeah, I think I remember you. It's a long night, maybe we can have a rematch?"

"Oh, I'd love to watch that," Keith says. Behind a cupped hand, he stage-whispers to me, "I'll be rooting for you."

Raahi shoves him. "Thanks for the support, bro."

Keith's shoulders jiggle as he holds back another laugh. He points towards a group huddled around a picnic table. "Lorna's down there if you want to check in with her."

"Ok, thanks. Nice to meet you."

"Oh, we'll meet again," Raahi says, trying to act sinister.

I bite my lip to suppress the laugh and wave as I walk towards the bigger group.

"Shane, can you ask a couple of the guys to help with the water?" Lorna says to a girl with the longest, lilac-coloured hair I've ever seen. Shane walks towards Raahi and Keith, her hair swishing behind her.

I stand by a few people, trying not to be in the way, to take on a task.

"You came," Harrison says, stepping beside me.

My stomach unclenches with his presence. "Hey."

"You look nervous."

"I do?"

"Anything you wanna talk about?"

I hug my waist as my stomach flips. "No. I'm ok."

"Lorna," Harrison calls. "You want us to start carrying stuff in?"

Lorna pulls herself out of a hug to turn Harrison's way. She locks eyes with me and beams. "Oh good, you made it safely." Her arms stretch wide and she moves my way. "I was going to send someone to the road to make sure you weren't lost." Her *Midnight Oil* t-shirt is tied under her bust and as she hugs me, she is so obviously not wearing a bra.

"Thanks. I've been coming up here since I was a little kid. Just took me a while to make it up."

Lorna rubs my back, grinning. "Well, you're here now and we couldn't be happier." She pulls me aside, digging into her bum-bag. She pulls out a string with a plastic whistle on the end of it. "Take this. All of the guys here are great, but there are a few newbies I can't vouch for. If anything makes you uncomfortable, blow it and we'll find you."

Panic cuts through my air and I look over my shoulder in Harrison's direction.

Lorna squeezes my hand as a faint laugh escapes her. "Not him. He's a gentleman, believe me."

I slip the whistle in my jeans pocket and blow out a breath. "Ok. Thank you."

"Nothing has ever happened in our group, but you hear stories, you know? I just want everyone to feel and to be safe."

"Thank you for the thought."

Lorna pulls me into another tight hug. "No problem, sister."

I play with her bright red plaits and close my eyes, and for a moment, believe it's a Kellie hug. Like Kellie sent her. Thanks, Kel.

"These bags are ready, Lorna," a girl says from the table.

Lorna lets me go and smiles at the girl. "Thanks Tegan. Harrison, yes, you can carry things in."

"You wanna partner up with me, Charli?" Harrison says, his lips curving right and highlight his stubble.

I nod. "Sure. Where are we taking it?"

Tegan hands me a canvas bag filled with fruit as Lorna moves onto newcomers for their welcome hug. Harrison takes a bag and gestures behind him. "We're going further into the national park."

"How many of these rallies have you done?" I ask, following him on the trail.

"Ten or so with this group."

"Wow, I didn't realise there was such an active group in Sanford."

"Most of the time we go into the city for protests, which means linking up with bigger groups."

"Are there any more city protests coming up?"

Harrison looks over his shoulder and smiles. "While the world keeps messing up, there'll always be something to protest. I can't wait for the day when there is nothing left to protest."

"You think that day will happen?"

"I like to stay positive, but..." He slows his pace so we walk side-by-side. "If I think about the end game, it just makes me sad."

"Not to sound rude, but why continue doing it?"

"It's about education," Harrison says. "If we can change the mind of just one person, the effort is worth celebrating. That person then goes back to their community and they might change the mind of another person." He nudges me and smiles. "Like you. We now have one more mind on our side."

"Oh man, I hope I wasn't against you guys before."

"You probably didn't factor the environment into your decision before?"

I shake my head slowly. "I mean, I always enjoyed being outdoors, but no, not really."

"And that's ok. Loads of things go on around us we have no idea about. Then something makes us stop and think about it."

Harrison shows me to a clearing, and we place our bags down.

"I think travelling overseas did it for me," I say. "It opened the world up to me."

"That's awesome. Where did you go?"

"Spain. It was a school exchange."

"Fantastic. You know, there are loads of travel opportunities for building projects, teaching English, and taking care of injured or abused animals. You see the world, meet locals, and help restore communities.”

I breathe out a long, slow breath as every knot of tension dissipates from my back. “That sounds wonderful.”

We bring in a few more bags and, once Lorna has given us a pep talk and introduced the film crew, Harrison takes my hand and pulls me further into the thick trees. We stand on the lush grass. Tingles race up my arms as our fingers lace.

“It felt a little crowded,” Harrison whispers, with a perfect smile.

I nod, hypnotised by his hazel eyes. “I agree.”

His face edges closer to mine. “Would it be ok if I kissed you?”

I flinch. I don’t think anyone has ever asked me if they can kiss me before. Hell, I don’t think I’ve asked someone if I can kiss them.

“Yes, please.” *Yes, please?* Is that really how I answered that question?

His lips press into mine and my wayward thoughts disappear. My fingers latch onto his and I add extra pressure to his bottom lip.

He pulls back and lets out a murmured laugh. “You’re a good kisser.”

“Thanks. You too.”

“I haven’t stopped thinking about you since we met, but I didn’t want to seem like I was rushing anything.”

My cheeks prickle red. “I’ve been thinking about you too.”

“Splendid.” He nods to the direction of the others. “We should probably get back.”

Do we have to? “Yeah, we should.”

It doesn’t take long for us to be alone again. Lorna flits between people, talking quick and bubbly. We set up along a bank of trees. Harrison and I pair up at the last tree in the row. This is difficult because Harrison is Mr Popularity. Everyone wants to stop him for a chat, but he assures them he’ll make time for them later with, ‘We have all night.' I'm so lucky he wants to start the night off with me. He's magnetic. He's wonderful. I want to know everything about him

As we sit on the soft, cool grass, a shiver runs down my limbs in the best way. His light brown eyes have specks of bright green in them and they round in a way that makes me feel like I'm the only person in the world.

"I feel so lucky to have met you," I say.

He laughs. "How so?"

"You're so present," I say, letting my eyes wander over him. "And I feel calm around you. Something I need more than ever right now."

His face becomes serious. "Why's that?"

I swallow hard and shift on the ground. My arms cross loosely above my lap and my gaze falls on some nearby shrubbery.

"Charli?" he pushes gently.

I shrug. "I just don't have anyone right now."

"What's happened?"

My stomach quivers. Why can't I just keep my mouth shut? Will telling him I just got out of rehab send him running?

"Hey," he whispers, touching my arm. "It's ok."

I find his eyes. "I've ruined all my relationships."

His eyes narrow. "You mean with boyfriends?"

I swallow roughly. "With everyone." I slide his hand off me. "Actually, maybe I should go. No one would really want me around."

"What?" Harrison questions with a nervous laugh. "Why would you say that?"

"I shouldn't have kissed you," I say, scooting backward. "You don't even know me."

He moves closer. "Sure, but we can change that."

"You won't want to."

"Why don't you let me decide?"

I sigh a breath and my shoulders droop. "You're too good. You won't want to know me."

His eyebrows rise. "What did you do?"

I press into my stomach and rush out, "I just got out of rehab."

"Really?"

"For drug use."

"Oh." His expression is blank. "What did you use?"

"Weed mostly."

His expression brightens and a timid smile curves his lips. He digs in his pocket. "So, I should get rid of this?" he asks, lifting a joint he retrieved from his pocket.

I'm dizzy at the sight of it.

"Shit, sorry. I shouldn't have done that," Harrison says, quickly stuffing it into his pocket. "You just said you have a problem with it and then I go shoving it in your face."

I wave him away, trying to settle my nerves. "It's ok, I just didn't expect to see it again anytime soon."

"I tried to make you feel less alone," he says. "Maybe not the best move, but I wanted you to know I smoke it too."

I hold my hands up. "To be clear, I don't anymore."

He takes hold of my hand. "Hey, that's ok, I would never force you. And I promise not to smoke it tonight."

"Don't on my account."

He squeezes my hands. "I would never put you in harm. So, when did you get out?"

"Recently." Our hands stay clasped together. "Being home is weird."

"Because of family?"

I nod. "Yeah. My parents don't trust me, my friend won't talk to me, and my sister... I've ruined things with my sister."

"Is she the older or younger sibling?"

"We're twins."

"Ah, that'd be hard. Your bond feels broken?"

"Shattered."

He moves to sit beside me and wraps his arms around me. I tear up. I didn't realise how much I'd missed the touch of someone.

"You just got home," Harrison whispers. "It's natural for there to be an adjustment period."

"Nah-uh." I shake my head. "I ruined things months before they sent me away."

"Want to talk about it?"

"I have weekly group therapy. Believe me, I talk about it enough." I lean into him. "I thought you should know before getting to know me more. I didn't want to turn you off."

"You haven't turned me off."

"This past year really changed me. In a lot of ways. Most of them bad."

"You don't seem like a bad person to me."

"I'm trying to find myself again." I hug him back because right now I really need it. "But I don't know if I ever knew myself. I used to strive for *top-of-the-class* grades to impress my dad, but I failed miserably in every way. Now I dread the thought of going back to school."

"Education is important."

"It doesn't feel like it."

"It's good because it gives you options," Harrison says. "But actions do as well."

"At least being at school means I won't have to be home. I think being away from my dad will be a bonus."

Harrison holds me tighter. "He's not abusive, is he?"

I shake my head like it may pop off. "No, no, not at all."

"It's an overbearing thing?"

I settle into his arms. "Yeah."

He plays my hair and whispers, "Hopefully, tonight helps you to forget about what's happening at home. The world out there is so big. Maybe your family will be as brave as you and see that too."

"I don't know if I'm brave."

"You are. I'm a stranger and you told me about where you recently were."

"I didn't tell you where it all started."

He kisses my forehead and says, "And you don't have to."

I rub my heart. Maybe I want to.

"Will you tell me something about you?" I ask, wanting a distraction. "Did you grow up here?"

"In Sanford?" he replies. "Tully, actually. I haven't lived here full-time in about three years, but I love coming back to hang with Lorna and the gang." He rubs my back. "And maybe I can see more of you too."

My blush returns with the silliest of girly giggles.

Harrison tells me about his first rally. He goes into detail about a fight that broke loose between two protestors, but all I can focus on is the pocket where the joint is. My fingers have that familiar itch, my temples sweat, and my heart throbs.

I pull away from him and blurt, "Can you get rid of it?"

Harrison pauses mid-sentence, his mouth hanging open.

"The joint," I elaborate. "It's all I can think about and I'm scared I'll light it."

Harrison hesitates. "Oh, sure."

"Just give it someone else to hold?" I suggest. "I'm so sorry, but

I'm scared of what I'll do if I know where it is."

Harrison holds my shoulders and finds my eyes. "Charli, it's ok. I'll get rid of it."

My eyes fog over, and I shrink away. "Thanks."

Harrison turns my body so I'm facing away from the group and he walks away. I blow out a heavy breath, shiver, and hold my torso. This is dangerous. Will I be able to last all night knowing it's here?

I meant it, right? That I'll never do it again.

Brittany.

I don't do it so I can have Brittany in my life.

My lungs fill with fresh air and my back straightens.

I can do this.

Harrison lands beside me and I'm quick to say, "I'm sorry."

Harrison's hands move up the sides of my face. "Don't be. I should have done it right away."

"I… I just—"

Harrison's lips press onto mine. My arms slide around his shoulders and I push my body against his. I tease my tongue against the opening of his mouth and move my hands down to his hips.

His lips pull away and his breathy laugh tickles me. "Are you going exploring?"

I bite my lip and search his eyes. "Can we go somewhere more private for exploring?"

His eyebrows lift and he latches onto my hands. "You sure?"

I nod, smiling. "Just for a little bit?"

He smiles and nods, walking backward. "I know a good spot."

The fact that Travis' first time was with GiGi has never left me. *"It meant nothing,"* was what he said. Like ticking something off the to-do list.

I kinda want that. I don't want to hold out for that special someone, a soulmate, a love of my life. I want to give in. Be free; spirit and body. Harrison is well-liked by everyone. Loved, even. He's a great first choice. No one from school is here. No one will pass a rumour in the corridors. It'll be for me. My memory. Oh, and for Harrison.

How many times has he done this?

I almost ask, but I don't want to know. I'm more than positive it's not his first time. He's too travelled, too popular, and plus, he's older than me.

I'm going to trust him.

I pull Harrison forward by the collar as I lean against a tree. I kiss him with rough passion. His hands cup my waist and I smile when they slip inside my shirt. I run my thigh against him until it's hooked in place. My hands slide down the back pockets of his faded, ripped jeans and I giggle as I cup his bum.

"Cheeky," he whispers, kissing below my earlobe.

"Can't help myself with you."

We slide down to the ground and my knees drop to the sides to keep Harrison close to me. Pulses of excited nerves rush throughout my body and I'm not super focused on my khaki shorts when they slip off. My fingers dance along his rippled torso and my heart knocks as he rips open the condom wrapper.

He kisses me once he's put it on and asks, "You sure you still wanna do this?"

I nod and lift the string around my neck that holds the whistle Lorna gave me.

When I go to take it off, Harrison stops me. "Don't."

"What?"

"In case you want to stop and are too scared to say anything," he says. "Keep it on and don't be afraid to blow it at any point."

"No, I wouldn't," I say, clutching the whistle.

He kisses me again and smiles. "I want you to feel safe. Remember, we can stop at any time."

I smile and nod. "Ok. Thanks."

Being with him is warm, thrilling, overwhelming, and wonderful. He's gentle and sweet. I focus on the green specks in his eyes and relax into the gritty yet damp earth beneath me.

It's different to what I'd imagined. Though I had no clue what to expect. I didn't know I'd feel this good afterwards. My heart flutters with the natural high.

Harrison lays beside me and pulls his arms around me. "You ok?"

I smile and exhale slowly. "Yeah."

He kisses my cheek and we nestle together for a few minutes before getting dressed.

My face is red hot when I walk back to the group hand-in-hand with Harrison. Will they all know what we just did? Is it way obvious? Shit, could they hear us?

I gulp as I meet eyes with Keith, but he talks with Raahi like I'm the most uninteresting person ever.

Phew.

Maybe it's all ok?

Eww, what if it's a regular thing for people to have sex out here? What if more people are doing it?

Well, that just makes the whole thing less special, doesn't it?

Harrison cuddles up to me in the row of protestors, and my qualms wash away. He's amazing. I just want to stay in his arms. I could stay like this forever.

The producer of the documentary comes our way and I slouch over, hugging my knees. *Please don't talk to me. Please, please,*

please.

When the cameras lights highlight us, the producer asks about the plight of the rainforest, and how a small-town crowd could make a difference.

Harrison fields the answer. "Anyone can make a difference. It doesn't have to be something big. A small conversation can make a difference. Or listening. Education is what's missing in modern society. We take so much for granted. Even the minor act of recycling is skipped by most of the population. It's unbelievable. People trap themselves in a bubble, and that's not necessarily their fault. How will they know what's going on if no one tells them? No one shows them. Connecting to this land, that's practically in their backyard, is a good start."

I swear I'm glowing. Oh, he was a great first choice. He's a dream.

The producer asks me why I joined the rally and, with Harrison's arm around me, I feel stronger. I pull my wild curls to the left and look into the camera lens. "Because I was alone. I felt purposeless. I wanted to make a positive difference." I look to Harrison and smile. "And then I found wonderful people like this guy."

Harrison kisses me and I laugh in the kiss, embarrassed and happy they caught it on film.

The producer explains the release I need to sign before I go home. I'm fine being in a documentary, there's zero chance my parents will see it, but I'm not so cool with my face in the local paper or on local TV news. The producer says they can ensure I won't appear on local media and he and cameraman leave us. Harrison and I lean into each other as my lungs fill with relief.

"I should probably talk to the guys I snubbed earlier," Harrison whispers, his arms wrapped around me.

I press my hand on his thigh. "Nah-uh."

Harrison laughs and it makes me feel lighter than air. "I haven't seen them in ages. You wanna walk down with me?"

I pull out of his hug and smile. "It's ok, you go catch up with them. I'm gonna stare at the stars."

Harrison looks up, grinning. "Great show tonight, isn't it?"

I kiss his cheek. "Sure is."

"Ok, I'll be right back," he says, getting up.

I clutch his arm and tug him back. He locks eyes with me, and I laugh, letting him go.

He laughs and moves away, waving. My body screams at me to call him back.

"Trav—" I call out and immediately slap a hand over my open mouth.

My eyes are wide when Harrison turns around and says, "Huh?"

I lower my hand and shake it off with a playful smile. "Nothing."

Harrison turns and moves over to the boys. I slide down the tree to the ground. I'm breathless as my heart thuds.

Did I seriously call him that?

Travis' face refuses to leave my mind.

Dammit.

18

Brittany

The worst summer break in history. On paper, it shouldn't have made me so miserable. Madi and Tayla sit either side of me as we paint our nails. Zach and Lenny yell at each other while playing a video game, and Reece taps his knees as he watches his video console from home. Nick said he overheard Mrs Watkins tell Reece he wouldn't like it being out of the house, but Reece wanted to try. We have nothing like that at Dad's as Nick isn't a gamer and Charli hasn't brought anything over here.

Nick sits next to Reece and pats his shoulder. "You ok?"

With Nick next to him, Reece seems to relax. They are so cute together.

I take in the room, and it should make me happy. All I've ever wanted is *genuine* friends. And I have that now. I never question their actions or look for ulterior motives. They *are* my friends.

"Is Charli here?" Tayla asks, dipping the brush in the electric blue polish.

I nod. "In her bedroom."

Tayla finishes her right pinky finger then tightens the lid of the polish. She jumps up and rounds the couch. "Imma say hi."

I bite my lip, hard. My stomach tosses and turns like a boat on an angry sea. If they get to talking, I might lose one of my friends. I shouldn't think this way, but I have the same fear when Reece is over. They were her friends first, but now they are on my side. I don't want to lose friends again.

Madison double-takes at me, and then calls, "Tay, hold up."

Tayla backtracks. "What?"

Madison gestures to me. "Maybe, don't?"

I wave my hands. "No. No, it's cool. Say hi."

Tayla looks between Madi and me sceptically. "You wanna ostracize her?"

Madi's mouth opens in reply, but she falters, looking to me. We share the same look. We were both left for dead by Chloe. Were we really going to copy her?

Tayla creeps to our couch and curls up on the armrest by Madi. "Don't you wanna get closer to your sister?"

"You think she can forgive her?" Madi asks.

"What would you do if it were Maggie?" Tayla asks her.

Madi looks up as she thinks it over.

"Charli and I have never been close," I cut in.

Madi pats Tayla's knee and smiles at me. "Maybe it'd be nice if you were?"

I frown. "Well, if *you're* saying it..."

Madi *tsks*. "And what's that spose to mean?"

Tayla giggles, sliding off the armrest. "You're a hard-arse, Madi."

"Where are you going?" Lenny asks, eyes glued to the TV.

"To see Charli," Tayla replies, venturing up the hall.

My gaze pans over Nick and Reece. Nick gives me an apprehensive smile and Reece keeps his gaze on the TV. That boy is too hard to read, I have no idea if he heard me or not.

The room's energy shifts and I sink lower into the couch and take everyone in. Hanging out with them all summer should have made me happy. I mean, it did, but there was always this gnawing feeling in the pit of my stomach.

Bryce wasn't there.

It's been weeks since I saw him last.

He's texted me a dozen times, but I've never brought myself to reply. All I said was I needed a break. A break means no texting and not seeing each other for a while.

I twist the ring around my finger. I've kept the stones turned on the inside of my finger, but I can't bear to take the ring off. That would be an agony I couldn't endure. Plus, I never said we were over.

How much time is he spending with his friends since we took our break? I imagine Sean and Naveen on either side of him saying things like, *"Finally got rid of the cripple, BK."* My stomach spasms.

I can't imagine school without him by my side. What will that be like? He hasn't texted me in a week. Will he ignore me at school? I'm queasy just thinking about it.

"What are you thinking about?" Madi asks and I snap out of my thoughts to see the worry on her face. "You look like you're gonna puke?"

"Brit?" Nick asks, leaning over to see my face.

I wave off their concern. "No, I'm fine."

"Charli or Bryce?" Madi whispers.

Oh *geez.* I swallow to put pressure on my twirling stomach.

"Both, I guess."

I hear Tayla and Charli in the hall. Tayla's giggle goes up an octave and my heart pounds as their friendship rekindles mere metres away.

Their footsteps sound closer and my body tightens into one big knot.

"Brit," Madi whispers harshly, grabbing my arm. "Breathe."

Nick stands up. "Brit?"

My neck snaps to the hall and I spy feet first. My heart blasts in my ears. Tayla returns and no one follows her. The drumming of my heart slows, and my shallow breaths resume their normal pace. When it seems the hall is clear, my hands relax from their cramp-worthy fists.

"What?" Tayla asks, eyes wide as she takes in all our eyes on her.

Lenny nudges at the space beside him for her to sit and when she does, he cuddles her and kisses her forehead.

Tayla looks past him to me. "You were freaking out?"

"*Ha!* Just a bit," Zach laughs.

Nick moves down the couch to punch Zach's thigh.

"*Ow!*" Zach whines. "What the hell?"

I glance to the hall and then to Tayla. "Did she go back to her bedroom?"

Tayla nods, mute for the first-time-ever.

I let one big, long, slow breath out and stand.

"Where are you going?" Madi asks, looking more freaked than I've ever seen her.

"To see if I can knock on her door."

She stands. "I'll go with you."

I shake my head. "I'll go alone. I dunno, with all of you here, I have a safety net if things go horribly wrong."

Madi sits. "Ok. We're all here for you."

I smile and my lungs refill. Friends. I have friends.

I push myself up the hall before I can chicken out. I pull my hair into a messy bun with a band from my wrist. The back of my neck is sweating like crazy. *She's your sister, just try.*

I stop in front of her closed door and my knees knock. I lift a hand to knock but it's like I'm on freeze-frame. I don't know how long I stand there like a statue before the doorknob turns.

The door pulls open and Charli stands in front of me.

I lower my hand. "Hi."

"Hi," she replies almost like a question. "I thought I heard someone out here. Are you ok?"

I bite my lip and then look towards the living room. I turn to her and ask, "Do you wanna join us?"

"Oh," Charli says, hesitation lingering in the air. "It's ok. You don't have to."

"Have to what?"

Charli's eyes flick to the hallway then to me. "They don't want me in there. And let's be real, neither do you."

I smooth down my t-shirt and summon all my courage. "Do you want to be?"

Her eyes go glassy. She sucks back a breath and hints at a smile. "I'll make it awkward."

"School's about to start," I counter. "What are you going to do when we go back? Sit around with no friends?"

"That's familiar." She shrugs. "Besides, they are making me repeat a year, I won't be in anyone's classes."

I hang a thumb over my shoulder. "So, you don't wanna come out?"

She eyes the hallway, a sour look twisting her lips and she rubs her stomach. She could be a mirror of me.

"Can I come in then?" I ask.

Her eyes brighten and she steps out of the doorway. "Really?"

I walk into her room and look around the bare walls. The desk is bare except for two books and the bed is an unmade mess she's obviously just crawled out of.

"You really haven't made this room homey, have you?"

"It never felt like home."

I sit on the edge of the bed as she wall-hugs. "You should give Tara and Nick a chance. They're nice to us."

She nods. "I know."

"And Dad's just angry because he didn't see it coming. You know, you and the—"

She pushes herself off the wall and furrows her brow. "Is this the stuff you really want to talk about?"

I slide my hands under my thighs and sigh. "No."

She edges toward me. "Can I sit?"

"It's your room."

She gingerly perches beside me. "I missed you."

"I've been missing you for a year."

"I'm sorry I didn't check on you in the hospital. You were right, it was nice that we'd talked so often when I was overseas. I threw it away like an idiot."

My heart tears. "It felt like you wanted me to die so Kellie could live."

A soul-sucking gasp erupts from her. She clasps my shoulder, her jaw dropping. "Oh, my goodness! I never intended for you to feel that way." Charli's eyes puff up with tears. "I'm so, so sorry. It was never like that. I was petrified you were going to die, and that sent me over the edge. Brit, you looked so broken in that hospital bed that a huge part of me died."

I slide her hand off me. "A huge piece of me died too. I'm not the same person anymore."

"Because of dance?"

"And so many other things."

"You want to talk about it?" she offers.

I rub my heart. "Not really."

"I saw Bryce after I got back. I've noticed he hasn't been around here."

I need to puke. "We just needed some time apart."

"You broke up?"

I rub my unsettled stomach. "I don't want to talk about it."

She hangs her head. "Sorry."

"I'd like a sister though."

Her hand presses on mine. "I'd like that too."

"Thanks for trying to talk to me since you got back. It's just hard."

"Believe me, I get it."

"I just wasn't ready to be around you. But I was wondering, what was rehab like?"

"You really want to know?"

I nod. "I couldn't stop thinking about it while you were gone. Yeah, we visited, but it seemed like they were 'putting on a show.' Was it rough?"

She tilts her head side-to-side, wincing. "I hated it at first, but now I look at it as a positive."

"Were you locked up?"

Charli splutters a laugh. "No. I was free to move around. It just involved a lot of therapy and exercise. And random craft, which I didn't care for. I now have an addiction to yoga."

"Oh." It comes out like I'm disappointed. "That doesn't sound as bad as I thought."

She laughs again. "Same. I look back on it and wonder why I was such a zombie for the first few weeks." She meets my eyes and smiles. "Our birthday brought me back to life."

I frown. "That was rough."

"It still blows my mind that we were apart on a birthday." She shakes her head. "I never thought that would happen."

"I wanted to call but they wouldn't let me."

"Thanks. They wouldn't let me either because of the no-contact policy." She smiles at me hopefully and suggests, "Maybe we could do yoga together sometime."

"Ah," I begin, and an awkward gulp ends the word. I smooth over my unfit mid-section. "I dunno. I don't think so."

"Oh, no worries," she replies quickly, taking the suggestion back.

I nod to the doorway. "C'mon. Join the others with me."

Hopefulness twinkles in her eyes. "Reece is out there."

"Yep." I squeeze her hand. "C'mon."

She pulls her hand away. "No, I can't. Reece doesn't want me around."

"Charli," frustration takes over my tone, "I'm trying here."

"I want to try to." She moves off the bed and to the doorway. "Lead the way."

I get off the bed and walk past her and toward the living room. I don't hear footsteps and look over my shoulder. She hasn't broken the threshold of the doorway, trepidation paling her face.

Screw it.

I'm not waiting for her and keep moving into the living room.

"How'd it go?" Madi asks, hugging her knees.

I stop by Tayla. "What did you talk to her about?"

She plays with a lock of her hair. "Kellie."

It takes me by surprise. "Really?"

She nods, smiling. "Kellie was an amazing person. I don't want us to forget her." She looks over her shoulder to Reece, who now has a controller and is still transfixed by the TV.

Lenny rubs Tayla's back as sorrow dulls his eyes.

"I asked her to join us," I say making my way to space by Madi.

"Where is she?" Madi asks.

I shrug. "She didn't follow." I flop my head back and close my eyes. A headache drills through my skull. "I'm tired."

"Maybe you should take a nap," Nick suggests.

All I can think about is how much I want to be in bed and curled up in Bryce's arms.

I open my eyes and pull my phone from my pocket. I snuggle into the corner of the couch and start scrolling. "Yeah, maybe I will."

I open the Bryce text chain and skim his last texts.

(Bryce) I don't get why we can't talk.

(Bryce) Just tell me how to fix it.

(Bryce) I never wanted anyone else.

This is so stupid.

I didn't reply because every single text made me angry. I could not have been clearer about the fact that I didn't want to be around Chloe. How she'd made me feel… How she'd stand close to Bryce and touch him… What she made the boys say behind my back, and possibly to Bryce's face…

I just wanted him. Me and him. Alone.

My gaze pans my friends. I wanted Bryce to get along with them. Did I force them to be friends?

My teeth grit at the middle text. Tell him how to fix it? He could have just listened.

But I have to stop being angry with him. It's not fair.

(Me) **Do you want to talk?**

My fingers tremble and I put the phone in my pocket. Terrified to see the response or, more honestly, the lack of response I'm expecting. Why would he respond after I hardcore ignored him?

My stomach knots and my neck fills with cement as I tense on the couch. My mind races, *will Charli walk in* and *will Bryce reply?*

Agony.

My phone buzzes in my pocket. My stomach somersaults. Puking imminent.

I hug my stomach and curl up on the couch. There's a reply on my phone. That's all I need right now. I don't need to look at it... just yet.

# #

Bryce and I texted for two days before I agreed to let him come over. It wasn't like the texting we'd had before. It was like we didn't know each other.

I'm sick to my stomach as I wait for him to arrive. His house isn't far from Dad's so I'm expecting him to walk, but I still look out the window for his car.

My stomach launches into my throat when he approaches the path. I step away from the window and plant myself against the wall. My fingers tremble as his footsteps near the front door.

His knock startles me even though I knew it was coming. I'm such a wreck. Maybe this was a bad idea? My biggest fear is that he's going to yell at me and then everything will be officially ruined.

Tara pops her head out from the kitchen. "You got that, hun?"

I bounce from the wall and fuss with my hair. "Yeah, I got it."

Tara smiles and returns to the kitchen.

I clear my throat and turn the doorknob. He smiles on the other side of the doorway. It's the same rosy kindness I've always known, but his eyes... There's something different in his eyes. He's looking at me differently.

"Hi," he says, almost like a question.

"Hi?"

He looks at me expectantly. I frown until he points behind me. "Can I come in?"

I shake my head to play it off. "Oh, yeah. Come on in."

I lead Bryce through the kitchen. Tara says hello to him but doesn't ask a follow up question like she normally would. I filled her in on everything the morning after Madi slept over. Tara is way easier to discuss things with than either of my parents.

Bryce follows me into the living room. We share the same couch, but we sit at either end of it.

"This feels weird," Bryce whispers.

"Huh?"

"I don't know how to act."

Somehow that makes me more guarded. I tense as I look him over. He looks the same but there's something about him that's so entirely different. Like, his energy, or something? Something has shifted.

"What made you finally text me?" he asks, and the light dancing in his eyes makes me feel less on edge.

I rub the back of my neck and look away. "I dunno. Maybe the fact that Charli is back?"

"How's that going? You know, I wanted to be here with you when she got home."

I wave it off. "Doesn't matter. I was out when she first got home."

"Have you two talked?"

I eye him. "I heard you two talked."

He grows pale and his eyes dart to the hall, then to me. "Not really. I just saw her on the boardwalk."

"You two talked about me?"

He shakes his head. "No. I just told her to look out for you."

My eyes roll. "That's like telling a dog to meow."

"Brittany," he says with exhaustion. "I don't get why we're not together. Why does there have to be hostility between us? It can't be because I asked you to go to a party?"

I groan, letting my frustration get the better of me.

"Why don't you talk to me then?" he blurts.

I shift closer to the armrest to be further away from him "It felt like you weren't accepting me."

"What?" he snaps. "Where did you get that from? We've known each other for almost two years. How can you say I don't accept you?" His eyes round with confusion. "I love you."

"I know that."

"I don't understand," he counters, sliding towards me.

I put a hand up. "Don't."

He takes my hand. "Don't, what?"

I fling his hand away. "I said, don't."

He rushes off the couch and paces to the other side of the room. "Why did you invite me over? To break up with me twice?"

"No."

"I don't need you to break my heart again. What do you want from me?"

I rub my chest, eyes welling. "You're not the only one that's heartbroken."

His demeanour softens, and he makes his way over and kneels in front of me. "I want to be with you."

"We were drifting apart. I needed time to think."

"And?" hopefulness lifts his voice. His head tilts as he notices my other hand. He lifts it up as surprise coats his face. "You're still wearing it?"

I make a fist, feeling the stone of the promise ring against my palm. My voice is weak as I say, "I never wanted to break up. I just asked for a break."

His mouth stays ajar as his eyes stare directly into mine. Something familiar returns to the crystal topaz of his eyes. The knots in my back loosen.

He places his hands on my knees, the watch I gave him snug around his wrist, and looks down as he whispers, "Why are we letting distance get between us?"

"I'm sorry," I whisper, tears escaping my eyes. "I'm not ready to get close to you again."

He looks up, sadness clouding his eyes. "What?"

I frown and wipe my eye. "Don't get me wrong, I want you in my life, but..."

"But, what?" he pushes.

I slide my legs away and sit in the middle of the couch. "Don't crowd me."

"How can you say that?"

"What?"

He stands. "We've always sat close together. We've always touched each other. Now you've banned me from seeing you for weeks and you want me to keep my distance?"

"Exactly. We haven't seen each other for weeks. I don't want to rush into anything."

He turns his back on me and sighs. "That's rich."

"Excuse me?"

He whips around with an irritated expression. "You don't want me to rush things but you're the one who was always pressuring me into sex."

I gasp. "What?"

He shakes his head and turns away again. "I don't want to fight over it."

"You think I pressured you into sex?" My heart throbs. "Do you regret when we did it?"

He turns around, eyes cloudy. "No, of course not."

"Then why are you making me out to be the bad guy?" my voice warbles with a sob.

He moves beside me and sits down. "I'm not. This is stupid. It's this hostility. I don't like it. I'll say something I don't mean."

"I wanted to be with you, but I didn't want to force you."

"It's just that the time apart made me overthink everything. Like that time at Chloe's party."

My defences fire up. "I told you she convinced me I had to do that."

"But I would have thought you'd talk to me about it first." He shrugs. "It could have been a big first time for us."

I huff and throw my hands up. "Fine. I'm the worst."

"Can you stop that?" Bryce mutters. "I told you that I hate hearing you put yourself down. Or is it only ok for me to be the bad guy?"

This time I'm the one off the couch. I pace across the room and say, "We're going around in circles. Maybe we're not good together."

Bryce leans over and hides his head in his hands.

I hug my waist and chew my lip, preparing for my next question. "You still hanging with Jace and Chloe?"

He lifts his head, agitated. "I hang with the whole group. Are you still fixating on her?"

"They ask about me?"

"I didn't announce I was single, if that's what you're asking."

"Did you hear what they did to Nick's guitar?"

"No. What?"

"Well, it wasn't them directly, but after Mermaid Cove a heap of them got drunk and found us at the skatepark. Sean hurled Nick's guitar into the skate bowl and destroyed it."

His face screws up. "You serious?"

I nod.

He stands. "You know I've never really hung with Sean. It sounds like him. He's a dick."

"We can have better friends," I say, taking a step toward him.

"It's fine to not like one person in the group."

"It's more than one for me."

His eyes half-roll, like he caught himself halfway through.

"Madi agrees with me," I add, hoping to build some weight behind me.

"Why do we have to keep arguing about other people? Other people shouldn't be the reason we are together or not."

"But they are."

We stand, mute, tense, and avoiding eye contact.

Horrible.

I excuse myself for the bathroom, unable to stand it. He doesn't stop me, and I amble my way down the hall.

Once in the bathroom, anger courses through me. He won't give them up. Not even for me. Why are we bothering? I should tell him to leave.

I fix my hair and leave the bathroom, ready to tell him to go. As I approach the living room, I hear Charli's voice. I freeze, listening to the two of them talk.

"I don't know what you've been working through," Bryce says to

Charli, "but I wanted to let you know that I think it's ok that you did what you did."

"That I did drugs?" she questions.

"All I mean is, you were abandoned by your family, just like I was. Our families put all their attention on someone else and ignored our problems. Yeah, we dealt with them differently, but we both harmed ourselves." I peer around the corner as Charli sinks into a couch. Bryce sits close to her. "I understand why you did it, and I know what it's like to lose someone. I'm sorry I didn't pay attention to you either."

"Oh, man." Charli sighs. She leans into him. "Thanks for that."

He hugs her, and their embrace sends shivers down my body.

"I had no idea," I blurt out.

They break apart and stare up at me like they were doing something wrong.

I walk towards their shared couch. "I never thought like that. Like Charli was going through what you went through. I was so worried about you when you went away, Bryce. You were the only thing in my thoughts." I turn to Charli, "But I never thought of you the same way."

Charli stands. "It's ok. I didn't deserve your attention."

"Don't say that," I reply.

"I ignored you first remember," she mutters.

My eyes move from Charli, to Bryce, and back to Charli. "I still should have noticed."

She hugs me. I don't hug her back, but I lean on her. I lean on her like the sister she is.

"I'm sorry," she whispers.

"Don't be," I whisper, and my tears fall.

"I should probably go," Bryce says, getting off the couch.

Charli and I pull apart and I wipe my face. "You don't have to."

He looks between us and says, "No, you two should talk this out. It's more important."

"Bryce, I'm sorry," I say and my heart races. "I want to fix this."

He nods but doesn't seem to believe me.

"You two were in the middle of something," Charli says, stepping away. "I don't want to ruin anything."

"No, stay," Bryce says to Charli and rubs her back. He turns to me and says, "Talk to your sister, and I'll see you at school."

Gulp. "Ok."

He leans in and kisses my cheek. Oh boy, I could melt right now. It was a quick peck, but his warmth lingers on my skin.

What are you doing, Brittany? Don't let him go.

"Bye," he says and walks toward the front door.

"Bye," Charli and I reply.

Bryce leaves and Charli and I stare at each other.

"You want to sit?" Charli asks, breaking the silence.

"Ok."

We sit and she says, "I didn't know he was here. He called me in when I was on my way to the kitchen."

"I was about to ask him to leave," I say, rubbing my forehead.

"What happened with you two?"

"I don't know." My eyes well up again. "We were drifting apart. It's so stupid. I'm not friends with Chloe and that group anymore, but he still is. And, and *ugh*."

"Oh. That's rough. Did you have a fight with Chloe?"

The question makes laugh. "Not at all. She used the wheelchair to ditch me. By the time I was out of it I was already phased out."

"*Bitches*. But I'm glad you're away from them."

"Plus, she was mean to Nick."

Charli grimaces. "What did she say?"

I shudder. "I don't want to repeat it."

"A year ago, there were rumours I had a threesome and beat up my boyfriend, so I can imagine they can come up with something just as foul for you."

"I should have listened to you about her."

Charli laughs and it makes me smile.

"What?"

She falls back, holding her belly as she laughs.

I grab the cushion from behind me and boff her on the head.

She takes the cushion and hugs it. "You should have listened to me? What a crack up."

I shrug, grinning. "Maybe going back to school would have been easier?"

"Seems like you've made new friends easily. I was only gone for two months."

I avoid her eyes. "Are you mad I'm friends with Reece?"

"No. If you two make each other happy, I'm glad. Plus, I was horrible to him when I got home from Spain."

"It was a weird time for everyone."

"I don't really want to do this gig," Nick says as we leave the car.

"Why not?" I ask, waiting for him to retrieve his electric guitar.

He pulls the strap over his shoulder and locks the car. He nods to the sign *Sanford Beach Lifesaving Club*. "Because it's the exact kinda place our band would never play. Madi was freaking out, saying we *had* to do it."

"I'm sure it'll be fine." I nudge him. "Are you annoyed I never stuck with the ukulele?"

He puffs out a laugh. "No way. It was just something I thought would pass the time. Did you think it was lame?"

"No, it was fun. Though I didn't love the indents it left in my fingertips."

Nick smirks. "See, not a true musician."

I laugh. "Whatever."

I follow Nick inside and notice guilt panging inside of me for not inviting Charli. We had a nice talk. Neither of us tried to pick a fight. So unlike us.

But it's Nick's night and he doesn't seem interested in hearing Charli out. He's protective of me and he'd worry if Reece showed up. It's too much drama. We need to ease in. Once Charli and I work stuff out, I'm sure it'll be easier to let her back in. To *deal* with her fitting in.

Part of me wanted Bryce here too. It's too weird going to Nick's band gig when the first one I went to was right after Bryce and I ended things. Things were so weird and intense at my house. Everything turned into a fight. Is there anything left to save?

I look down at the ring on my finger and remember the kiss on my cheek. I guess I'll have to see what school brings.

Nick moves ahead of me to the stage. Madi and Zach are standing by the drum set. They could be talking, but it looks more like arguing. Zach stands tall, arms rigid as he lifts his chin, listening to her. Madi waves her arms about while she talks. When she doesn't get the answer she wants, she takes Zach's wrists and tugs. Zach's chest puffs out and then his shoulders droop. He nods and Madi grins.

Nick jumps onto the stage and moves over to Zach to whisper something. Zach shakes his head and moves behind the drums. I'm guessing Zach had a problem with the location too and Madi wasn't happy about it?

I take a seat at the front and wave at Madi.

She smiles, slides off the stage, and makes her way over. "Hey, how are you? How'd it go with Bryce?"

"Loaded question."

"You didn't get back together?"

"No, but we didn't make it any worse." I blow out a breath. "I almost did, but weirdly, Charli saved me from opening my big yap."

Madi's nose crinkles. "Charli? How'd that happen?"

I shake my head. "It was intense. I don't think I can get into it right now."

"Ok, fair enough."

I nod to the stage. "What was going on up there?"

Madi *tsks* and rolls her eyes. "The boys being drama queens. They think this place is too snobby for them. They only like playing in West Sanford."

I smirk. "It's just the lifesaving club. Sure, it's a new building, but there are plenty of fancier places in town."

"I think the boys are still getting used to this side of the train tracks." She stands up. "Well, I should get up there. Oh, Lenny and Tay just walked in. Good, you won't be sitting alone."

"Break a leg," I say.

She winks. "Thanks." Madi waves to Lenny and Tayla and jumps on stage.

Tayla sits beside me, her glittery eye makeup playing against her tanned complexion. "This is a way better venue, huh?"

I smile. "Yeah. I wasn't a fan of *Gina's* but Nick and Zach seem to love it."

"Didn't Nick say he used to go there a lot with his sister?"

I nod. "Yeah, I think so. I think Charli went there with Shae too. Speaking of, how would you feel if Charli hung out with us?"

She grins. "Are you kidding? I'm the one who wanted her to join us first. Is she coming tonight?"

I shake my head. "I didn't invite her. I didn't want to make things weird, but I thought school could be a good start to making things right."

She nods. "For sure."

"Hey," Reece says, landing on my other side.

His entrance startles me. "Oh, hey. You came?"

Tayla waves. "Hey, Reece."

"Yeah, I thought I'd give it a go," Reece says. He frowns at the stage. "But I don't think I can be this close."

Tayla stands. "We can move back. My family and I come here a lot and sit in the booths off to the side because it's not as loud."

I stand. "I'm cool with that."

"Reece," Nick calls from the edge of the stage. "You came?"

Reece nods. "I wanted to hear you play."

"We're just going to move to a booth," I call out.

Nick gives me a thumbs up and sends his smile in Reece's direction.

As we settle into a booth, my stomach jitters at the thought of asking Reece about Charli joining in. Tayla was easy to ask. Reece didn't seem pleased that Charli was coming home from rehab. He never asks about her. But maybe that's just Reece?

Oh, *geez*. Reece didn't overhear me talking about Charli, did he?

I look his way. There's no expression to read.

Great. I'll just sit here with a churning stomach, shall I?

My body eases when Nick addresses the crowd from the microphone. The crowd is a mix of people, who are turned towards the stage or moving to the restaurant, bar, or the patio smoking area. Not exactly an engaged audience, perhaps Nick and Zach have a point? The people at *Gina's Coffee House* were enthusiastic to have a live band.

The band play mostly the same set as their last gig, but I'm pleasantly surprised when Nick sits at the keyboard Zach and Madi brought. Nick plays two songs at the keyboard and his voice becomes the star. One song I remember well. An original I heard him play repeatedly one weekend. The other is the original he filmed with Madi.

I'm covered in goosebumps by the time the set is over.

The band leaves the stage to heads to our booth. A woman in a grey blazer and pencil skirt stops Nick and beckons him off to the side. Instinctively, Reece, Tayla and I crane our necks to get a better look.

"Who's he talking to?" Tayla asks.

"Does she work here?" Reece asks.

"Should we go over?" I ask as I pan my gaze over the other band members, who are standing a few metres from the pair. "Why is she only talking to Nick?"

"Lenny's coming over," Tayla says. "Maybe he can fill us in."

Lenny slides in beside Tayla.

"Who was that woman?" she asks.

He shrugs. "Beats me?"

Reece and I groan.

Tayla whacks Lenny's arm. "I need to teach you how to eavesdrop."

Lenny laughs. "Nah-uh. That's your job, Babe."

Madi and Zach walk over, but Nick is still talking to the woman. The woman is Asian, and I have this urge to ask Madi if she knows her, but she's already called me racist once before, so I bite my tongue.

"Who is that?" Tayla asks, about to burst.

"*Shoosh*," Madi hushes. "I don't want to jinx anything."

"You know her?" I blurt out and feel my cheeks blush.

Madi doesn't answer me and instead keeps her gaze over her shoulder at Nick.

After what excruciatingly feels like forever, Nick walks over.

"Who was that?" Tayla and I both yell at him.

He stops mid-step and then laughs and stands by the table, placing a card down. *Wendy Chen, Platinum Management.*

Madi squeals, bouncing on the spot.

"Spill," Lenny says, tangled up in Tayla's bouncy energy.

"She's a talent agent," Nick says, almost shellshocked. "She wants me to record a track and be an opening act on a new band's tour."

"What?" we all erupt.

"She was sent the link to a video of mine," Nick says, side-eyeing Madison.

"Madi," I gasp.

"What?" Madi says, giggling. "I can't believe she came."

"You set all of this up?" Zach asks.

Madi nods. "Ahuh. This is the place Wendy wanted to visit."

"Madi, you're incredible," Tayla says, impressed.

"I can't believe you were talking to an agent," I say.

Madi nudges Nick. "I told you I wanted the world to hear your music."

"It's a small east coast tour, not the whole world," Nicks says, his smile growing bigger.

Zach loops an arm around Nick's neck. "Congrats, Coop. That's awesome."

"When does this happen?" Lenny asks.

"Soon," Nick says, his eyes rounding like it's all just hitting him. "Sorry guys, I tried to tell her she wanted the whole band but—"

Zach shakes his head. "Dude, no."

"You're a star on your own," Lenny says.

Tayla hugs his arm, *awe*-ing.

"This is your moment, Nick," Madi says, hugging his waist.

"You've earnt it. You write the songs. You're the complete package."

"I don't know if I can do it." He sighs and looks to me. "What do you think, Brit?"

"Ah." My mouth hangs open and it takes a while for more sounds to follow. "I think this is great."

Nick squints at me. "You seem worried."

At that, I smile and shake my head. "No, I'm super-dooper happy for you. I guess my mind just went straight to how much I'll miss you."

"I'll miss you too," Reece pipes up.

Nick pulls out of all the arms wrapped around him and slides by me and Reece. "I'll miss you guys too. So much."

Zach laughs. "I can just imagine Tara's reaction now. Losing her baby to the big, scary world."

Nick frowns. "You reckon she won't let me go?"

"Please," I reply. "She spends all her money on your music. This is her return investment."

Nick smiles and relaxes against the vinyl booth, a dreamy look in his eyes.

19

Charli

"C'mon, it'll be fine," Brittany says, dragging me inside *John Thomas High*.

I'm sick to my stomach. Imagine the rumours the school produced because I was in rehab rather than school. And what they snowballed into over summer.

I'm gonna puke.

"Snap out of it," she whispers, nudging my side. Typical Brittany bluntness.

"I'm sorry, but it's not like I'm thrilled to be back here."

She huffs and rolls her eyes. "Like I was any more excited when I came back after being stuck at home or in hospital?"

"Ok, ok. I get it. You've had it no easier than me."

Brittany's eyes wander up the corridor and I follow her gaze to Reece. My stomach flips. This is not going to be an easy day.

"Why haven't you talked to him yet?" Brittany asks.

"I tried. He doesn't want to talk to me."

"You didn't apologise correctly."

I eye her, mouth falling open. "Excuse me? What?"

"You've disappointed a lot of people," she says, looking me up and down.

I swallow dryly as she looks at me the way I feared other students would. "I thought you were on my side today."

"I want to be friends with you," she says, but there's something behind the look in her eye. "But I'm not going to fix everything for you."

She walks ahead and waves to Reece. Reece nods at her and glances over her shoulder at me, then looks away.

Screw it.

I catch up with Brittany to speak to him before we make this so much worse. "Reece."

The bell rings for homeroom and Reece seizes the moment to make a getaway.

Shit.

And the rest of the day was no better.

I know *of* people in my classes, but being a year older, I've never hung out with any of them. No one is outright rude to me, but my name is in their whispers. I was MIA most of last year. They don't find the overseas part interesting, it's the rehab part that fascinates them.

One girl asked me what it was like.

I told her it was fun, and she rolled her eyes and went back to whispering with her friends.

The only thing that got me through was knowing I would be seeing Harrison after school. Walking into *Gina's*, he looks as good as ever. He's been in Melbourne for weeks, so I only saw him a few times after the rally night. Not complaining. Any time with him is good time.

"Hey," he says, embracing me in a hug and kissing the top of my head. "How are you?"

"I'm good now." I huff and sit beside him. "School was horrible."

"First day blues?"

"I just don't want to be there. I think I spaced all my classes. And it wasn't like last year when I was taking things to make me zone out, I just didn't want to pay attention." I blow out a breath. "I hate it."

He cups my hand and smooths back my hair. There's a frown on his face and I don't like it, so I try to cheer up.

"School shouldn't make you feel like that," he says seriously. "I want to tell you to stay in school because knowledge is power, but if it makes you miserable, that's not good for your wellbeing."

I shake my head. "I'll figure it out." I pat his hand and smile. "How was Melbourne?"

His smile breaks through. "Good. Something happened I need to tell you about." Cue nausea. "My mate has a project coming up in Peru and had someone drop out. He asked me to take the place."

"Oh. Well, that's awesome. When do you go?"

"Friday."

I chew inside my lip. "Oh."

"I know. I would have liked to spend more time with you, but I feel like I need to go."

I nod. "Totally, I get it."

"It'll be at least three months, maybe four."

I squeeze his hand. "It sucks, but there's always *Skype*."

He twists his lips and shakes his head. "There's no internet where I'm going. I can reply to emails when I go into the town at an internet café."

I'm out of breath. "Wow. That's unreal."

His eyebrows lift. "You could always come with me."

I sink into the chair. "Really?"

His smile grows. "Sure. It's something you want to do, right?"

My heart slingshots against my chest. "That would be crazy. Crazy amazing."

"Take some time to think about it," Harrison says, his eyes entrancing me. "Your passport is in date? If you wanna go, I'll have my mate organise your flight. We can go together."

My heart is in my throat and I tremble with fear and enthusiasm. "Ok, I'll think about it."

After an electrifying coffee date with Harrison, I walk into Dad's as a living room conversation takes over the house.

"I just don't know whether I should go," Nicks says, perched on the couch, leaning on his knees.

Dad and Tara sit beside him.

Tara rubs Nicks back. "This is something you've always wanted."

Nick hugs his stomach and gulps. He eyes Dad. "Won't you be disappointed if I miss school?"

Dad pats Nick's knee. "We will support you. I read over *Platinum Management*'s contract. They are ensuring time with a tutor. If you keep up to date with your schoolwork, you can still graduate on time."

I bite inside my cheek hard as the warmth in Dad's eyes softens his face with a display of love for Nick. Support. Support for Nick. Where was my support? Where *is* my support?

Nick's smile brightens his face. "Thanks, Rob." He turns to his mum. "I can go?"

Tara wraps him in a hug. "Yes, hunny. I've wanted this for as long as you have."

Nick rubs his mother's back as she sniffles tears. "Thanks, Mum."

They haven't noticed me by the doorway. I taste blood from biting my tongue and cheek. Infuriating.

A creak sounds behind me and I peer over my shoulder to see Brittany spying into the living room. I hold my breath for a moment, looking her up and down. What will she think of me going to Peru? Will she care more about Nick leaving than me?

I breathe again when she slides her eyes my direction. It was brief and she moves past me and into the living room. Dad moves away from the couch and turns in my direction.

I fold my arms and pierce him with a steely gaze.

"What's wrong, Charli?" he asks.

"I can't believe my ears," I reply. "You would never let Brittany or I leave school to pursue something non-academic."

"I would if she had a passion for something," he replies. He walks towards the kitchen and I'm hot on his heels. "I'd support you, but I don't see you sticking with anything or choosing something."

"How can you say that? I spent so much time trying to impress you with no return."

"Yes, you joined a debate club and chased high marks, but then you threw it all away." He grabs a coffee cup and gestures to another one for me. "The year before that, it was watercolours, the year before that was surfing. I'd love to see you stick to something."

I groan and flap my arms as I turn toward the hall. "I know I won't find it in school. I don't want to go back."

"Don't say something so ridiculously stupid."

"You hypocrite! Nick is leaving school and I can't even mention it to you."

"Nick is pursuing music while continuing to study. You can't quit to do nothing."

"I won't do nothing."

"Just go to your room or something. I don't know who you are anymore."

"I'm dropping out of school," I say with a stomp of my foot.

"Get out of my sight!" he yells, pointing to the hall.

The tears line my eyes and I run to my bedroom, slamming the door behind me. A scream burns inside me. My fists curl and my nails cut into my palms.

I'm about to let rip when a noise grabs my attention. I turn to my closed door and see a piece of paper slipping its way underneath. I scuff towards it and recognise the expressive colouring as an Alyssa creation.

My mood softens and I open the door to find her crouching in the hall.

"Hey," I whisper.

She waves, standing up.

I pick up the picture and it's adorable. "This is incredible. How did you get even more talented?"

She blushes and pushes out her stomach as she grins.

"You wanna draw with me?" I offer.

"Where did you go?" she asks.

"When?"

"You were gone a long time," Alyssa whispers.

"Oh. Um, it was like a hospital."

She tilts her head, squinting one eye. "You broke your leg too?"

A faint laugh escapes me. "No, nothing like that. All you need to know is I'm better now."

"Ok," Alyssa says with a determined nod. She beckons me to follow. "Come to my room. Mum got me more pencils."

"Can you walk in there? You already have so many," I joke, following her to her room.

Alyssa *tsks*. "Don't be silly."

I blush and laugh again. Why can't everyone be as forgiving and direct as kids? "I picked up a few techniques at an art class. Do you wanna try painting?"

Her face screws up. "You painted in hospital?"

"It was a different kind of hospital."

Alyssa waves an arm, shaking her face, determined. "Nope. I only use pencils. I don't paint."

I grin, loving her pure confidence.

Mr Ferguson rants in front of the blackboard. I rub my temples and shut my eyes. This is another class I daydream my way out of. It's so hard to care. I hate all the bullshit in this town. No one cares about what happens outside of this town, out in the world. Hell, they don't even care about the *real* stuff that happens in town.

It's like everyone's forgotten Kellie. It's like none of it matters. Was it always like this? How long did it take for her to no longer matter? I know I hid from everything, but people can't be this small-minded and self-involved, can they?

Mr Ferguson calls my name and I lift my head with boredom in my eyes. "Yes?"

His face tenses and frown strengthens. "Are you paying attention, Charlotte?"

I blow out a breath and slide down my chair. I play with a pen. "No."

The bell sounds and Mr Ferguson walks up to my desk. "Stay back. We need a word."

Sniggers and remarks pass my desk as the rest of the class leaves. I stare hard at my desk. Like I give a damn.

"I know it's a big adjustment," Mr Ferguson begins. "But it's a new year, a fresh slate. You need to apply yourself."

I push my chair back and stand. "I will. Can I go?"

Mr Ferguson tilts his head, unimpressed. His looks at the ceiling and sighs before nodding.

I dart out of the classroom.

The corridor smells briefly of freedom but I'm still stuck here for a few hours. Bummer.

There are bigger things for me to think about. Things I can do to make a difference in the world. Meeting Harrison has opened my eyes. I have a reason for living. I have a way to honour Kellie.

I hug my books and meander down the corridor. The sound of something colliding with metal grabs my attention. Ahead, along the row of lockers, a brute pushes Nick against a locker, holding him up by his collar.

"West Sanford scum dirtying up our school," the over-hormoned boy spits.

Nick squirms, attempting to get loose. My mind whirs with panic when Reece gets between the two. My heart palpitates at the thought of him getting hurt. The bully releases Nick and faces Reece, hesitating. In a second, Reece's fist connects with the bully's stomach.

The bully hunches over with an awful moan and Reece grabs Nick's wrist, telling him to run.

The boys run down the corridor and my heart is in overdrive. What the hell did I just see? Flashes of Reece from a year ago with a skateboard as a weapon appear in my mind.

I run down the corridor, hoping to catch them to check if they are ok. I bust out of the east wing door and search for them. I tiptoe around the path and spot them in an alcove.

Nick holds Reece's hand and they stare into each other's eyes. Nick holds Reece's eye contact. Gulp. Nick steps closer and thanks

Reece. Nick's lips press against Reece's and I'm about to keel over as they kiss, soft and slow.

They pull apart and Nick is smiling while Reece is expressionless.

"I have to head to class," Nick says. "See you after school?"

Reece nods.

Nick brushes Reece's cheek and then heads into the school building.

I hide long enough so Nick doesn't catch me, but short enough to grab Reece. I run around to the alcove where Reece is shaking. He looks at me and I am terrified he'll run from me.

His eyes are round and his body trembles. He's in freak-out mode. The mode Kellie always fixed.

I edge closer to him and he blurts, "I need Kellie."

I freeze and the pounding in my ears intensifies. "Ok. Ok, let's go see her."

It's still easy to skip school. We are quiet as we walk to the cemetery and I'm glad I get to do it with him. We sit down in front of Kellie's tombstone and take in the shade of the overhanging trees while the warm breeze coats us.

Reece sits cross-legged, staring at the tombstone. There is a two-person gap between us. We feel miles apart. I clear my throat and stare at Kellie's name. "You know, I used to come here a lot. I can feel her here. I talked to her here."

Reece's eyes stay fixated on the stone and he nods. "Me too."

I purse my lips and stay quiet, realising he's talking to her. My hands clasp over my heart. *Oh, Kellie. Please take care of him.*

About five minutes later, Reece shifts his position. He seems slightly more relaxed.

"So, what was that?"

He fidgets. "Whaddaya mean?"

"You and Nick? So... so close."

He shrugs. "We're friends."

"Reece. You two kissed. I saw you."

He bows his head and sighs. "Charli, I don't know. I like him a lot but..."

"I didn't know either of you were..." Gay?

"I like him," he whispers. "He makes me feel good about myself but... not we're not romantic or anything. I don't have those feelings for anyone."

"You mean, at the moment?"

"At all."

I take a few moments before asking him what he means.

"I dunno. I've talked about it with my therapist before. I don't know what that stuff is and I don't see anyone in a romantic way. It's not in me, I guess." He pauses and glances at me. "I always thought if I did, it would be you."

My chest rises and then plummets. Me? Did he think about *me* like that? What about the time at the skatepark on my sixteenth birthday? He could not have seemed more repulsed.

I bypass all of that. Way too awkward right now. "So, what are you going to say to Nick?"

Reece shies away from me.

"Reece, he's expecting to see you."

"What do I say?"

"I don't know. Why did he kiss you? Surely there was build up to this?"

"We are friends," he whispers.

I have an overwhelming urge to hug him. He won't like that, so maybe a topic change. I spot the frayed edges of a paperback in his slightly unzipped backpack. "What's the latest read?"

"I'm rereading *'Wuthering Heights'*."

"Oh, good one. I just read *'The Colour Purple'*."

He spins to look at me. "I just read that."

"Shuddup."

"Seriously."

"I loved it, made me cry."

"The back and forth between the sisters made the story, in my opinion. Their stories could not have been more different."

I swallow uncomfortably. "Speaking of sisters. You and Brit are friends now?"

He shrugs. "Yeah."

"How did that happen?"

"Because of you."

"Me?"

"You left and I was alone. I wanted to help her because I didn't know how to help you. She asked me to keep her company."

We walk to Reece's house and he says I can come inside. I haven't been in his house since before Spain, so I jump at the chance.

"Sammy!" I squeal as Reece's dog runs up to me. I kneel and pat him as he licks at my neck. "It's been too long, buddy."

We take Sammy into Reece's bedroom and boot up his latest video game. I'm so rusty. I never played games when I was overseas, so it has been months since our last match.

"Reece," his mum calls from downstairs. "Nick is here."

Reece drops the controller and stands, eyes bulging.

"It's ok," I say.

He lunges for the window. He opens it and hops a leg out.

I grab him. "What the hell are you doing?"

"I'm climbing down. You talk to him."

"*Um*, no," I say, pulling him inside. "Get back in here and talk to him. It'll be worse if you leave it."

"I can't talk to him."

"Yes, you can. You said it yourself, you are friends. Just tell him what you told me."

He trembles. "No, I can't."

"I can't do it for you. It'll be ok. I'll be here if you need me. Go see him."

I turn Reece to the door quickly, so Nick doesn't come in here first. I don't want Nick to see me. I really don't want to get in the middle of whatever this is.

Reece goes downstairs and I creep onto the landing so I can hear what is going on. I want to be here to help if Reece freezes and can't handle it.

Reece meets Nick at the bottom of the stairs. I peer through the railing at Nick, who smiles and brushes Reece's side-swept hair aside. A shiver runs down my spine. Nick is mesmerised by Reece's eyes.

Nick goes to take Reece's hand, but Reece flinches and takes a step back. Nick's smile droops and he asks what's wrong.

"Did I do something wrong?" Reece asks.

"Wrong?"

"To make you think we were more than friends."

Nick's cheeks redden and he stumbles backwards. "I'm sorry, I thought..."

Reece steps closer to him. "It's ok, I still like you, just not like that."

Nick's hands cover his face and he puffs air out.

"It's not you, I'm not like that with anyone."

Nick lowers his hands. "Whaddaya mean?"

"I'm not into anyone, I'm not straight or gay, I'm... I'm nothing."

Nick steps closer to him and rubs his arms. "You're not nothing."

They are so close together, looking at them feels wrong. I look away and hear Reece tell Nick that if he'd be with anyone, he'd be with me. My stomach plummets.

Reece, no.

I look through the railing and see them both looking up at me. My jaw hangs open.

Nick moves back. "What, you're setting me up so you can laugh at me?"

I stand up. "Nick, no. It's not like that."

Nick shakes his head. "I'm such an idiot."

"Nick, wait!" I call out.

He runs out of the house and I'm breathless while racing down the stairs.

"What should we do?" I ask Reece.

Reece stares at the doorway. "I don't know what is happening."

"Should we talk to him?"

"And say what?"

I throw my hands up, defeated.

He turns to me. "Can we be ok?"

"It's up to you," I whisper. "Reece, I love you and it hurts me every day that I abandoned you. We both lost Kellie, but I could only see how it affected me. I'm sorry."

Reece pats my back.

I giggle and whisper, "Can I give you a proper hug?"

He nods and I pull him in for a gentle squeeze.

"Wanna play a video game?" he asks.

The biggest smile spreads across my face. The purest sign that we will be ok. "Let's do it."

It's still weird between Reece and me, but silently levelling up in the game was a huge step for us.

I take my bike from home and ride to Dad's house.

I enter through the back door.

Inside, I hear Brittany whisper, "You and Reece?"

I creep towards the hall as Nick walks into his bedroom.

Brittany fidgets in his doorway. "Since when?"

I slip into the bathroom as Nick replies, "I dunno, I like him, ok? I thought he was like me."

"Gay?"

Silence.

"Nick, it's ok."

"I feel so stupid," his voice wavers. "I really thought he liked me."

"He does like you."

He groans. "You know what I mean."

"But you know Reece is different. Like, his brain works differently."

"I don't care about any of that stuff. He's beautiful."

I peer through the doorway as Brittany *awes* with her hands clasped under her chin. "Oh, Nick."

His hands run through his hair. "Like it matters. Everyone's gonna kick my arse now."

"No, they won't. We won't let them."

"Reece won't." He sighs. "Maybe I should go on tour. Leave all this mess behind."

"Don't run away."

"It'll be easier."

"What are you going to tell your mum?"

"Huh?"

"About you and Reece."

Nick moves to the doorway, arms crossed against his chest. "Why should I have to say anything?"

"Don't you want her to know?"

"Straight kids don't have to announce who they love or make a big production about liking the opposite sex. Why should I have to say anything? It's unfair. Can't everyone work it out for themselves?"

Brittany frowns at her shoes. "I didn't know."

Nick's eyes shine. He bites his lip and nods. He puts a hand on Brittany's shoulder and looks to the side, right at me.

My eyes grow as wide as his and Brittany looks my way.

"You're eavesdropping?" Nick accuses. "Again?"

"Again?" Brittany asks.

I put my hands up. "No, I—"

Nick groans and backs into his bedroom, slamming the door.

Brittany plants her hands on the door. "Nick? Nick, can I come in?" Her head snaps toward me. "What were you doing?"

I emerge from the doorway and whisper, "I saw them kiss."

She tiptoes toward me. "At school?"

I nod.

"And he's mad about that?"

I shake my head. "I was at Reece's and I heard them talking."

Her eyes widen. "You and Reece were together?"

A smile plays at my lips. "Yeah, I think we might be ok."

Brittany looks over her shoulder at Nicks closed door, then back to me. "Don't stuff it up. He misses you."

I nod. "I know. I miss him too."

Brittany edges to Nick's door and knocks.

Nick won't open his door, and Brittany and I retreat to our own bedrooms.

#

"I can't go with you," I tell Harrison outside *Gina's* the next day.

He clutches my hand. "That's ok. You're still in school. That's what's important."

I bite my cheek and inhale loudly. "It's more my friends and my sister. I need to make things right. If I leave, I'll be running from them again and I'll never fix it."

Harrison kisses my lips softly and whispers, "It's ok. They are important to you. I would never want you to give them up."

I throw my arms around his neck and lean my body into him. "I'll miss you so much."

"I'll look you up when I get back."

"You'd better."

20

Brittany

"Britty."

My fingers curl around the straps of my backpack and I hold a breath as I turn around. Bryce jogs toward me in the north wing corridor.

"Hi," I say.

"Walk you to your locker?" he asks, stopping by me.

"Ok," I say, continuing in the corridor.

"How are you?"

"Fine."

"You and Charli ok?"

"Yes."

"What's with the one-word responses?"

"Nothing."

"Brittany."

I groan, stop, and roll my eyes.

"I'm trying here," he says, moving to face me.

I avoid eye contact.

His hand brushes my arm and I flinch.

He huffs. "Just tell me if we're broken up or not."

"I can't fling myself back in." I meet his eyes. "We need to be friends again."

"I'm trying to be friends."

"I don't feel it." I shake my head. "I mean, I feel like *I'm* not trying."

He steps back, his eyes widening. "What do you want to try?"

"Remember when we first met?"

"Yeah."

"You made us be friends first before we dated. Can we re-do that?"

He smiles. "Ok."

"It's like we're missing something," I whisper. "We have for a long time."

"We don't talk," he replies. "Not really."

I nod. "Not really."

He holds out his hand. "Do you want to try it?"

I eye his hand and bite my lip. My heart *ba-booms*. He's never taken off the watch. My hands slip into my pockets. "Maybe tomorrow."

He drops his hand, smiling. "Ok."

I walk by Bryce. It's nice, but I can't help feeling sad. Nick's gone. I've gone to school with Nick for months, and now he's missing from my daily routine.

Shae came home to talk Nick through his identity crisis. Tara called her straight away because she could see something was up with

Nick. Maybe telling his mum scared Nick because of the whole church thing? Shae's studying to be a counsellor, so I guess she's good at that stuff, but it made me feel like crap. Shae is his *real* sister. He'd talk to her about stuff before me. They've always been close. Always shared things.

Look at the sibling train wreck that is Charli and me. It's a no brainer that he'd choose Shae over me after seeing what my sibling relationship looks like.

I don't know why Nick hesitated to tell Tara. *Duh*, she was supportive. I'm so glad I've got her as a step mum. She's the most grounded out of all three parents. I don't understand how her old partners didn't want to keep her. But it was a good thing she ran from Nick's dad. He sounds like a nightmare.

Watching Tara and her three kids in our living room made me so jealous. Before the divorce, my family of four was never close-knit.

But anything could make me mad now. I'm still not over the fact the button of my jeans popped this weekend. Like, what the hell? How was that even possible? *Ugh*.

Nick is in Sydney for some studio time before leaving on his tour. He gets to record a single and do backing vocals for the band he's touring with. It's an awesome opportunity and I miss him like crazy already. He's caring, comforting and loyal. When I was next to Nick, I felt safe.

I watch Bryce's profile. He's calm, mind adrift, and familiar. Watching his expression, I almost know what he's thinking about. I bet it's the beach.

"What you thinking about?" I ask.

He shakes his head as he springs out of his thoughts. He smiles. "That time after your sweet sixteen when we escaped to the beach."

I swear my heart has swelled to three times its size.

"I wished we'd had more times like that this summer," he says.

I avoid his eyes, purse my lips and nod. Guilt rises inside me. I push it down. We didn't see each other for a reason. As the homeroom bell sounds, I spy the reason. Her platinum blonde hair moves into her classroom.

Chloe waves to Meah, who is further down the corridor. She is a skinny, fake blonde. A Chloe Clone. Damn. I looked that stupid a year ago.

I move inside my classroom before she approaches. I wave to Bryce as Meah tries to get his attention. I find a desk, so I don't have to pay attention to her.

At lunch, I find Reece walking toward the quad with Charli. My hands press into my stomach as I chew my lip. They have history. Everyone ditches me eventually. I'm so stupid for not seeing it coming.

"Hey Madi," Fiona calls out across the corridor. "Sad your little boyfy's left town? Too bad you don't have a dick to make him want to stay in town."

"Oh, shut the fuck up," Madison snaps, walking behind me.

Fiona giggles and skips toward Sean.

"Are you ok?" I whisper, holding out a hand to her.

Madi links arms with me and forces a smile. "She's a dumb bitch. Not worth my time."

"You two were best friends," I say. "It has to hurt."

She eyes me. "And what about you and Meah?"

"Point taken."

"You're heading outside?"

"I think so."

Madi nods up the hall and unravels her arm. "I'm heading to the music room. I feel like I want to continue practicing." Her eyes gleam with sadness. "You'll be ck?"

"Yeah, totally. You go."

Should I ask to go with her?

She's quick to move further up the hall and I take the hint that she wants to be alone. We wave goodbye and I know she misses Nick. Me too.

I fidget, contemplating whether to go out to meet Charli and Reece. A sing-song giggle bounces above the noise of the corridor. I turn, smiling, to find Tayla.

Tayla's arms are draped over Lenny's shoulder and her eyes are fixated on him. I wall-hug by the exit to the quad and the pair pass me like I'm invisible. I slouch and my sight falls to my shoes.

My feet drag through the corridor. I don't need a crutch to walk anymore, but the dull ache hasn't left. I approach mess hall and take in a big breath, considering whether to go in.

"Hey."

I jump as a hand touches my back and plant my hand on my pounding chest as Bryce rounds me. "Oh, hi."

"She looks shocked to see you," Chloe says, laughing behind Bryce.

My eyes roll as I angle my face away from them.

"C'mon, Chlo," Jace says, and from the corner of my eye, I see him tug on Chloe's arm toward mess.

"Whatever, Jace," Chloe says, pulling her arm from his grip.

"You coming in?" Bryce asks me, nodding at mess.

"Uh," I start. My eyes pivot between mess hall and Chloe.

Bryce looks at Chloe and Jace. "You guys go in. We'll be in later."

"Chloe," Jace huffs in the doorway of mess hall.

"Bryce, you need support," Chloe says, stepping close to Bryce.

"Jace, he's one of my best friends and he's going through something major right now. I can't leave him."

I shoot my hands up and walk away from them. "Whatever."

"Brittany," Bryce says, pulling away from Chloe and following me. "If you don't wanna go into mess, I'll go outside with you."

I stop and turn to him. "Now? You'll do that now?"

"Yeah. Wait. What do you mean?"

I roll my eyes and turn away.

"Brit?"

Over my shoulder, I reply, "I was asking you to do that for months and you're going to start now?"

"I'm trying," he pleads.

Chloe *tsks* behind him, popping a hip.

Why doesn't she just piss off?

I turn back to Bryce.

On second thought, why don't I?

I move as fast as my body will let me down the corridor, a hand stretched behind me to indicate I'm not to be followed.

I push my way into a bathroom and lock myself in a stall. I blow out a breath, cradle my head in my hands and anchor my elbows on my knees. This sucks. I should head straight to the library at lunch instead of trying to find a friend. Studying will help me ignore all this crap.

"Hi."

I exit the school building after my last period and look side-to-side for the voice. It's Reece.

"Hey," I reply.

"You waiting for Charli?" he asks, fiddling with the headphones around his neck.

"Oh, um, I wasn't. Sophia's car will be out the front."

"I'm waiting for her. I'm going to your place with you guys."

My stomach tightens oddly. "Oh, ok." I feel the heat rising to my neck. Will they play video games and ignore me?

"Where were you at lunch?" Reece asks.

"I was wondering the same thing," Charli says, landing beside me. "Were you with Madi or Bryce?"

"No," I answer quickly. "I'm ready to go home."

Charli nods, concern crossing her face. "Ok, let's go."

We walk towards the line of cars and find Sophia's. I take the front seat, Charli and Reece slide into the back. Sophia asks us about our days, and all three of us answer in murmurs.

When we walk into the house from the garage, I slink behind Charli and Reece. I expect them to chat amongst themselves, but they are silent too.

I turn toward the stairs.

Charli says, "You coming?" and nods to the living room.

I point to my chest. "Me?"

Charli looks to Reece and then to me with apprehension. "We were gonna play a video game, but we don't have to if you think it's lame or something."

I shake my head. "No, I don't care if you play. You really want me to hang with you?"

Charli and Reece share a look and then deadpan at me. "Yeah."

I laugh nervously. "I thought you two would want to hang out like you used to."

"Nothing's like it used to be," Reece says.

"Why did you think we wouldn't want you around?" Charli asks, taking a step forward. "Did I do something wrong?"

I bite my lip and then smile. "No, I guess not. I just expect people to exclude me."

"But we're friends?" Reece questions.

I pinch the bridge of my nose and scrunch my eyes closed. *"Ugh. I feel so stupid."*

"Brit, we love you," Charli says, placing her hands on my shoulders. "Don't be alone."

I lower my hands and smile at my sister. "Ok."

"You're in my routine," Reece says, making his way to the living room. "Don't go missing on me."

I link arms with Charli and follow him into the living room. "Ok, I'll stick with you guys."

We sit on a couch and Charli asks, "Where were you at lunch?"

My stomach flips. "I don't want to even think about it."

"Tell me," Charli whispers, her eyes widening as she audibly swallows.

We sit and I pat her knee. "It's ok, just Chloe being Chloe."

"I thought you weren't hanging around her anymore."

I shake my head and sink into the couch. "Believe me, I avoid her where I can. Bryce was talking to me and she kept butting in."

"Are you and Bryce ok?" she asks.

I shake my head. "I dunno."

"Wanna invite him over?"

"No, I'll see him at school."

Reece boots up the video game console and hands Charli a controller. He offers one to me and I laugh and wave him off.

"You should give it a go," Charli says. "Knowing you, you'd be a natural and beat our high score."

"I'm happy to watch." I fiddle with my phone and repeat in my head, *do not look at Instagram.* I bet Chloe would post a pic of her and Bryce just to get at me.

I toss the phone on the coffee table and blow out a breath. "Ok, show me how the game works. Maybe I will have a go." My desperation level for a distraction is high.

"Charli's bad at explaining," Reece says, selecting *start* on the menu. "I'll walk you through it."

Charli *tsks*. "How am I bad at explaining?"

I whack her arm. "*Shoosh*. Let him explain."

Reece pokes his tongue out and then explains the game. I catch five percent of it because Charli and I are in a fit of giggles. My stomach aches in the best way. I wave my hands in front of my face, gasping for a decent breath of air.

"*Shoosh*," I try to say, but only laugh more.

Charli sinks into the couch and rests her forehead against my shoulder. Her jiggling body reverberates through mine.

I push her off and laugh. "Stop."

An explosion sounds from the TV and Reece swivels to us. "And that's how you win."

Charli wipes her face and sits up. "Dude, you killed me."

Reece smiles triumphantly. "That's why rule number one is *pay attention*."

Charli sits on the edge of the couch and grips the controller. "Ok, it's on."

She looks so determined as she plays, I just can't help it. As her concentration deepens, I poke her between the ribs.

Charli jerks away from me. "*Oi*. Beat it."

But I don't. I poke at her continuously until the same explosion sounds.

"*Dammit*," Charli grumbles. She pushes the controller at me. "Ok, ok. Let's see how you do."

I laugh and slide away from her. "Nah-uh."

Charli keeps prodding me with the controller, so I give in and take it. When Reece starts the game again, I get up and move over to Reece's couch.

Charli laughs. "No fair."

I poke my tongue out at Charli and she falls back in giggles as I realise Reece's tongue is poked out too.

Reece and I focus on the game, ignoring Charli as she composes herself. The TV is split screen and my character is on the right. I try to follow what Reece's character does but end up looking at the wrong side of the screen and getting my character trapped in the corner of a room.

Reece takes my controller and gets me out of the room. He hands over the controller and points to the green button. "Press this one to fire and the red one to defend."

"Defend?"

"Yeah, for when I do this."

Flames approach my character as Reece's character launches a flame-thrower.

"*Oi*," I squeak, jamming my finger on the red button. An opaque shield protects my character. It fractures and eventually the explosion takes over my side of the TV.

I flop backward and drop the controller. "And this is fun for you guys?"

Charli pounces and snatches my controller. She retreats to her couch, saying, "Yes. Now I'm really gonna get you, Reece. No more distractions."

I return to my proper position as spectator and somehow watching these two goofballs makes me forget about all the crap at *John Thomas High*.

#

"I hope you and Bryce can work it out," Charli says as we meet up at lunch the next day. "I like him."

"We're just in a weird place," I say as we cross the quad.

"Can I help?" she asks.

"How?"

"I dunno."

"I think we'll be ok. I think school seems to make everything feel worse."

"Then you should see more of him outside of school."

"He never wanted to hang out with the people I was with."

"Like Reece and Nick?"

"Yeah. It was uncomfortable."

"Has he changed or something? He's always seemed nice when I've been around him."

"He's not mean or anything. Just not engaged, you know?"

"I'm surprised," Charli says as we sit by a tree. "Even Travis tried with Kellie and Reece, which should have been super weird."

I smile. "Never thought I'd want Bryce to act like Travis."

Charli hugs her waist and looks to the clouds. "He wasn't all that bad."

"He wasn't the poster-boy for boyfriends though."

Charli shrugs. "Anyway, that's in the past."

"I don't know if I can be with Bryce if he keeps hanging with Chloe."

"It sounds like a simple decision," Charli says. "Who in their right mind would choose Chloe over you?"

I lift my palms. "Lots of people."

"If Bryce won't be with you because he wants to be friends with

Chloe, he needs to be institutionalised.”

I laugh. “Ok, whatever ya reckon.”

My phone buzzes in my pocket. I pull it out and read *Incoming Call: Bryce.*

“*Ohmigawd*, he’s calling me.”

“Answer it.”

“I can’t.”

“Talk to him.”

“Nah-uh.”

“Givit.” Charli takes my phone as I gasp *no*. She slides her finger on the screen and raises the phone to her ear. “Hello?”

“Charli,” I hiss.

“No, it’s Charli... No, she’s here with me... Where are you? ... We’re by the quad... Ok, see ya soon.”

She hangs up and I blurt out, “What?”

“He’s gonna come out and sit with us.”

My heart pounds like a paddleball. Breathlessly, I reply, “Ok.”

“What’s wrong? You wanna see him, right?”

“Yeah. Yeah, it’ll be fine.”

“I’ll stay with you,” she says, taking my hand.

I gently squeeze her hand and smile. “Thanks.”

I’m on edge as the minutes pass by. My stomach swishes when Reece approaches and my tension ramps up as I wait to see Bryce. Tayla and Lenny join us too, and still no sign of Bryce.

“He definitely said he was coming?” I ask Charli.

She nods. “Yeah. It hasn’t been that long. You look freaked. Are you sure you’re ok?”

“Yeah. I want to see him and don’t want to see him, you know?”

“Maybe he got held up by a teacher or something? Or is in a changeroom or at his locker?” Charli suggests.

"What's this?" Tayla asks, scooting beside us. "Bryce?"

"He just called to ask where Brittany was," Charli replies quickly. "He'll come out and join us."

I edge closer to Charli and whisper, "I dunno if I want to sit with him with everyone else. It seems so on-display."

"But you want me around?" she questions.

I nod.

She nods. "Ok, it'll be fine. When he gets here, we'll figure it out."

When I see Bryce walk across the quad, I squeeze Charli's hand.

"Don't be nervous," she whispers. "You two are friends, right?"

I nod, unable to take my eyes off him. I stand and pull Charli up with me.

"Don't strain yourself," Charli says, putting her other hand on the small of my back.

Bryce jogs up to us. Something's wrong. I see it in the shine of his eyes.

"What is it?" I ask, almost breathlessly.

He rubs his jaw and looks away from me.

I drop Charli's hand and step close to him. "Bryce?"

"I need to talk to you," he whispers.

"Go ahead."

He eyes Charli, then drops his gaze. "I wanted to talk to you alone, if that's cool?"

Something is wrong. I nod and rub his arm. "Sure."

"You're ok?" Charli asks me.

I nod and move away with Bryce.

"I got this text," he says and slips his phone out of his pocket.

I notice the way his hand shakes as he taps on the phone. I touch his hand. "Are you ok?"

He wipes his brow and taps the phone screen quickly. He takes a breath and then moves the phone closer to his chest. "I don't want to have to show you."

Colour drains from my face. "Show me what?"

He moves to a bench and plonks himself down.

I move over and sit slowly. "What is it?"

He gulps and lowers his phone. "Will. He's coming back."

My chest constricts. "What?"

Red lines form at the base of Bryce's eyes. "Everything from the accident came racing back when I saw his text." His breaths draw in hastily. His face drops to his hands. "Shit."

"Charli," I call out. I wave her over. "Come over here." I turn to Bryce and lower my voice. "She has to know. Is it ok if she comes over?"

Bryce nods in his hands. "Yeah."

Charli walks over sheepishly like she's worried we're dragging her into a fight. "Yeah?"

I press into my flipping stomach and eye Bryce. He looks like he's moments from being physically sick and there's no way I will let that happen. I rub his back, lean my head against his, and whisper, "It'll be ok."

"What's happened?" Charli asks, landing at our feet and soaking in the devastation.

I rub circles on Bryce's back. "Will's back."

Charli's jumps back a step. "What?"

Bryce sits up and wipes his forehead. "No, he's *coming* back."

"He texted you?" I clarify.

"Yep."

Charli lowers to the ground and kneels by our feet. "Why?"

Bryce lifts his phone and sighs. "I never got that far. I just saw the message and then called Brit."

Charli pulls at her hair. "I don't want to see him."

"He's coming back to school?" I ask.

Bryce shakes his head. "I don't know."

I hold out my hand. "Can I?"

Bryce hands me his phone and I steady my fingers to reply to Will's message.

> **(Will) Hey man. I'll be back in Sanford soon.**
>
> **(Bryce) Back to John Thomas?**
>
> **(Will) Nah. Back for my dad. He's getting out.**

I drop the phone to my lap. "His dad is getting out of prison. That's why he's coming home."

Bryce bounces off the bench and paces, shaking his out arms, an unsettling moan escaping him.

I get up and move to him with urgency. I stop him in place and wrap my arms around him, gripping with the intensity he needs to become grounded. I smooth his butterscotch hair and whisper that it'll be ok.

His arms lock around me and the trembling of his body halves.

"Charli?" I find her on the ground. "You ok?"

Charli wipes her palms over her eyes. She stands and clears her throat. She peers over her shoulder and then down to the ground. "We have to tell Reece."

I reach out a hand and she takes it. "We'll do it together."

She tries for a smile and nods.

Bryce's face nestles beside mine and I drop Charli's hand to hold him tighter.

"You're still on your medication, right?" I whisper.

He nods against the nape of my neck and relief fills my chest.

"I need you," he whispers.

I twist the emerald ring on my finger. "You have me."

21

Charli

Brittany and I sit in Reece's kitchen as his mum places fresh, hot brownies onto a plate.

"You are the best, Mrs Watkins," I gush as I take a gooey brownie from the plate.

It's easy being around Reece's mum. When Reece and I played video games after the Nick incident, she pulled me aside to apologise for slamming the door in my face all those weeks back. Mid-ramble about being in mum-mode and Reece being her number one priority, I stopped her and said all was forgiven. Especially when I still had so much to make up for.

"Chocolate is truly the way to my heart," Brittany says, a smile brightening her face.

"Don't hype them up too much before you try them," Mrs Watkins says with a laugh.

"As if, they're always so—" I interrupt myself with a bite and it's as gooey, crispy, and chocolaty as I remember. "*Ohmigawd.*"

"*Ohmigawd*, indeed," Brittany says with a mouthful of chocolate.

Reece takes a bite and gives his mum a thumbs up.

Mrs Watkins laughs and moves to the sink. "Thanks, kids."

I move onto my second brownie as the texture and flavour sooth my queasy stomach. I'd been thinking about something all day and hadn't the courage to bring it up. I shake off the tremors. Just say it.

"Kellie's birthday is coming up," I say in a low voice, eyes focused on the brownie my fingers are picking at.

Reece fidgets beside me, his head low. He's been thinking about it.

"Her eighteenth?" Brittany asks awkwardly.

I drop the brownie on the napkin in front of me and sigh as I slouch on the chair. "I can't believe she didn't make it to eighteen."

"You know, I've been thinking about her birthday too," Mrs Watkins says, staring off to the side as she dries a dish. She laughs and looks to Reece. "She was over here for her last five birthdays."

The slightest curve upturns the corners of Reece's lips as he eyes the table.

"Why don't we hold a memorial on her birthday?" Mrs Watkins suggests.

"A memorial?" Brittany and I say at once.

"Yeah!" Mrs Watkins eyes light up. "Like a big birthday bash and celebration of her life. We all know the funeral didn't display her life well, but who could blame the family? They lost their daughter without warning after she went out with her friends. A celebration on her birthday could act as closure for everyone."

I look to Brittany and her eyes water. Her smile grows. "I love that idea."

I smile back and turn to Mrs Watkins. "That would be amazing."

"I agree," Reece says, and he shifts his body closer to me.

"Oh, perfect," Mrs Watkins cheers. "I'll call the Saunders and get their seal of approval. You kids make a plan. What do you think Kellie would like? Then we can start on the details."

Mrs Watkins grabs her phone and leaves the room, as giddy as if she were planning a surprise party.

"This is a weird yet fun idea," I say.

"Yeah. I like it," Reece replies.

"It would be cool if you made it more like a birthday party than a stuffy memorial," Brittany says, taking another brownie. "What would she like?"

"We always had small parties," I say to Reece. "But a memorial has to be big."

"I think she wanted a big eighteenth," Reece replies.

"If she had let Will plan it, it would have been so loud," Brittany smirks.

"*Ugh*," I mutter. I rub my temples and exhale. "He's coming home, and it brings up so much pain. Like the fact that her death is my fault."

"*What?*" they screech.

I cover my face and nod.

"Charli, you weren't driving," Reece says.

"I ignored her calls and texts. There was something important she wanted to talk to me about," I whimper through cupped hands. "Kellie wanted to talk about breaking up with Will and if I had been there for her, I could have saved her life."

"*Um,* I think you're wrong," Brit says.

I lower my hands to view her.

"Kellie and Will were together non-stop," she continues. "They were in love."

My head spins. "Love?"

Reece nods. "That's what she told me."

It's still not sinking in. "Love? She said, *love*?"

Brittany raises her palms. "Maybe that's what she wanted to tell you."

"*Fuck.*"

They stare at me in shock and I mouth an apology. Kellie and Will were in love? She was in love? In love with him? They were inseparable?

My head continues to spin.

It was all just a dumb accident.

She was happy.

Her life was cut short.

And I made it all about me.

"I'm so dumb," I whisper behind cupped hands.

Brittany rounds the table and throws her arms around me. "Don't do that. You were overseas, you didn't get the chance to see them fall in love."

"I shouldn't have gone to Spain."

Brittany squeezes me. "Don't. You needed it. You're not the crazy control freak anymore. Yes, you went off the rails. But you're ok. You'll be ok."

I lower my hands before wrapping my arms around my sister. "You're the best older sister."

She kisses my forehead and releases me. "I'm not super thrilled about seeing Will either, but we will get through it together."

Reece slides his brownie away. "I've already organised to see him."

My eyes become round. "Really?"

Reece nods. "Mum and I are going to sit down with him and his mum."

"Think he'll wanna go to the memorial?" Brit asks.

"Kellie's parents wouldn't let him go to the wake," I mutter. "I doubt they'd want him around."

"They'd have to let him go. He loved her. If Kellie's parents are uncomfortable, surely Will knows to keep his distance," Brittany says and sits down. "I don't get why he had to text Bryce. Bryce doesn't want to see Will. It's sad, they were best friends."

"We all lost a best friend that day," I whisper.

"Such a stupid thing that caused so much chaos," Brittany says with a huff. "It rippled through Bryce and me." She gestures to me, "Sent you off the deep end. I mean, a positive came from that, I'm glad we're all hanging out."

I nod. "You definitely got some better friends out of the deal."

"Maybe Mum will know if Will is invited or not," Reece says eyeing the doorway and listening for his mother's phone conversation.

"I'd suggest we have a small gathering for Kellie's birthday, but you're right, a memorial should be big. It should be open to the entire town to celebrate Kellie." I laugh and look to Reece. "It'd only get gate-crashed like that games night in grade ten."

"That was horrible," Reece replies.

Brittany scrunches her hair. "*Ugh*, that party. I got so wasted and the hangover was hell."

"And it trapped you in Chloe's lair," I joke.

Brittany laughs. "The beginning of the end."

Mrs Watkins enters the room, humming a cheery tune. She waves her phone. "The Saunders love the idea."

We look at each other and say in unison, "What about Will?"

Mrs Watkins stares at us. She gulps. "We didn't bring him up."

If Kellie was truly in love with him, she'd want him there.

Wouldn't she? Does she forgive him for her death?

How could she possibly do that?

I push away from the brownies. Suddenly, they don't seem as appealing anymore.

"I had a good talk with my sister," I say to Mariah and the rest of my therapy group. "I think we're beginning to see eye to eye on some things."

"See, told ya," Yasmine pipes up. "You need to put your family first if you want a good relationship with them."

Pan groans and rolls his eyes as he crosses his arms.

Yasmine is so pretty. When I first saw her, she made me think of Maja. *That kiss.* Sometimes, I wish I let Maja kiss me again. I was warming up to the idea and thought there would be more time. What would the trip to the Greek Islands with Maja be like?

A girl can dream.

Mariah lifts her hand. "Yasmine, let Charli continue."

"It feels easier," I elaborate. I try not to look at Yasmine. She's beautiful but needs to learn to shut her mouth. "We're talking about having a memorial for my friend that passed away."

Mariah smiles. "That sounds lovely. Do you think it will help bring you closure?"

I nod. "Yeah, I learnt about some things that happened while I was overseas. I feel better. Slightly."

"Want to elaborate?"

I shake my head. "It's not important. I just feel clearheaded."

"What do you talk about in therapy?" Brittany asks that afternoon as Sophia fills our glasses with pomegranate iced tea.

"Anything, really," I reply. "Whatever we're thinking about, whatever is bugging us, or whatever happened that was good." I take a glass and smile at Sophia. "Thank you."

Sophia warms me with her cheery smile. "My pleasure."

Having her support again helps me feel better about my place in this wonky world. Sophia has always shown me love and kindness. Seeing the hurt in her eyes when I was at my lowest point was truly devastating. I never want to disappoint her again.

Brit pats my shoulder. "I'm glad you're still getting the help you need."

I sigh. "Me too."

"Speaking of help," Brittany says, peering at our notebooks and textbooks on the breakfast nook. "Do you want me to help you with your homework?"

I laugh. "You wanna be my tutor."

She shrugs. "I'm ahead with my work, so I don't mind."

"You should take her up on it, Charli," Mum says, walking into the kitchen. "Brittany is doing extremely well in all her classes."

Brittany leans against the island bench, a nervous smile bringing a blush to her cheeks. "Mum, I was thinking I might have good enough entry marks to study law at uni."

Mum's mouth falls open as she sets her laptop and paperwork down on the benchtop. She brushes Brittany's cheek in awe. "Oh Brit, that would be wonderful."

A headache pings between my eyes as my feet try to settle in this topsy-turvy foreign world.

I slide into the breakfast nook with my iced tea and Brittany says, "Shall we hit the books? Which subject are you working on?"

"Modern history."

"Oh, I did that one. Vietnam War?"

I turn my notes toward her and she nods.

"Yeah, I can help with that."

Mum smiles, taking a cup of coffee from Sophia. "So good to see you girls working together. Keep it up, ok?"

Brittany smiles across the table at me and it is more than easy to smile back.

The only important thing at school for me is watching out for Brittany. Now that I'm repeating a freakin year, it's only possible at lunch and between classes. There are the odd days where she'll have a limp and I see the way people look at her from their lockers. I don't want anyone to say anything mean to her and I don't want her to feel like an outcast. I'd rather distract people by giving them something horrible to say about me instead. I can take it.

My mind drifts to Harrison and the night in the forest. It opened my world. He's now in Peru doing wonderful, empowering things, and I'm dawdling through the corridors of *John Thomas High* feeling useless.

Useless.

The word tugs at me. It tugs me towards the guidance counsellor's office.

"Uh, hi?" I say, knocking on the doorframe of the open doorway.

"Hello?" Mrs Hendrix, the guidance counsellor, says and turns her chair away from her monitor. "Oh, Charlotte, hi. Feels like just yesterday I was helping you get ready to leave for Spain."

I bunch my curls to the left and sigh. "Yeah. Do you have a minute to talk?"

Mrs Hendrix beckons me in. "Yes. Come in, come in."

I scuff my way into her office, scanning the motivational posters and the images of cities from all over the globe.

"How are you fitting in with your peers?" Mrs Hendrix asks. "How are you adjusting to repeating grade eleven?"

I sit on a chair and shake my head. "Not well. But even if I was still in my grade, I don't think I'd be managing."

"Why's that? You were always such a diligent student."

"I don't think I care anymore."

"What do you care about?"

I twist a curl around my finger and choose to be honest. "Illegal logging in rainforests, vulnerable people in developing countries, clean drinking water, carbon footprints, animal abuse…"

She smiles. "Just to name a few."

"I want to be out helping the world."

"You do know there are many subjects you can take that cover these things?"

I shake my head. "I can't be in a classroom anymore. I was hoping you could tell me how I go about dropping out."

Mrs Hendrix sucks in a breath and grows pale. "You sure about that? Have you discussed this with your parents?"

"I've brought it up with them, but they quickly shut it down."

"You aren't eighteen yet, so they will have to sign off on it."

"*Dammit*," I hiss. "Can I get the paperwork started anyway?"

Mrs Hendrix turns to her monitor and taps on the keyboard. "Oh, boy," she says. "Your grades really have dropped, haven't they? You know they planned to expel you?"

I blow out a breath. "Now I wish they had. It'd be easier."

Mrs Hendrix looks over her shoulder at me. "No, you don't. If you ever wanted to get into university via another pathway, you don't want an expulsion on your transcript."

"What other pathway?"

"You can do online classes or finish grade twelve and final exams at technical college."

"Can I do that in a year or so?"

She nods. "At any age."

"My parents couldn't be mad if I made that an option, right?"

Mrs Hendrix smiles but can't mask her hesitation. "I know your parents. They will take a lot of convincing. Perhaps I should sit down with them?"

I shrug. "You can try. Would I have to be there?"

"Your presence would help to lead us to the best outcome."

My stomach flips. "If we can avoid it, it'd be better."

"Dropping out of school?" Mum yells when she gets home from work. "That's what your guidance counsellor tells me. Charli, what are you thinking?"

"Mum, stop yelling," I say, getting up from the couch.

"You wanna drop out?" Brittany deadpans.

"It's out of the question!" Mum yells.

"Can we talk about it?" I ask, my heart pounding in my ears.

"Your father and I will not support this decision," Mum says, lowering her tone.

My knees knock. "You talked to Dad?"

"He was in the conference call with Mrs Hendrix. We are shutting this down, Charli. You get your act together and focus on your grades."

"But I don't want to be there," I plead.

"You're not leaving school and sitting around the house," Mum orders. "If you leave school you're out of the house."

"What?" I gasp.

"Mum!" Brittany pipes up.

"Your dad is with me on this one," Mum adds, crossing her arms.

My heart tears in two as it smashes against my ribs. Tears prick the corners of my eyes and I'm breathless.

I slide past mum to the front door. "Fine."

She grabs my arm and twists. "Where do you think you're going?"

"Charli," Brittany whimpers.

"You want me out, I'm out," I snap.

"That's not what I—"

I don't let Mum finish. I wriggle my arm free and reef the front door open. I slam it behind me and race to Reece's house.

I'm panting by the time I get to his front door. I bash my fist against the it.

Mrs Watkins opens the doors, a shocked expression on her face. "Goodness, Charli. What's the matter?"

I wipe my face and the wetness makes me realise I was crying as I ran past the two houses in-between my house and here.

"I'm sorry," I whimper.

She shakes her head, concern shifting the shock. She pulls me inside. "Don't be sorry. What's got you so upset? Is it thinking about the memorial?"

I let out a breath like I'm gasping for oxygen. "No... No, it's nothing to do with Kellie."

"Reece is in the living room," she says, patting my back. "Go sit down and catch your breath and I'll brew you a green tea. You still like green tea, right?"

My eyes fog with tears. I press my lips together so the rush of tears surging in my throat don't spurt out. I nod and want so much to thank her, but it will come out as an ugly cry.

"Go on, love," she says, smiling. "He's playing one of those videos games."

I wipe my face and walk up the hall to the living room. Sammy stretches out in the doorway and the sight of his long, fluffy body dries up my tears.

"Hey, boy," I say, leaning over to give him a pat.

"Hey, what are you doing here?" Reece says, eyeing the screen. He must have seen me when I was patting Sammy and gone straight back to his game. I wipe my face one more time.

"Just needed to get out of the house," I say, moving to the couch. My voice was much too nasally and gets Reece's attention.

His eyes widen and he pauses the game. "What happened?"

I avoid his eyes. "Nothing."

"Charli."

The way he says my name causes my tears to resurface and ugly lines crease my face. I cover my face with fists and hear him shift closer.

"Tell me," he whispers.

"I had a fight with my mum," I croak.

"What about?"

"Leaving school."

"You wanna drop out?"

"What?" Mrs Watkins' voice enters the room and I lower my hands to take her in. "Charli, that's not like you. Why do you want to leave school?"

I frown. "It hasn't been the same for a long time. I hate it there."

Mrs Watkins sets my green tea on a coaster on the coffee table. "Since Kellie's passing?"

I shrug. "I've kinda hated it since my dad got remarried."

"Oh, Charli," Mrs Watkins says with a disappointed edge to her words. "You can't put the blame on your dad."

I rub my chest, a tear rolling down my face. "I'm sorry, Mrs

Watkins, I can't have another person telling me my feelings are invalid."

Mrs Watkins gasps, taking a step back. "Oh dear, sorry, I didn't mean... Perhaps I'll leave you kids to talk this through."

"I didn't mean to be rude," I reply quickly. "I was just saying the truth."

Mrs Watkins smiles and pats the top of my head. "Ok, I believe you." She turns and leaves the room, carefully stepping over the dog who happily sleeps in his same position.

"You really wanna leave?" Reece asks.

I nod. "Definitely."

Reece smiles limply. "Ok, then do it."

"My parents want to kick me out of home if I leave school."

Reece's chin drops. "What? That's crazy."

I sink into the couch and pat my eyes dry with my sleeve. "That's what Mum said."

"They're not gonna kick you out."

"Honestly, I wouldn't put it past them."

My phone buzzes in my pocket. I pull it out and read *Incoming Call: Brittany*.

I answer it. "Sorry Brit, I'm ok."

"Charli, what the hell?" Brittany rushes. "Why didn't you tell me you were dropping out?"

"I dunno. It's a hard thing to bring up."

"*Geez*, it was like an ambush."

"I didn't think Mum would go ballistic like that."

"Where are you?"

"Reece's. Don't tell Mum."

"*Pfft*. As if. You want me to come up?"

"No, it's getting late. You stay home. Tell Mum you know where

I am but I'm not coming home tonight."

"Charli, don't. Come home. Don't make this worse."

"I can't, Brit. But I'll call you in the morning."

Brittany huffs. "Ok. Please think things through."

"I will, I promise. Love you."

"I love you too." And she hangs up.

My heart pitter-patters and I rest my phone on my lap.

"Is Brittany ok?" Reece asks.

"Yeah, she's fine."

"You wanna stay here tonight?"

I exhale and find his eyes. "I'm sorry, I didn't even ask, but do you think it'll be ok?"

Reece nods. "It will."

I smile and slide my hands by his. Immense relief shoots through my body as he latches onto it.

"Mum arranged *Horton Park* for Kellie's memorial," Reece says.

"That's awesome," I say with a flat tone, but I'm beginning to feel human again.

"Mum was talking to my aunty about it and my aunty told Travis." Our hands squeeze together at the same moment. "Travis asked if he could make a video montage. Apparently, he has videos and photos of us all from when you two dated."

I take in a breath and choke, spluttering a loud cough.

Reece lets go of my hand. "You ok?"

I cover my mouth and pat my chest. My hands tremor at the thought of his involvement. "Travis?"

"I'll talk to him about it," Reece blurts. "Don't worry about it."

I take a moment to catch my breath.

"Is it too weird?" Reece asks.

I shake my head. "No, it would be nice if he made something. At least we know it will be well made.”

“You look worried.”

“It’s just the thought of seeing him…” Flashes of being cuddled in his arms as we marathoned Hitchcock movies fill my mind.

“He’d email it, not come over.”

I fan my face, nervous. “It’s been a big afternoon.”

“He wants us to check the videos and images are ok,” Reece adds. “But I’ll do that.”

I nod. “Ok.”

Lines of poetry filter through my brain. The lines I wrote about him. The memories of him picking up my notebooks and the security I felt at him reading my words. He’s the only person I let do that. Not Brittany. Not Kellie. It may have ended in a shitty way, but everything we had as boyfriend and girlfriend was solid and real. It meant something.

Travis was safety.

Travis was love.

I was relieved when Mrs Watkins agreed to let me stay over. She made me tell her everything and promise to talk to my parents in the morning. Mrs Watkins hated my parents not knowing where I was, so she called my mum and somehow got her to agree to let me stay the night. Mrs Watkins should go into mediation if she can take down my lawyer mum like that. I guess we all need breathing room.

“Your mum will call your dad,” Mrs Watkins says, handing me a night-shirt from her wardrobe. “This will probably be too big for you.”

“It’s fine. Thank you so much for this.”

“It’s more than fine. My husband’s onboard a ship and the rest of the boys are away. Reece and I could do with more company.”

“Glad to be your company.”

Mrs Watkins walks me down the hall to the guest bathroom. "I got a reply from *Platinum Management*. They are considering letting Nick, and the band he's touring with, play at the memorial."

I gasp. "Wow, how did you manage that?"

"I asked if they'd like a 'good news story' for their PR."

I laugh, giddy. "Mrs Watkins, you are too much. Thank you for everything."

She kisses my forehead. "Take a shower and get ready to relax. We need you to take care of yourself."

"I will. I promise."

22

Brittany

This upcoming memorial is a nightmare. I love the celebration for Kellie, but I hate the pity surrounding me. Mum keeps hugging me and reminding me how grateful she is that I'm alive. *Yep, got it Mum, enough now.* The plans for the memorial have brought back every thought and feeling from the car accident. Everyone's treating me like I'm back in hospital.

As I leave class, Mr Palmer makes a reference to the memorial and tells me I need to seize the day. Cold shivers form bumps on my arms and I want to vomit. The look in his eyes is the same as all the pairs in the corridor throughout the week. *Pity, pity, pity.*

Grateful I'm alive. *Gawd*, I'm so sick of hearing that. Should I be grateful my whole world has been flipped upside down? Should I be grateful I was forced to abandon my dance classes and got kicked off the cheer squad after I made captain? Should I be grateful that I feel too awkward to go to parties and no longer have a lean body? Should I be grateful that I keep my boyfriend at arm's length and I'm too afraid to have sex with him? Should I be grateful for all the raised scars across my hip, abdomen and leg?

(Tiffany) Hey Gurl. I know you said you were done with dance, but we'd love to have you back. I'm happy to do 1-on-1 classes with you, til your confidence comes back.

Tiffany's efforts to get me back to dance class have increased. It's nice she misses me, but it's not the same. I know everyone's intentions are nice, but they need to stop. I don't need the constant reminder. They have no freakin idea what it is like to be me. I don't need them telling me how I *should* feel.

"Are you sick?" Bryce asks as we meet by my locker.

"Huh?"

"You look pale."

The concern on his face draws me in. I flick hair off my face. "I'm fine."

He steps in. "You don't look fine."

His eyes are different. Different to everyone else at school. Concern is different to pity. It's genuine.

I clutch his hand and lean into him. "I hate everyone reminding me I was in the accident with Kellie."

His hand rubs a circle on my back with perfect pressure. "Tell me about it."

"You get it too?"

He rests his head against mine. "I've been seeing the accident over and over again. It sucks."

"I'm sorry," I whisper.

"It's not your fault."

I wrap an arm around him and bite my lip. "It's no one's fault."

"No one? Someone was driving."

"I don't want to hold a grudge against him."

Bryce pulls away. "It's not that easy for me."

I squeeze his hand and find his sorrowful eyes. "I know. You don't have to see him."

He shakes his head. "I won't be seeing him."

"Hey," Charli says in a gloomy voice, stopping by us. She flips her phone around so I can see the screen. "Tara texted me, telling me to come home."

My heart speeds up. "That's good. You should come home. I'm sick of packing up your stuff to dump in your locker."

Charli drops the phone and frowns. "But Tara asked. Not Dad. Not Mum."

"So what? She's here for you. She's here for us."

Charli slips the phone in her pocket and shrugs, moving away. "I dunno. I'll think about it."

"Don't disappear," I say, dropping Bryce's hand and reaching for her. "Stay here with me."

"I'm sorry I left you at home," Charli says. "I just can't be there."

I turn to Bryce and smile. "Maybe I'll leave home too."

"What?" they both question at once.

"Pretend it's two summers ago when I spent all my time at Bryce's house." I wink at Charli. "I'll protest. I'll come home when they talk to you like rational human beings."

Charli smirks. "Don't ruin your relationship with them on my account."

"*Pfft.*" I laugh. "As if it's not all *their* doing."

Bryce tugs on my hand, and his smile crooks to the left. "I'd love you around more."

After school, I wait in *Shakes* while Bryce is at therapy. My palms sweat and my throat catches. Bryce doesn't want to see Will, so this is the best time to see him. I didn't mean to go behind Bryce's back. He never said he didn't want me to see Will. Knowing Bryce will be with his doctor for an hour puts me at ease.

"Hey, Brit." It's low but there's no doubt it's Will's voice.

I turn to his tall stature and sun-bleached blond hair.

I move to stand. "Hey."

"Don't get up." He moves to the other side of the table and sits. "How are you?"

I sit. "I'm ok. You?"

He rests his chin in a hand, and his eyes drift up. "As good as I can be, I guess." His eyes meet mine. "It's weird to be back."

"Which school did you go to?"

"Gilmore Boys Academy."

I smirk. "An all-boys school?"

A smile plays at his lips. "An all-boys boarding school. Yep, as hellishly fun as it sounds."

I tilt my head, looking at him. "You seem different."

"Yeah?"

"Really different. You were always so loud and bouncy. You filled up a room all on your own."

Will shrugs. "Maybe two years ago."

I blow out a breath. "It's been a huge adjustment, I guess."

"I'm the quiet guy at my new school."

"Shuddup," I laugh. "No way."

He nods. "I sit in the back corner, don't make comments, and do my schoolwork."

"Wait," I deadpan. "You do your work? What about all those times you bugged me in science and sat there doing nothing?"

He pushes back on his chair and sighs. "It was time to change."

"I've missed you," I whisper.

He shakes his head. "Really?"

I nod. "Really. We were close. Then you were gone."

"I had to go. I hurt you."

"It was an accident."

Will grows pale and I notice the sweat building at his hairline.
"Will?"

"I was texting," he whispers.

"What do you mean?"

"I was texting while driving. That's why we crashed."

My eyes prick with tears. "What? I didn't know that."

"Your mum got the Saunders not to press charges. I got a
negligent driving charge, but I wasn't proven to be at fault. My family
and Kellie's family talked via your mum, and we agreed I should leave
town so nothing would escalate."

"Wait, my mum knew about the texting?"

"Bryce told her at the hospital because he didn't tell the police.
She took the information and helped me and my mum. It was easy to
leave Sanford when it no longer had Kellie in it."

My heart pounds in my ears. "Bryce knew about it too?" No
wonder he didn't want to see him. "You stupid dickhead, Will. You
know Bryce saw everything. He saw Kellie die. Who would you need
to text when your girlfriend was sitting next to you?"

Will groans, growing sickly. "I know. It's the most stupid thing I
could ever do. It was a stupid group chat about nothing important. It
cost Kellie her life. It ruined your life." He reaches across and takes my
hand. "I'm sorry, Brit. I'm so, so sorry."

I don't pull my hand away. I watch the sincerity in his eyes.
"You're an idiot, but I don't hate you."

A hint of colour returns to his face.

"I believe you're sorry."

"Don't say you forgive me." He clears his throat and pulls his hands back. "Where's Bryce?"

"Therapy. He doesn't want to see you."

Will nods. "Fair enough."

"I haven't told him we're meeting. I don't know if I should."

"Don't lie to him."

"I wouldn't know where to begin." I notice a raised red bump above his cheekbone. "What's that?"

Will runs his fingers over the area. "Oh, that's a scar. From the accident. It's my constant reminder of Kellie. That's why I'm trying so hard at school. I need to honour her memory."

I smile. "She'd like that."

"I see the scar in the mirror and it's like seeing her face. I don't need this town to remember her."

"You're not moving back now your dad's out?"

He shakes his head. "No, I'm never moving back. I'm done with Sanford and *John Thomas High*. The only thing I miss is my morning surf."

"No beach where you are?"

"Nope. Hey, how's Charli? I heard about her going to rehab. I had to get Mum to repeat herself ten times. It was so hard to believe."

I slump in my chair. "I know. She's another idiot."

"Is she ok now?"

I nod, smiling. "She's much better."

"You think she'd wanna see me?"

"I don't know." I pull out my phone and call her. "Let's see."

We move out onto the decking when Charli cycles across the boardwalk.

"Thanks for coming," Will says as she approaches us.

Charli moves beside me and avoids Will's eyes.

"How are you?" Will asks.

"I'm ok. You?"

"Ok. I'm sorry about everything you went through. I'm sorry I caused it."

Charli lifts her head and meets his eyes.

"If I could trade my life for Kellie's I would," he whispers.

Charli chews her lip. "Me too."

"Sorry I tried to force you to talk to me last year," Will says to Charli. "I wanted to apologise, but I shouldn't have gotten in your face."

"You weren't in my face," Charli replies. "Besides, I was high, I wouldn't have listened no matter how you approached me."

Will's eyes round. "Oh."

"It's not your fault I was stoned all the time," Charli says. "That's on me."

"I wish it had never happened," Will says.

Charli pats his arm and smiles. "Me too. Are you going to the memorial?"

Will winces and shakes his head. "I can't believe it's her birthday. I'll take her present to her cemetery plot and spend the day with her. I'd love to be at the memorial, but I don't want to distract people from thinking about her. I don't want them to focus on her death."

Charli's eyes well and she nods, smiling.

"You're doing ok, now?" Will asks her.

"Besides getting kicked out of home, yes."

"What?" Will asks, shocked.

Charli tells Will about moving into Reece's house and dropping out of school while I check the time.

"Bryce will be here real soon," I say. "I'm going out front to meet him."

"D'you think he'll come in?" Will asks, hopeful.

I doubt it. "I'll ask. If I'm not back in ten minutes, it's a no."

Will nods. "Sounds fair."

I touch Charli's shoulder. "Will you be ok if I go?"

She nods. "I'll stay with Will for a few minutes."

"I hope I'll be back soon, but don't hold your breath," I say, waving goodbye to the pair.

I make my way out front as Bryce leaves his car.

"Hold up," I say, planting my hands out like stop signs.

"What?" he says, stopping by the footpath.

I move toward him. "Will's inside."

He exhales loudly. "What? Why?"

"I wanted to talk to him."

Bryce frowns and crosses his arms.

I hold his shoulders. "You don't have to see him. We can leave right now."

His eyes flick past me. "What's he like?"

"He's ok. He's quiet."

His eyebrows raise. "Quiet?"

I smile. "Yeah. Apparently, he doesn't joke around anymore."

"*Pfft*," Bryce smirks.

I throw a thumb back at *Shakes*. "You can see for yourself."

A shiver jolts Bryce's shoulders. "I dunno."

I take his hand. "How was therapy today?"

He shrugs. "It was ok. I talked about him. I don't know, maybe I'm not that mad. I just wish it could all be erased. Like, if Will could undo it all... It's dumb."

"It's not dumb. We all feel like that."

Bryce kisses my cheek. "I love you and I'm glad it was good for you to see him, but I can't."

"Ok, let's go home then."

"It's ok?"

I wrap my arms around him and take in his oaky cologne. "More than ok." My emerald ring turns around my finger. "I love you."

Hand-in-hand, we move toward Bryce's car. His grip on mine squeezes and he halts.

"You ok?" I ask.

"Maybe I should see him," he whispers.

"Don't push yourself if you're not ready."

He turns around and pulls on my hand, walking towards *Shakes*. I keep a half-step behind, letting him make up his mind.

We walk into the seating area and he asks, "Where is he?"

I nod ahead. "Back decking. With Charli."

He takes in a weighted breath, and I cup his hand with mine. He takes another step and then shakes his head. "Maybe I shouldn't."

"It's up to you, B."

He looks into my eyes. "He was ok?"

"Yeah. Just sad."

Bryce looks ahead to the deck and chews his lip. He takes a few more steps whilst apprehension takes over his face.

"Stop," I whisper, gently pulling him back. "Don't do it if you don't want to."

His eyes shine. "You'll be with me?"

I smile. "Of course."

Our fingers interlace and we walk out onto the back decking.

Charli spots us first, her smile growing. "You came."

Will turns on his seat and offers a weak smile as he meets Bryce's eyes. "Hey, man."

"Hey," Bryce replies.

We are still a few steps away from the table and Bryce isn't budging. I don't want to push him, but does he need me to nudge him??

He fidgets in place and then walks to the table. "How are you?"

I let go of Bryce's hand to sit near Charli, but he holds me tighter.

"I'm doing ok," Will says. "You?"

Bryce shrugs and this conversation feels like pulling teeth. I pull him to the table and apply pressure to his shoulder so he will take a seat. I sit beside him, resting my hand on his thigh.

"Will was telling me about his school," Charli says, breaking the awkwardness.

"An all-boy school," I tease.

Will smiles and leans back on his chair. "It's not that bad."

"Brittany was saying you're not the class clown anymore," Bryce say.

Will's shoulders relax at Bryce's effort. "I didn't feel like fitting in when I got there."

"There's no way you're doing homework though," Charli says, eyeing Will with scepticism.

Will lifts his palm, a blush to his cheeks. "What can I tell you? Kellie got through this knucklehead."

Charli smiles and her shoulders jiggle in a silent laugh.

Bryce pushes back on his chair and his palms run over his eyes.

I rub his arm. "Are you ok?"

A weak groan slips out of him and he drops his hand. "Just hearing you say Kellie," Bryce says to Will. "I got a flash of being in the car."

Will's expression drops and his cheeks sink with his frown. "I'm so sorry, man. Honestly, I wish I could take all of it back."

Bryce sighs. "But you can't."

Will wipes under his eye and murmurs, "I want her back."

"I saw her die," Bryce says.

"I know."

I press on Bryce's arm as I watch Charli. "B, don't..."

Charli clears her throat, slouching in her seat. "I'm ok."

"Oh, I'm sorry," Bryce says. "I didn't mean to blurt that out."

She waves a hand, staring at her knees. "Really, it's ok."

Bryce stands, his chair skidding backward. "I should go."

Will stands. "You don't have to."

Bryce looks to me. "Will you come with me?"

"Sure," I say, standing. I ask Charli, "Will you be ok?"

She throws a thumb backward. "I got my bike."

"I'm glad I got to see you," Will says to Bryce.

Bryce turns from the table. "I'll text you, ok?"

"Ok."

"Bye, Will," I say, following Bryce.

"Bye, Matty. Thanks for coming."

The nickname makes me smile.

"Are you really gonna text him?" I ask Bryce when we get onto the footpath outside *Shakes*.

Bryce huffs and his shoulders droop. "I just said it."

I go home with Bryce and we retreat to his bedroom. We pull the comforter around our bodies and stare into each other's eyes.

"Why don't we kiss anymore?" he whispers.

"What?"

"We don't kiss like we use to. We hold hands, we hug, but we don't kiss."

"I'm in your bed with you."

"I know, and I love that, but I miss kissing you whenever I want.

It feels like I'm not allowed to."

I pull the comforter tighter around my body. "It's not like that. I dunno, it's me, I guess."

"You don't trust me or something?"

"No, no, it's not that. I guess, uh, I dunno. It's like I realise I'm keeping us apart and it's not what I want, but maybe I need time."

His lips quirk as his hand slides under my side of the comforter. "After today, I've realised how much I need you."

I pan my gaze over the bed and rest my eyes on him. "You have me. Or does it only count if we make out?"

"No. But if we do make out, it makes me feel more secure. Like, we really are back together."

My hand smooths over my *no-longer-flat* belly and I force a smile. "I feel changed. Like, I'm not the girl you fell for."

His finger traces my jawline. "But I never fell out of love for you."

I lean close and kiss his lips, keeping the lump of bed covering between us.

"I'm sorry if seeing Will was too much for you," I whisper. "Is it bad that I didn't say anything?"

"We ripped off the band-aid," he replies flatly.

"Do you want to see him again?"

"It was so awkward. I dunno if I wanna do that again."

"If you want me to go with you, I will."

He smiles and kisses the top of my head. "Thanks, Britty."

"Why didn't you ever tell me Will crashed the car because he was texting?"

His eyes become round with shock.

"Will told me," I say.

"I saw it right before he veered off the road. I couldn't stop him.

I'm sorry."

"It's not your fault he did it."

"I didn't want him to get into trouble," he whispers, sadness clouding his eyes. "I didn't want you to know. I wanted to protect you and I didn't want you to be mad at me for not stopping it."

"You need to stop blaming yourself for other peoples' issues."

His expression lifts. "Have you just met me?"

Lazy giggles seep out of me. "I'm kinda tired. Mind if I sleep here?"

His smile slides to the left. "Only if I get to cuddle you."

I swallow hard and remove the mess of comforter between us. I shuffle closer and let him wrap up his smaller spoon. I interlace his fingers with mine and they rest beside my body.

I'm excited to see Nick perform on stage. He's performing the single he recorded in the studio, plus a bunch of covers the management picked for him. I can't believe he's transforming into a popstar. That's so freakin cool!

But does it have to be at an event commemorating the day I almost died? Ok, ok, I know it celebrates Kellie's birthday, but the images of lying in a hospital bed keep flooding into my mind. I worked hard to hide the memories of nurses showering me, Mum feeding me, the pain of sitting, and the agony of relearning to walk.

As I clasp my earrings in front of my dresser mirror, Bryce paces the length of my bedroom. He will wear the carpet thin, he's so frantic. I turn from the mirror and Bryce's breaths quicken. His face is ghostly white except for the dark circles under his eyes.

"B, are you hyperventilating?" I wrap my arm around his shoulders and move him to the end of the bed. "Sit down. Just breathe.

Slow. In and out, nice and slow."

He hunches over, chest heaving, but his breathing slows and becomes more regular.

I rub his back. "You ok?"

"I don't think I can go," he whispers. "I know I have to. That I should. But I can't. I keep seeing her dying over and over."

I slide my hand across his cheek and whisper, "We don't have to go."

"Huh?"

"We were the last ones with her. We will always remember her. This party is for everyone else. Why don't we go to the beach? We'll be alone while the rest of the town is at *Horton Park*. Why don't we use tonight to celebrate moving on?" I rest my forehead against his and close my eyes. "Together."

He nods against my forehead. "Ok, let's do that."

"I'm sorry I shouldn't be making tonight about me," Bryce says as we hold hands and walk across the sand.

"What?"

"You had it worse than me and Kellie... I just shouldn't be—"

"Stop," I say while tugging on his hand and dropping a throw rug onto the sand. We sit. "Don't say things like that. You're entitled to hurt."

"I should be taking care of you," he says, playing with the ring on my finger. "You never took this off."

"I never will."

"You want to stay with me?"

"Forever." I lean in and tease his lips with a light brush of mine.

His breathy laugh tickles my lips and his arms lock around my waist. "Can you just kiss me already?"

I laugh so much it ripples through my gut. I toss my arms around his neck and push my lips against his. I kiss him like it's the first time. Like it's the first time it's mattered. I kiss him like he's the only person who matters. The person I love the most. My person.

We pull out of the kiss and I open my eyes to the biggest smile.

"We're ok." He says it, doesn't ask it. "I'm never letting you go."

I snuggle into him and watch the moonlight glisten over the dark, crashing waves as the salty air becomes mist around us. "We're stronger together."

23

Charli

At group therapy, Mariah suggests not to delve too deep when planning Kellie's celebration. The panic attack triggered by the mention of Travis told me to focus on having a good time at the event. The party of Kellie's dreams.

Ha! Party of her dreams? I don't know if Kellie would want the whole town at *Horton Park*. I think she'd prefer to be in the forest, smoking something green.

Eep. I gotta stop thinking about that stuff. I plant a hand over my chest and inhale deeply, exhale slowly. Kellie would have quit if she had seen me abuse the stuff. She'd be the best support system. If Brittany's life had been taken and Kellie was still here, she would never have let me fall as far as I did. Even if I kept shutting her out, she would keep opening the door between us.

Not that Brittany was able to do that for me. Brittany was a victim and I failed her.

Tonight, is about rectifying everything. All the pain, all the loss. We need to heal and move forward. I promise to be a better person every single day. I promise to rethink every selfish thought. Mariah suggested counting to five, but I don't believe that works. I just need to think of others instead of myself. That's why I want to leave this town. I want to leave and help those who have no one.

Reece's brothers came home for the memorial and his dad made it off the ship in time. It's good to see Steven again to apologise for snapping at him all that time ago. He gives me the best hug. A bunch of us are going, so we take two cars to *Horton Park*. Mrs Watkins made me promise to talk to my parents tonight. It's a big ask, but if I'm going to be less selfish, I have to start somewhere. Why not tackle the hardest thing first?

Reece and I break away from his family as we enter the park. A stage is set, ready for Nick and the headlining band to perform. We walk around the groups of people and I'm surprised so many have turned up. The decorations are green and purple, Kellie's favourite colours. Some local restaurants set up food stalls along one end of the park and Mrs Watkins organised the Tully Beach Arcade to setup games at another end. The behind-the-scenes logistics have been insane. I'm kinda glad they kept me out, I'm spinning at just the thought.

"There's a lot of people here," Reece says, just loud enough for me to hear.

"I know, it's crazy. Think Kellie would like it?"

He nods. "She'd like it."

"Oh, look," I say. "It's Kellie's family. We should go over and say hi."

We move over to the Commander and Mrs Saunders and I wave to Kellie's younger brother, Bailey.

"Charli, Reece," Mrs Saunders says, smiling with shiny eyes. "How are you both?"

"We're good," I reply. "How are you guys doing?"

The Commander places a hand on his wife's shoulder and nods with a firm smile. "This was a superb idea. Kellie will be looking down, annoyed she can't enjoy this with us."

I nudge Bailey and smile. "She's here though."

He gives me a limp smile and nods.

"Do you want to hang with us?" Reece asks Bailey.

Bailey looks to his parents. "Can I?"

"Sure, go ahead," Mrs Saunders replies.

"We'll just be a little further up," I tell them.

We find a spot close to the stage but off to the side, and I ask Bailey, "How old are you now?"

"Ten," he replies.

"*Wowza,*" I say. "No wonder you're so tall."

"Whatever," Bailey laughs, lively like Kellie.

I ask Reece, "Did you want to get something to eat first?"

"Nah, let's watch him perform first," Reece replies.

I smile and sit on the grass beside him. Seeing Reece excited for Nick to perform is cute. It weirds me out I didn't see their friendship happen, but if Nick makes Reece this happy, I can't be mad. Hopefully, they will be ok when they see each other after how things ended. Being pulled between the two of them after that kiss was awkward.

We sit in silence on the grass and, before long, the crowd cheers. I crane my neck and see Nick walking over stage, his guitar strapped to his shoulder.

Nick waves to the crowd and I eye Reece, standing as he does.

"Hi, everyone," Nick says into the microphone. "Unfortunately, I didn't know Kellie. Sometimes, she would visit my house with my sister Brittany when they would hang with their boyfriends. Kellie was always nice and I remember hearing her laugh at her own jokes. I wish I had gotten to know her. She seemed like a cool person. You always think there will be more time." Nick strums a few chords as he continues, "Kellie was especially close with my friend Reece and step sister Charli. She meant a lot to them and I'm so sad that they lost their best friend. I hope tonight they remember the good times and know no one is ever really gone. I was told this was her favourite song."

Nick steps away from the microphone and strums a different tune as someone steps behind the drums and other musicians take the stage. My heart hammers and my eyes weep as I instantly recognise *'A Case of You'* by Joni Mitchell.

By the stage, a tall and wide white screen lights up and images and video of Kellie filter in and out. I sniff back a tear as another two roll down my cheek before I can catch them.

Nick's voice is magnificent. His cover of the song is low and slow. It's different, in a perfect way, and it complements the slideshow. My chest grows tight as I imagine the work Travis put in to make the slideshow so captivating. A video of Kellie and I cuddled on the couch crosses the screen and I dip my face into my hands.

Arms wrap around me and I lift my head to double take at Reece hugging me. His eyes are red. I lay my head against his. I take in Nick's performance and shivers run down my limbs. There's an overwhelming feeling that Kellie is hugging us too.

The rest of Nick's set is upbeat and poppy. From what I remember of his band with Zach, they were into rock music, so it's an interesting change of pace. Nick sways with his guitar, stamps his foot with the drumbeats, and bops to the pop rhythm.

Girls from school—the likes of Chloe, Meah and Fiona—dance in front of the stage, squealing and jumping to the song covers they recognise.

"I wish Brit were here to see this," I say to Reece.

"Where is she?" he asks.

"She texted to tell me that she's spending the night at the beach with Bryce. They might come by later, but they're finding it too hard to cope with."

"Hey, Charli," my step sister Shae says, landing by us after Nick finishes his performance. "How are you? Haven't seen you by the house."

I chew inside my lip, eyeing her apprehensive smile. "You know why."

Shae sighs, looking away. "I know. I'm sorry. I wish you and your dad could see eye-to-eye. I'd be happy to mediate for you before I go back to uni."

"I dunno. To be honest, I don't wanna talk about that stuff tonight," I say. "Just because you're becoming a social worker, doesn't mean you can fix the mess at home."

"I get that." Shae rubs my shoulder and her smile grows genuine. "I miss you and want you to be happy. Did you like Nicky's set?"

I nod, grinning. "He's crazy talented. I loved his interpretation of 'A Case of You'."

Shae rubs her heart. She's smiling and her eyes are shining. "Oh gosh, he was up all night because he was worried he would mess up.

And the video was so moving. I literally teared up. Who made that?"

I throw a thumb back at Reece and blurt, "His cousin."

She nods to Reece. "Ok, cool. Mum's backstage with Nick. Wanna see him?"

I go to answer 'no', but Reece gets in before me with, "Could we?"

The enthusiasm brightening his face warms my heart, so I nod to Shae. "Ok, let's go."

We walk Bailey to his parents and then move backstage to meet Nick. A playlist of Kellie's favourite songs plays through the sound system before *Faux Wish* appears on stage to end the night.

"No, Mum, I feel like a fraud," Nick snaps as we make our way backstage. "Did you see those people dancing in front of the stage? At school, they hate my guts, but then I sing some songs I didn't write, and they like me? No way. It makes me sick."

"Nicky?" Shae asks, hurrying her pace to meet her brother. "What's going on?"

Nick turns to his sister, hunched and exhausted. He wraps his arms around Shae and buries his head in the nape of her neck.

"Nicky," Shae says, rubbing his back. "Why are you upset? You did such an amazing job."

Nick pulls out of her arms, shaking his head. "I can't play what I want to play. Everything they get me to record is so unlike me. They want me to play this role. I thought I could do it, but seeing those girls dancing in front of the stage..."

"They liked it," Shae replies.

"But that music is not me," Nick says, tapping his chest. "It's not *me* they like." He huffs and pivots away from her, getting a glimpse of Reece and me. "Oh, guys, hey."

"Hey," I say as Reece lifts a hand to wave.

"Charli," Tara says, moving close to me. "It's been a lovely night, hasn't it?"

"Yeah, it has." I look at Nick and say, "Thank you so much for playing. Your cover of *'A Case of You'* was perfect."

Nick's face softens. "I'm glad. That was my favourite part of the set."

"Kellie would have loved it," Reece adds.

"Would she have hated the rest?" Nick asks, his anxiety peaking.

"No," I say quickly. "It was hard to get Kellie to hate anything."

"She liked Joni Mitchell and I played that crap afterwards," Nick says, pain in his eyes.

"She made me listen to K-pop," Reece says.

I smile at Nick. "She would have liked it, don't be so hard on yourself."

"Coop!" Zach cheers as he rounds the stage. "What a legend!"

I step back as Zach bear-hugs Nick.

Tara moves with me. "Your father is being his stubborn self, but he wants to talk to you."

"He does?"

Tara places a hand on the middle of my back. "Will you come out with me and see him?"

"I'm not in the mood to be yelled at."

"Hunny, I'm not going to let that happen." Tara smiles and pushes back one of my curls. "Tonight is about healing, right? Just talk to him for a few minutes."

The pain in my stomach radiates throughout my torso. Reece is by the other boys so perhaps this is the best time to get the Dad issue over and done with.

I sigh. "Ok, let's do it."

"Nicky, I'll be right back," Tara says, but Nick barely

acknowledges her because he's wrapped up with Zach and Shae.

I follow Tara out into the crowd and my stomach sloshes. I was lucky, this week I was able to avoid talking to Dad. I replied to a few texts and ignored the rest. Thankfully, he never came around to Reece's house. But I'm never going to get what I want if I don't talk to him.

"Charli?" Mum calls out.

I stop dead and find her to my left. She paces toward me, her face a mix of concern and annoyance.

"I've been looking for you," Mum says, her eyes flicking to Tara as her jaw clenches.

"Hi," I answer, not knowing what else to say.

"We were just going to Rob," Tara says. "Do you want to join us so we can—"

"Excuse me," Mum rushes. "Are you suggesting I let you arrange an important discussion with my daughter and her father?"

"No," Tara says, shrinking. "I wanted you to join us. It's a family discussion, after all."

"You don't have any say over her," Mum snaps.

I throw my hands up. "*Ugh*, forget it!"

"Charli," Mum and Tara both say, but I move away.

"I'm not doing this right now," I say, quickening my pace to get away from them.

I flex my fingers, focusing on lowering my body heat, when someone taps my shoulder. I turn around and almost fall over at the sight of Kimmy Jones.

"Hi," she says softly. "Can I talk to you for a minute?"

I smile with surprise. "Yeah, sure."

"This is a really nice night," Kimmy says. "Thanks for making it an open invitation."

"Thanks for coming," I say, not sure I mean it.

Kimmy blows out a breath, looking down and shifting her feet. "Look, I'm sorry for being a bitch to you at school."

My eyebrows lift and I'm too stunned to reply.

She meets my eyes. "I was obsessed with popularity. I literally didn't care my friends were bitches. I was in, and I liked it."

"Ok?"

"But I got ditched last year." Her eyes gleam with sadness. "I still hang with them, but I know they want me to get lost. You heard what Fi did."

She says it like a statement, but I have no idea.

"Sean cheated on me with her," Kimmy elaborates.

"What?" I gasp. "Isn't she your friend?"

Kimmy shrugs. "I thought so. And no one even cares. No one said anything to her." She waves her hands. "Anyway, that's not the point. It just hit me like a freight train. I had this amazing kickass friend I ditched for no reason. That made me sad, but then I remembered our fun adventures and they made me happy."

A hint of a smile tingles my lips. "They were epic. Especially finding the cave at the base of the lookout."

"We had so much courage together. I didn't realise how much I missed that."

I fidget in place, an unexpected sorrow washing over me. "Me too."

"I'm sorry about Kellie," she says. "She was an actual friend. Losing her was not fair on you. I've feel like I've had no one and that made me realise how bad you must have felt. I wanted you to know I was thinking about you."

"Wow," I murmur as the weight of this hits me. "That's really nice of you, Kim."

She hangs a thumb behind her. "Anyway, I'm heading home.

Maybe I'll see you around sometime."

I nod. "Maybe."

She walks away and I feel like there's an anvil on my chest. Did that really happen?

I meander through the crowd, letting a mess of thoughts swim around in my brain.

It's as if the crowd parts perfectly on cue and all the streetlights shine on him. His chocolate curls, his broad shoulders, the fullness of his lips. Travis.

He waves and mouths, 'Hi.'

My feet sink into the earth. I'm immobilised.

He takes a step forward and waits for me to react before taking another step.

I manage to nod and he continues towards me.

"Hi," he says, standing in front of me. "How are you? Ah, sorry, that was dumb."

My heart knocks in my chest as he winces. I swallow hard and say, "I'm good. You?"

He nods, trying to smile. "I'm good. You look good."

My eyebrows lift. "I do?"

His smile spreads. "Yeah. I'm glad I got to see you. Just… sorry for the reason."

I clear my throat and almost meet his eyes. "Me too. Thank you for the video. It was amazing."

He takes in a sharp breath. "Really? I was so nervous about it. I didn't want to stuff it up or make it uncomfortable for you."

I shake my head and smile. "It was great. Really, thank you."

His shoulders relax. "I'm glad. It was no problem. I could never get rid of the footage, I still had it on a hard drive. My aunt has a copy for you."

"Ok."

"You're living with them, right?"

I nod. "Reece's family? Yeah."

"A lot has changed over the past year."

"Ahuh."

I bunch my curls to the side as he shifts his weight.

He fidgets like there's something he wants to bring up. Something like 'what was rehab like?'

"Uh," we both say at once.

He laughs with nervous awkwardness. "Sorry, go ahead."

"No, it's ok," I say, gesturing for him to speak.

He rubs his lips together, thinking over his words.

I take the opportunity to change the subject. "How's uni?"

He puffs out a breath. "It's going, I guess. I'm in my second year of the business degree my dad wanted, so he's happy."

I hug my waist. "What about film?"

He shrugs. "I dunno."

I drop my arms and take in the beautiful lines of his face and carefree waves of his hair. "You were happy when you were working on films, right?"

A smile brightens his face. "Yeah. I was. I am."

Staring up at his face, I can't help it, I have to say it. "You look really good too."

His dark brown eyes shine with familiar warmth. He whispers, "I've missed you."

I take in a breath and nod. *Me too.*

"I tried to get in touch," Travis says, sliding his hands into his pockets. "I'm sorry, I probably made it worse. I didn't know where to start."

"It wasn't you," I say. "I wasn't in a good place."

"I get that," he says, staring into my eyes. "I understood at the time too, but I wanted you to know I was thinking about you."

My heart *ba-booms* and for a moment I forget how to breathe.

He takes a step in and places his hand by mine. "How are you doing?" he whispers. "This can't be easy, having all the memories brought back."

"I'm doing ok," I reply. "I've talked about it a lot in therapy to prepare myself and this is the fun stuff. I can see Kellie laughing and being goofy here."

Travis laughs. "Yeah, I can see that too." His face grows serious. "I'm glad you're getting help."

I bite inside my cheek and nod. "Me too. I really didn't want help, but it's a real lifeline now."

"I'll bet. I hate that you felt so alone."

My eyes well. "Trav, I..." my voice quivers so much I can't bear to finish the sentence.

His expression drops and concern rounds his eyes. "What? What's wrong?"

I want to tell you I miss you. I want to tell you I forgive you. I want to tell you I want to be with you.

But my stomach churns and my knees knock.

I close my eyes to dry the tears and rub my arms. "Nothing. Just cold."

"Well, here."

I open my eyes to him, slipping off his jacket. "Oh no, you don't have to."

He drapes the jacket over my shoulders. "Better?"

His cologne lingers around me and I feel a mix of being home and wanting to keel over. "Thank you."

His hands stay on my shoulders and slip down my back. I watch his neck as he swallows and I'm sure I hear his heartbeat.

"How long are you in town?" I ask.

"I—"

"Travy!" a squeaky voice calls out from behind me.

I grit my teeth, looking over my shoulder as Meah skips towards us with Chloe strutting along behind.

Travis and I break apart as he replies to his sister. "Yeah?"

Meah jumps to a stop beside me with her hand out towards Travis. She goes to respond to Travis, but double takes me. "Oh, hey, Charli. Nice party. Good job."

"Thanks?" I say.

Meah nods. "Seriously. It really seems like Kellie. You should be proud."

I almost gasp. "Wow, thanks, Meah."

Meah turns to her brother, palm flat toward the sky. "I need cash."

"I'm not your ATM," Travis replies.

As they bicker, a hand grabs my shoulder and yanks me back. I spin with alarm and find the smiling faces of Tayla and Lenny.

"Need saving?" Tayla murmurs, her fake smile faltering.

"Ah, I—"

"Come with us," Lenny says, cutting me off.

I look back to Travis. Chloe drapes an arm around him, saying, "*John Thomas* hasn't been the same without you."

He lifts a finger in my direction, signalling to give him a minute and he'll catch up with me.

Not wanting to see another moment of Chloe in action, or to hear Meah's squawking, I go with Tayla and Lenny. When he's clear of the fake blonde girls, Travis will find me to retrieve his jacket.

Lenny hugs his arm around me and Tayla walks on my other side, keeping me close and away from danger.

When we reach the other side of the park, I say, "I was ok."

"It seemed awkward," Lenny says, stepping away from me.

"Only because I haven't seen him in over a year," I say. "But I was fine. We were fine."

"We wanted to give you an out if you needed it," Tayla says.

"Thanks. I guess it could have taken a wrong turn eventually. At least you got me away from Chloe and Meah."

"Amen to that," Tayla jokes.

I slip my arms into the sleeves of the jacket and pull it closed. I eye the direction we came from but don't see Travis through the crowd.

"Do you know where Reece is?" I ask Lenny and Tayla.

"Yeah," Lenny says, craning his neck to peer around the food stalls. "I saw him not too long ago with one of his brothers."

"He wasn't with Nick?" I question.

"We haven't seen Nick," Tayla says. "I've been busting too though. I'm dying to tell him how well he did. Wasn't that performance epic?"

I nod. "I agree, but Nick wasn't very pleased with it."

"What? Why not?"

I shrug. "Something about it being too pop."

"Yeah, it didn't seem his style," Lenny agrees.

"Oh," Tayla says flatly. "Well, I still liked it."

"There they are," Lenny says, pointing to the left.

I turn and see Reece. He's trailing behind Nick, who's talking with Madi and Zach.

"Should we join them?" I ask hesitantly.

Tayla grabs my hand. "C'mon. Let's catch up to them before they get further away."

The three of us jog towards them, Tayla calling out for them to 'wait up.'

Lenny and Tayla fall into easy conversation, while Reece and I hang back.

"How are you doing?" I ask Reece.

He nods. "Good. But there's a lot of people here."

"Ironic. You're here for Kellie when we know Kellie would have taken you home by now."

A smile cracks his face. "Yeah. But it hasn't been too bad." He looks up to the sky. "It's like she's up there telling people to be orderly and not so loud."

I laugh. "Sounds like her."

"All right, everyone," Lenny calls our attention. "Best Kellie story you've got."

Tayla swats a hand, grinning. "Easy. The time she pinned down Greg Francis when he stole my backpack."

"What?" My gasp mixes with laughter. "When was this?"

"Sixth grade," Tayla continues. "He was calling me names and she held him down until he took them back."

I grin. "I didn't know about that."

Tayla giggles, nodding. "That girl freakin rocked."

"The one time she tried skateboarding," Reece says, his smile growing.

I tear up and smile. "Oh, that was such a good day."

Reece gazes at the starry sky and smirks. "She was so bad at it."

I wipe my eyes dry as Lenny recalls the story of how Kellie saved him from detention by giving him a crash-course study session. It's all too real that our smart and cool friend is gone. She brought us together and it sucks that tonight will be our final story of her.

"I'm sorry I didn't get to know her that well," Madison says, eyeing me with sincerity. "There was this time she tried to get out of

P.E. and Ms Harvey was having none of it. Chloe tried to target her with a basketball, but Kellie had quick reflexes. I dunno. She always seemed like a cool chick."

I swallow hard as my stomach wobbles. I don't love that her story is twisted with the stories of mean girls, but it's a nice reminder that Kellie didn't take any shit. Even from me.

"If she were here, she would have shaken sense into me months ago," I say, sniffing back a tear. "She'd have done it gently. She knew how to get me talking. She'd ask the right questions or distract me with anime. At the time it sucked, but I love looking back to when we cycled into the forest after I found out my dad was leaving."

Reece rubs my arm and Lenny fidgets in place, crossing his arms and looking up at the stars with a smile. Nick's lips press firmly together, and he backs slightly away from the group.

"Kellie was my biggest cheerleader and comfort," I say. "Man, such great hugs."

"*Such* great hugs," Tayla agrees, looping an arm around me.

Laughter seeps out of Reece. "Such great hugs."

The night drifts to an end and I give Mrs Watkins the biggest hug, thanking her for all the effort she put in to put this together.

"Make sure you let your step brother know how much we appreciate his efforts tonight," Mrs Watkins says as we break apart.

"You coming home with us?" Shae says, staring at me like she's trying to hypnotise me.

"Ah, no, I..."

She gently touches my arm. "Why don't we go for a walk? We can talk things out on the way and you can decide where you want to spend the night. I'll drive you to your friend's house if that's what you want."

My shoulders bunch. "I dunno."

"You don't have to," she says, "but it could be good to talk to someone new. Get things off your chest?"

I look past her to Dad and Tara, opening the doors of the car. "Ok. If you don't mind the walk uphill."

Shae's arm slides around my shoulders. "Not at all. Mum, Charli and I will walk."

Tara beams at us. "Ok, hunny. Stick to the lighted paths."

Dad peers over the top of the car. "You're coming home, Charli?"

I nod. "Maybe."

His smile is weak. "I hope so."

With Alyssa and Nick in the backseat, the family drive away.

"Call me later tonight," Mrs Watkins says, moving to her car.

"I will."

"Have a nice night?" Shae asks as we start along the footpath.

"Yeah, I can't believe so many people turned up."

"Kellie must have been a very special person."

I grin. "She was."

"I hope Nick's ok," Shae whispers. "He was so upset after his performance."

"Did he talk to you while he was in the studio?"

"Yeah, he said it was a lot of work and long hours, but as far as I could tell he was enjoying it."

"I hope he sticks to it. I mean, it's his dream, right?"

Shae nods. "Right. And what about you? What's your dream? You wanted to be a lawyer?"

I shake my head and scuff my shoes. "Nope. That dream is long dead and buried."

"So, what do you want?"

I rub my palms over my eyes. "That's a loaded question. I feel so scattered.”

“Is that why you want to drop out of school?”

“I just don’t care enough to try.”

“That doesn’t sound like you.”

“I dunno, maybe it is me. I think it’s the first time I’ve ever tried to find me. When I was a kid, I constantly looked for adventure. Then in high school, I put all my focus into impressing Dad and got no results. I think I want adventure again.”

“You’ve only got one more year of school. You can’t push through?”

I smirk. “Did my dad ask you to say that?”

Shae laughs. “Your dad would want me to be a lot more direct than that.”

“Yeah. *Push through. It’s one year.*”

“Wow, wonderful Rob impression.”

“Heard it a few times,” I snigger. “I just can’t push myself. I didn’t mind being a loner, but now I’m a total outcast. I don’t fit in with the people I used to fit in with.”

“Is that because of Kellie?”

“*Ugh*, it’d have to be my reaction to losing Kellie. She helped me focus on school. Without her, I went wayward. I also hate the idea of staying behind another year with Brittany at uni. That would be hell.”

“But what are you going to do without your high school certificate?”

“I don’t need a piece of paper to do things,” I say with a huff. “I want to go overseas and volunteer. Like build houses or teach English.”

“*Habitat For Humanity?*”

I nod. “Something like that.”

“That’d be a great thing to do. But isn’t it usually something you do during the summer between high school and uni? Like, a gap year thing?”

“No. I’ve met people who do it constantly. They get a job to save up money and they complete a few projects each year.”

“And that’s what you want to do? Have a crummy retail job and fly to other countries to help *their* vulnerable people?”

I stop walking. “Why do I detect some resentment in your voice?”

She stops and turns to me. “It doesn’t sound like much of a plan.”

My teeth grind and fingers flex. “Why? Because it’s not: go to uni and study something I might end up hating?”

Shae swats a hand. “Forget it. I don’t want to upset you. Especially not tonight when you’re supposed to be filled with happy thoughts of your friend.”

A pain radiates between my eyes and I plonk down on the gutter. “Kellie would ask me all these kinds of questions too.”

Shae steps beside me and crouches. “Really?”

“Well, in a nicer way,” I say with a smile.

“Sorry,” Shae says, sitting. “Have you thought all this through?”

“Yes. I hate school. And this town. I don’t want to be here anymore. I want to move to the city, find a job, and save to go overseas.”

“You don’t want to find a job here in Sanford?”

“No. Here, my mum and dad will constantly remind me I’m wasting my time and should be in school. They wouldn’t be supportive.”

“You want to be far away from them?”

“Just not in the same town. I still love them and all, but it’s too hard. They always make me feel like I’m doing something wrong. The only way I can thrive is to be away from them.”

“Come back to the house with me,” Shae says, resting her hand over mine. “I’d like to suggest to Mum and Rob that you come to

Sydney with me."

My eyes widen. "What?"

"You're miserable here and my couch folds out. I can help you find a place and a job. If you want?"

I bite inside my lip then smile. "You'd really do that?"

She rests her head on mine. "We're sisters."

My eyes become wet and I nod. "What will Dad say?"

"Will he prefer you to be happy or unhappy?"

A nervous laugh tumbles out of me. "I don't know. Whichever one makes him happy?"

"Charli," Shae whispers. "He loves you. He wants you to be happy."

We get to Dad's and I let Shae take the lead.

"So, Charli's been living with her friend because you and her mum can't come to terms with the fact that she wants to quit school," Shae begins.

"Quitting isn't the answer," Dad argues.

Shae lifts a hand. "Rob, please hear me out."

Dad crosses his arms and puffs out his chest, but his face softens as he waits for Shae.

"She shouldn't be away from her family," Shae says, rubbing my shoulder.

Tara nods, looking me in the eyes.

"But she doesn't want to be here." She takes in a big breath before continuing. "That's why I've offered for her to live with me for a while."

"What?" Dad snaps.

"Oh, Shae, that's nice but..." Tara trails off.

"Why are you enabling her?" Dad asks.

I roll my eyes. "*Dad*. Shae is actually listening to me. *And* Tara, for that matter. Why can't you be reasonable?"

"And what exactly are you going to do in Sydney?" Dad asks, a cocky smirk at his lips.

"Find a job and apartment," I say, trying to stand tall.

"*Ha*. With what qualifications? With what money?"

"Rob," Tara hushes. "Don't put her down."

"She's a child," Dad argues.

"I'll work it out," I say, stamping a foot. "I'll stay with Shae till I find a job, then find a room to rent. I have confidence in me, I wish you would too. When I quit or find a new direction, it isn't a reflection on you. I want to be my own person."

"Give us a moment to discuss this," Tara says to me with a wink.

I'm not entirely ready to stop arguing, but my dad listens to Tara, so I leave the kitchen and head toward the living room.

"I'm sad you're not going on tour," Brittany says, sitting by Nick on the couch. "But I'm so happy to have you home. I've missed your face."

Nick smiles. "Thanks, Brit. I've missed you too."

"Sorry, I missed your performance," Brittany says.

"Oh, that's ok. Don't worry about it."

"I wanted to see you, but Bryce was having panic attacks," she says. "His doctor said he probably has that PTSD thingy from the accident."

"Oh," Nick says, worry creasing his face. "Would you have it? Because you were in the same accident?"

Brit recoils. "No, I don't think so. I mean, everyone else talking about it is more of an issue than my own head."

"Maybe it wouldn't hurt to see someone about it," I suggest, moving further into the room. "A counsellor or something."

"No," she snaps. "No, I don't want a therapist."

"But if you know it helps Bryce and me…"

"No. I don't like that stuff."

I put my hands up. "Ok. Is Bryce ok?"

"He's doing much better," Brittany says. "Not going to Kellie's memorial tonight was a good idea. I hoped you liked it."

"It was great."

"Where were you?" Nick grumbles at Shae as she enters the room.

"You know I was walking home with Charli," Shae says.

"*Well*, I need to talk to you too," Nick complains.

"Don't get huffy. I'm here," Shae says.

Nick storms up the hall to his bedroom with Shae following.

"He's leaving the tour?" I ask Brittany.

She nods. "They don't let him play any of the originals he wrote. Dad tried to talk him around, saying it was a stepping stone to playing his own stuff, but Nick doesn't want to budge. He said he feels like a fraud."

I move back into the kitchen to find Dad. "You're letting Nick quit?"

"He's going back to school," Dad replies, irritated.

"How can you be so supportive of him but not me?"

"He's pursuing a career. You don't have any direction."

"Yes, I do! It's just not a direction you approve of."

"Please, do you two have to repeat this?" Tara whines. "Alyssa's gone to bed. I really don't want her getting up again."

"Promise me you'll sign the paperwork to get me out of school," I say, burning a hole through Dad's eyes.

He throws his hands up in surrender. "Fine. If you want to throw your life away, I won't stop you."

"Not totally encouraging," I say, backing away. "But I'll take it."

I move back to the living room where Brittany's eyes bulge from their sockets. "You're really dropping out of school?"

"I hate it, Brit. I don't want to be there for another second."

Her eyes shine. "This sucks. I'm gonna miss you so much."

I drape my arm around her shoulder and play with her lush hair. "The school year will be over soon, then you can move to the city too."

"I want to come with you."

"Stay and get through school. You're good at it. Besides, you have Bryce and everyone else to support you."

"They'd all support you too."

"I can't do it anymore."

She pulls me into a hug. "I know."

Heavy footsteps come our way.

"What's wrong?" Brittany asks as Nick enters the room with a huff.

"Just a stupid argument with Shae," he murmurs.

"About leaving the tour?" Brittany asks.

Nick smirks. "Nope. About church."

"Why?" she asks.

"She asked me about service in the morning," he says, "and I told her I wasn't going."

"You're not?" I ask.

"It's not exactly the most welcoming place for me now," he says, flopping on the couch.

"Because you came out?" Brittany asks, horrified.

"Before I left, I felt the distinct shift in how people treated me," Nick says. "I don't want to go back and be around that."

"That's fair," I say. "You shouldn't have to be around people who treat you like shit."

Nick eyes me like he appreciates what I said, but wishes it came from someone else's lips.

Why do I bother with him?

Brittany's ringtone buzzes from her pocket. She pulls out her phone. "Oh, it's Bryce. I'll be right back."

When Brittany leaves the room, I have a massive urge to follow her out. *Don't leave me alone with him.*

"I see you stole Reece while I was gone," Nick mutters.

A stabbing pain shoots through my gut. "What?"

"He went running back to you after we kissed." Nick runs his hands over his face. "He picked you."

"Reece is my best friend," I argue. "And he didn't *pick* me. We have a history, but at least he let you kiss him."

Nick's frowns. "What?"

I sigh and shrug. "When I tried to kiss him, he pulled away. You're close to him in a way I can never be." There's an ease to Reece's relationship with Nick that he doesn't have with me. I crack my knuckles. "Stop throwing it in my face."

"Throwing it in your face? He said if he chose to be with someone, it'd be with you."

I roll my eyes. "He didn't know what he was saying."

"He doesn't lie."

"Don't get mad at Shae for talking to me," I fire back, anger boiling my veins. "I didn't come in here all agitated because you were talking to Brittany."

"Whatever," he mumbles.

I groan and leave the room to find Brittany. Maybe it will be a good thing to leave with Shae if Nick comes home. The last thing I need to see is him getting on better with my family than I do.

I wrap Travis' jacket around me in the hallway. I didn't see him again to return it, but I think it will be nice to go to bed wearing it.

24

Brittany

Charli's gone. It was only a few months ago that I didn't want her to come home and now I miss her like crazy.

"She left so soon after Kellie's party," Reece says when we're on the topic of Charli during our library study session.

"Shae had to get back for classes," I say. "But she was desperate to leave town."

"She's doing ok?"

"Yeah. Why, are you two not talking?"

"No, we text. I was making sure she wasn't just putting on a brave face."

"Oh. As far as I can tell she's having a good time. I think she's happy. She's free."

"I'm glad."

I sigh. "Mum's so mad."

"Because Charli left?"

"Because Dad and Tara left her out of the decision-making. She was backed into a corner and felt forced to agree to Charli leaving school and moving away."

Reece shrugs. "She was already living with me."

"But that wasn't permanent." I bite my lip and add, "She refuses to talk to Charli when she calls."

"Poor Charli."

"Every time I think she will make up with Mum and Dad, there's something else that drives a wedge between them."

"As long as she's happy."

"It's so weird without her. I know she was overseas for months and then she was in rehab for weeks, but this time is different. I felt like we were actually becoming friends."

"I know. We were good too."

I nudge him. "At least we will all be in the city next year."

His lips twist. "I'm not ready for that change."

"Your brothers are there, aren't they?"

"Sometimes. Depends on their work."

"We'll work it out together."

"It will be weird."

When we finish our notes, we leave the library for the quad. On the way, Tayla and Madi slink out of the gym, giggling to each other.

"Hey, what's going on?" I ask.

They link arms as they try to shake their giggles.

"Just watching cheer practice," Madison smirks.

Tayla splutters a laugh. "They're terrible."

"Terrible?" I say, grinning.

"I don't know what happened," Madison says, suppressing her laughter. "But they've lost the plot."

"Or did they always look that bad?" Tayla asks. "And we never noticed because we were in it?"

"Oh, c'mon. *We* were never that bad," Madison says.

"Sounds like they're missing you guys," I say.

"Maybe they've gone too long without you on the squad," Madi suggests.

I shake my head. "Uh, no. It's got nothin to do with me."

"What will Queen Bee Chloe be like next year with no high school to run?" Madi asks, a devilish smile playing on her lips. "She must be freaking out."

I nod as a grin pushes at my cheeks. "It'll all be over soon."

"What were you guys doing?" Tayla asks.

"Working on our economics assignment," I say.

"*Eww*," the girls say in unison.

Reece shrugs. "Has to be done."

"Did you see Nick in there?" Madi asks.

"Nick?" I question.

"He and Nav got assigned to work on a project in our religious studies class. They said they'd work on it at lunch," Madi says. "I was wondering where they were hiding out."

"Haven't seen them," Reece says.

"I need to eat something," I say. "Either of you seen Bryce?"

"Maybe mess hall," Tayla says. "At least it'll only be the boys in there."

At that, I grin. "True. Wanna check it out with me?"

The girls agree to follow me and when Reece screws his face up at mention of the dining hall, Tayla tells him Lenny and Simon are out on the quad.

With Reece on his way outside, the girls walk with me to the mess hall. This strange queasiness takes over me every time I walk into it. This place was once my safety net but now I'm walking a tightrope without a harness.

As we approach their table, Sean gestures in my direction. "BK."

Bryce swivels in his chair and smiles when we lock eyes. "Hey." He hugs me. "Finished your study session early?"

"Yeah, I need food."

He kisses my cheek and holds my hand. "Then let's get you some food."

We move to the food line and Bryce wraps his arms around my middle, resting his chin on my shoulder. Having him this close to me is magical but as his hand moves along my stomach, I flinch and move his hand away.

"What?" he whispers. "You've never had a problem with me touching you in front of people before."

"Nothing," I whisper, which I realise doesn't answer his question. I take his hands so we're still close, but he's not touching me. This year, I had to ask Mum to order me the next size up of my school uniform and it still feels tight. Ever since I stopped dance and cheer practice, I've put on weight. Putting on weight at the hospital made sense, but I've never been able to lose it. I've even put more weight on. The thought of not being able to have kids nags at the back of my mind. It's something I shouldn't have to think about. It's not fair. Anytime it pings in my mind, I want to curl up on the couch with chocolate and a rom-com.

Bryce is still being nice to me. He hugs and kisses me like I haven't changed, but I don't feel good. I'm in too much of a funk to do anything about it. I know I should exercise, but I get scared I'll do something to hurt my hip or leg. Aisha only gave me gentle exercises to help me walk again. I don't know what I can do now and I feel too dumb to ask after all this time.

"What are you thinking about?" Bryce asks.

"Just schoolwork," I lie.

After school, Madi comes to Dad's place with me. We said we'd study, but that never happens with Madi around. Bryce is at therapy and says he'll come over after. He's doing so much better after the PTSD diagnosis. I know he wants off antidepressants, but he's dealt with so much over the years, he needs to stick with them.

"You're sure you don't want to talk about it?" I ask Madi as we curl up on a couch.

She swats me away. "Brit, I'm fine."

I don't push it. She and Zach broke up on the weekend. They never looked super serious together, but a breakup is never easy.

"Oh, hey girls," Nick says, walking past the living room toward his bedroom.

"Come sit with us," I say.

"Can't," he says, continuing on. "Naveen and I are studying."

"Oh, fine then," I say, feeling ditched.

Madi shoves her phone in my face. "Which do you like better?"

I push her phone back and blink to get my vision back. "What are you showing me?"

"Formal dresses, *duh*," Madison says. "I've got it narrowed down to these two."

"Oh yeah, that's coming up."

"What do you mean, *'oh yeah'*?" Madi deadpans. "You're going to the winter formal."

I shrug. "I dunno."

Madi whacks my arm. "Yes, you are."

I twirl a piece of hair around my finger and stare at a shadow on the wall.

"Why? Are you and Bryce having problems again?"

"No, we're great."

"Then what's up?"

"I missed last year's formal because I was in hospital, and a few weeks ago Bryce and I were struggling through preparations for Kellie's memorial. I don't know if I want another event to worry about."

"It'll be fun," Madi says sweetly, her oval eyes shining with hope. "It's the last one we will ever go to."

"I don't have a dress," I answer, lips curling at the thought of going.

Madi squeals and grabs onto my arm. "We'll go shopping. This will be way fun."

"I'll talk to Bryce about it first."

"As if he won't jump at the chance to take you. He's gaga over you."

"Are you going with someone? Is Zach taking you?"

She shakes her head, showing me the dresses again. "Nick and I said we'd go together, but that's as friends, not a date."

I grab her phone and roll my eyes. "*Hello*. Nick will decide. He's good at making quick decisions."

I get up and race toward his bedroom as Madi calls out anxiously, "What? No, Brit, wait!"

I pull open Nick's door as she reaches me. "Nick," I start, but the rest of the words suck out of me.

Nick is on top of Naveen, who lies back on his bed. Their faces are so close. I've interrupted a kiss.

Naveen pushes his hands into Nick's chest, sending him stumbling backward. Naveen sits up, staring at us wide-eyed as his chest rapidly rises and falls.

My eyes flick between Nick and Naveen, my jaw dropping.

"Brit," Madi whispers, tugging my arm.

Nick wipes his mouth with the back of his hand and a hint of a smile curls his lips.

"You two are...?" My mind is still catching up as I look to Nick for confirmation of what I just walked in on.

Naveen whips off the bed, hands out to his sides, trying to take control of the situation. "Nothing was going on."

"C'mon," Madi says, squeezing her grip around my wrist. "Let's leave them alone."

A lightbulb flicks on in my brain. I turn to Madi. "You knew?"

She sighs, letting me go and looking away.

I turn to the boys. "How long has this been going on?"

"Nothing's going on," Naveen replies, his jaw tensing.

"Relax," Nick says, "Brittany won't tell anyone."

I can't help but smile. It has been so long since I've been in on gossip. "It's a secret?"

Naveen groans and plonks on the bed.

"I'm teasing," I say to Naveen. "I won't tell anyone. But why can't I?" I look at Nick and giggle. "You two look cute together."

Naveen runs his hands over his face. "Don't."

"He wants to stay closeted," Nick says.

"That's unfair," Madi says.

The excitement from my face vanishes as Madi defends Naveen. I back away, my stomach knotting at the thought I've made something so much worse.

"I was just filling Brittany in," Nick says defensively.

Naveen groans. "It's not like it's what I want."

"Wait," I say, excitement tingling under my skin. "What about Meah? Does she know?"

Naveen shakes his head, expression blank. "Nope."

I throw my head back and laugh. I clasp my hands in front of my face, the biggest smile hurting my cheeks. "Oh, that's too good."

"I wouldn't have had to involve her," Naveen says, looking to Madi, "if someone played along."

Madi's eyebrow arches as her arms fold against her chest. "I'm nobody's beard. I'll support you all I can, but that's a line I can't cross."

My lips twist as my eyes narrow at her. "I've seen the two of you make out."

Madi shrugs and points to Nick. "I've made out with him too. What's your point?"

My face drops purely from surprise.

Madi winks at me. "I'll make out with you too, if ya want."

"Shuddup," I say with a laugh.

"Ok," Nick says, ushering us out. "We got more studying to do."

I poke at his ribs. "Oh yeah, right."

"Buh-bye," he says, loud enough to get his point across.

The door closes in our faces and I rub the tension from my stomach. "Well..."

Madi takes my hand and moves me into my bedroom. "Seriously," she whispers, shutting my door behind us. "You can't say anything. His parents are super conservative. Nav wants to come out after high school, when he's moved out of home. It's up to him. We can't tell anyone."

"I won't tell anyone," I promise. "It was just a shock. I didn't expect to find them tangled up in each other."

Madi smiles. "They are cute together, aren't they?"

"Yeah, they're both way too handsome. I'm kinda glad it's behind closed doors or I wouldn't be able to stop looking at them together."

"I know. Mega eye candy."

A half hour later, Nick and Naveen leave his bedroom and Naveen is quiet as he leaves the house. My heart aches for Nick seeing the distance between the two. But I guess that was the deal going into it.

Madi leaves with Naveen. She must be giving him a pep talk.

I follow Nick into the kitchen and lean against the bench, deciding if I should ask what had been playing on my mind. *Geez*, why not?

"So, what about Reece?" I ask.

"What about him?" Nick asks, perusing the fridge.

"I thought you liked him."

"I do," Nick says, shutting the fridge door. "But Reece rejected me. Naveen wanted to hook up. It was a better opportunity than sitting around for Reece to *maybe* look me in the eye."

I frown and rub his back. "Sorry."

Nick smiles. "Don't be sorry. Have you looked at Naveen? The caramel skin, dark hazel eyes, and sexy half-smile. A guy could do a lot worse."

"I can't believe Madi's known about his orientation for years."

"We can't go off your judgement. You have the worst gaydar ever."

"It's not my fault I'm not good at finding out people's secrets. I figure people are talking about me behind my back before guessing they have their own stuff going on."

"Don't worry," Nick says, backing out of the kitchen. "Naveen and I haven't talked about you for one second when together."

"I don't need the details," I tease. "So, did Madi set you two up?"

"She may have had a hand in it." Nick waves, heading up the hall. "I have a song to finish for my assignment. Catch ya later."

"No worries, Bryce will be over soon."

"Hey, how was your afternoon?" Bryce asks when I let him into the house.

"It was *in*teresting."

"Tell me," he says, following me into the house.

"Just Madi, Nick and Nav made for an interesting dynamic." I leave it vague, remembering how much Naveen pleaded with me to not tell anyone.

"Nav? What was he doing here?"

"A group assignment with Nick."

"Oh, ok. So, what, did Nick and Nav not get on?"

I giggle. "Um, no. They get on great."

Bryce's cheeky smile slides left. "What? What are you not telling me?"

I grab Bryce's hand and race him into my bedroom. I shut the door behind us and lean against it. "If I tell you, you promise not to tell anyone?"

"Ok..." he says warily.

I bite my lip, my cheeks burning with nervousness. "I tell you everything, so it'd be weird to keep this from you."

His face drops. "What is it?"

"I mean, maybe you already know."

"Britty, tell me. You're making it so much worse by dragging it out."

The worry on his face makes me laugh. I move towards him and whisper as quietly as possible, "Nick and Nav."

His eyebrow arches. "Yeah?"

I bite my lip then laugh. "They were making out."

His mouth drops. He takes a step back and his face screws up. "Sorry, what? Did I mishear that?"

I grin, shaking my head. "It's true. I saw it."

Bryce sits on the edge of my bed, his face a mess of confusion. "That... That... Naveen?"

I sit on the bed beside him and curl my legs up. "I know. I didn't see it coming either. Hell, I didn't see it coming with Nick and Reece either. But Nick and Nav are super cute together."

Bryce throws a palm up. "What about Meah?"

I grab his forearm, my smile larger-than-life. "That's the best part. She's his beard and has no idea."

He tries not to smile. "You're enjoying that a little too much."

I place a hand over his heart. "You can't say anything. Nav doesn't want anyone to know."

Bryce's eyebrows pinch together. "How did I not know?"

"He's been playing it straight. Madison was the only person who knew."

"You're kidding."

"She's a good friend, huh?"

Bryce smiles. "Yeah, she is."

"You won't be weird around Naveen, will you?"

Bryce tilts his head, frowning. "As if. I don't care who he likes. But I get why he wouldn't say anything about it at school. People get picked on for the stupidest shit."

"Apparently, it's more about his family than people at school."

"Ah, that sucks."

"Yeah, I know. I'm so glad Nick belongs to a supportive family."

Bryce kisses my cheek. "With such an awesome sister like you."

I giggle and meet his lips with mine.

His hand runs down my back and he slides me against the bed. My hands run up his neck, under his ears, and into his hair. His kiss increases in pressure and his hands slip around my waist. I'm hyper aware of each of his fingers moving against my body, the bloated lump

I am.

I push his hands off me and a weird whimper squeaks out.

"What's wrong?" he asks.

"I don't feel good."

He pushes himself up. "You're sick?"

"No." I sigh and close my eyes. I may as well just say it. "I'm fat."

He laughs with surprise. "No, you're not."

I slide out from under him, lips pursed in a frown.

"Brit," he whispers, running a hand up my arm. "You're beautiful."

"Stop," I whine, pushing him away.

"Don't push me away."

"I don't want to," I whisper, covering my face, "I just..."

"Come here," he says gently, holding his arms out.

"It got away from me," I say, not budging.

He edges closer. "Britty, I love you."

It's so sweet it makes my eyes well up. I twirl the emerald ring around my finger and suck in a breath. I lower my hands and take in his crystal blue eyes.

"I love you too," I whisper.

He curls a finger under my chin and tilts up my face. "You're beautiful. There's nothing wrong with you."

A lump in my throat makes me whimper. I wipe my eyes and then wrap my arms around his neck.

"Is that why you've been pulling away from me?" he asks. "Because you think you've put on too much weight?"

I nod against his shoulder.

He strokes my hair and I listen to the rhythm of his heart.

"I love you for you," Bryce says. "You're the perfect girl for me."

My hold on him tightens. I bury my face in his chest, not caring that my tears are wetting his t-shirt.

"Do you believe me?" he asks.

"Mhmm," I answer, unable to look up at him.

"We can still take things slow. There's no rush. I just like being near you."

"I like that too," I say in a croaky voice.

He pushes me down to the bed, cradling me in his arms and playing with my hair until I'm ready to reveal my face.

"I'm so lucky to have you," I say, locking my arms around his back.

He kisses the top of my head. "You wanna watch a movie or something?"

"Maybe, but I'm happy just lying here."

"Me too."

"Madi was asking me about the winter formal," I whisper, hugging his arm against me.

"Yeah? You want to go?"

"I don't know. I'm kinda anxious at the thought of it."

"We can do something else. Like, go out for dinner or something."

I smile and brush his cheek. "You'd be ok with that?"

His rosy lips shine as he smiles. "Yes. If it's with you, I don't care where we go."

I kiss his cheek and then flop my head against his chest. He plays with my hair and this is our position for the rest of the evening.

I fix a bejewelled, floral hairpiece to the back of Madi's messy bun. She's a bombshell. Her ruby red, satin dress hangs from her neck and waves around her body, finishing at her ankles. Her warm skin tone is highlighted in the most delicate way, as her dress shows off her back, shoulders and arms.

"Thanks, Brit," Madi says, stepping away from my mirror. "I could never get it to sit right."

"No problem. I love playing with hair and makeup," I say, eyeing the winged eyeliner and shimmer eyeshadow I had applied.

"You're a lifesaver," she says with a wink. "You sure you're happy not going?"

It's the night of the winter formal and she has asked me this all week. "Yes, I'm fine."

Her shoulders bounce up to her ears. "Sorry, just checking."

"Don't feel sorry for me."

"I don't," she rushes.

I follow her out of my bedroom and we stop by Nick's closed door.

"Ready yet, Prince Charming?" Madi calls through the door, giving it a knock.

"Give me a minute," Nick calls out.

"C'mon," I say, giddy, "I wanna see."

The doorbell sounds and Madi sighs loudly in relief. "Finally," she says and gestures for me to answer the door.

"What?" I ask, my eyebrows squeezing together. "Who are you waiting for?"

She pushes me up the hall. "Just get the door."

My stomach flip-flops as I walk to the door. Why is she being weird?

I open the door and smile at the sight of Bryce, but my smile quickly falls as my jaw drops. "What's this?"

He's wearing a navy dress shirt and tailored black trousers and holding a dress bag.

"Hey," he says with a cheeky grin.

"Bryce, what did you do?" I whisper.

"We don't have to go to the dance," he says, stepping into the house, "but you love getting dressed up. We can go to dinner or something. I don't care, but I didn't want you to regret not going."

My hand claps over my heart. "*Ohmigawd*, aren't you the sweetest?"

"He's here now?" Nick asks, emerging from his bedroom.

I turn and throw my hands up at him. "You were stalling?"

"You would have shooed us out of the house otherwise," he replies.

Bryce holds up the dress bag. "You wanna try it on?"

I take the bag, trembling at the thought of it not fitting.

"C'mon, Brit," Madi says, beckoning me to my bedroom. "I'll help you."

I give Bryce a quick peck on the lips, still in shock that he turned up like this. I follow Madi into the room and blow out a breath.

She claps. "Open it up."

I swallow hard and unzip the bag. I choke at the sight of it. I lay it on the bed and pull out the blush pink, A-line skirt of the delicate chiffon dress.

"Do you like it?" Madi asks, bouncing beside me.

"Did you help pick this out?"

"Your boy tried to help, but Tay and I were there to save the day."

"*Ohmigawd*," I whisper and chuck my arms around her. "I have the best friends."

She rubs my back. "Tayla even *FaceTimed* Charli for her input."

I pull out of the hug and wipe my eyes. "Oh, stop or Imma lose it."

"*Aw*, you're so cute. Now get dressed."

I look at the dress, down at my body, then to Madi. I want her out. I look back at the dress.

"What? Do you not like it?"

"No, no, I do," I say in a whisper.

"Then, what?"

I face her. "Sorry, can you give me a minute... alone?"

Her eyes widen and she backs away. "Um, yeah. Ok."

Madi leaves the room, shutting the door behind her and I flop on the bed, the beautiful dress spread out beside me. It's not like there's anything I want to think about. I'm blank. I'm overwhelmed. It's such a sweet gesture, but I'm so anxious about the dress. Everyone staring at me. Snooty girls judging the hell outta me.

"Britty," Bryce's voice gently sounds through the door as he knocks. "You ok?"

I scrunch the bedding in a tight grip. I hunch over and take laboured breaths.

"Brit?" he asks again.

I want to say I'm ok. To let him know not to worry. To tell him I just need a moment. But my heart pounds and stomach twists. I grit my teeth so hard that pain shoots down my neck.

My door opens and I stop breathing. Bryce slips into the room, shutting the door behind him. His face elongates when he sees me.

He rushes and kneels in front of me, resting his hands on my knees. "I'm sorry," he whispers, "I didn't mean to upset you. I thought it'd be romantic. I'm sorry, it was stupid."

I plant my hands on top of his. "It is romantic. It's so sweet I could cry. I've always dreamed of having something this magical happening to me. The guy of my dreams coming over with a magnificent dress to take me out. I don't know why I can't be excited."

"If you don't want to go, we can forget it."

"B, you understand me better than anyone." I touch his face and smile. "When I was helping Madi, I was jealous. I wanted to be in a formal dress and having my hair styled. I just feel like I don't belong anymore."

His face tilts as his eyes stare into mine. "Don't belong? It's for the entire school."

"I know. It's just... I've gone to the formal with Chloe & Co and know the kinds of things they say about people and..."

Bryce groans. "Her again? Can't we forget her and have a fun time together?"

He's right. But so am I. I eye the dress and sigh. "You think I'd look good in it?"

"Gorgeous. Will you let me see?"

I nod.

He stands, clasping one of my hands. "Do you want me to stay?"

I shake my head. "Let me get changed then I'll come out. You know, like a big reveal."

He grins and kisses my cheek. "Sounds great."

When he leaves, I hope I sounded confident because I sure as hell don't feel it. I've spent the past year hiding in books and avoiding who I used to be. Somehow, putting this dress on feels like I'm doing it all over again. A scared girl trying to impress people who don't give a crap about her.

I take off my clothes and slip into the dress. I pull it up over my arms and press the fabric against my stomach, moving towards the mirror with closed eyes. Do I really wanna see? I slowly open one eye. It's a blurry version of me but isn't grotesque. I open the second eye and scrutinise myself. I turn to the side, smoothing the dress to make sure no rolls are showing off my figure. The dress is double lined so it's super flattering. I catch myself smiling in the mirror.

"Madi," I call out.

She's in like a shot.

I turn my back on her. "Zip me up?"

"Brit, you look so good."

"Thanks," I say, playing with my hair to decide whether I should put it up or down.

"Down," Madi says, reading my mind.

I pick up a spray bottle filled with water and start working on my hair. "And curls," I say. "Bryce likes them, but I never leave my hair curly. Hell, maybe I should start."

When I finish with hair and makeup, I walk into the hall, Madi tailing me. I walk into the living room where the boys are waiting. Both their jaws nearly smack the floor. It sends me into nervous giggles.

"I didn't think I'd look like this tonight," I say, pulling at the skirt of my dress.

Bryce meets me with a kiss. "You look stunning."

"Thanks. Just trying to match you."

"I'm no match for you."

"Barf," Madi mutters behind me.

"Let me see," Nick says, scooting between me and Bryce. "What a babe."

"Shuddup," I snigger.

"Ready to go?" Madi asks, picking up her silver clutch.

"You guys go," I reply. I look to Bryce. "Is it ok if we go together a bit later?"

"Yeah, Baby," he says, brushing the back of his hand against my arm.

"Ok, c'mon Nicky," Madison says, moving towards the front of the house.

Nick looks me up and down. "You're coming though?"

I don't answer. "Have fun."

His lips purse. He smiles for my benefit and waves goodbye.

Bryce pulls out his phone and an uneasiness swirls inside me.

"What is it?" I ask.

He taps a few buttons and then music sounds from his phone. Bryce tosses his phone onto the couch, scoops one of my hands in his, and presses the other against my lower back.

"Can I have this dance?" he asks, with a ridiculously handsome smile.

I bite my lip to stop my grin from exploding. "Why, of course." I'm such a dork.

He leads, gliding us around the room. He spins me out and when he pulls me in, dips me. As he lifts me up, I'm quick to lock him in a kiss.

"You're too much," I whisper.

"I love you."

"I love you. With all my heart."

"You wanna stay in tonight?"

I bite my lip and bat my lashes. "Wanna do something crazy?"

Nervous laughter seeps out of him. "What?"

"Wanna order pizza and eat it on the floor in these fancy clothes?"

His head tilts back as he laughs loudly.

"No?" I ask with a laugh.

"That sounds awesome. I'm so down."

I pull him into a kiss. "It'll be the most perfect date ever."

"It's not like you to avoid a dance," Bryce says when we're on our second slice of pizza. We get the house to ourselves because Dad and

Tara took Alyssa to see a new kids' movie.

"School's not the same anymore. I used to hang with people who would say the nastiest stuff. I don't wanna look over my shoulder, wondering what they're saying about me."

"Why do you think they're talking about you? I haven't heard anything. And you're walking again."

I blow out a breath and stare at the pizza slice. "I'll tell you because I know it was hard for you to talk about the accident and Will texting after so long." I suck in a breath. "This is so hard."

He rubs my arm, tilting his head to find my eyes. "What is it?"

"I heard the boys call me a cripple."

Bryce's mouth falls open and his slice drops to the cardboard box. "What? Who did?"

I shake it off. "It doesn't matter. It just never left me."

He sits up straighter, intensity in his eyes. "Britty. Tell me who."

"Sean. There were other boys laughing with him, but I didn't see who."

His chin drops. "They were laughing at that? Why didn't you tell me?"

My eyes well. "I was embarrassed."

He scoops me into his arms. "Embarrassed? Brit, they were pigs. I wished you'd told me."

"I'm sorry."

His arms tighten around me, my body pressed against his. "This is why you didn't want me hanging with them? I didn't know. I never heard anyone say that stuff about you."

"I was scared they were telling you to dump me."

He kisses the side of my face, his hug still strong. "Never gonna happen. I love you so much."

"I love you too." I swallow hard. "I couldn't bear to let the word *cripple* out of my mouth."

"I get it. It's foul. I can't believe they said it. Now I'm glad we didn't go to the formal."

I try a laugh. "You mean, you weren't enjoying our pizza party?"

A faint laugh seeps out of him as his arms unravel. "Nah. You were right." He kisses my lips mid-sentence. "This is the most perfect date ever."

I stare into his eyes and my skin warms. "Do you want to talk about getting closer again? Like, next level stuff?"

Light dances in his eyes as his smile grows. He nods and says, "Yes, I do."

"Maybe we can start easing into that stuff?"

An easy chuckle comes out of him. "Hard-core make out session tonight?"

I laugh and lean into him. "Deal."

25

Charli

It took two weeks to get a job. Not bad, considering I'm a high school drop-out who never had an after-school job. All those debate matches prepped me to be on my toes during the interviews. I think I sold myself too well. Who knew waitressing was so hard?

I don't like the looks the patrons give me when I ask them to repeat something or when I take too long to recall all the ingredients in a salad. Like it's a massive deal or something. *No need to get all huffy with me.* I feel bad for anyone who's ever waited on my parents before. I never noticed it from the other side of the table. I am now overly polite every time I order a gunpowder green tea.

"Got plans tonight?" my supervisor Mike asks when I join him behind the bar.

I'm not allowed to serve alcohol until I turn eighteen, but I can restock fridges and clean glasses. I bolt when a customer walks up to the bar. This is a ritzy bar though, so most patrons wait for a server to come to them.

I run a hand over my messy bun. "Going to the salon."

"Gonna chop it all off?" he asks, smirking.

"Ah, no. My hair is super long. It's like a trophy. But just wait, it will be extremely different."

"You said you wanted to look different," the hairdresser says when she lowers the flat-iron.

"Wow, you didn't disappoint," I say.

My reflection is completely altered. Coffee-coloured, sleek straight hair sits either side of my face and runs over my chest.

"Glad you like it," she beams, taking the cape off me. "Fresh look for the new you."

I get off the chair, fanning my hair out. "That's what I'm hoping."

I swear I walk taller when I leave the salon. Something about the new look gives me mega confidence. I rub my hip where I got extra added to my tattoo this morning. Curving around my purple-green peace sign in gorgeous cursive writing is *Kellie*. I'm truly set for my new life now.

"*Geez*, Charli," Shae says, surprise lifting her face when I enter the apartment. "I thought you were some random person walking into the place."

I gulp, playing with the ends of my darkened hair. "Do you like it?"

"Are you kidding?" she says, walking towards me. "I love it. It suits you, even though I never pictured you as a brunette."

"I hadn't either. Just had an impulse."

"You're definitely leaning toward this free-spirit side," Shae says, moving towards the kitchen. "You hungry? We're thinking about pasta for dinner."

"Sounds great," I say, leaning against the kitchen bench. "Can you teach me how to make it?"

"You've never made pasta?"

"I've never cooked anything."

"How did Mum never get you in the kitchen?"

"I wasn't exactly close with your mum."

Shae nods, pursing her lips. "Hopefully, that'll change when we go back to Sanford."

"It will. I'll make more of an effort. Without her, I wouldn't be here."

"She adores you."

I smirk. "I don't know why. I was nothing but rude to her."

"You met her when you were upset over your parents' divorce. She gets it. Mum's a forgiving person."

"Maybe too forgiving." I laugh. "Maybe that will be what keeps her and Dad together."

"Hey, he's good for her too," Shae says, filling a pot with water. "She's a lot more level-headed than before. Her emotions run high and she can be impulsive."

"For their sakes, I hope they stick together."

Shae grins. "Me too."

Shae sits the pot on the stove and ignites a burner.

"You boiled water before?" she teases.

"In a kettle," I reply, poking my tongue out.

She laughs and opens the packet of pasta. "This is easy-peasy. Once the water boils you stick the pasta in and in about ten to fifteen minutes, it's ready."

"How do you know if it's ten or fifteen?"

"By feel and taste. You stir it a few times and it changes texture. Don't worry, I'll show you. First, let's make the sauce." Shae retrieves an onion from the cupboard and shows it to me. "Cut one of these before?"

"I've cut vegetables for Sophia before," I reply. "But not for long. Once I get bored, she ushers me out of the kitchen."

Shae groans. "*Ugh*, no wonder you lost interest if they didn't make you stick with it."

Shae shows me the proper way to dice the onion and I watch her sauté it in a pan with olive oil and garlic. She adds different herbs and tells me if I have basil and oregano at my new place, I'll be right.

When the onions have browned and smell sinfully delicious, she opens a tin of chopped tomatoes and pours it into the pan. She adds the pasta to the boiling water and says it's time for the ingredients to 'do their thing.'

"It's that easy?" I ask.

She nudges me. "Sure is, kid."

Shae's boyfriend Reynold joins us for dinner. They're a weird couple. They hug for two-seconds and I've never seen them kiss. Shae's focused on her religion, so maybe that has something to do with it? He's never spent the night, he just comes for dinner and sometimes a movie, and sometimes they have their dinner and movie out on a proper date. I suspect their dates look like two acquaintances randomly seated together.

She must judge me hard sometimes. Imagine the look in her eyes if she knew about my night with Harrison in the forest. Luckily Tara's so open-minded that Shae didn't become an fundamentalist.

The apartment is tiny and I'm still sleeping on the sofa with the hella lumpy mattress. We had agreed to me staying here until new years' because I plan to go back to Sanford to spend time with Brittany for our birthday. That way I'm not spending rent somewhere without making an income. But my time here is wearing thin. Shae and Reynold sit on my folded up 'bed' and I don't want to third-wheel it while her roommate is at the university library.

I take my laptop out onto the balcony to show Brittany my new hair over *Skype*. I've already discovered the sound doesn't travel into the living room, so it's about as private as it gets in this matchbox.

Opening my laptop, an email notification pops up. My heart skips a beat. An email from Harrison. The first one since he left for Peru.

My fingers tremble as I hit *open*.

Hola Charli!

I hope you're well. This is the first time I've been near internet in weeks. I'm eager for your reply, but please keep in mind it may be weeks until I read it.

Today, I'm in a larger village to gather some supplies for the build site. Man, you'd love it here. I've met the cutest kids, who are desperate to teach me Spanish, and I do a terrible job at teaching English. I am in no way a teacher!

But the people here are awesome. The team is full of big hearts and well-travelled souls. I get why you couldn't come, but someday soon we will have to go on a tour together. You would have fitted in perfectly here.

I think about you all the time. I hope you've worked things out with your family and friends and are living a happy, fulfilling life.

Harrison.

I push away the laptop. *Whoah.* I don't know where to start. At least he says it'll be weeks till he sees the response. I have ample time to write back.

I gather my hair to the side. I laugh at how weird it feels to not have big curls in my hands. My hair is so shiny it almost slips through my fingers. I comb my fingers through it, watching the light pick up the different tones of brown. I focus on a chocolate tone, which reminds me of Travis.

Over my shoulder, I eye his jacket hanging on a chair inside. With all the arguing at my dad's house and then at Mum's, I didn't have time to contact him. I've stared at his text message countless times. It said he needed to get back to uni, but he was glad to see me. I saw it a few hours after he'd sent it and wasn't sure how to respond. Now, three weeks later, I still haven't replied. Part of me wants to tell him I'm in the city, part of me wants the memory of him and nothing more.

I wore his jacket to work the other day. Maybe he knows I'm here. Maybe he's seen a clue on *Instagram*. I weaned myself off checking his *Insta* feed while in Spain. I had Maja and Miguel to distract me.

Ugh. I was the absolute worst to them. I cut off all contact the minute I got to Sanford. I had a million crippling thoughts in my brain, but I can imagine how bad it must have felt to be left completely in the dark. Not knowing if I was ok. I don't know what the school would have told them. I had nothing to do with cancelling my enrolment, Dad took care of that.

I should get in touch. To let them know what went down. Not stacks of detail just that I'm okay. It's been over a year since I've seen them. I wonder if Miguel told Maja about the trip to the airport. The two never spoke to each other when I was at school, but maybe that changed after I left? That would be nice.

I shake off the mess of thoughts, deciding to draft the emails later tonight, and open *Skype*.

"*Ohmigawd*," Brittany squeals through the screen. "Your hair! What did ya do?"

I tussle my hair. "You like?"

"It's so different," she says, moving closer to the screen. "When did you do it?"

"Today."

"It's stunning. *Gawd*, you couldn't have done it when we were at school together so people could tell us apart."

"*Pah*-lease. You were already dying and straightening your hair two years ago. People have been telling us apart just fine."

Brittany giggles, sitting back. "What else you been up to?"

"Just work."

"How's that going?"

"My boss is way cool. He lets people work whenever they want. You can say you don't want shifts over a few weeks if you're travelling or studying for exams."

"And that's what you want, to travel more?"

"Yep. Gotta get more use outta the St Christopher pendant you gave me."

"Wear it now. You're already on a big adventure." She sits her chin in her hands. "So, what else is going on other than work?"

"Shae's boyfriend is here."

Brittany winces. "Still a robot?"

I grin. "Pretty much. Don't get me wrong, he's very nice. They just need to loosen up a bit."

"I couldn't imagine not cuddling up with my boyfriend."

"No one's calling you a prude, Brittany May," I tease.

"Shuddup. As if you wouldn't be all over a babe like Bryce."

"Not my type."

"Gorgeous is everyone's type."

I puff out a laugh. "Sounds like you and him are on good terms."

She grins, nodding. "Very much so. Anyway, when are you coming back?"

"The day of our birthday."

"That long?" she whines. "Come back a few days earlier."

"No, I can't. I'm staying until you graduate so I don't want to add on too many extra days."

"I'm that bad to be around?"

"You know it's not you."

"What about Reece and everyone else? We will hang out with our friends. We won't be home with parents."

"Sorry, Brit. I've already organised it with Shae. She had to arrange shifts at work and her classes, and I don't want to push it too early and miss too much work. I'll be home for a while once I get there."

She pouts. "I guess that'll have to do. Have you found a place to live yet?"

"No, I'm staying with Shae till the end of the year."

"*Or* you could come home."

I frown. "Brit."

"I know, I know," she says, curling her hair behind her ear. "I'm just playing."

"Everything at home has been ok for you, hasn't it?" I swallow dryly at the genuine possibility that our parents' frustrations over me are being taken out on her.

"You know they like to wrap me up in cotton wool. I dunno, it's weird at either home. I've been spending more time at Bryce's house."

I sigh with relief. "Ok, good. I'm glad you have such a wonderful guy."

"And what about you? Seen any cute boys?"

I laugh, looking away from the screen with discomfort. "No, haven't really had time to look."

"Maybe you will once you're eighteen and can get into clubs."

I shrug. "Maybe."

"I feel you're holding something back."

"I'm not."

"There *is* a guy, isn't there?"

I grin and roll my eyes to show her she's way off track. "Whatever, Brit. I gotta go anyways. Sleep well."

She blows a kiss. "You too."

We end the call and I push the laptop off my lap. My mind works over the email and my eyes fixate on the jacket hanging on the other side of the window.

I slink down on the chair. "*Ugh.* Get outta my head!"

Chocolate and charcoal,
Freedom and shackles,
A heart and a mallet,
Distance and closeness.

Time and wounds,
Ripping and tearing,
Shattering and mending,
Growing and shrinking.

A missing puzzle piece,
A true love,
A fleeting moment,
Another thing of nonsense.

26

Brittany

Charli's found a job and is adventuring around a big city. I wish I could be there with her. She gets to move on so much quicker than me. But graduation is coming up. Then I can join her.

These months apart have been so weird. Last year, I never thought I'd miss her this much. At least our *Skype* calls are regular. We upgraded from every-other-day to nightly chats.

Without her around, I really had to find myself. I needed to stop tying my identity to someone else. To not be a twin or a hot guy's girlfriend. With Nick back at school, I easily could have used him as a crutch too.

My life changed so much over the course of a year. I never went back to cheer or dance. I needed to find something else I was good at. Who would have thought that was studying? I made top marks in a couple of classes. I must have been bored if being good at my classes was my new hobby. But the feeling of accomplishment and pride was something I didn't expect. It was like a high. I wanted to beat my previous mark with each new test. It was kinda fun.

Ha! Nerd Alert!

Charli's coming home. It's our eighteenth birthday and the only thing we want to do is spend it together.

I would love to travel to her. Live it up for a few nights in the city, but she wanted to come home. Graduation is coming up and she figured it might be the last time everyone's together. One final big farewell. Lenny's having a party, and everyone agreed to go. I think everyone from school is invited. It'll make for a crazy night.

"Yay! You're home!" I cheer, pulling Charli into a hug as soon as she enters the foyer.

"Hey," she says wearily, slumping in my arms.

"You alright?"

She pulls out of the hug. "Just tired. I worked this morning."

My face screws up. "You worked on your birthday. *Ick.*"

"I want to make a good impression," she says with a shrug.

Sophia moves in behind Charli with her luggage. "I can't believe my angels are adults." Her eyes shine and she pinches Charli's cheek. "I'm so proud of you for looking after yourself."

Charli grins. "I learnt from the best."

Sophia waves her away. "*Ha.* I've never seen you vacuum or dust. You can give it a go this weekend, if you like?"

"*Eww,*" I interrupt. "You know it's our birthday, right?" I poke Charli's arm and ask, "How was it at Dad's?"

"Fine," Charli replies. "It was quick, thanks to Sophia."

"The only problem was the little one wouldn't let go of Charli," Sophia says with a giggle.

"Alyssa," Charli adds, grinning.

"That's so sweet. I was over there for lunch," I say.

"I can't believe you two are going into the big world," Sophia hushes.

"What's your plan, Sophia?" Charli asks.

"Yeah," I say. "Are you going to stay with Mum or go back to the Philippines?"

"The plan was always to return home," Sophia says, eyes distant. "This is so much house though. I can't leave your mother stranded."

"She can get a non-live-in housekeeper," Charli suggests.

"Or you stay so we can visit," I say with a giggle.

"We can visit the Philippines," Charli says.

"Charli," Mum says, entering the foyer.

Charli stiffens at the sight of her.

"Happy birthday," Mum says, resting her hands on Charli's shoulders. The way Mum deliberately left out *Pumpkin* stings.

"Thanks, Mum," Charli replies and they engage in the most awkward hug ever.

"I'd like to talk to you about staying," Mum says to Charli.

Charli hisses, sliding backward. "Mum."

"I just want you to think about it," Mum rushes. "You have so much potential. I don't want you to throw it all away."

"I'm not," Charli argues, backed into a corner. "Why don't you start supporting me instead of questioning me?"

"Mum, it's our birthday," I grumble.

Mum raises her hands in surrender. "I won't say another word. I want you two to have a good evening."

Charli pulls herself out of the corner.

"Well," Mum says, clasping her hands and shaking off any discomfort. "As promised, the house will be cleared out for you two." She eyes me. "You're sure you don't want a big party?"

I nod, flicking my eyes to the door. "Yes, Mum. *Adios.*"

"Yes, Ms Matthews," Sophia says, touching Mum's shoulder. "Brittany gave us very strict instructions to vacate."

"Ok, ok," Mum says. She collects her handbag and car keys and makes her way down the hall to the garage with Sophia.

"So glad she's gone," Charli mutters under her breath.

I pull her bags to the bottom of the stairs and tug her into the living room. "What else did you do today?" I ask as we curl our legs up on the same couch.

"Nothing."

I deadpan. "Stop it. Just tell me."

"I did. I worked and came here."

"As if Shae wouldn't have organised something."

"She did make an awesome breakfast. Pancakes with all these different berries."

"Nice. We had our traditional pastries. I made sure we left some for you."

She chews her lip, eyes falling to a spot on the carpet.

"You should have come home earlier."

She huffs. "Don't."

"I just mean… because you're sad. If you were here in the morning, you wouldn't have missed out on anything."

"And, what?" she says meeting my eyes and the hurt is unmistakable. "So Mum could make me feel like shit for longer? You know she's stopped calling me, right?"

I swallow dryly and blink back a tear. "I know."

She bats her hands and sits back on the couch. "Forget it. I didn't come home to discuss all that. I'm here for you."

"*Us,*" I correct. "It's *our* birthday."

At that, she grins, and I instantly feel better.

"I'll get popcorn?" I suggest.

She stands with me. "What do we have to drink?"

"Sophia gifted us Moscato. Wanna try it?"

"I'm game."

"I hate that we were apart on our last birthday," I say on the way to the fridge.

"I wasn't going to let it happen again," Charli says, pulling glasses out of a cupboard.

"Those are water glasses."

Her lip upturns at the glasses in her hands. "So?"

"Get the wine glasses," I snigger. "It's our eighteenth, be fancy. *Geez,* some bartender you'll make."

"Technically, I'm a waitress," she says, finding the right glasses. "I wasn't allowed behind the bar because I was under eighteen, but they secretly let me practice."

"You gotta try anything to get in trouble, don't ya?" I tease.

"Shuddup."

I shove the popcorn into the microwave. "You got a cute guy teaching you?"

"I wouldn't exactly call Mike *cute.*"

I laugh. "I knew there was a guy."

"Just pass the bottle," she says with an eye roll.

"Are you seeing anyone?"

"Nope." She pours the reddish-pink wine into the glasses. "How are things with Bryce?"

"Really good. I think I might be ready to take things further with him again."

"Again?" she questions. "You mean…?"

I bite my lip and narrow my eyes. "Didn't I tell you?"

Her eyes widen. "Tell me?"

I giggle. "When Bryce and I had sex."

She gasps. "When?"

"Oh *geez*, over a year ago now. His seventeenth birthday."

"Wow. That's so long ago. And you didn't tell me. What the hell?"

"I was going to on a *Skype* call, but then I ended up in hospital and… you know."

"And I dropped off the face of the planet," she mutters. "You never did it again once you got out of the wheelchair? Like, over the summer?"

I shrug. "We weren't seeing each other last summer. And," I pause, taking a moment to tip the popcorn into a bowl. "And, I have these huge, ugly scars. I was too self-conscious."

She blows out a breath and nods. "I get that. Well... I guess keeping big news from each other is our sisterly thing."

My heartbeat speeds up as I follow her into the living room. "What?"

She grins and flops on the couch. "I lost my virginity too."

I let loose a squeal.

Charli whacks me. "*Shoosh.*"

I fall beside her. "Who? When?"

"It was a while ago too," she says. "It was when I got home from rehab."

"No way."

"Yes way. His name is Harrison and we did it in the forest."

"The forest? *Eww.* Why?"

"It wasn't *eww*," she laughs. "It was perfect."

"*Ohmigawd*, Charli. How long had you known the guy?"

"Like a week," she says with a cheeky grin.

I *tsk* and shake my head. "Why couldn't you have waited for a guy you'd been with for a while? Don't you think it'd be better to be in love with the guy?"

"I've been in love before and it wasn't perfect."

"But aren't you afraid you'll regret it once you fall in love with someone else?"

"I really don't feel like that."

I take a handful of popcorn to avoid her eyes. "I guess. How did you get away with this? Weren't you on lockdown after rehab?"

Her lips twist and she shrugs. "When your parents don't check where you are, it can be pretty easy to sneak out." Her mood lifts and she pats my thigh. "I'm excited for you and Bryce. I'm glad you're doing so much better."

"We've been spending a lot of time together. We lost our friendship for a while and it seemed important to build it up again before rushing into sex."

"Look at you, being all grown-up."

"I have a new rule. If I don't know what to do, I ask myself, *'what would Chloe Benson do?'* And then I do the opposite."

We fall back in laughter.

"We should have already known about this stuff," I whisper, linking arms with her. "Can we please promise to act like sisters from now on?"

"That's all I want." Charli snuggles against me. "Bryce was ok not spending your birthday night with you?"

"Not really." I smile. "But he gets this is important to me."

"Maybe tonight could have been the perfect night for you two to get busy," Charli teases.

"Are you trying to get rid of me?" I kid.

"Totally," she jokes. "Seriously though, it's so cool to spend the evening just with you."

I clasp her hand. "I agree. I want us to stay close."

"Me too. I can't wait until you move to the city."

"That's if I get the marks I need to get into uni," I say and suck in a breath.

"You will," Charli says, squeezing my hand. "You've worked so hard. And you're annoyingly brilliant at everything you try."

"*Ha*, no I'm not."

"You beat me at *'Night Crawler'*." She flings my hand and deadpans. "A game I'd been playing for weeks, then you pick up a controller and, in an hour, beat my high score."

I giggle and flick my hair. "Pick a harder game then."

Charli splutters a laugh. "Bitch."

I laugh hard, holding my gut.

"What movie do you want to watch?" Charli asks, lifting the remote.

"I dunno. We never agree on anything."

"Because you like the dumbest shit."

"I like *fun* movies."

"You need a new definition of fun."

"Whatever. You pick something." I stretch out on the couch and say, "I can't believe graduation is so damn close. High school will be over. In a way it's sad, but I also can't wait."

"You're ok with going to the party?" Charli asks, scrolling through *Netflix*. "You said the thought of going to the formal tripped you out."

"It must be that I've lost some nerves with school ending," I say. "I think it'll be fun. I mean, it's at Lenny's house. That has to be safe."

"But they invited the whole school."

"On our turf," I say, confidence building inside of me.

She grins and pats my hand. "It's good to see you sure of

yourself."

"Remember, you've promised to go."

"Don't you worry, I'll be there if you're there."

"Reece says he's going."

"I know," she replies, worry wrinkling her face. "I'll have one eye on you and the other on him."

"You can go to have fun," I assure. "I'll have Bryce and Reece will have Nick."

She deadpans me. "They're a couple?"

"No, I mean they'll be close by each other. We will band together. The stupid comments about Nick didn't return after his record deal. He made a good impression at Kellie's memorial."

"Does he hate that? He seemed to hate himself after his performance."

"Doesn't make him like Chloe & Co more, but it gave him confidence in his stage performance. And not getting bullied is always a good thing."

"Definitely." She stops on *'Save the Last Dance'*. "Didn't you like this movie?"

My insides twist. I watched it last birthday, when she was gone. "I did, but I'm over it. Put on one of those shit sci-fi movies and I'll see if I like it."

Her left eyebrow arches mega high. "*One of those shit sci-fi movies...*" she mocks. "Yeah, that's an open mind."

"Yeah, it is."

Charli keeps clicking. "What about a slasher movie? See who screams first."

"It'll be you for sure."

Charli selects *'Child's Play'* and says, "Wanna bet."

I take a sip of wine and it fizzes on my tongue. I set the glass on the table and memories of how alcohol changed me into someone else tumble into my mind. *A Chloe Clone,* Charli called me.

Charli takes a sip and smiles. "Oh, it's actually nice."

"Sophia has nice taste," I reply, hoping I can get away without drinking more.

"Do you like it?"

"Yeah, it's fine."

We recline with the popcorn nestled between us, giggling at who will be the first to scream and knock it over.

It's so her.

#

I walk out of my bedroom and hear from below, "Is it all right if I go upstairs?"

My heart *ba-booms* as my mum tells Bryce he can come upstairs. Should I go back in and let him knock or meet him on the landing?

Before I can decide…

"Wow, what a stunner," Bryce says, bounding up the stairs.

My cheeks flame as my hands run over the beaded sequins of my sleeveless sky-blue and white cocktail dress. "This dress is ok?"

His larger-than-life smile and the sparkle in his eyes fill me with confidence. "Yeah, Babe, you look hot."

Bryce moves closer, his hands moving into my freshly cut and curled hair that now sits above my shoulders. I breathe in his cologne and close my eyes as his lips taste mine. His kiss burns of passion and he pulls me close, our bodies pressing together as his tongue glides into my mouth.

I giggle as I pull out of the kiss. "You're in a good mood."

His hands tighten around my back. "Don't think I'm letting you go."

"You don't want to go to the party?" I say, giddy.

"We can go," he replies, "we just have to go clung together."

I swat at his arm with a nervous giggle. He bends his knees and snags my lips again and he kisses me like it's the end of the night and we're headed to bed.

I gasp when our lips part. "My lipstick is on your lips."

Bryce wipes his lips and I pull his hand away.

"Don't smudge, you'll make it worse."

I tug on his arm and drag him into my bedroom. I pull a makeup wipe from my dresser and swipe it across his lips. With a deep breath, I turn to the mirror to inspect the damage.

"*Ugh*, I need to fix my makeup."

"Don't bother," Bryce says, his arms draping over my shoulders as he stands behind me. "I will only mess it up again."

I playfully push him off me. "Stop it."

He laughs, plonking on my bed. "What? I can't help it."

"What's gotten into you?"

"I'm just crazy about you."

I laugh as he throws himself onto the bed. I wipe off my lipstick and the foundation around my lips. As I dust powder on my face, my fingers shuffle through my glosses and lipsticks. I dig out a smudge-proof raspberry lipgloss. I test it on the back of my hand and rub my finger vigorously over the top of it.

"Aha!" I cheer. "You won't be smudging this one."

"Good," he says, sitting up. "So, I can kiss you all I like without you pushing me off."

"Whatever," I say, turning to the mirror to apply the gloss. I fix my hair and shift my dress. The best thing about going up a dress size is the extra cleavage. I've never looked so good in a strapless dress before.

"Should we go?" I suggest.

Bryce gets off the bed and wraps his hands around me before pulling me to the bed. I laugh much too loud and he kisses my neck as my hair fans over my face. The crystal pendant from the necklace he gave me for my sixteenth birthday swings and rests against his chin. I pull myself up and scoop my hair back.

He grins. "Ok, we can go."

I smooth my hair in front of the mirror.

He stands behind me and asks, "Want me to help?"

I puff out a laugh with a hint of frustration. "No."

"You're fun to annoy."

I whack his arm. "Stop."

He laughs and heads to the door.

I fasten the crystal stud earrings he bought for my latest birthday to my lobes and curl my hair behind my ears. With a quick fan of my face, I follow him out onto the landing.

I knock on the adjacent bedroom door. "Charli? You ready?"

Charli's door opens and I feel instant disappointment. Her brunette, blow-dried hair is in a loose plait over her left shoulder. She's wearing an old t-shirt under a tartan shirt, ripped jeans and ratty sneakers.

"That's what you're wearing?" I deadpan.

She gestures to me. "What? We're going to a fancy ball or something?"

"It's the last party of school. You should make an effort."

"Newsflash," she replies, chucking her hair over her shoulder. "I don't go to this school anymore."

"I can find you a dress," I say, cuffing her wrist.

She flings me off. "A dress? Get real."

"Leave her alone, Brit," Bryce says.

Charli grins. "Thanks, Bryce."

"Uh, you're supposed to be on my side," I say to him.

He clasps my hand. "C'mon, let's get to Lenny's. You two look exactly like who you are."

Charli nudges me, a shy smile to her face. "You look pretty, Brit."

"Thanks, Scruffy," I reply, rubbing her back.

I backtrack to my bedroom and snatch my crutch.

"What's wrong?" Bryce says, his expression turning fearful as he eyes the crutch. "You need that?"

"Just in case," I reply quickly. "There's gonna be loads of people at the house and I think it's gonna be hard to move around." I take in Charli's worry and say, "I promise, I'm ok."

I leave out the part about the dull ache that's flared up around my hip in the past day and a half. It's nothing new. The flare-ups happen occasionally. It's just my normal now. I look down at the silver flats on my feet and smile. Once upon a time, I wore stilettos to parties. Now, I feel confident in these bad boys.

We head downstairs for the obligatory photo in the foyer. Charli reluctantly takes my offer to join us in the photo as Mum intensely stares at her, desperate to pull her aside and convince her not to leave home again. I feel for Mum and I'd love Charli to stay too, but her mind is made up. Mum needs to learn to give it up.

We leave the house, pile into Bryce's car, and stop three houses down to pick Reece up.

"I'll go get him," Charli says, exiting the backseat.

Bryce's hand runs through my hair and I love how his eyes glimmer in the darkness of the car. "I love you," he says.

"I love you too."

He leans in and kisses me. I slide my hands along his jawline and gently suck his bottom lip. We stay glued together until a harsh succession of knocks pound against the window.

We break apart, and I see Charli outside Bryce's door.

"*Eww*," her muffled voice sounds through the glass.

I roll my eyes and lean back against my seat.

Charli and Reece slide into the back and Charli says, "Can you guys keep ya hands off each other for two seconds?"

"Sure, for two seconds," Bryce jokes.

I turn in my seat. "Hi, Reece."

He waves. "Hey."

Bryce pulls the car off the curb, his hand cupping mine as he smiles at the road. He's too damn cute.

We get to the party and I'm so glad I brought the crutch. My arm stays linked with Bryce's as we move through the crowded rooms of the house. I keep my eyes peeled for Lenny and Tayla, but so far I only see every other student.

Fiona squeals on top of a table, shimmying her hips as she holds a half-empty bottle of vodka to the ceiling. Sean grabs her and pulls her down into his arms, pinching her butt. It's only ten pm and these people are loose.

"Sis!" a voice yells out.

I spin and find Nick, shirt half-unbuttoned, bopping in the middle of the makeshift dancefloor. His hands are up beckoning me over and I can't help giggling at his tipsiness.

"You want a drink?" Bryce asks me.

"Just a Coke or something," I say. "Do you mind if I dance with Nick?"

"Yeah, go for it. I'll be right back," Bryce says, and moves toward the kitchen.

Nick pulls me into his arms. He then notices the crutch and his eyes widen. "You alright?"

"I'm fine," I yell over the music. "Don't worry about it."

"Charli!" Nick yells too close to my ear. "Come ere, Charli! *Ohmigawd*, Reece. Come ere."

Reece is quick to move further into the house and when Charli tries to follow, I reach out and catch her.

"Nah-uh, Sissy," I say, pulling her close. "You're dancing with me."

"Brit, you look fab," Nick says, close to my ear. The distinct smell of raspberry vodka, something I'm too familiar with, lingers on his breath.

"Thanks, Nick. You look hot."

Nick moves his arms from me to Charli. "Shae said she loves living with you," Nick yells. "Thanks for being such good company for her."

Charli nods, smiling and trying to get some space between them. Nick keeps a hold of her, not noticing her struggle, as she says, "Shae's awesome."

"Boyfriend's here," Nick says, nodding ahead.

I turn to see Bryce squeezing between two groups of dancing friends.

"It's crazy in here," he says, looking around at all the people in the room.

"Have you seen Tay or Madi?" I ask, taking a can of Coke from his hand.

Nick taps my shoulder. He points across the room, saying, "Madi's over there. Watch out, she's tipping vodka down people's throats."

"Oh, so that's what happened to you," Charli says to Nick, hanging off his shoulder.

Nick screws up his face and dips his shoulder to slide her off.

"As if she's not right," I laugh, poking Nick's ribs.

Nick leans in and kisses my cheek. "I'll catch up with ya later, ok?"

"Ok."

Nick moves further through the crowd towards Madi. I wonder if I'll see him cosied up with Naveen somewhere. Madi said they ignored each at the formal and I never see them talk at school. I haven't seen Naveen near Meah either, but the rumour mill hasn't given word on a breakup.

Charli says she will find Reece, and that's my cue to wrap my arms around my guy's neck. Bryce kisses my forehead and his eyes dazzle as he smiles at me. I ignite as his hands run the length of my back. We move close enough to a table to set our drinks down and then continue to wrap our arms around each other, the grip around my forearm dragging the crutch with me.

He holds me close as the dancefloor gets rowdy. We squeeze between gaps; him walking me backwards until I press against a wall. In his arms, in our own space, I'm secure. I run my hands up to the sides of his face and kiss him slow. He leans in closer, our kiss burning.

"Open up," Madi's voice erupts beside us.

We break apart to her holding her vodka bottle high, ready to tip by Bryce's face.

"Get real," he says, blocking the bottle.

"Oh, c'mon," Madi slurs. "Everyone needs a drink from the same bottle. It'll bond us all for graduation."

"Going to the same school was enough of a bonding experience," Bryce says with a laugh. His arm slips around me, hinting at Madi to leave.

She holds the bottle up to me. "Brit?"

"No." I really have no desire to drink tonight, especially not straight vodka. That's a mistake you only need to make once.

Madi shoves the bottle at Bryce and he laughs, saying. "No, get lost. I'm driving Brit home tonight. Go bother someone else."

"Whatever," she whines and then tips the bottle to her own lips. She pulls it down after a large guzzle, gasping.

Madi moves into the crowd and Bryce says, "She's still as crazy as ever."

"I will and won't miss her partying ways."

"We will see her," Bryce says. "We will all be in Sydney. Surely we'll all meet up, even if we are at different universities."

"True. I hope so."

"Anyway," he says, playing my hair. "Where were we?"

I giggle as his lips move back to mine. I tease his bottom lip and hold onto his hips. I squeeze my hands around him and slip my hands into the back pockets of his dark jeans.

His lips move to my earlobe. He whispers, "This party sucks, we should leave."

I bite my lip as he kisses my neck. If I could snap my fingers and be magically alone with him, I'd do it. I'm glad all these people are drunk, so in a way we are alone. Invisible in everyone's beer googles.

"We have to stay longer for Lenny and Tay," I say, breathless. "But not too long."

"Deal."

I push us back to our drinks, saying, "C'mon, let's go say hi to people."

He groans, grinning. "Do we have to?"

"Goof," I laugh.

"*Aw*, Brit," Chloe says in a baby voice, flicking my crutch. "Don't ya look super cute?"

I eye her with suspicion. "Thanks?"

She twirls a piece of hair around her finger, waiting for a compliment. I grin, feeling power by not giving it to her.

She rolls her eyes and pushes past me to get closer to Bryce. "Hey, Brycey."

"Hey Chlo," he replies. He nods ahead. "We gotta go. See ya later."

Her jaw flexes and her eyes bulge while she tries to seem cool. "No probs, cutie. We're all hanging out front. Make sure you come join us, okies?"

I clasp onto Bryce's hand and he follows me without another word to Chloe.

Hmm, that couldn't have gone better. She has been off her game since they laughed her off the stage at her second *L'Amour Dance Company* audition. Tiffany sent me a cheeky text message about the entire thing. The fact that high school is ending is cracking Chloe's confidence.

We open the door to the back deck and I press into my stomach as the happiest laugh tumbles out of me. Tayla is dancing in a white tutu dress with glitter-frosted white wings, a silver tinsel halo, and illuminating glitter makeup.

"Tay, what's with the outfit?" I ask, giving her a massive hug.

"The art of not giving a fuck," she announces with a boisterous cheer.

She returns to dancing in a circle, holding a wine cooler to the sky. Lenny sits off to the side, guitar on his lap, grinning at his girlfriend. I join Charli and Reece on a nearby bench.

"She's outta control," Charli says, watching Tayla.

"She's having fun," I reply.

"You want some wings?" Reece asks, nudging me.

"I dunno, they might look good on you though," I say, nudging him back.

Charli nods to the house. "Crazy crowded in there."

I nod and tap my crutch. "Yeah, I was a little worried."

Worry spills over her face. "You didn't get hurt or fall, did you?"

"Don't panic," I answer quickly. "I'm fine, but Bryce and I might leave early."

"I can take you home," Charli offers.

"No, I'm staying at Bryce's."

"Did you tell Mum or Dad?"

"*Pah*-lease. We're at our pre-graduation party. They'd expect us to pass out here on the floor."

Charli smirks. "You'd know. All those parties you got wasted at."

"Don't even try to act high-and-mighty, Charlotte Jane," I tease. "Your innocent days are long behind you."

Charli laughs, holding a hand up to block my face.

After some more mingling and awkward dancing, Bryce and I are ready for more kissing. This time in private. We say goodbye to our friends and head to his car.

It's kinda been like the summer before we had sex. We've taken baby steps until we could go all the way. This time, I put up the roadblocks. I've spent so many nights in Bryce's bed, loving it. We got down to underwear a few times. His hands didn't explore, he'd hugged me and didn't look under the covers.

I'm so comfortable around Bryce. We talk all night or lay in complete silence and both are perfectly beautiful. Now, I stand in his bedroom with my back to him, awaiting for him to unzip my dress.

"You sure?" he whispers.

I look over my shoulder and smile at him in the darkness. "I want to be with you."

He slowly unzips my dress and I shiver in the good way. My dress falls to my ankles and his hands sit above my hips.

"Can I see?" he asks.

I know he means the scars. I turn, feeling confident in the darkness. He kneels and kisses my bolted-together hip. My hands glide through his hair and circle around to his chin. I lift his face and he stands.

We kiss and move to the bed. I fall backward, arms above my head, hands entwined with his. My eyes fall closed as his lips move down my neck and follow my collarbone.

I free my hands and wriggle to unclip my strapless bra.

He grins. "Getting ready?"

"Oh, yeah." I snag the bottom of his shirt and pull it over his head.

He removes his pants and we move to the top of the bed. My legs curve around his hips and I love looking up at him.

"You ready?" he asks.

I nod, biting my lip which sends his smile to the left in that cheeky and handsome way.

"Tell me if anything hurts," he whispers. "I'll stop."

"I'll be ok," I whisper, "I'm ready. I love you."

He kisses me softly. "I love you too."

27

Charli

I had followed Brittany and Bryce into the house when they left. I made a break for the bathroom while the line was small and now I need to find my way through this maze of a party. I spot a familiar face. It's crazy dark in here and a million voices mix with the dub beat.

Kimberley stands against a wall, holding a drink with little interest. There's a loneliness about her and my heart tugs at me to go over to her. After how sweet she was about Kellie, maybe we can leave high school with a mended relationship. I don't expect us to rekindle a friendship, but to get rid the animosity and harsh words could be nice.

I step towards her and we lock eyes. She looks down at her drink and then to the other side of the room. She pulls herself off the wall and walks in the other direction. Her path leads to Chloe and Fiona. *Ick*. No, thank you.

It's not totally surprising she'd head their way, but we could have talked. It's hurtful. I guess that's the way I'm destined to always think of her. Don't know why I tried. I don't understand why she's choosing to be around them when school is ending. Is she that insecure?

I move to the back of the house and find everyone sprawled out on the grass in the backyard. Moving closer, my forehead wrinkles as I focus on the space between Reece and Nick. Their hands are planted on the ground and their fingers are spread and interlaced. Holding hands?

I try to wipe the confusion and jealousy from my face as I round the group to sit on the other side of Reece.

"Hey," I say softly to him. I eye their hands again, I can't help it, and Reece doesn't seem to notice. He knows he's doing it, doesn't he?

I wrap my arms around bent knees, smile at a waving Tayla, who sits on Lenny's lap as he talks with Nick. Nick's distracted enough for me to steal Reece's attention. I drop my knees and stretch my legs. I shouldn't have to steal my best friend's attention.

I look to Reece as he turns to me. "What's wrong?" he asks.

"Nothing. Why?"

"Because you look pissed off."

I wave him away, panning my eyes across the moonlit grass. "Must be coming back here with all the schoolyard bullshit."

"Mhmm." Reece nods, tilting his head pensively. "It must've been good to leave early. Sometimes I wish I had let Mum home-school me."

"Really? Why didn't you?"

He shakes his head, brow furrowed, but then releases with a laugh. "Kellie, probably."

A smile tingles at my lips. "Makes sense."

"Cooper!" Madison calls from the back door, pointing a near-empty bottle of vodka at Nick. She squeals drunkenly, skipping in a curvy line towards our spot in the backyard.

Madison leaps towards Nick and straddles him, tipping the bottle to his lips. Reece pivots closer to me and I smile as his hand jerks away from Nick's.

Nick coughs as the bottle is taken away from him. He swallows, wincing, and Madi grabs his shirt collar and pulls him toward her and kisses him long and hard.

When Madi lets him go, she taps his face, ordering, "Come dance with me."

Dazed, Nick agrees and follows Madi into the house.

Reece turns to me with wide eyes. "She's scary."

"Very dominant," I snigger.

"You guys having fun?" asks the angelically dressed Tayla, who is crawling over to us.

I nod and look over to Lenny. "I feel much more comfortable here than any other *John Thomas* party."

Lenny falls backward to view the stars. "Because I'm awesome," he cheers.

"Yes, Baby," Tayla replies and then mimes drinking to us, mocking Lenny.

I laugh loudly. I've never seen her do anything other than fawn all over him.

"What do you plan on studying at uni?" I ask Tayla.

"I'm not," she says with a proud grin. "I'm going to take a gap year."

My insides bubble with excitement. "Really?"

She throws a thumb backward. "Me and Lenny are going to backpack through South America. I'd love to check out the place where my grandparents came from. Not to mention all the awesome hiking trails."

My jaw wants to plummet to the ground. "That's way friggin cool. Finally, someone speaking my language."

"Maybe we can meet up on a trip somewhere," Tayla suggests.

"You're on."

"Reece, would you want to travel somewhere?" Tayla asks.

Reece's expression is blank. "I don't think so."

"How do you feel about moving into a dorm?" I ask him. "D'you think you'll go ok with the adjustment?"

"Tay Tay!" Lenny calls, moving his limbs against the grass like a starfish.

Tayla giggles and crawls over to him, snuggling beside him.

"I think it'll be ok," Reece says to me. "We visited the *USyd* dorms and Steven is close by."

"And Brit and Bryce will be at *USyd*," I add. "And I can check in. We could have a weekly catch up. Or more than once a week, if you want."

"It'd be good to have you close by," he says, "like a sister."

"I should have stepped up right after Kellie..." I murmur. "Steven asked me too."

"It's ok. Kellie left a big hole behind. Her death was a shock." He shakes his head and looks beyond the yard to the crashing beach below the cliffside. "It doesn't seem like she's gone. I swear, since the memorial, I talk to her for real every day."

I slide my hand over his. "I'm glad. We can't forget her."

He smirks. "As if she'd let us forget her."

We sat around in silence for another hour, breaking the silence every now and then with funny memories of high school with Kellie. Pulling her out of the science lab, re-watching our fave animes, or easily beating her at video games.

"One way to make yourself feel better was to verse Kellie at a video game. She even sucked at *'Mario Kart'*," I say with a laugh.

"But what a mistake it was introducing Brittany to video games,"

Reece says bluntly. "How did she get so good so quick?"

I throw my palms up. "I know. Was she secretly playing all this time?"

"Anyway, we were saying we were gonna go?" Reece says, getting ready to stand.

I nod and stand with him. "Yep. Let's say goodbye to everyone then head out."

Tayla and Lenny wrap us up in a four-way hug. Reece and I squirm our way out and thank them again for a party we could actually stand.

Inside the house, Chloe Benson and Jace Wilson suck each other's faces off in the middle of the living room. I retch and hope it's the last time I lay eyes on the pair. People are still squealing, dancing, and jumping around. In the hall, I spy Nick and Madison.

They hang off each other, hunched, laughing loudly at nothing.

"Crap. They're completely wasted." I hold Reece's arm firmly, so he knows to listen to me. "We need to get them home. No way are they getting there by themselves."

"How?"

"Did one of them bring a car? Did Nick drive you?"

"His sister drove us."

"Yeah ok, I can call Shae. There's no way I can take him to Mum's. She'd flip it if one of Tara's kids crashed in her house. We've gotta go to Dad's."

"How do I get home from there? Will Shae drive me?"

"Just stay over at Dad's with us. Text your mum, she'll be fine with it."

He pulls out his phone and asks, "Are you going to tell your Mum?"

"*Pfft*. She can work it out for herself. I might send Sophia a text in the morning to let her know, but I don't wanna wake her up at three am."

Once Reece finishes texting, he slips his phone into his pocket and winces at Nick. "*Ehck*. I don't wanna hold up a drunk person. What if he pukes on me?"

I smirk. "He's too busy dancing to puke."

Reece's eyebrow arches. "What about when he stops dancing?"

"You wanna deal with Madi instead?"

Reece's face drops and loses colour. "Nope. I'll be right."

"Nick," I call out as Reece and I get to them. "We've gotta go home."

Nick throws his arms around me and announces, much too loudly, "Look, it's one of my sisters."

Madi slides a hand over my head and slurs, "See, don't you see, brunettes really have all the fun."

"Do you have someone picking you up?" I ask Madi, trying to keep her focus.

She grabs Nick's jaw and squeezes his cheeks. "I'm climbing into bed with this stud-muffin."

"Ok, whatever," I wave off their silliness, "Let's get outside and call Shae."

Nick groans. "She'll only give me a lecture. Don't call her."

I push him towards the front door. "What, you'd prefer your mum?"

"No, call your dad."

"Yeah, right. Not gonna happen."

We get outside and Madi stops dead. She links arms with me and has a stunned expression. "Wait," she drawls. "Are we gonna walk?"

"Are you gonna dawdle?" I ask.

"We can't walk," she says with disgust.

I pull her down the path to the road. "You won't even notice. We'll be there in no time. My dad's place is only a few streets away."

Madi laughs at me. "You mean Nick's house."

I unravel my arm from hers, already regretting this.

Madi skips ahead of me, zigzagging her way down the road. *Eh*, at least she's headed in the right direction.

"*Whoah*," Nick hushes behind me. I turn, and he's staring at the sky. "The stars are way blurry."

I clap in his face. "Ok, Nick, focus. We gotta get home, ok?"

He pushes my hands away, an ugly grimace to his face. "Why don't you get out of my way so I can walk?"

"*Um*, ok. No need to bite my head off," I say, stepping out of the way and biting inside my cheek to stop the word *jerk* from flying out of my mouth.

Reece follows Nick onto the road and I trail behind. Madi is ahead and sitting in the gutter. I know I should catch up and pull her to standing or hold her hair back if she's puking, but I also have a massive urge to ditch these two and get Reece and I home to his house. Waking up in the morning to his mum's cooking would be perfection.

Madi lies down on the tar road and a groan reverberates out of me. *Shit.* I jog up to her to check how conscious she is.

Her eyes are wide open when I get to her.

"What are you doing?" I ask, crouching beside her.

She giggles. "Waiting."

"Dude, get up," I say, stretching a hand out to her.

Thankfully, she gets up with ease and we wait for the boys to catch up. I can tell Nick's slowed his walk so he doesn't have to be near me, so I press on with Madi beside me.

When we approach our street, I check behind us to make sure they're following. I crane my neck to the intersection to check their silhouettes are still moving. Nick's back is facing me as he stands super close to Reece. A kind of closeness that makes my skin crawl. A kind of closeness I wish Reece would push away. I try to work out how close their faces are, but it's so hard to in the dark.

I turn when they start walking again and I decide their mouths weren't as close as my eyes believed.

Once we're in the house, I try to *shoosh* Madi. I don't need my dad getting up. True to her word, she pushes Nick into his bedroom and closes the door behind her.

"I don't get their relationship," I whisper.

Reece shrugs a response.

"I guess you can crash with me," I suggest with tingling hope. "I mean, it's a double and all."

"Maybe the couch would be better," he replies.

There's a stab and twist to my heart. I've put all my messed up feelings for Reece behind me, but is it crazy I don't want Nick near him? Nick shouldn't get everyone that's close to me.

I open Brittany's door. "Take her bed. She's staying with Bryce tonight."

Reece chews his lip as he stands by the open door.

I dash to my bedroom. "Good night," I say, trying to not make a fool of myself.

I don't fully close my door. If he wants to come in, he can. It's not like I wanna hook up, I just want him next to me. Like a best friend. We should be able to do that. I wanna do that.

I toss and turn for an hour. Reece won't leave my head. I throw off the covers, needing to talk to him. To tell him that I wanna stay close. I wanna be his person. The person he shares secrets with, the person who looks out for him.

I push my door open and turn up the hall. The wind is knocked out of me as Nick goes into Brittany's bedroom. I return to my bedroom and want to scream. Now I wish I had been drinking. Does Dad have a liquor cabinet somewhere?

I peer into the hall. His bedroom is next door. Did he accidentally go into the wrong room after a drunken stagger from the bathroom?

Fuck.

I pull my phone from my bedside table and fit my headphones into my ears. I crank up the metal music and crawl under the covers. Staying in a ball until sleep takes me.

I wake up in the morning with a dry throat. I pull myself out of bed and am thankful I now wear my hair straight because I can only imagine the mess my big curls would be in.

I walk the hall toward the kitchen and am distracted by loud retching in the bathroom. Gross. Poor Madi. But it's no surprise.

"*Ugh*," Nick groans, hunched over the island bench, shirtless and rubbing his temples. "Rob, do you have to be so loud?"

My dad is at the stove, frying up a delicious smelling breakfast. He laughs. "Just because you're eighteen, doesn't mean you can drink everything under the sun."

"Who's vomiting?" Tara asks from the hall. "Is it Char— Oh, hi hunny." She masks her surprise with a wide grin.

"It's Madi," I reply.

"*Eww*, gross!" Alyssa shrieks, bolting past the bathroom.

I laugh and tussle her hair.

I move further into the kitchen and Dad scrutinises me, asking, "And how much did you have to drink?"

"Nothing," I reply, sitting on a stool a few places away from Nick.

Dad stares me down like he can't possibly believe me. I stare at the marble countertop before he can catch my eye roll.

"Charli was sober, like me," Reece says entering the kitchen. "We had to carry these two home."

Nick rubs his face and mutters, "We weren't that bad."

"*Ha!*" Reece and I both blurt out.

"Madi may have drunk more, but she could handle her liquor better," I say.

Nick points up the hall. "Who's the one puking?"

"Who's the one who puked all night?" Reece counters.

A guilty smile crosses Nick's face and the thought of Reece comforting Nick makes my stomach wobble.

"How do you want your eggs, Charli?" Dad asks, spatula in hand.

I take a moment to take in his features as he changes the subject. His way of apologising without saying sorry. There's a touch of remorse on his face, but not enough for it to be genuine.

Man, I really made the right decision in leaving this place. No one, not even my father, will take me seriously. I'm always going to be the girl who fucked up after her friend died and then abandoned her sister for months.

Once Brittany graduates, I'm outta here.

28

My last time in this stupid uniform. No more tartan skirt, no more blazer, and no more tight-fitting neckerchief.

I'm so freakin nervous. I shouldn't be. I'm ready for this. I wanna grab that certificate and run. Well... as close to running as I can. I wanna be out of here. I wanna be like Charli. Free from our parents standing either side of me, telling me what I should do and what I'm doing wrong. So much noise but it'll be over soon.

University, here I come!

Fingers crossed, Bryce and I get accepted into the same dormitory. *Ohmigawd.* I can't imagine how grown up that'll feel.

"You ready to go?" Charli asks, knocking on the doorframe of my bedroom door.

I quickly apply another layer of lipgloss, not entirely happy with my reflection, but I can stop looking in the mirror.

"Yep, let's go." I follow Charli to the staircase and ask, "You sad it's not your day too?"

Her lip upturns. "*Please*. I was flunking my grades by the end of grade ten. I was never gonna make it."

"What a special day," Sophia cheers at the bottom of the staircase.

A massive case of butterflies disperses throughout my stomach. Something about her *uber* cheery smile makes me more nervous. Nervous in the *I-don't-want-to-disappoint-her* kind of way. I nudge Charli and she gives me the same nervous and happy smile.

I land at the bottom of the stairs and wrap Sophia in a gigantic hug. "Thanks for everything," I whisper in her ear.

"Not a problem, Sweetheart," she whispers, rubbing a circle on my back.

"You've done so much for us," Charli says, a tear in her eye. "Thank you for always being there for us, no matter how bad things got."

Sophia smiles sweetly and brushes Charli's face. "That's what you do when you love someone."

"Girls," Mum calls from the garage. "Ready to go? Brit, we have to meet the photographer before the ceremony."

My eyes roll. "Yes, Mum."

At school I get a photo with Mum, a photo with Dad, and then it's like pulling teeth to get them in a photo with me and Charli. All three might hate it now, but future them will be grateful, especially Charli. I know she'll love this photo once she gets a copy.

I pull Charli in for a photo, then we add Nick, and then I get a photo just with Nick. As we take the photo, he gives me the best hug. We add Tara and the rest of the family for one big family photo. Mum refuses to join.

When the family scatters after our turn with photographer ends,

Charli sneakily pulls Sophia in front of the backdrop and asks for one more photo with the three of us. Sophia is a ball of tears once they snap the photo.

"I'm nervous," I say to Charli, pulling her to the side. "Maybe I should have brought my cane."

Charli takes my hands. "No, you'll be ok. You can walk fine now."

"What if I stumble? What if I faceplant?"

She squeezes my hands and looks into my eyes, a sweet smile on her lips. "You'll be ok. I can walk you to the stage if you want."

I smile. "Really?"

"Sure. Doesn't bother me."

"That actually makes me feel more confident. Thanks, Charli-Wharli."

"*Eww*, don't start with that nickname or I'll take back my offer," Charli jokes.

"I'm proud of you," I whisper. "You've really turned yourself around."

Her shoulders bunch. "You don't feel like I abandoned you again?"

I brush back her hair. "You needed to leave. You're a better person now."

Her eyes well. "Thanks, Britty. You pulled yourself out of a hazy situation too. Look at the new friendships you made and how well you did at school."

"I'm so excited for next year," I say, clamping her hands.

"Brittany May," a voice calls behind me and my heart *ba-booms*. Bryce.

I spin around, grinning, as he stands at the backdrop, his dad and sister moving away from the photography backdrop.

He smiles and points to the space beside him. "Front and centre, gorgeous."

I hug Charli. "I'll be ok. If I fall, I fall. But I'll do it on my own."

She rests her forehead against mine. "I'll be there if you need me."

Charli leaves the room to find a seat in the audience and I strut my way to my beautiful boyfriend.

He hooks a finger under my chin and kisses me, soft and sweet.

"Ok, it's not the winter formal," the photographer says with a laugh. "Huddle together and look studious."

I squeak a laugh when Bryce pinches my bum as the photo is snapped.

"Ok, you two," the photographer says, throwing a thumb over his shoulder, "move along."

"It'll be a good pic," Bryce says, his smile sliding left.

"Definitely."

Waiting in my seat for my name to be called is infuriatingly nerve racking. My insides nearly explode when it's my turn. The eyes of the audience makes me want to fade into nothing. My hands tremble as visions of dance concerts flood my mind. All those times on stage when I wanted to vomit. My stomach sloshes for a different reason. Even though concerts made me nervous, the thrill of performing a routine always made me buzz. It's been a year and a half since I felt that rush. No stage and no sidelines of a football game with the cheer squad.

Emptiness fills my stomach.

The applause and cheers of my name wake me up. I focus, moving one foot in front of the other. I fumble up the steps leading to the stage.

Graduation is not what I expected. Everything before my senior studies pointed me toward going to design school. I pictured myself working in fashion and studying my dresses on a runway. Never in a million years would I guess I'd pivot so drastically to something academic. *Law*. Me. *Me*, studying law. It sounds so crazy. But it's fun. I like memorising the cases, statutes, and torts. Most importantly, I'm good at it. I like feeling good at something, especially when so many things I had enjoyed were snatched away from me. The pain I feel while walking is a constant reminder. If studying heavy material distracts me from the life I once had, I'm going to let it.

I shake off my nerves and cross the stage. The principal extends his hand and I shake it before collecting my certificate.

I did it.

I'm done.

Hell yes!

"We did it!" Bryce says after the ceremony and wraps his arms around me before spinning me in a circle. "Officially out of this place."

"I'm so glad to have you with me," I say, nestling against him. "I feel so dumb for all the time we wasted."

"Don't go there," he whispers. "We got through it, that's all that matters."

Nick and Madi's music teacher pulls them aside to congratulate them for getting into the Australian Institute of Music. They'll only be a bus ride away from my university!

Bryce and I join Charli, Reece, Tayla, and Lenny as they are lost in conversation.

"Where do you see yourself travelling first?" Reece asks.

Charli looks to the sky, her eyes darting between all the possibilities. "Honestly," she says in an airy voice. "There's so many places on my list, I don't know where to start." She looks down with a smile. "Peru, Cambodia, Ireland. You name it, I'll go there."

"Afghanistan," Lenny blurts out.

"You never know," Charli replies with a cheeky grin. "In two decades maybe it'll be a thriving tourist destination. The next, Dubai."

Reece shakes his head. "Don't bet on it."

"Don't shoot her down for being an optimist," Tayla says.

Charli laughs. "Yes, thanks Tay."

"She's brave," I say with a pinch of fear.

She takes my hand. "I'll be fine. I mean, you are all brave too. Moving away from home."

"Going to uni is the normal and safe thing to do," Bryce says.

"It's still a huge move. No parents around," Charli says. "But it's so good once you do it."

"Can we make a pact," Tayla suggests. "This time next year we meet up, no matter what we've been up to or if we've stopped checking in, we all mark our calendars to have one big group meet up."

"Wait," I say before anyone can respond. "Nick and Madi need to be a part of this."

Lenny wolf-whistles, beckoning the two over.

They move over and Tayla explains the pact.

"I'm in," Nick and Madi say together.

Everyone reaches into the middle of the circle and says, "I promise."

"Brit?" Charli asks. "Can I talk to you for a minute?"

"Sure."

We move away from everyone else.

"You ok?" I ask. I've been scared she'll break down from regret about dropping out.

"I want you to know you're my whole world," she whispers. "You're the only person I care about and I want you to know no matter where I go, I'll always be around for you. Don't be afraid to call me when you need help. No matter the country I'm in, I'll be there for you. Distance won't stop me."

"*Aw*, Charli," I whisper, thankful she's sure about herself and her decisions. I need the certainty of one of us living with confidence. "Thank you. That's so sweet. I don't want you to worry about me. Know you will always get calls and texts from me. You don't have to act brave or like you have it all together. You call me whenever you need help."

"Thanks, Sis," she replies. "I will."

I hug her. "Let's always remember we are not only sisters; we are two halves of one being. When one of us is hurt, we're both hurt."

"I love you."

"I love you too, you goofball."

To be continued...

THANK YOU FOR READING

To complete the **In It Together** Series:

      #1 – In Mirror

      In Fiji - Companion Novella

      #3 – In It Together

      #4 – In The Beats

      And many more to come!

Other books by Emily Bourne are the **Happily After When** Series, look out for the following books:

      #1- JAZZ

      #2 - ARIA

      #3 - CARA

      And many more to come!

CONNECT WITH THE AUTHOR

Visit author **Emily Bourne** in the following places:

Website: www.emilybourne.net
Instagram: @iemilybourne
Twitter: @iemilybourne
Facebook Page: Author Emily Bourne
YouTube: Emily Bourne